Praise for the compelling suspense of Lowen Clausen

Seco...

"Clausen's sturdy new novel takes us to the same street-level policing as did his debut, *First Avenue*. . . . Clausen is good at finding the slice-of-life details that bring his characters to life. . . . Further heft is provided by the tension between the easygoing lives of many of the book's characters and the gritty story of police work, dead kids, and killers."
—*The Seattle Times*

"Equal parts police procedural and character study, and the two halves are balanced to perfection. . . . Chilling. . . . Fascinating."　　　　　　　　　　　　　—*Publishers Weekly*

First Avenue

"Sights, sounds, smells, and—most of all—real emotion mark this novel as a winner! Clausen is a natural, and I hope *First Avenue* is only the first in a series. I loved this book!"
—*New York Times* bestselling author
and
former Seattle cop Ann Rule

"Lowen Clausen has written a cop novel that is really about people, and an atmospheric mystery that is actually about the resiliency of the human heart. *First Avenue* is as moody as Seattle in the rain, and just as alluring. It's a skillful, memorable first novel."
—*New York Times* bestselling author Stephen White

"A thoughtful police drama, filled with insight and empathy. More than a shoot-em-up, *First Avenue* offers a glimpse at the human beings who can be found in the shadows of skid row. Clausen is a fine writer with enough talent and personal experience to keep us reading for many more books."
—Bestselling author John Straley

continued . . .

"A solid debut marked by unfussy prose and straightforward plot lines. . . . The book's chief pleasure, however, lies in its evocation of seventies-era First Avenue."

—*The Seattle Times*

"Strong narrative style . . . admirably real people. . . . Much of the pleasure of Clausen's book comes from seeing that despite the blue uniform, the lives of beat cops are much the same as anyone else's." —*Seattle Weekly*

"A quick, compelling, literate read about a Seattle cop whose determination to solve a particularly horrible crime entangles him in unsuspected mysteries and secrets of his own life." —*Footnotes*

"A satisfying mystery with honest, hardworking characters you hope are based on real people. The authenticity of these characters shines through."

—*Herald-Citizen* (Cookeville, TN)

"Lowen Clausen provides a fabulous tale that will leave . . . fans anxiously awaiting his next book."

—*Midwest Book Review*

THIRD
&
FOREVER

Lowen Clausen

A SIGNET BOOK

SIGNET
Published by New American Library, a division of
Penguin Group (USA) Inc., 375 Hudson Street,
New York, New York 10014, USA
Penguin Group (Canada), 10 Alcorn Avenue, Toronto,
Ontario M4V 3B2, Canada (a division of Pearson Penguin Canada Inc.)
Penguin Books Ltd., 80 Strand, London WC2R 0RL, England
Penguin Ireland, 25 St. Stephen's Green, Dublin 2,
Ireland (a division of Penguin Books Ltd.)
Penguin Group (Australia), 250 Camberwell Road, Camberwell, Victoria 3124,
Australia (a division of Pearson Australia Group Pty. Ltd.)
Penguin Books India Pvt. Ltd., 11 Community Centre, Panchsheel Park,
New Delhi - 110 017, India
Penguin Group (NZ), cnr Airborne and Rosedale Roads, Albany,
Auckland 1310, New Zealand (a division of Pearson New Zealand Ltd.)
Penguin Books (South Africa) (Pty.) Ltd., 24 Sturdee Avenue,
Rosebank, Johannesburg 2196, South Africa

Penguin Books Ltd., Registered Offices:
80 Strand, London WC2R 0RL, England

Published by Signet, an imprint of New American Library, a division of
Penguin Group (USA) Inc. Also published in a limited hardcover edition by
Silo Press.

First Signet Printing, April 2005
10 9 8 7 6 5 4 3 2 1

To the memory of Mary Youngdahl
—LC

Chapter 1

He walked across the gravel parking lot toward the borrowed car, disguised outwardly from others and inwardly from himself. He carried a paper sack in his left hand. Upon reaching the car he stood motionless for a moment and listened. It was long past midnight and the night was quiet. Lake water lapped against the pilings of the boat dock.

He didn't like to feel confined and once inside the car moved the driver's seat as far back as it would go. He stuffed the paper sack beneath the seat. From the breast pocket of his sports coat he removed a pair of glasses, opened them, and put them on. The glasses did not change his vision. He started the engine and drove out of the parking lot along the one-lane drive. After turning on the headlights he dimmed the green dashboard lights so that his reflection disappeared from the windows.

He drove cautiously, checking the speedometer often and stopping after several blocks for a traffic light at the first hint of yellow but not because he cared what a traffic light directed. In the night he took no directions from anything or anyone. As he waited for the light to change, he watched two people walking on the sidewalk—a young woman and a man, talking, a couple. The woman was attractive, probably a student, nineteen or twenty, her painted lips opening and closing in conversation. She wasn't looking beyond her partner, but she would. Someday she would.

While the others slept, he was free. Their rules didn't apply to him. Possessed by desire at times resisted but overpowering, he felt compelled to search without knowing where, to act without knowing why, to find relief without knowing who.

The university campus reminded him of the island where he grew up—perfect houses with perfect yards tended by the Filipinos and Mexicans who crossed the bridge in the morning and left before dark. On their way to work in downtown skyscrapers, his father and the other island fathers passed the Mexicans and the Filipinos on the bridge and skirted the section of the city that they warned their sons to avoid. Stay away from there, their fathers said. In the evening shadows of the skyscrapers, those prohibited and uncontrolled streets were so far from their island that they seemed to be in a different country. Yet they were so close that the sons had a primal awareness of them—could almost smell them, touch them, taste them.

He remembered the first night a carload of his friends crossed the bridge to the prohibited streets. The boldest of the boys, it wasn't he, rolled down a window and beckoned the black girl to come closer—close enough for them to see her teasing smile as she bent down to look in the car window, so close that they could smell her perfume, hear her breathing. They were not buyers, these boys. The whore could tell at once and turned away in disgust at the pimpled white faces in the car. But they returned, this carload or another from their perfect island streets, and once in a while a whore would negotiate, and the boys would become thrilled by talk of the pleasure each would receive. It was only talk. The whores never entered their cars, and the boys howled with unfulfilled desire as they sped back over their bridge to the quiet curving streets of their perfect island.

The island girls held no mystery for him. He had no interest in them or in the expectations they formed if he smiled back. From his mother he knew all about expectations. He disliked their voices, their smiles, even the way they walked beside him with their arms hugging books to their breasts and eager to begin their demands.

One night he crossed the bridge alone, trembling with virgin fear as he turned toward the streets where the women walked in shadows. He rolled down the car window beside him and the window on the other side. He had money in his pocket. He believed it sufficient. Beyond that he knew nothing.

He pulled to the curb for the first whore he saw, a tall girl no older than he with boots so heavy that he heard them on the sidewalk as she walked to the car. The girl looked in the window, looked right through him.

"Your daddy give you enough money to have a good time?"

He followed her directions into an alley behind a burned-out house where garbage lay scattered on the ground. He gave her the money and unzipped his pants himself when she demanded to see it. His erection failed as she pulled on him in disinterested silence. This was not what he had imagined. He had followed all her directions for nothing.

"What's the matter with you? You queer?" she asked. "You better not be fooling with me."

"I'm not queer," he said.

"You need more money if you want me to keep doing it. I ain't doing all this work for nothing."

"I don't have any more money."

"Then you come back another time when you're ready."

She was no older than he, but she treated him like a child. He wasn't a child. He looked past her silhouette. A streetlight from the next block shone through the trees, but darkness surrounded them. He reached over and found her arm.

"What are you doing? You keep your hands off of me."

His fingers encircled her skinny forearm and closed upon

themselves. No longer indifferent, no longer dismissive, her demands became more forceful and fearful as he tightened his grip. When she tried to open the door, he jerked her back. Her fist was nothing to him, and he struck her face with the back of his hand. He found her throat, closed his fingers tightly around it, and hit her again. She stopped fighting. Her fingers clung to his arm, but they were no longer trying to pull his hand away. Her strangled voice begged him to let her go, begged him to stop, to start, whatever he wanted. He pushed her down onto the car seat, and her body molded into any place he pushed it. Rising above her, he released the pressure around her throat and ripped away her clothing to expose her. He crushed her breasts and groped between her legs until his fingers penetrated the dry shell of her sex. Although he couldn't see her face, he heard her open mouth gasping for air, and there he released his rage and dominance.

He left her on her hands and knees in the alley gagging. He could have taken his money back, but he didn't. He wanted to pay. He had come to her streets a trembling boy, but he was trembling no more. If he had brought more money, he would have dropped it on the ground beside her when he pushed her out of the car. She deserved it.

When he woke the next morning, the night was a distant dangerous dream where desire, hunger, and anger had been beyond his control. For days, for weeks after, he had feared the loss of control. He vowed to himself that it wouldn't happen again. Gradually the fear left him, and he remembered the whore beckoning him, her debauched smile, her final desperate repetition of the word—yes.

That night had been years earlier, and now another night had come. He drove away from the bright streets in the University District and entered a district of darker streets. He saw a face in the shadows. Was her smile derisive or inviting? Did it matter? He turned the car around at the next intersection and drove into the shadow.

Chapter 2

When she was a child playing hopscotch on the rectangular blocks of concrete that formed the sidewalk on Ballard Avenue, she would not mark the blocks with chalk as other girls did in other places. She drew the pattern in her mind, a secret for herself. Uncountable times her footsteps laid their invisible impression over other footsteps, upon the concrete hard as rock that showed no sign of her or anyone else. After she jumped and skipped her way to the end of the sidewalk, to the tip of the triangle formed by two streets that marked the divide of where she could and could not go, she pirouetted on one foot, sometimes the right and sometimes the left, and retraced her invisible steps back to where she had begun in front of Rigmor's store: hours spent in a game with carefully constructed rules that only she understood.

When Grace thought about the little girl on the sidewalk, there was always an ache in her heart for the child, as if the little girl was somebody else, not her, as if the rules the little girl followed were not rules for her. The child had been careful not to step on any of the cracks in the sidewalk. *Step on a crack, break your mother's back.* It was a silly, cruel, unthoughtful rhyme, but the little girl had not wanted to take a chance. It was difficult enough to skip on the uneven sidewalk where the loose, unfirm, irregular blocks of concrete tilted precariously beneath her feet without placing her mother's well-being into the game, but it wasn't her choice to make. The rhyme had been chanted long before she could make any rules to counter it.

Grace Stevens walked the same sidewalk now, looking for the trouble she had never wanted to find as a child. Beside Grace was her beat partner of five months, Katherine Murphy. Grace's long stride had shortened over those months to accommodate her partner, and Katherine's had lengthened. Grace could now sense Katherine's presence without seeing her. Wes Mickelsen, Grace's previous and only other partner in the police department, was so big that there had never been any difficulty knowing where he was. But Katherine was different—smaller, not as assuming; quieter, yet more persistent.

When Wes Mickelsen had told her that he was planning to retire, Grace had considered quitting rather than trying to find a new partner. He had been her partner since she left the police academy; her mentor, the man she had known on Ballard Avenue since childhood. For her it was always difficult to begin with someone new. Wes understood her and she understood him. She could tolerate his habits and practices even when she disagreed with them. If he lifted a drunk roughly from the sidewalk, she knew it was because there had been too many drunks. If his anger flared in the middle of a bar dispute, she remembered the kindness he had shown her as the little girl he met in Rigmor's store on Ballard Avenue. She still carried the police whistle he had given her; she still remembered the day he had taken her hand, walked up and down Ballard Avenue with her, and introduced her to every business owner on the street although most of them already knew her, or knew about her. "This is Grace," he had told them, looking each merchant straight in the eye and holding her small hand in his huge one. "She's with me."

In addition to his kindness, Wes Mickelsen was a devious

man. "Call Murphy," he had said after he told her he was retiring. "I hear she's pretty good."

He had smiled his devious smile. Women had never been partners before in the police department: Men had been partners since the beginning of police partnerships, and then came the forced pairing of men and women, but never two women. Wes was gone, and Katherine had taken his place. No, not his place. Katherine had taken her own place, just as she had.

With summer at an end, a few early leaves had fallen to the street. Their dry brittle skeletons crunched beneath her dusty black shoes. Above her the mercury vapor lights came on one by one as sensors on the poles reacted to the fading light. The lighter blue of the vapor lights stood out against the background of darkening sky, the time of twilight, of light without shadow.

"It's Wes's birthday today," Grace said.

"How old is he?" Katherine asked.

"Fifty-eight, I think. After he reached fifty, he didn't want to keep track."

"So it's not just women who feel that way?"

"Don't tell me that you're worried about getting older?" Grace asked.

A car passed slowly with its headlights on, and Katherine turned away from Grace to watch it. It was the only car moving for several blocks. Headlights weren't necessary yet.

"I'll be thirty pretty soon," Katherine said. "I'm not so happy about that. You're still a baby, so you wouldn't understand."

"You don't look thirty," Grace said. "Anyway, my mother says that her fifties have been the best time of her life. Finally, she doesn't have to take care of anybody. My father has even learned how to do his own laundry. It took some prodding, but he finally learned. And she said that sex is better at fifty than when she was twenty-five."

"Your mother said that?" Katherine asked. "My mother would never say anything like that."

"Does your father know how to do his own laundry?"

"Probably not."

"Well, there you have it."

"I'll keep that in mind."

"Mom volunteers every Tuesday and Thursday for Planned Parenthood. I think she's getting used to talking about sex. But something happened when she turned fifty. Mom said it was because she was healthy enough and ornery enough to finally enjoy what it took those fifty years to learn."

"Something to look forward to," Katherine said.

Grace looked for a piece of wood on which to knock to ward off envious spirits as her mother always did when she said something to tempt them. There was no wood at hand, only a brick building beside them. At the corner was a light pole, and she would knock on that when they reached it.

Katherine pointed across the street toward the front door of the Shev Shoon Gallery. The door was slightly ajar. Grace recognized the owner's blue and white station wagon parked on the street. The tailgate of the station wagon was open, and there were several cardboard boxes stacked behind the rear seat. It was late for Linda to still be at the gallery.

They crossed the street together, and Grace pushed the door open a little more. The front of the gallery had only the dim light of twilight coming through the large windows, but there was an electric light on in the back room. Oscar, the owner's Labrador, raised his head from where he lay close to the front door. He recognized Grace and stretched back comfortably on the cement floor. Grace heard a shuffling noise in the back room.

It was a strange job, Grace thought, always to look for the worst, and never, almost never, to completely believe what she saw. There was or could be something hidden just beyond what seemed evident. It had changed her—this job. Grace knew that she had to change to do her job well, but she didn't like it. At home, with friends, on a simple trip to the grocery store, there was some part of her that remained alert for trouble. She resisted the change whenever she was conscious of it, resisted it as much as she could, but the change came anyway, slowly and inexorably tiptoeing into her conscious thoughts and finally into the unconscious.

Linda came out of the back room carrying a broom and waved to Grace without alarm. Grace waved back.

"You're here a little late tonight," Grace said.

"I'm trying to clean up," Linda said. "I hate to throw any of this stuff away, but if I don't, I won't have any room to work. Do you want any pottery? I've got boxes of the stuff here that students have left behind."

"No thanks," Grace said. "I'm not so big on pottery."

Grace looked at Katherine, whose subtle expression was clear enough. Katherine was no bigger on pottery than she.

"Do you think Rigmor would like any?"

"Probably," Grace said, "but she's got so much stuff in her apartment I don't know where she would put anything else."

"Well, tell her she can come down and look if she wants any."

"I'll tell her," Grace said.

Grace closed the door, and she and Katherine resumed walking. It wasn't until they came to the next light pole that Grace remembered that she hadn't yet knocked on wood. Surely it was too late for such nonsense. Nevertheless, she placed her hand on the rough splintered pole and tapped her fingers twice.

When working with Wes Mickelsen, she had followed his zigzag course on the beat without question. Irregularity was the only regular pattern to follow, he had said, and he determined what that irregular pattern would be. As she recrossed Ballard Avenue with Katherine, Grace realized that they had made the decision without discussion or without one following and the other leading. And yet they zigzagged as frequently and irregularly as Wes, even on one of his best days.

They arrived at the hardware store, which had closed for the day and would remain closed through Sunday. On the glass panel of the worn front door a cardboard sign announced the extension of Saturday hours from noon to 4:00 P.M. The cardboard had been there so long that it had faded from prominence, just as had the Milwaukee tool sign in the plate glass window and the taped crack that ran the length of the glass.

Shiny new cars—German, Swedish, and Japanese models—filled the parking spaces on the street in front of the hardware store. When the hardware store was open, beat-up pickup trucks and delivery vehicles occupied the spaces. The owners of the shiny foreign cars were not customers of the hardware store. Weekends and early evenings were the busy times for the athletic club across the street. Seekers of health from the affluent neighborhoods to the north and from downtown offices flocked to the gym on their way home or on their days off, while the ship workers, plumbers, and carpenters who bought hardware sat on bar stools in Hattie's Hat or the Smoke Shop farther up the street—at least some of them did. It was possible, she supposed, that a few of the workers were over in the athletic club becoming fit. She had never checked to know for certain.

In the next block beside the secondhand store, which was next to Rigmor's Grocery, Grace saw a shopping cart heaped with plastic bags. It was not uncommon to find a bag lady or a bag man north of Ballard Avenue on Market Street, or even one in the park behind the Bell Tower, but she had known only one who had ever ventured down Ballard Avenue as far south as Rigmor's Grocery.

The cart was at the bottom of a wide stairway that led up to the apartments above the secondhand store. A woman in her fifties, approximately the age of Grace's mother, sat halfway up the wooden stairs, looking over their heads through the tunnel created by the walls and ceiling of the enclosure. She had a spiral notebook propped on her knees and a pencil in her hand.

"What are you doing up there, Edith?" Grace asked.

The woman looked up from her notebook. Her eyes widened with alarm.

"We're down here," Grace said, "on the sidewalk."

The portable police radio, which Katherine carried in a case buckled to her holster, squawked with static as the dispatcher sent a University District car to a disturbance call on Brooklyn Avenue.

"Did you hear that?" Edith whispered. "Listen. That one. Did you hear him?"

Edith looked up at the ceiling of the stairway to locate the voice. Grace slowly ascended the creaking steps.

"Edith, do you remember me? I'm Grace. Do you remember?"

Grace continued to repeat her questions, keeping her voice soft and even so that she would not startle the woman. Slowly, reluctantly, Edith looked down at Grace.

"Of course I remember. Why do you ask such stupid questions?"

Grace stopped on the step below Edith's feet, but off to the side so that she wasn't directly in front of the woman. Katherine had followed her and took a position below Grace and on the opposite side of the stairway. Katherine turned the volume down on the police radio.

"You went away to get well," Grace said. "What happened?"

"They tortured me," Edith said, "but I wouldn't tell them. Did they send you to find me?"

"No," Grace said. "I'm on your side. Don't you remember?"

Edith stared at Grace. The older woman wore a green knitted hat and heavy winter clothes although winter was still months away.

"You're lying. They sent you."

Edith had penetrating blue eyes.

"I'm telling you the truth," Grace said.

"Swear it, then."

"Edith, did they give you medicine to take?"

"I thought so," Edith said. "You black ones are the worst. You tie me down, and you know what happens after that."

"I've never done that to you, Edith. Does your daughter know where you are?"

"I don't have a daughter."

"Yes, you do. Her name is Elizabeth."

"Not any more. I changed her name. You don't know what her name is now."

"Edith, do you have medicine that you're supposed to take?" Grace asked again.

"I have to go now," Edith said.

Edith stood abruptly and closed her notebook. Grace didn't move, although the large woman stood menacingly above her. Katherine moved one step closer, but Grace cautioned with her hand not to take another. Edith was harmless unless she felt trapped. At least she had been harmless before she went away to get well.

The stairway was narrow, and there wasn't room for Edith to pass unless Grace and Katherine moved out of the way. Grace thought back to the long ordeal she and Wes had gone through with Edith and the daughter, Elizabeth—all for nothing. Grace slowly backed down the stairs. Katherine did the same, a step behind her, all the way down to the sidewalk. Edith didn't move until the two police officers were off the stairs; then she walked straight down to her cart without looking at either one of them.

Edith talked to herself and to the voices above as she hid

her notebook beneath the plastic bags. Ignoring the silent police officers, she pushed her shopping cart down the sidewalk across the irregular concrete blocks. A few of the loose blocks tilted with the weight of the wheels. At the first intersection Edith turned in the direction of Shilshole Avenue and the railroad tracks.

"What was that about?" Katherine asked.

"It's a long story," Grace said. "I guess she doesn't have much use for black people."

"I'm sorry she said that."

"Why are you sorry? Edith is the one who said it, and she's crazy."

"She probably doesn't like the Irish either."

"You can ask her next time," Grace said.

"What happened before? Where is her daughter?"

"San Francisco, the last I knew. That was a year ago—maybe it's more than a year. God, I hate to tell Elizabeth that her mother is back on the streets. Edith used to have an apartment close to Ballard Hospital, but she lost it when she started hearing those voices. She sort of lost touch with this world. When the toilet plugged up in her apartment, she used five-gallon buckets instead. The apartment was full of them when the landlord finally evicted her. Her daughter, Elizabeth, flew up from San Francisco. She had been trying to get her mother help for months, but I don't think she knew how bad Edith was. Elizabeth found her mother here on the streets, and it's where she found Wes and me, too.

"Edith wouldn't commit herself or allow her daughter to do it, and if you can't prove that she's a danger to anybody . . . "

"Then nothing happens," Katherine said.

"That's right.

"With the daughter, Wes and I chased Edith all around Ballard. We tried to convince Edith to ride along with us to Harborview where we could get her evaluated, but she wouldn't go. She might be crazy, but she isn't stupid. So the daughter and Wes and I tried to talk to her and keep her in one place long enough for a mental health worker to meet us and evaluate her on the street. Sometimes we felt like tying her to a tree.

"Edith said her daughter was dead, or if she wasn't dead, she was part of the group who wanted to torture her. She said terrible things about her daughter, things you would never say to your child. It nearly killed Elizabeth. She spent a week in a rental car following her mother around day and night.

"Then one day Edith agreed to get treatment. I don't know what happened. Maybe Edith had a flash of lucidity, or maybe she finally felt sorry for her daughter who was about to go crazy herself. I don't know. Wes and I took Edith and Elizabeth to Harborview Hospital, and Edith signed herself in.

"Elizabeth was so grateful. She showed Wes and me the notebooks her mother kept. Edith has beautiful handwriting, and there were wonderful sentences scattered among the pages. They didn't make any sense when you tried to read the whole page, but some of the sentences, when you read them separately, were clear and beautiful. I was going to remember a few of them. Elizabeth cried and cried over those notebooks. I don't know how I'm going to tell her that her mother is back. I don't know if I will."

"It's not fair," Katherine said. "Some process goes wrong in the brain. Who knows why? Just one little thing goes wrong, and you're living out of a grocery cart."

Grace looked down to the concrete blocks of the sidewalk; she remembered but could not see the invisible steps of her childhood that always led her back to Rigmor's store. Before coming upon Edith, they had been working their way there. It was the place where they began most shifts and ended them all. Rigmor's Grocery, beyond the secondhand store, was one reason Grace had backed down the steps and let Edith walk away. Their shift was almost over, and Rigmor was waiting.

The bell above Rigmor's door jingled when Grace opened

the door. Grace smelled freshly cooked *frikadeller*. Although she had eaten thousands of Rigmor's meatballs, her mouth still watered.

"Hello, *skat*," Rigmor called to her from the back counter, the accent and words of Denmark still marking her speech forty years after leaving the old country. "Is it that time already?"

Every night except Saturday, the last chore of the walking beat was to close Rigmor's store, to bring in the fruit and vegetable tables from the sidewalk, to make sure that Rigmor was fine—she wasn't so young anymore, she said. Every night they stopped last at Rigmor's store to receive her benediction before leaving the street and going home. On Saturday nights the poker players, a group of current and retired police officers who had worked the Ballard Avenue beat in the years before Grace and Katherine, carried in the fruit and vegetable tables and closed the store, but Grace and Katherine stopped anyway.

Grace walked up the center aisle between shelves stacked full of Scandinavian grocery items and walked behind the cash register and refrigerated display to the work counter where Rigmor made the *frikadeller* and everything else that was good. On the counter were two rows of thinly sliced Danish rye bread, buttered and waiting to be completed into open-faced sandwiches for the poker players. Katherine remained on the other side of the cash register, still not sure what she could do to be helpful. It took a long time to know what to do in Rigmor's store.

"And how are you, Katrin?" Rigmor asked. "Ready to go home, I'll bet, and then with two days off. You'd better take some of these *frikadeller* with you so that you will have something good to eat over your weekend."

"You made them for your party tonight," Katherine said. "I wouldn't want any of the poker players to go hungry."

"There's no danger of that. I've made enough for an army."

Grace opened the oven door and lifted the lid from Rigmor's largest roasting pan. It was full of meatballs, hours of work.

"How many are you expecting in this army?" Grace asked.

"Six, seven, eight, who knows? Put some in a carton for Katrin and some for you."

Grace knew better than to resist Rigmor's commands. She reached under the counter for two Styrofoam containers.

"Bigger ones than that," Rigmor said.

Grace put the containers back and brought out two that were larger.

"Is Wes coming tonight? It's his birthday, you know."

"Is it? Well, he'd better come, then. But I'm sure he will. He comes every time, and he always wonders how you and Katrin are doing. Of course, he doesn't think anybody could do as good a job as he did when he worked here, but I told him that nobody even misses him now. We don't want him to have a big head, even though he taught most of these men, including the chief, how to be police officers just like he taught you. But he could have stayed here if he wanted. He wasn't so old that he had to go off and retire. What if I did that? What if I retired and collected my pension? Then where would these men go? *Hvad?*"

"Where would all of us go, Rigmor?"

"No *ja*," Rigmor said, combining the English no and the Danish yes, as she did whenever she resigned herself to the unknowable. "Someday you'll come to the poker party, too, when you become a big shot like the chief and leave us here."

"What if I don't leave?" Grace asked.

"That sounds good to me, but then you don't come to the poker party. But I think you will. That's why you're going back to school, *hvad?*"

"Maybe I just want to learn something new."

"That's always a good idea."

"I'll help you with these sandwiches. Then Katherine and I can carry them upstairs for you."

"Oh, that would be nice. What shall you do? Do you want to spread the pâté or put on the garnish, or shall we do both together?"

"Let's do it together."

"*Leverpostej,* a little slice of bacon, gherkin fanned just so, sautéed *champignon,* and there we have it. You remember how to do that, I suppose."

"I remember," Grace said. Nevertheless, she watched Rigmor's skilled hands just as she had watched when she could barely see over the counter.

"Yes, of course you would."

"I helped you make these sandwiches before Wes ever came here."

"That's right, but you don't do it so often anymore."

Grace placed her hand gently on top of Rigmor's hand, which had settled beside one of her finished sandwiches.

"It's not something I'll forget."

"No *ja,*" Rigmor said again. "I should know that. My sons forgot how to do this as soon as they could, but not you. Now, your sister, she was something different. I almost had to tie her down to make her learn anything."

"We must have been a pain in the neck for you, two little girls running around here while you were trying to run a business."

"No. You were a joy. Always a joy."

"You're lying, Rigmor."

Rigmor laughed to herself the way she always laughed when she alone knew the joke and didn't intend to share it.

Chapter 3

Gasping for oxygen, Grace leaned into the slope and forced herself to continue running up the steep hill to the bluff above Golden Gardens. Her legs quivered from the unaccustomed exertion. It was a race to see which would give out first, her legs or her lungs. Getting back in shape was a more painful process than she had expected. During the academy the daily exercise had gotten her into reasonable condition, but she had not been in truly great shape since playing on her high school soccer team.

In the small park at the top of the hill she stopped to rest. She grabbed the backrest of a concrete bench with both hands and stretched slowly and carefully. Maybe she had pushed too hard on the last stretch up the hill. Her hamstring muscles felt as if they were ready to cramp.

The park was halfway between her house on the east side of the hill and her parents' house on the western slope. When her parents' house had belonged to her mother's parents, the park was the place where she and Evangeline escaped during the long Sunday afternoons of their mother's visits. Their father usually stayed home and worked, except on special holidays. She and Evangeline almost always had the park to themselves. The view was so spectacular that she wondered why everyone in the neighborhood didn't come every day.

From the park she could see all the way across Puget Sound to the Olympic Mountains on the peninsula and could imagine the unending ocean beyond.

Grace sat on the bench and grimaced as she extended her toes. She should have taken the car. She might have to ask her father for a ride back home.

She and Evangeline hadn't come to the park as often after her mother and father bought the house and their grandparents moved to the retirement village in California. She wondered why. Was it because they could see Puget Sound from the living room windows, or was it because there was no longer a need to escape?

When she and Evangeline were children, Evangeline had told her that their grandparents moved to get away from them. "Why?" Grace asked. Evangeline shook her head in disbelief that Grace could be so ignorant. Grace was only six then. Evangeline was nine and knew everything.

"Because they're white and we're not."

It seemed that Evangeline always saw color better than she did. Was that it, or did Evangeline just imagine that she could? By that time Grace knew there were no other mothers and fathers in the neighborhood who were like theirs, but she was still trying to grasp why that mattered.

"Mom is," Grace had told Evangeline.

"But we're not," Evangeline had said.

It was downhill from the park, and the pain shifted to her shins. She couldn't imagine how she had ever enjoyed running. At one time she had been able to run from the house all the way to Golden Gardens without even breathing hard. It would be a long time before she could do that again.

Morfar, her mother's father, was a stern, white-haired man. Grace remembered that he always sat very straight in a chair. She didn't think he was ever comfortable. She could never tell what he was thinking, and because of that, she was a little afraid of him. He wore a suit and a white shirt all day on Sunday, and she always felt that she should be careful not to disturb his Sunday clothes. He might like her, she had thought, if he would just not sit so straight.

Mormor was never well. Her heart could not stand much excitement. *Mormor* and *Morfar* had moved to California where it was dry and good for *Mormor's* lungs. She had bad lungs in addition to the bad heart that could not tolerate excitement. Grace remembered the special Norwegian cookies *Mormor* baked for the girls at Christmas when she still lived in Seattle. Grace liked eating the cookies very much, but she always wished that *Mormor* would show her how to make them. *Mormor* and *Morfar* were both gone now. Her mother baked the same cookies and had shown her how, but it wasn't the same.

When Grace was a block from her parents' house, she slowed to a walk so that she would have time to cool down. She should have begun walking a block earlier, two blocks. She was still sweating when she reached the backyard where she planned to let the breeze dry her before she went inside. Her father was there with a saw in his hand. He was using his knee to hold down a long stake that extended beyond the end of a picnic bench. He looked up when Grace entered the yard.

"Why are you limping?" he asked.

"I'm not limping," Grace said. "I'm a little stiff, that's all. I decided to run over here today. What are you making?"

"A few more stakes for the tomatoes. It's going to be a good year if I can get two more weeks of good weather."

Grace walked over to the wooden fence where the tomatoes grew. It was the sunniest place in the yard. Her father had already tied up all the vines that she could see, but there must be more. Her father had a mysterious communication with his tomato plants and was continually trying to give them some added advantage to make up for Seattle's short growing season. Each spring he started the plants inside on the back porch. When he transplanted them to the garden, he covered them with clear plastic for the first month. He did everything possible to increase heat for the plants—black rocks in the dirt to hold the heat, aluminum foil on the fence to reflect it. Still, every year at the end of September came the same plea—just two more weeks.

"What kind are these?" she asked.

"Nebraska Reds. Aunt Margaret sent me the seeds."

"They look more like Nebraska pinks."

"I know. Just two more weeks. That's all they need."

They didn't need it in Nebraska. She remembered how hot it was in Omaha on their summer visits to her grandparents, her father's parents. She would lie in bed and sweat and wait for the darkness to cool her. Surely, she had thought, the dark would be cool, but even darkness was hot in Omaha.

"I miss Grandmother Bess and Grandpa Joseph, don't you?"

Her father lowered the saw to his side and looked at her.

"Sure, I do."

"What do you miss?" Grace asked.

"Just hearing them talk, I guess."

She missed Grandmother Bess's lap, where she would wake up in the morning. Her grandmother might be in the kitchen drinking coffee and talking to her father and grandfather, or she might be on the back porch snapping beans or husking the sweet corn that Grandpa Joseph brought in from the garden. Wherever she was, Grace would stumble groggily out of bed and find Grandmother Bess. It was a delicious way to have the first taste of morning, much better than the green beans from the garden, better than the fresh sweet corn, better even than the huge red tomatoes. She could still smell the rich soil on the knees of Grandpa Joseph's overalls. The bare dirt in her father's garden always reminded her of that smell and of the contented sound from Grandpa Joseph as he unhooked the straps of his overalls on the back porch and let them fall.

Grandmother Bess and Grandpa Joseph came to Seattle once, but it wasn't the same. She remembered them sitting stiffly in their best clothes on the couch watching the rain fall on Christmas Day. It wasn't nearly as delicious to sit on Grandmother Bess's lap in Seattle.

"They didn't like it here very much, did they?"

"It wasn't what they were used to. You get used to something, it's hard to change."

Grandpa Joseph died when Grace was eight, and Grandmother Bess died four years later. Grandpa Joseph died in the winter, and only her father had gone to his funeral. The airplane was too expensive for them all to go. Her grandmother died in August when the Omaha garden was at its peak of fresh corn and red tomatoes. They all went then, two days in the car without stopping for anything.

Grace returned to the picnic bench and grasped the end of the stake that her father had been cutting before she interrupted him. She had held many boards for her father. He lined up the saw inside the cut and finished it with a few quick strokes. Grace stacked the cut piece beside the others on the ground. Her father slid the stake forward on the bench and lined up the saw again. She grasped the new end. The old wood was dense and difficult to cut. Drops of sweat gathered around his few remaining clumps of short hair.

"How does it feel to be going back to school?" he asked.

"The students are a lot younger than I remembered."

"I'll bet. They're not going to get any older either. It's a smart decision—school, I mean. It's good to have something to fall back on."

Her father had never been pleased with her decision to become a police officer. If she moved into administration, he might think differently. The captain from Personnel was trying to get her to transfer to Community Relations. Her father would like that. He thought she should go further than the walking beat in Ballard. They didn't talk about it directly anymore.

"I'm sure there will be no end of opportunities for an anthropologist with a master's degree specializing in the communal structure of coastal peoples," she said.

"The degree counts. You'll see."

Maybe he was right and she would see. What she saw now was that it would be an enormous amount of work. Her father wanted her to go on until she got her doctorate. Was that why she had gone back to school, to please him? Or was there something within herself? There was something within, although she couldn't yet pinpoint what it was. The field was interesting, incredibly interesting, but the work . . . how would she ever find the time to do all the work?

"Are you going to finish cutting this, or am I holding on for nothing?"

He drew the saw back through the stake, creating a shallow cut against the angle of the saw teeth.

"I can't believe they don't start classes here until the last week of September," he said. "Then you're done by Christmas and start again with a new quarter. The football season is half over by the time the students show up. It's no wonder you never got very interested."

He pushed the saw forward, but it skipped out of the shallow cut.

"I was interested enough," she said. "I remember that one game we went to and it poured all afternoon. I couldn't believe that people would sit in the rain to watch a football game. I couldn't believe that we did."

He pulled the saw back through the wood one more time.

"They sit through snowstorms in Nebraska."

"So what does that tell you about the intelligence of those people?"

"Are you holding on?" he asked.

"I am."

She held the stake tighter while her father sawed through it with rapid strokes. Then he laid the saw on top of the picnic table and sat down with his forearms resting on the table. Grace put her length of stake onto the table beside the saw. Its cut edge looked new and fresh compared to the weathered gray of the rest of the wood.

The tomatoes were all he missed from Nebraska, he said, that and the football team. She could understand the tomatoes, but the football team was another matter. Even Evangeline cheered for the football team. It was beyond Grace's comprehension. But the tomatoes—she could understand the tomatoes.

"I was just kidding about the people in Nebraska."

"I know. Aunt Margaret said it froze last night in Omaha."

"Already? Just a month ago it would be so hot that you couldn't sleep at night."

"They have air-conditioning now. You can sleep anytime you want. It's not like it used to be when we visited Mom and Dad."

"I wish they were still there."

"I do, too."

Her father began to smile, the sad but accepting smile of old memories that both hurt and sustain, but a troubled look came into his eyes and changed his whole face. Her mother could hide problems for days, or forever, but her father's face registered them the moment they appeared.

"What's the matter?"

"I'm not supposed to say anything yet."

"About what? What's wrong?"

"Your mother has a lump in her breast. It might be just a fatty tumor and nothing to worry about, but the doctor is worried. She has a biopsy scheduled tomorrow."

"Tomorrow? Why didn't anybody tell me?"

"You know your mother. She didn't want you to worry—it being the first day of school and all."

Grace stood up and looked toward the house. Her father remained sitting at the picnic table, turning one of the newly cut stakes over and over in his hand. Stiffly, more from fear than sore muscles, she walked to the back door and opened it.

"Mom," she called tentatively.

"In here," her mother said with a voice that was no different from the voice Grace had heard the week before, no different from the voice she always heard.

Grace walked into the kitchen, where her mother sat at the table in the breakfast nook with the newspaper spread before her. She looked up at Grace over her reading glasses.

"Your father told you."

Grace nodded. She couldn't trust her voice.

Her mother took off her glasses and slid out of the breakfast nook, rising to nearly the same height as her daughter. Smiling, her mother held out her arms. Grace stepped into the embrace, but she was too tall to bury her head into her mother's breast as she had done as a child.

"My Grace," she said. "You always feel enough for all of us."

Chapter 4

Detective Anne Smith unlocked the door to the Sex Crimes office on the fifth floor of the Public Safety Building and flipped on both light switches. She dropped a file folder on top of her desk and pushed her swivel chair forward to where it belonged. Horace had always placed the chair exactly in the center to leave a message that he was doing what he could to give her a good start, but the new janitor merely shoved it in the general direction. All the chairs were that way; hers was not singled out. She missed Horace, even if his dust mop never quite reached the spot behind the far desk leg closest to the wall.

She pulled the electric cord from the back of the silver percolator, which had sat on top of her file cabinet and reigned over the lineup of coffee mugs from her nieces and nephews for more years than she wanted to remember. If it ever stopped working, she would have to retire. She doubted they even made percolators anymore. Now everything was Mr. Coffee, a cheap plastic device promoted by a baseball player who wouldn't know the difference between a good cup of coffee and a slug of chewing tobacco.

In the women's restroom Anne filled the percolator with water, one cup at a time, using her Space Needle mug. The hand sink wasn't deep enough to set the percolator under the faucet. Anne looked at her face in the mirror and released the first sigh of the day. Her lipstick had already faded, and the applied blush had not brought the advertised color to her cheeks—not that anybody here would notice. They might break their necks trying to glimpse the backside of the new Mona Lisa clerk in Records, but she couldn't remember the last time any of them had broken his neck over her. Why was it that Monday mornings were always a long time from everything?

In another year she could retire with a full pension—fifty percent of her salary, increasing each year as long as she lived. She could do something else, something she always wanted to do and might actually think of doing if she left. Maybe she could sleep an entire night in deep forgetfulness. It would be wonderful to sleep. Or, like other aunts, she could knit stocking caps for the nieces and nephews, for the great-nieces and great-nephews. What would they say to that? The little ones only wanted to see her gun and badge. She wouldn't show them the gun, but she brought out the badge, let them touch it, and watched their eyes grow big and wondrous. Would they find wonder in stocking caps?

Her hard-heeled shoes rapped loudly on the tile floor as she headed back to the office. It was too early for the buzz that happened at eight every morning when the clock watchers showed up with a minute to spare. They seemed to think it was a crime to give the taxpayers an extra minute or two of their precious time. Of course she might only be jealous that they could still sleep, or that they had something else to do and somebody to do it with. She filled the strainer with ground coffee, fastened the lid, and plugged the electric cord into the wall socket. Immediately, almost immediately, she heard the gentle hiss of the element heating the cold water. The percolator worked another day; not yet time to retire.

Anne walked down the back stairway one flight to the fourth floor and unlatched the halfdoor at the counter of the

Records Bureau. Sylvia was standing at the copy machine with her back to Anne. It was Mona Lisa's backside, or whatever her name was, and not Sylvia's that caused the hallway stir. Anne walked over to the tall, slotted cabinet where Sylvia sorted the reports by category. After the weekend there was a mountain of paper. If as much work were done as paper used, the world would be a better place. It still amazed her, sometimes, that it wasn't.

They exchanged good mornings, and Anne removed from the Sex Crimes slot the weekend accumulation of reports that came up from Patrol. From the absence of officer statements she could see that there had been no arrests.

"Slow weekend," Sylvia said, without moving from the copy machine. Anne appreciated that Sylvia always had the reports ready by the time she arrived in the morning.

"This old world is getting better every day," Anne said.

"Tell me about it."

Sylvia slipped a larger stack of reports into the Auto Theft slot. It was certain that none of those guys would be in early to get them, and why should they? They arrest a kid for auto theft, and he's back home before the arrest report is done.

She ought to be happy that her stack was small. She ought to be happy that she could feel her fingers pressing though the paper. As she walked back up the stairs and down the hall to her office, she flipped through the reports in her hands: a rape on Capitol Hill, a flasher in the U-District, a groper at a bus stop in Chinatown, one attempted sexual assault on Beacon Hill, and a few other minor offenses—perversion spread democratically across the city. Sometimes there would be a series of assaults in one geographic area, and that was always a worry.

Now and then Sergeant McHenry arrived before her and picked up the reports, but he didn't mind if she ran the errand for him unless she still had the reports on her desk when he arrived. She never tried to pick her cases, but she had discovered long ago that Mac would usually assign one to her if she had an idea or two about it to share with him before the other detectives arrived, especially if she accompanied her ideas with a fresh mug of coffee.

She read the rape report first: a warm night with an open window, ground floor apartment, suspect with a knife. The victim never saw the suspect's face, but he had black hands. He cut the telephone cord and escaped through the entry window. The victim waited an hour before she knocked on the stranger's door across the hall and asked for help. An hour. What would the young woman, twenty-two years old, think about for that hour? Sometimes a victim waited days before calling for help. Often, she never called. Anne had long ago stopped making judgments about them, about the women who called or didn't call, about the children who didn't know how to call. There was more than enough opportunity to make judgments about the rapists and molesters, more than enough for that.

The attempted sexual assault was a strange case, if it was a case. The suspect picked up the victim from a bus stop on 12th Avenue, somewhere close to Jefferson Street. The suspect was a tall white male, late twenties, thin build, white shirt and a suit coat. "Victim stated that she wanted the suspect to take her home," the report said, which Anne knew meant that the patrol officer writing the report probably didn't believe her. Instead the suspect took the victim to a vacant lot close to Public Health Hospital on Beacon Hill. From there the victim could see the freeway below her. After parking his car the suspect attempted to grab the victim. The victim broke free from the suspect, fled from his vehicle, and flagged down the reporting officers who were on routine patrol on 12th Avenue SE. The officers searched the area for the suspect's vehicle but couldn't locate it. The victim was not certain of the color or make of the car and was not able to show the officers where the attempted assault took place.

Anne read the remaining reports and knew that nothing would happen with them without a lucky arrest. The rape case had potential. The patrol cops had been diligent and had lifted fingerprints from the windowpane. The suspect had probably been watching the woman and others, waiting for the right chance. He was active and dangerous. Everyone would work hard on that case, but the case on Beacon Hill was different. 12th and Jeff—a few blocks from Yesler, a few blocks from 14th which was a district known for prostitution—a trick gone bad probably. The victim had no telephone number where she could be reached. Everyone had a telephone these days. Anne would have doubted the address, too, if the officers had not taken her home. Uncooperative victim, incomplete information, so why bother? There were plenty who wanted help. There were plenty who somehow struggled through the hell that was no fault of theirs, who helped as much as they could, and endured. Somehow, most endured.

Sergeant McHenry came into the office at seven thirty. After he had read through the reports she had stacked neatly on his desk, Anne poured a cup of coffee and took it over to him. In the summer his nearly bald head was tanned from spending every weekend on his boat. He always looked healthier then, happier. During the winter as the tan faded and the paunch grew within his expanding belt, he became more irritable and less willing to smile when she brought him a cup of freshly percolated coffee.

"Fishing any good?" she asked him as she sat on the empty corner of his desk.

"Always good," he said. "The salmon are still running at Neah Bay. Someday we'll have to get you out in the boat."

Mac leaned back in his swivel chair and cupped his hands behind his tanned head. He looked almost handsome with his summer tan.

"Not me," Anne said. "I get seasick in the backseat of a

car. Do you remember that guy we had a few years ago who was picking up prostitutes in Chinatown? I was trying to remember his name. Redford, wasn't it?"

"Renfro," the sergeant said.

"That's right. Whatever happened to him?"

"He got twenty years, I think. He won't be out yet. Besides he's too old and too short to be this guy."

The sergeant nodded toward the reports that lay on his desk, overlapping each other in a single column with the headings exposed.

"I know. It's just that these perverts who prey on prostitutes bother me. They always think they'll get away with it. They think nobody will care."

The sergeant rocked forward and pulled a report from the column on his desk. He dropped it in front of her.

"Nobody does," he said.

She picked up the report from the sergeant's desk.

"How late do the buses run on Jefferson?" she asked.

The sergeant paused before answering.

"I don't know."

When she returned to her desk, she dug into her purse and found the day planner she bought each December. She flipped through the worn pages and saw that she had a meeting with a deputy prosecutor at nine thirty and nothing after that until one o'clock. She had time after the morning meeting to visit the victim, but what do nineteen-year-old girls do in the morning if they're not working, if they're not in school? Occupation—none, the report said. The earlier the better, she decided.

There was a computer terminal in the office that was hooked up to the Records Bureau and to NCIC and who knew what else, but she hated the thing. Whenever she tried to use it, nothing happened. Blink, blink, blink went the little underline mark that demanded the right sequence of keys but was too dumb to tell her what they were. And whoever wrote the instructions needed to go back to school. It was faster and less irritating to walk down the stairs and ask Sylvia.

Anne didn't like checking on her victim before talking to her, but if this girl was a prostitute, it was better to know right away. This time Sylvia's computer had nothing to provide. The victim had no arrest record and no contact as a past victim or witness.

She signed out a car at the property room window on the third floor and took the elevator down to the first floor where the car was parked on B-deck. Since her last checkup she felt guilty every time she took the elevator. Her doctor had told her she should walk more, take the stairs instead of the elevators, maybe even buy a set of dumbbells. What a ridiculous idea. Besides, he didn't look so good himself, and he should follow his own advice before he handed it out and made everybody else miserable. On the first day after the checkup she had taken the stairs to the fifth floor and nearly died.

Her car was parked so closely to the adjacent car that she had to enter it through the passenger door. She checked her side mirror repeatedly as she inched back into the aisle. Just as she was about free, she heard a light scraping from the left front of the car. She stopped abruptly.

"Damn," she muttered.

She inched the car forward slightly and winced as the scraping continued. There wasn't room to get out and check the damage. Another few feet and she would have been free.

She straightened the steering wheel and backed out again. This time she made it into the aisle without additional scrapes. She got out of her car and walked over to the other car. There was a small scratch on the rear door. She looked around and saw no one else on B-deck—not that it mattered. She examined the scratch more closely and rubbed off a few flakes of paint. The scratch was barely noticeable. It was a banged-up old police car, not some Cadillac on Fifth Avenue. She got back into her car and headed up the ramp to the exit door. She could always fill out an accident report later if she had the time.

As she drove up the steep incline on Cherry Street, traffic poured off each side of the elevated freeway that separated Capitol Hill from downtown. She passed beneath the freeway and continued east. A few blocks made all the difference. Once she passed the freeway, she could poke along without feeling that she was delaying every car in the city.

Anne drove to 12th and Jefferson. There was a playfield on one corner, an abandoned lot on another—not much to attract anybody. Seattle University was a block or two away, but it wasn't likely the young woman was coming from there. Where was she coming from at three in the morning? A block south and a block east would put her in an area of known prostitution, but maybe she was waiting at the bus stop as she said.

The victim lived in a three-story brick apartment building on 20th Avenue E and East Madison Street next to Jimmy's Cafe. Two cars were parked in the tall unkempt weeds and grass on the planting strip in front of the building, and an old refrigerator lay tipped onto its side next to the front door. There was no directory at the entrance. The door was unlocked.

Anne walked down the hallway and smelled frying bacon. It never smelled good unless she was making it for herself. The hallway was a neglected gray and had a dark streak a few feet above the floor where kids, as kids would do, had rubbed their hands along the wall. Most of the hallway lights had burned out.

Anne stopped at the apartment door listed on the report, removed her badge case from her purse, and knocked politely. She heard a noise inside, but no one came. She knocked again, louder but still not demanding. The door flew open and a little boy, three or four years old in undershorts and a T-shirt, stared up at her without saying a word. For a moment Anne said nothing herself and didn't raise or open her badge case.

"Is your mother home?" Anne asked.

The boy didn't answer, or move, or blink. He seemed to be as surprised to see her as she was to see him.

"What's your name?" Anne asked.

The boy still didn't answer, but he did move. Without closing the door he ran into another room. Its door was also open. Anne waited in the hallway and surveyed the apartment. A worn couch stood against the wall opposite from where she waited. A pillow and blanket lay on the floor beside the couch. A television flickered images without sound. On the coffee table in front of the couch, a half-filled bowl of cereal sat in a puddle of milk. There was another plate beside it with leftovers from a previous meal. An empty metal table and empty metal chairs stood close to the archway opening into the kitchen. Table, chairs, coffee table, television, and couch—the entire inventory of furnishings. There was not a picture on any of the walls, a bookcase or books, a clock or plant, a light other than the light bulb hanging from the center of the ceiling. The fixture had lost its shade.

A young woman in a long nightgown and shorter robe came out of the bedroom where the little boy had run. She looked older than nineteen, the age of the victim. When she saw Anne waiting in the doorway, she stopped, turned back, and shouted into the bedroom, "I told you not to open that door."

Anne wondered if there would be another greeting, or if that was it. When the young woman looked back toward her, Anne raised her badge.

"I'm Detective Smith. Are you Lucy Means?"

"Supposing I am?"

"I'd like to talk to you about the man who tried to grab you."

"I already told the police all I know about him."

"I'd like you to tell me. Do you mind if I come in?"

"You can come in if you want, but I already told them everything. Antonio, you come out here and fix this mess. Antonio!"

Lucy Means turned her back on Anne and waited for the boy. The boy emerged from the bedroom. He stared at Anne with wide-open eyes as he picked up the cereal bowl and carried it into the kitchen. Anne closed the hallway door and crossed some part of the distance that separated her from the mother. There was another part that she knew would never be crossed.

"Now you come here and get the rest of this," the mother said. "I told you not to leave your food out here."

Antonio picked up the plate, smiling at his mother's harshness that was all make-believe to him. "Go on now," she said.

Antonio marched into the kitchen with such exaggerated steps that Anne had to smile as she watched him.

"He reminds me of my nephew at that age," Anne said. "Now he's a smart-aleck lawyer in Washington, D.C."

"This boy won't live that long if he doesn't start minding his mama," Lucy Means said as she picked up the pillow from the floor and dropped it onto the middle section of the couch. Then she folded the blanket into a neat bundle and placed it on top of the pillow. "You want to sit?" she asked.

"Thank you," Anne said.

Anne sat at one end of the couch and took a pen and notebook from her purse. Lucy Means sat at the other end. Antonio tried to crawl onto her lap.

"You go over and watch the TV," his mother told him. "Big Bird is on. You can turn it up a little bit."

After Antonio had settled in front of the television set and had focused his wide-open eyes on Big Bird, Anne flipped through the notebook until she came to the first blank page.

"I'd like you to tell me what happened," Anne said.

"Where you want me to start?"

It was a good question, Anne thought. Lucy Means looked away from Anne before she could answer, looked toward her child and the television where no one looked back at her. There were two children, Anne realized. One stared directly into her eyes, and one had to look away—the result of a few, too few, intervening years.

"May I call you Lucy?" Anne asked.

"That's my name."

"It is, isn't it? The police report says that the man offered you a ride while you were waiting at the bus stop. Is that where you first saw him?"

"Where else would I see him?"

"I don't know. Tell me what happened at the bus stop."

"I was waiting there and this man stops and asks me if I want a ride. I'd been waiting there a long time, and I didn't know if that bus was ever going to come. My mama takes care of Antonio when I go out, and she doesn't like it if I stay out too late."

"Where does your mother live?"

"Upstairs, but I don't want you talking to her. She's got enough on her mind. We used to stay with her, but we don't anymore. We're here now. I don't want you to be bothering her about this."

"I won't bother her. So you decided to accept the ride?"

"That's what I said. He looked okay. He didn't look like somebody who would try anything."

"How could you tell?"

"You can't, I guess. Next time, I'll just keep waiting for that bus."

"What happened after you got into his car?"

"I told him where to take me, but he went on down 12th Avenue instead. I asked him what he was doing, and he said he wanted to show me something. I told him I didn't want to see anything, but he doesn't turn around. I'm not scared yet because he's still real polite and calm, and I can't think he's wanting to do anything, you know. He wants to talk, he says. I tell him I don't have time to talk, but he's driving and he's not stopping. He goes over that bridge to Beacon Hill, and he's talking the whole time, telling me that people should get along better, stuff like that. He asks me if I have any kids, and I don't tell him about Antonio because it's none of his business what I got. I'm looking for a chance to get out, but he doesn't stop until he comes to this place where I can see the freeway down below me. I should have jumped out right away. I know that now, but he didn't seem like that kind. He starts telling me about his wife and how he wishes he could have kids, but she doesn't like being intimate. He thinks there's something wrong with her, and he's trying to figure out what it is.

"He keeps on talking like that, and I'm wondering if he's lonely and wants something from me. He seems nice, though, and sort of touches my shoulder like he's shy or something. He starts to move closer, and that's when I tell him that I got to go home right away. He doesn't want to listen, and I tell him I'm getting out of the car right now if he doesn't start it up and get me home. He puts his hand on my arm, and he tells me I'm not going anywhere. That's when I see that yellow rope in his other hand."

"Rope?" Anne asked. "He had a rope? The police report didn't say anything about a rope. Did you tell the officers about the rope?"

"They wasn't interested in what I said. Maybe I said it and maybe I didn't, but the man had a rope."

"Where did it come from?"

"How do I know? When I see that rope I wasn't going to stop and ask any questions. I pulled the door handle and jumped out before he could do anything. He was meaning to hold on, but I didn't intend to stay in that car with no rope. I took off running as fast I could. I was afraid he would follow me, but he took off the other way. That's when I see the police car. I guess they wrote down what happened after that."

The rope changed everything, Anne thought. The patrol cops would have included it in the report if she had told them. Why wouldn't Lucy tell them the most important part of the story? Maybe she was making it all up; it didn't seem like it, though. Once she had begun, Lucy's story had flowed without pause. Some of it had to be true, but which parts? Anne wondered if Lucy knew. To establish a crime, if there was even a crime to establish, it didn't matter whether Lucy was turning tricks or waiting for the bus as she said. It wouldn't matter to the prosecuting attorney or the judge; it might not even matter that much to a jury. But it did matter to Lucy. Anne suspected that it was early in Lucy's career, that she was still denying that she had turned the corner. She was still creating illusions for herself: *I'm on the corner and some man comes by, and he wants to give me some money. It just happens, and it doesn't mean that I'm a prostitute.* Anne knew that it was easier to work with the veterans. They had no illusions about the corners where they stood.

"Lucy, can you give me a physical description of this man?" Anne asked, beginning with a question that took Lucy away from herself, to make it less likely that she would lie. "How tall was he?"

"I never saw him standing," Lucy said, "but he was tall. You could tell by the way his head almost touched the roof of the car."

"Over six feet?"

"Antonio's father is six feet. This man is taller than that. At least that's how he looked sitting in the car."

"The report said he had a thin build."

"I didn't say that," Lucy said. "I said he wasn't fat. Trim, you know. He didn't have a gut hanging over his belt like some men do."

"Muscular?"

"I didn't see any muscles."

"What was he wearing?"

"He had on a white shirt and some kind of suit coat that didn't look like it belonged on him. I mean, there was a lot about him that didn't add up. It was like he was trying not to look good. He was wearing these heavy glasses that nobody wears anymore, and his suit coat didn't fit either. It looked like it came from the Salvation Army or something, like maybe he was trying to hide who he was. That's what started to get me scared, and then he put that hand on me and I saw the rope. That hand was strong. I don't know about anything else, but that hand sure was. If I hadn't jumped right then, I might not have got away."

"What did you think he was going to do with the rope?" Anne asked.

Lucy didn't answer immediately. Too early, Anne thought. Simple facts first. Don't let her dig a hole with a story that she can't get out of.

"First," Anne said, "tell me about his car."

Lucy didn't answer the simple question immediately either. She again looked at Antonio, who was sitting cross-legged in front of the television set, rocking in time to the music on *Sesame Street*.

"There wasn't anything special about the car," Lucy said at last. "It was an Oldsmobile or Buick or something. Nothing special." Lucy answered the question, but she was thinking beyond it.

"Two-door or four-door?" Anne asked.

"Four," Lucy said. "Why are you asking me what he was going to do? What do you think he was fixing to do with that rope?"

"I don't know," Anne said.

This time it was she who turned her eyes away. Anne looked at the little boy sitting on the floor and then beyond him to the moving picture on the television screen. Big Bird was surrounded by small friends, and he took the hand of each laughing child as he skipped among them. When Anne turned back to Lucy, the girl was still looking at her.

"I don't know," Anne repeated, "but I'm glad you never found out."

Chapter 5

D o you want a ride?"

Maria peered beneath the shelf suspended above the stove.

Her father stood outside the Dutch door that opened from Silve's kitchen onto the grooved-concrete pedestrian ramp in front of the restaurant. His blue police uniform filled the upper opening.

"Sure," she said. "I'll be ready in ten minutes."

"You go now, Maria," Silve said. "Don't keep your father waiting."

The old man left the counter where he had been talking to a regular customer and joined her at the stove. He took the handle of the sauté pan from her.

"Big day today," he said and shook the pork adobo she was finishing off for the Philippine omelet. "Big day, Sam," the old man called loudly to her father, who had opened the half door and stood inside the kitchen.

Silve didn't need to bend down to see through the space between the great black stove and the overhead shelf, and he didn't need to shout to be heard. But he did anyway.

"Now this Maria is an upperclassman, and you and I are still here on the bottom." He chuckled as fire shot up from his pan. "We're still here," he said more softly.

Maria removed the orange chef's jacket that matched Silve's, his favorite color, and hung it in its place next to the hand sink. She scrubbed her hands and looked into the small mirror above the sink. Her straight black hair survived everything, even the steam of the adobo.

Maria looked out the west window where the morning had advanced without her notice. Silve's restaurant was nestled into the west side of the Pike Place Market above the busy viaduct. Below them, beyond the viaduct, Elliott Bay stretched out before the jagged horizon of the Olympic Mountains. Sometimes, when the order rack above the stove filled with green slips of paper, she forgot to look beyond the tiny kitchen and the wants of the customers in the dining room. It was a million-dollar view, her father had said when he had stood with Silve at the stove earlier in the morning, and it was true. Up the street, only a block or two from the restaurant, were expensive condominiums that people bought so they could see what she saw anytime she turned around and looked.

"The dishes are done, Silve," Maria said, "and the oxtail is still in the oven."

She pulled the omelet order off the now clear order rack and slapped it onto the finished-order spindle on the shelf above the stove. "I still think you should have Henry come at nine o'clock instead of ten."

Silve looked at Sam again. His chef's hat flopped down over his eyes, and he pushed it back. He could never find one small enough.

"This girl has been worrying all morning," he said. "She doesn't think I know how to do this anymore."

Silve laughed as he poured the remaining juice of the adobo over the omelet. He was in a particularly good mood, as if he were the one getting ready for the new school year.

Maria slipped behind Silve and picked up the omelet plate. She set the plate on the counter in front of the customer she called Silent John and filled his coffee cup. Silve was right; she had been worried. It had been her idea a year ago to stop hiring the morning waitress because of the difficulty of finding someone reliable. Wouldn't it be better, she had asked Silve, if they did it themselves?

Silve liked the idea. He took care of the counter around the kitchen where his regular customers sat, and she handled the tables and booths down in the small dining room. They shared the cooking, and she made tips in addition to her salary. But now she had to take a class that was offered only in the morning, and she had to leave the restaurant before breakfast was completely over. She knew it tired Silve to walk up and down the steps to the dining room; she was learning the consequences of ideas. Ideas were like children. Once she produced them, she was responsible for them.

Then there was the problem with the tips. She knew that the waitresses lied about how much they earned, but she had given Silve a precise record of her tips, to the penny, so that he could report accurately to the IRS. "They'll think you're lying," he had said. "They won't understand that you work in the kitchen and earn a few tips on the side. They won't understand that you do two things at once. Maybe the IRS will audit you, and maybe they'll audit me and make everything complicated. It's better to keep the money and not report it. What they don't know won't hurt any of us."

Not wanting to make a problem for Silve, she kept the money and didn't report it. There had to be something wrong when telling the truth made so many complications.

Silve opened the sliding door on the cooler next to the windows and removed a paper sack from the bottom shelf.

"I made you lunch," he said, handing her the sack. "Chicken breast sandwich, a red apple, and a little chocolate from the Dilettante."

"When did you do that?"

"This morning before you came. You can give the apple to the teacher if you don't want it."

"Thank you," she said. She took the lunch from him and quickly kissed him on the cheek before he could turn back to the stove. "I'll eat the apple."

Silve rocked back on his heels and straightened his hat. The kiss had pleased him greatly.

"So now you study the fish," he said. "Soon you will know more than your father and me about all these things. We only know how to eat them. Isn't that right, Sam?"

"That's right," her father said.

Her father had not moved from the door. The kitchen was so small that an extra body could make it impossible to move around. When she and her father first arrived in the morning, he stood behind the stove with Silve. Sometimes the two of them looked out the window together, as they had this morning, as they had many mornings before she came. Today, there was new snow on the Olympic Mountains. It was a sure sign of fall, her father said, and winter after that, Silve added.

From the shelf beneath the cash register, Maria pulled out her backpack and jacket. She unzipped the pack and placed Silve's sack lunch on top. She hoisted one strap over her shoulder and walked back up the steps into the kitchen. Her father opened the door and waited for her to pass in front of him.

"Bye, Silve," she said. "See you tomorrow."

"Bye, honey. Learn everything you can."

Halfway up the concrete ramp that rose to street level, she reached around her father's waist and squeezed him as they walked. She wasn't sure how much he could feel through the bulletproof vest that he hated to wear. He put his arm around her and hugged her back, vigorously and briefly before they reached the top of the ramp. She turned around and saw Silve standing in the kitchen doorway below them. He waved, and she waved back.

"First day of school?" Zeke called from the City Fish stall at the top of the ramp.

"First day," Maria said.

Zeke lifted a purple banner tied to a long stick and waved it back and forth. "Go dogs," he said without the slightest tinge of enthusiasm.

Pike Place was packed with cars, and the cars barely moved on the one-way street. The sidewalk through the market stalls was equally packed with people. Her father knew most of the merchants by name, and it took time to walk with him a block in the Market. She liked that they knew her name and accepted her as one of them, but it was a mixed blessing. Sometimes the merchants came to the restaurant and found her when they couldn't find her father.

"Tell Sam to come and see me today," they would say, or "Tell him that Maximillian is out of jail and he wasn't supposed to come back here," or "Tell your father that somebody tried to rob Jolene this morning while she was walking to work." Sometimes they even came to her on her father's days off from work. "Well, tell him anyway," they said.

Her father unlocked the driver's door of the police car and slid behind the steering wheel. He pulled up the lock on the passenger's door, closed the lid of his briefcase that was on the front bench seat, and pulled the briefcase next to him. Her left knee brushed the shotgun that pointed toward the ceiling from the jaws of the locked steel rack bolted to the dashboard. She had become accustomed to the shotgun, just as she had become accustomed to the way people looked at her as her father drove up Virginia Street toward First Avenue. When she had first ridden with her father in the police car, she had wanted to communicate somehow to each of them that she wasn't under arrest, that she was just getting a ride, that the policeman was her father. It was an absurd notion. She wouldn't be able to explain any of it.

The voices on the police radio faded into the background.

She was learning to discriminate, just as he did, to pick up from the constant chatter those words that applied to him. She no longer felt slighted or ignored when he turned away from her midsentence and focused on the voice from the radio.

During the first months after finding him, he had not said a cross word to her, as if she were a mirage that would disappear with the slightest harshness. She had known of him before her mother's death, but he had known nothing about her and could not have imagined her as she had imagined him. Her mother had left her the thin fragile book of his poems—poems she had read so often that she memorized the words before she understood them. Through them she had imagined her father. Without the poems she might never have come to Seattle. She might have stayed in Anchorage with her stepfather and her stepsisters. She might have tried harder to become one of them. She might have tried to forget him.

"Ready for the new quarter at school?" he asked.

She turned toward him and wondered how long he had been watching her.

"I think so."

"You didn't get much of a break from summer quarter."

"It was enough."

She had gone back to Anchorage twice, once with her father. Everyone had tried to accommodate the new relationships—stepfather instead of father, father instead of stranger, daughter to both. It wasn't easy, and she had not gone back after the summer quarter, despite her stepfather's invitation. He would be busy teaching at his university. The timing was off; the vacation periods were different at the two schools.

When her father put his arm around her now, she didn't feel as if she had to hold on in fear of what would happen when he let her go. She thought she understood what love meant, what he meant when he said it, but maybe she didn't. With her mother it meant kisses all over her face until she laughed and ran away, or fingers dancing in stories about the raven or pushing away bad dreams in the night. Love was in her mother's eyes, which came so close when her mother held her face and rubbed her nose that she could see nothing else.

Sometimes she wished she could be a little girl with her father, as she had been with her mother, and crawl onto his lap as he sat at the kitchen table after dinner. She wished she could make her hands small and explore his cheeks, feel the whiskers that showed late in the day, tickle his ribs and make him laugh. He didn't laugh nearly as often as her mother, who had laughed until the end when even her eyes hurt and she could not get out of bed.

"Where shall I drop you off?" he asked.

They were crossing the steel grating of the University Bridge. Below them were houseboats floating on the northern reach of Lake Union. To the east at Portage Bay she saw the large brick buildings of the Oceanography Department rising above the few waterfront businesses that had survived the never-ending university expansion.

"Anywhere on Boat Street will be fine."

The southern portion of the huge campus was a campus by itself, smaller and more remote. On the main campus north of Pacific Street she sometimes felt lost, but among the familiar fisheries and oceanography buildings within sight, hearing, and smell of Portage Bay and the ship canal, she felt more at ease. Her father turned onto the broken asphalt of Boat Street and stopped in the first no-parking spot.

"Good luck," he said.

"Thanks for the ride."

"My pleasure."

She leaned over his briefcase, beyond the shotgun, and quickly kissed his clean-shaven cheek. Then she picked up her backpack from the floor of the car and opened the door. Outside, she bent down and looked at him.

"Be careful," she said.

"Always." He smiled as he always smiled when she told him to be careful. She told him every day.

Maria watched him make a U-turn on Boat Street and head back downtown. Would he go back to the Market and have breakfast with Silve, or would he have to answer a call that would turn out to be dangerous like one of the rogue waves that came from nowhere and washed over their kayak? He hadn't told the truth. He wasn't always careful.

With Silve's help she had prodded him into wearing the bulletproof vest issued by the police department. He didn't like it. It was too uncomfortable, he said, the same thing he said about the life jacket for the kayak, which he had stored behind his seat as if that would do any good. He now wore them, but she wondered what he did when she wasn't there. When they paddled the double kayak to work early in the morning, they stayed close to shore, especially in rough weather, but she knew he headed straight across the Sound when he paddled back alone. Knowing this frightened her sometimes; sometimes it made her angry; sometimes there was nothing she could do but laugh.

Usually she took the metro bus to school, but because her father had given her a ride, she was half an hour early for her first class. She walked to the small park at the edge of the canal where there was a wooden bench beneath a willow tree. It was her favorite place on campus. From there she could look across Portage Bay and see the cars on the freeway and the homes on the north end of Capitol Hill. She could even see the tops of some of the tallest skyscrapers downtown. They seemed far away. Water was always the great separator.

Opening her backpack, she removed the sack lunch and the textbook on intertidal systems. She had read the book during the break between school quarters. The book reminded her of the times she had explored the seashore of her mother's village in southeast Alaska—first with her mother, then alone.

"Sit quietly," her mother told her. "Watch what happens."

Maria sat quietly beside her mother and watched small crabs emerge from their holes. The crabs watched them warily with strange projecting eyes. They made her laugh, but she laughed quietly. Bees, wasps, and butterflies appeared with the crabs on the beach, or perhaps they were there all the time. When she sat quietly with her mother, she saw life on a smaller scale than she had seen before. She noticed the paw prints of raccoons, the talon marks of an egret, the slithering trail of a snake. With each wave from the ocean there was new life, and she saw it.

The same ocean current that flowed south from her mother's village in Alaska entered the straits between British Columbia and Washington and moved slowly but resolutely into the waters of Puget Sound. The fish, as Silve called her studies, made up some part of her interest, but the link with that current, that same water, was what held her.

It also frightened her. The first time she paddled on Puget Sound with her father in their double kayak, she had avoided looking down at the water. She looked over his shoulders to the shoreline, to the tall buildings beyond. Every unanticipated motion, every rocking of the kayak made her afraid that the kayak would roll over. The water was deep. She knew that much. How deep, she didn't know, and it wouldn't have mattered if it were twenty feet or two hundred. If the kayak rolled, she would have to swim in any case. Still, the idea of it mattered. Because she couldn't see more than a few feet below the surface, the water was unknowably deep.

She had gotten used to the roll of the kayak, to the way it moved with every wave and swell of the water. It seldom frightened her anymore. She had studied the glacial origin of the Sound and knew how deep it was. It was deep but not unknowably deep. Still, there was something down there, something unknowable about the water that frightened her.

She opened her lunch sack, removed Silve's apple, and took a bite. On the opposite shore of the narrow canal, a row of houses fronted the road to the yacht club. A small open boat with an outboard motor sailed up the canal, and the seaman waved to her as he passed by. The wake spread from the bow of his small boat and lapped softly against the shore below her.

Maria sat in the middle of the classroom with a new spiral notebook open to the first page. The professor, in his brown tweed coat and blue jeans, stood at the front of the room unpacking his worn leather briefcase. Maria recognized three students from previous classes, although she didn't know their names.

The professor turned on the overhead projector and placed a transparency on the lighted top. He began explaining the structure of the class, what he expected from his students, how they would earn their grades. Maria copied the outline from the screen into her notebook with a careful hand. The professor paused as a tardy student entered the room. Along with everyone else, Maria looked toward the door.

The student didn't slip quietly into a back row seat as Maria would have done, as most of them would have done. He stood confidently in the doorway while deciding where he would sit.

The professor gestured, but not impatiently, for the young man to find a desk. Maria recognized the student. He either threw the football or ran with it; she couldn't remember which. Her father would know. She wasn't a football fan, but she might pay attention now that the runner or thrower, whichever he was, walked to the row in which she sat and glided past two students who pulled in their legs to make room. He sat in a desk one removed from her but with no other person between them.

He smiled at her, gracing her momentarily with his full attention as the professor placed a second transparency on the projector. The football player was better looking than his pictures. His curly black hair appeared uncombed, but even the uncombed curls were handsome. She copied sentences from the screen but wrote nothing beyond them. While trying diligently to concentrate on the professor's words, she heard only scattered phrases as if she were listening on a telephone with a bad connection. The young man shifted toward her, his arm taking up the seat between them, his legs moving into the void, his body inclined in her direction.

It meant nothing, she told herself. He was used to taking up a lot of space. In the meantime she needed to concentrate on what the professor said. They had two papers to write, one on vertical migrations of zooplankton and another on population dynamics of local marine animals. There would be a field project that made up fifty percent of the total grade. She wrote it all down.

She wondered if she smelled like adobo.

Several times their eyes engaged accidentally. She forced normal breathing upon herself until she turned away; she forced her eyes not to blink, to disengage from his. It was a long hour that passed quickly. When the professor turned off the projector, she closed her notebook and drew her backpack closer. She slid the notebook past Silve's sandwich and waited for the football player to leave. He had nothing to delay him—one thin notebook and a pen that he clipped to the cover. He had no books, no pack, no coat. His plaid shirt hung loosely from his broad shoulders.

"That was interesting," he said to her as other students began leaving the classroom. "I wasn't so sure about this class when I signed up. How about you?"

"I need the class for my major," she said. "I think it's all interesting." She lifted her jacket from the back of her chair and wiggled into it while sitting in the desk.

"I admire you scientists," he said. "Studying some experiment year after year without knowing where it will lead."

"I'm not a scientist," she said.

"Not yet."

Now he rose, moved back a step without turning away, and waited. She stood and reached down for her backpack. Two students had gone to the front of the classroom to talk to the professor. They were students she recognized, serious students who had questions about the weekly lab. She should be there, too. It would be a good way to break away.

"My name is Paul," he said. He extended his hand with the same confidence with which he had occupied the space next to her. He had an enormous hand. Her hand would disappear within his grip.

"Maria," she said. She put her pack on the desk and shook his hand. His smile showed perfect white teeth.

"Glad to meet you, Maria. What do you have next?" he asked.

"An English class."

"Up on the main campus?"

"Yes."

"That's where I'm going," he said. "Do you mind if I walk along with you?"

She had an hour before the English class and had planned to remain on the south campus and study in the Oceanography Building lounge.

"Maybe you can tell me how hard this class will be," he said. He was already backing out of the aisle.

She decided that she could study on the main campus as well as anyplace and followed him out of the aisle and out of the classroom. He walked with a loose athletic gait that made her feel stiff and upright by comparison. Before they reached Pacific Street, he had learned that she was a junior thinking about graduate school. By the time they reached the north side of the fountain where she always looked for Mt. Rainier down the tree-lined boulevard to the southeast, he had learned that she lived off-campus with her father, below and beyond the Magnolia Bridge. He was inquisitive about her but said very little about himself. Maybe he thought she knew all about him. Walking with him through the campus was like walking with her father in his uniform through the Market. People noticed him and noticed her because of him.

She looked past the fountain and saw Rainier in bright sunshine. It was the final sign that convinced her that she was too warm. She would soon begin to sweat if she didn't get out of her jacket. Her right sleeve wouldn't come free, and she was stuck until he delicately lifted the jacket from her shoulder where it had become bound.

"Thanks," she said.

"It's a beautiful day, isn't it?"

"Yes."

"Where to now?"

"I think I'll go to the library for a while. I have an hour before my next class."

"I do, too. How about a Coke or something? We could sit out on the patio at the Student Union and enjoy the sunshine. It won't last long, you know."

"No, it won't."

On the patio a few tables away a beautiful girl with long blond hair had not been able to remove her eyes from him. Maria closed her eyes for a moment and arched her neck into the sun. She didn't think about herself as pretty or not pretty. There was too much else to think about. Her father complimented her, but that was her father. Perhaps Paul Renzlau, the full name with which he introduced himself after the first sip of Coke, had so much beauty in himself that he didn't look for it in others.

"What about your mother?" he asked. "Where does she live?"

Maria opened her eyes wide.

"She died when I was eight years old."

"I'm sorry," he said.

"I am, too. My father said she was the most beautiful girl he had ever seen, but he writes poems. He sees things differently than the rest of us."

"Maybe."

She looked across the table at the young man. The memory of her mother always made her sad, but time had tempered the sadness so that she could smile now with her memories. Mostly she smiled to herself, but occasionally she let someone else see it.

Mt. Rainier peeked at them over the top of the trees that followed the hillside down to Lake Washington. Her mother had a story about a mountain. Her mother had a story for everything. Maria had told the stories to her father, but only some of them. Some she wanted to keep for herself. She thought all stories must be that way.

He must have them, too, this beautiful young man who had chosen her for an hour. The hour would soon be gone, and she had not heard any of his stories. Maybe he wanted to keep them to himself just as she treasured the stories from her mother.

Chapter 6

Grace and Katherine walked along the east side of the hospital where there had been a rash of car prowls the last two weeks between noon and 2:00 P.M. Car prowling was seldom a high priority concern, but the time of day was unusual. Katherine had shown Grace the reports at roll call. Maybe, Katherine speculated, somebody was picking up a little extra money during his lunch break. The car prowls might not have interested either of them except that one of the victims was a nurse in the emergency room whom they had gotten to know. Katherine, especially, knew all the staff in the emergency room since the hospital had the only reliably clean bathroom in the neighborhood. From the beginning Grace couldn't focus on the search. Now Katherine stopped looking, too.

"When did you find out?" Katherine asked.

"Mom called last night. Her surgery will be next Monday. My sister is flying up from Los Angeles on Saturday."

It seemed impossible that her mother was sick. A little more than a week ago, she had helped her mother clean the basement. Her mother was so strong that she carried the heaviest boxes up the stairs herself and placed them on the curb for the Goodwill truck without difficulty. Her mother had always been strong, and she didn't look any different from the week before. Yet there was a cancer growing inside her breast. And what if it had spread someplace else? What if it continued to spread? What if there was nothing they could do to help? After her mother's call, Grace had not been able to sleep. She couldn't read anything either. She had piles of books to read, but she couldn't read them. All night she had listened to the Pia Zadora records that were her mother's favorites. All night she listened to the records with Lady, her gentle dog, on her lap and cried into Lady's soft coat. Without Lady the night would have been even longer.

She was glad she could finally tell another person. She couldn't talk to her father and Evangeline about the cancer: They were as scared as she was. Her mother was the strong one among them, especially now, but she couldn't burden her either. Her mother had enough to bear. Grace was relieved that Katherine was beside her. The worried look that appeared on Katherine's face somehow made it more bearable for herself.

"Is there anything I can do?" Katherine asked.

Katherine looked as if she were prepared to stop right there on the sidewalk and begin doing whatever it was that needed to be done, but that was the problem. So far, Grace hadn't thought of anything useful for any of them to do.

"I guess you can pray," Grace said.

Katherine did stop then, and for a moment Grace wondered if Katherine intended to drop to her knees and begin praying. Katherine had never given any hints of religious fervor before.

"I'm not very good at praying," Katherine said.

Her partner was absolutely serious, and Grace smiled at Katherine's serious and good intentions. She was also relieved that Katherine had remained standing.

"I don't know if I am either," Grace said, "but I decided it couldn't hurt."

"Does Rigmor know?"

"Not yet. I'll tell her after we finish this detail."

Katherine looked down the street where there was a car parked in every available spot. In addition to the cars on the street, there were cars in the parking lots and cars in the circular drive of the emergency room.

"Oh, hell," Katherine said. "This is like looking for a needle in a haystack. Let's go talk to Rigmor. We'll never find anything here."

From out of nowhere, or perhaps from the middle of the haystack, came the sound of a scream.

"That's mine! That's mine!" shouted a woman from the open door of an apartment halfway down the block. The woman followed a man out to the sidewalk. He was carrying something. Grace couldn't make out what it was, but it was heavy.

Grace looked at Katherine. Although both knew that they had to walk down the block and investigate what was happening, neither wanted to go. They had made the decision to leave, but now a woman trying to grab a heavy object from a man had changed their plans.

"That's mine. You can't take that."

It was a microwave oven that the man carried and that the woman was trying to snatch away from him. He ignored her as if he neither heard her voice nor felt her hands. He dumped the oven on the neglected lawn beside a mess of boxes that had been dumped with equal care. The woman quickly snatched the microwave from the ground. The man said nothing, but he clenched his fists. The woman backed away with the microwave oven. Then the man saw the two approaching police officers and eased the tightening of his fists.

"Is there a problem here?" Grace asked.

"Nope," the man said and walked back into the apartment. The woman followed him with the microwave oven. She was no longer simply yelling about retrieving the microwave oven; she now wanted him out of her apartment.

"Oh, shit," Katherine muttered.

Grace agreed. The last thing she cared about just then was somebody's microwave oven or, she suspected, anything else they would find inside the apartment. Grace pulled the radio out of its holster on her belt and told the dispatcher that they had come across a disturbance. She gave the street number for the apartment building and holstered the radio.

She and Katherine stopped at the apartment door. Inside were two men and the woman. The woman looked at them with bleary eyes. She had oily dyed hair and a voice that grated on the nerves. The two men might have been brothers. The one who had been outside was bigger than the other. Both had long hair, beards, and wore heavy black boots; they looked like the last two members of an aging outlaw motorcycle gang. The woman, the most attractive member of the gang, was clutching futilely at the hands of the smaller man, who was disconnecting the antenna wire from a television set. The saved microwave oven was upside down on the floor of the living room.

"That's mine," the woman said. "Don't you take that."

"Hey!" Katherine shouted. "What's going on here?"

"They're stealing my stuff," she said.

Grace and Katherine stepped into the apartment and moved a few feet apart from each other. The smaller man had finished disconnecting the antenna wire, and the bigger one lifted the television set. He took a step forward as if he intended to walk past them out the door, ignoring them the way he ignored the other woman.

"Stay right there," Grace said. She was losing patience with his surliness. "Whose place is this?"

"It's mine," the woman said. "I have the papers to prove it."

"Fine," Grace said without looking away from the man with the television. He had hard eyes, and she didn't trust him. "Let's see the papers."

The woman disappeared into another room. Grace pointed

at the stand where the television had stood. "Put it down until we sort this out."

With deliberate slowness that was more than reluctance, the man put the television set back on the metal cart. The woman came out of the room with a long sheet of paper and handed it to Grace. It was a rental agreement. Grace looked at the name at the top of the page.

"Are you Cecilia Thompson?"

"Yes, and all of this is mine." Her hand swept the room.

"It's my TV," the tall man said, "and I paid the rent. It doesn't matter what's on that paper."

"It does matter," Grace said, "unless you have receipts for the television and microwave and everything else you want to take."

The tall man looked at the shorter one. There were no receipts.

"He can take his clothes, but I want him out of here," the woman said. "I'm tired of his ugly face."

The woman pointed at the tall man's ugly face.

"That's enough," Grace said.

The woman had a fading purple and yellow bruise beneath her right eye.

The tall man bent down and picked up the television set again. "I bought this," he said. "No bitch is going to stop me from taking what's mine."

The smaller man laughed.

Grace pulled the portable radio from its holster. "2-Boy-8," she said sharply, "send us a backup unit now."

The man with the television walked toward the door. Grace and Katherine joined together to block his path. Grace heard the radio operator asking for a status report. Before she could respond, the woman hit the man in the face with her fist.

"Bastard," she said.

He turned with the television set in his hands and kicked her in the stomach. She flew backward and fell to the floor.

"You're both under arrest," Grace shouted. "Step back. Step back."

The man tried to push his way past them by using the television set as a battering ram. He was strong, and they were fast losing ground. Katherine brought her canister of Mace up to the man's face, aimed at his eyes, and sprayed. He screamed with pain but still held on to the television set as if it were glued to his hands. The other man charged forward and knocked Katherine to the floor. The tall man with the television began swinging it as a weapon, wildly and blindly, and knocked the portable police radio from her hand. Grace pulled out her nightstick and hit him hard across the forehead. The television fell to the floor, and the man dropped to his knees.

The shorter man was leaning over Katherine and trying to hit her with wild swings. She kicked him away and sprayed him with Mace. In a fury that nearly blinded her, Grace grabbed the man by his collar and flung him against the wall. She wanted him away from her partner. She wanted to throw him so hard that he would break through the wall and bring the whole house down on top of him. She wasn't seeing clearly. Mace fumes and anger hindered her vision, and it was becoming hard to breathe. The man, rebounding from the wall, held a gun in his right hand and was swinging it in a wide arc toward Katherine.

Grace dropped her nightstick and lunged for the gun. She grabbed the hammer of the revolver, pushed the gun away so it was no longer pointed at Katherine, and twisted the man's wrist until the gun fell to the floor. She continued twisting until the man screamed in pain and dropped onto his stomach. Grace forced his hand high onto his back. Katherine scrambled toward her and pressed her knee across the man's neck. She had her service revolver in her hand. Her face was deathly white.

"You okay?" Grace asked.

Katherine nodded.

Grace handcuffed the man's right hand and reached for the left. Radio was urgently asking them for their status. A number of cars called in that they were responding. A siren screamed outside. The man she had knocked down with her nightstick was trying to get up, while the woman he had kicked was groaning and clutching her stomach as she raised herself to her knees. It was a mess everywhere Grace looked.

"Check the other guy," Grace said. "He might have a gun, too."

Grace picked up the man's gun from the floor and made sure that it wasn't cocked. It was a revolver with a two-inch barrel. She popped open the cylinder and ejected the cartridges into her hand. Then she stuffed the gun into her belt and put the cartridges into her pants pocket.

Katherine forced the other man back to the floor with her knee. She frisked him with her left hand. Her right hand still held her gun. Morgan from Boy-3 appeared in the doorway. He hesitated a moment until Grace motioned for him to help Katherine.

"I'm sorry, Johnny. I'm sorry," the woman began to cry. "Let him go. He didn't mean it. Let him go."

Katherine holstered her revolver and unsnapped her handcuff case. Morgan pulled the suspect's right hand back and held it while Katherine slipped on the first handcuff. Two more officers appeared in the doorway. Morgan pulled back the man's left hand.

"Let him go," the woman pleaded. "Johnny, I'm sorry," the woman cried as she crawled toward the man beneath Katherine's knee.

"She's under arrest, too," Grace told the two officers and pointed at the crawling woman.

The two officers halted the woman's progress and lifted her to her feet. She slumped in their grasp and tried to drop back to the floor with Johnny. They straightened her again and clasped handcuffs on her wrists.

"Johnny," she cried as they dragged her outside. "Johnny, I'm with you."

They soon had more help than they needed. Four officers in two-man cars hauled the men and woman off to the North Precinct; two others brought the cardboard boxes inside and stacked them beside the television set on the living room floor. One officer opened all the doors and windows to clear the remaining Mace fumes, and another ran the serial numbers from the television set and microwave oven and any other appliance he could find. All the serial numbers checked clear.

Eventually every car except the two transporting prisoners went back into service. The sergeant arrived as the last backup car pulled away. There was nothing remaining for him to do, and he left a few minutes later.

Thirty minutes after they had heard the first scream, Grace and Katherine were alone in the silent apartment, which had been emptied of people as well as anger and fear. Grace didn't feel much of anything except the sickening knowledge of how close Katherine had come to being shot. If she had not grabbed the hammer of the revolver, the man surely would have shot Katherine. If she had been a split second later, he would have pulled the trigger, and it would have been her fault for letting anger overcome her reason. She had the nightstick in her hand. She should have hit him when he was on top of Katherine. She should never have thrown him into the wall.

The whole series of frustrating and pointless events had improved nothing. They could just as well have turned away or walked down another street for all the good they had done. There was no separation of original victim and perpetrators;

all three had gone to jail. She and Katherine, the police officers who were supposed to improve the street, were now the victims. The uselessness and meaninglessness of violence was what she hated most about the job. Katherine had almost been shot, and for what? The television and microwave oven lay broken on the floor.

Katherine stood in the living room looking at the wall from which the man had rebounded. She was so pale that Grace wondered if she was hurt. Katherine would never admit pain.

"Are you sure you're not hurt?" Grace asked.

"I'm okay," Katherine said softly.

"I'll write the report," Grace said. "You write your officer's statement. We can wrap this up in an hour or two."

What else could they do except wrap it up and put it away?

"I almost shot you," Katherine said.

"What?" Grace wasn't sure that she heard Katherine correctly. Her partner's voice was hardly above a whisper.

"I was squeezing the trigger when you jumped in front of me. I almost shot you."

The whiteness of Katherine's face had nothing to do with any pain she felt for herself.

"I was too close to him to do anything else," Grace said.

Grace thought back to the seconds that had passed from the time she threw the man into the wall and to the time she first saw the gun. Maybe she hadn't been as close as she first thought. How long had it taken her to reach the gun once she saw it? A second? Two seconds? Long enough for Katherine to draw her weapon. Grace had grabbed the hammer so that he couldn't pull the trigger, but how long had that taken? Unlike Katherine, he wouldn't have had the slightest restraint. Why hadn't he fired?

She removed the small handgun from her waistband and opened the empty cylinder. The revolver was a piece of junk.

She didn't even recognize the brand. The hammer felt strange, as if there was something wrong with the spring. Grace pointed the revolver at the floor and handed it to Katherine. Then she pulled out the five cartridges she had stuffed in her pocket. She carefully examined each one of them. On the fourth cartridge she examined was the unmistakable impression of the firing pin on the primer—a tiny indentation a fraction of an inch off-center.

Without saying anything she showed the cartridge to Katherine. It could have been anywhere in the cylinder, but they both knew where the bullet had been. She hadn't reached the gun in time after all. It had misfired.

Katherine took the bullet from Grace. Her hand trembled as she held the small brass casing between her thumb and forefinger.

"We'll be lucky if we ever get to Rigmor's today," Grace said. "This will take forever."

Chapter 7

In the rain Maria stood before a plate glass window looking at a pair of tall black boots. It had sounded simple from Paul's explanation—a small party at the fraternity house with friends. He could pick her up at eight and have her home before eleven. She should have said no. She didn't start thinking until she was alone. It wasn't at all simple.

Why would Paul invite her? He could invite any girl on campus, including any of the girls on Greek Row where the party would be. She had never been inside a fraternity house or a sorority, but she had an image of the people who lived there that was much different than the image she had of herself. The girls from the sororities were the ones with expensive hair, who put on makeup even for early classes and wore Italian leather boots like the boots she was staring at.

Was he curious about her, a darker face in the white sea of students in the oceanography class? Was that what her father had been about her mother—curious? And her mother, why would she go to him? She had been a girl then, younger than her daughter was now. Could a girl love a boy that much? Was that what was in the poems he had written or in the lingering longing mist in her mother's eyes, even at the end? Maria wanted to understand that longing, but she wasn't sure she could. Nevertheless, there she was because of it. There she was, this image she saw reflected in the plate glass window.

Two years earlier she had come to find her father, hoping that she might find herself, too, for better or for worse. She found him, but where was she? Here, she saw from her reflection; here, in front of a mannequin with straight black hair and a white china doll face, who wore black boots that matched the leather of a knee-length coat cinched tightly around a slender waist. The coat was like the one her father had given her for Christmas. At the time she wondered what he was thinking. Where could she wear such a coat? Perhaps he had also seen the black-haired mannequin.

She had worn the coat twice: once with her father when she had taken him to a fancy restaurant for dinner on his birthday and again to an art show on campus escorted by a young artist who was not one of the starving sort. He wasn't very good either—not that she could see. Then the winter was over, and the coat hung in her small closet, scenting all her clothes with its pungent new leather smell.

A coat like that required more—a dress or skirt that was short enough to match the length or long enough to completely escape its restraint. A coat like that required a silk blouse, the right collar, boots. Her father didn't understand that. He saw only the coat.

The boots had no price listed that she could see. The buyer must go in and ask. How much would she pay for such boots? Soft leather, two-inch heels, blunt toes. A week's wages at Silve's? More? She doubted that Paul Renzlau ever stood outside on the sidewalk. She had asked him how people would dress. He didn't know. What was he going to wear? He didn't know that either. He didn't have to know.

She had to be careful with her money. She had her job and money her mother had left her. Her father paid her tuition—wanted and maybe needed to pay it—but she would have to leave someday, to support herself, and there was no way to know when that would happen. Could she afford the boots in the window? Could she ever know how much such boots would cost?

Inside the store the young salesman gladly measured her foot and brought forward the gold box from the back room. His touch was so intimate that she held her breath as he folded her jeans above her right calf. He slipped on the right boot and zipped up the side. He stood back for her to take a step. She couldn't bear to look at herself in the mirror. She stared at the floor, moved her foot inside the boot, and heard his purring compliments. He knelt at her feet, rolled up the left cuff, and held her calf as he fit the second boot over her foot.

Is this me, she wondered—black leather coat, tall black boots? The boots would make a lot of noise when she walked. Did she dare walk with so much noise? Her father told her how quietly her mother walked, her body so still that she seemed to float over the gravel beach of her village in Alaska. He said that her mother told him that his feet were angry with the ground. Were these angry boots? Would they carry her too far from her mother's village where feet were quiet?

She didn't look at the price, didn't look until the amount appeared on the cash register. She wrote the check quickly, writing numbers without meaning, and showed the purring young man the identification he requested. This was her picture, her name. These were her boots.

"Rain gear tomorrow," her father said, meaning for the paddle to work. "This weather is supposed to last a while."

They had finished dinner at the table in front of the sliding glass door, and he was sipping from his second glass of red wine. He had grilled salmon on the deck, and steam rose from the top of the black grill as raindrops cooled the lid. The beach stretched before them, the view broken by the wood slats of the deck railing. The city rose beyond the water. It was too early to notice the lights in the tall buildings.

"I'm going out tonight," she said.

"Oh?" Her father was surprised.

"Paul Renzlau invited me to a party at his fraternity house."

"I see."

"I have to get ready," she said and began gathering the dishes. "He's going to pick me up at eight."

"Leave this," he said. "I'll clean up."

She had told her father about her class with Paul Renzlau but not about going to the Student Union each day afterward.

"I know you're wondering why he would invite me. It's just a spur of the moment type of thing. We were having a Coke after class, and he invited me. It's no big deal."

"I wasn't wondering why he would ask you."

"I am."

"Well, I wasn't, but you should be careful. These guys are used to getting everything they want."

"What guys are you talking about?"

"You know. Football players. Big men on campus. Those guys."

"He hasn't told me that he's a football player. I know that he is, but he hasn't said a word about it. I haven't talked about it either."

"Really? What do you talk about?"

"We talk about school, that sort of thing. He plans on going to law school. He already has enough hours to graduate. He's only taking this class because he thought it might be interesting. He seems like a really nice person."

"Maybe he is. That's what the newspapers say. Of course it wouldn't hurt if I strapped on my gun and met him at the door."

Her father smiled, but she didn't feel like smiling back. She smiled anyway.

"He doesn't know that you're a police officer. I don't think it helps when they find that out. I told him you were a poet. He probably expects to meet some old man smoking a pipe."

"I tried that once."

"What?"

"A pipe."

"You?"

"Yes. We could smoke in classes back then. In most of those English classes there was a haze of smoke from all the guys like me who pretended we were contemplating, but it was all smoke."

As she ironed a white blouse in her room, she tried to imagine her father with a pipe. How old would he have been? Her age. A few years older than the boy in the one picture she had of him and her mother. She raised the iron and looked at the framed picture on her desk—a boy and girl standing on the beach, the boy with his arm around the shoulder of the girl leaning into his body, wanting to be close—a moment caught by the camera never to change. He must still think of her that way. He never saw her grow older, although she never grew old. What must he think now, this boy who had grown older? What must he think when he sees the daughter who is older than the mother, the lover he remembers? She had shown him other pictures of her mother. His eyes blurred with tears, distorting the image in the photograph. She believed that the only picture he ever saw clearly was the girl on the beach.

She greeted Paul at the door. He had an umbrella with him that he had not opened. She led him into the living room where her father rose from his chair and extended his hand. Paul was bigger than her father, stronger. She wasn't used to seeing that.

In her boots with their two-inch heels she felt as if she were seeing everything from a different angle. Before her illusions disappeared, before the perfunctory greetings of the two men turned to questions, she put on her black leather coat and led Paul back out the door. He opened the umbrella, raised it over her head, and guided her to his car with a hand pressed into her back. He opened the door for her and lowered the umbrella once she was inside.

"What a great place to live," Paul said as he drove up the hill toward the Magnolia Bridge. "You must love it here."

"My father fixed up the house himself. It was in bad shape when he bought it."

"He's a lot younger than I expected."

"I know."

He twisted his head toward her, and she could see his smile from the light of the street lamps. He had a perfect smile, like an advertisement in a magazine.

"You look great tonight," he said.

"I wasn't sure what to wear," she said. "I hope this is okay."

"It sure is."

She began to relax. Paul's small car had the gearshift on the floor, and his right hand seldom left the stick. He seemed to enjoy the coordination required of his hands and feet. He drove faster than she was used to, but she wasn't concerned. He was skillful in avoiding any traffic problems.

"I won't be in class tomorrow," he said.

"Why?"

"Maybe I should have told you before. I'm on the football team. We leave for Oregon in the morning. That's why my fraternity brothers are having this party on a Thursday night."

"Why didn't you tell me?"

"I don't know. I get tired of talking about it. Most people already know. I think I was waiting for you to say something."

"I don't know anything about football," Maria said.

She hadn't expected him to laugh, nor to release the gearshift and squeeze her hands, which were folded in the curve between her legs.

"Great," he said.

His hand went back to the gearshift, and the car accelerated as he shifted into a higher gear.

The bus ride home from the university took an hour, sometimes more. She had to ride downtown first before transferring to a Magnolia route. Paul covered the direct route in ten minutes. Greek Row, the several streets where most of the fraternity and sorority houses were located, was at the top of a hill just north of the campus. From the top of this hill on 45th Street, she saw the floating bridge that crossed Lake Washington. Mostly she saw headlights and taillights moving both ways across the bridge in a heavy stream of cars. It was a long distance away. She knew students who had research projects in the lake marshes beneath the columns of an abandoned freeway. The freshwater lake didn't interest her the way salt water did.

Paul drove down an alley and slipped between two cars in a small parking lot behind a large brick house. The lot had been the backyard at one time. Without waiting for him she opened her door and got out. He came around the car with the umbrella. The sliding lever was stuck, and the umbrella wouldn't open. Finally it burst apart in an explosion of spindles and fabric. She laughed at the absurd look on his face. He laughed, too, and threw the umbrella into the backseat. Then he took her arm and ran with her through the rain around the house to the front door.

Perhaps thirty people were in the huge front room when they arrived. There were more men than women. Loud music played through speakers that surrounded the room. It was familiar music, but she knew no more about music than football. A young man in a beautiful purple sweater came up to them.

"Jim Robbins," he said, holding out his hand and welcoming her.

"Jim is our president," Paul said. "Be careful. He's always looking for votes."

Paul took her coat and disappeared with it into an adjoining room.

"How about something to drink?" Jim asked. "Beer, wine, soft drink?"

She looked around the room and saw others with beer.

"Beer would be fine."

"Light or dark?"

"It doesn't matter."

"Beer it is," he said.

He brought two beers, one for her and one for Paul, and then moved on to the next couple who were arriving.

Paul led her to one side of the room and introduced her to other people. The boys shook her hand, and the girls smiled with their names that she forgot as soon as she heard them.

A boy stood and offered her his place on the couch with a formality that surprised her. It was hard to get the boys in class to even move their feet out of the way. She didn't want to take his place, but with his gesture and Paul's, she felt compelled to sit on the couch beside another girl. Through a puff of cigarette smoke the girl asked her a question that got lost in the smoke and music. Maria smiled nervously and leaned toward the girl.

"I'm sorry. I didn't hear you."

"Friend of Paul's?" the girl asked again.

"We have a class together."

"Ah," the girl whispered. Maria recognized the response from the shape of the girl's lips as her head tilted back and she released another stream of gray smoke.

Paul sat on the wide arm of the couch, and the three boys who had gathered around him pressed closer. They were talking about the upcoming football game. Defense, she heard—some sort of corner, inside or out. The three game experts waved their long-necked bottles with growing excitement. She strained to hear what they said, to understand. Paul nodded in agreement, but he didn't say anything until he turned away from the football seminar and looked at her.

"Do you feel like dancing?"

She felt like doing anything that would get her off the couch, away from the other girl's smoky smile that hid her words. When she was a child, she liked to dance with her mother. They often danced together when they visited her grandparents. All the women danced together. Age didn't matter: They all danced. Certain steps, certain movements of hands and head, meant different things. Their movements told stories within the dances. Fragments of those stories came back to her when she danced to the party music, which was so loud it garbled words beyond understanding. She watched and imitated others on the dance floor, but eventually her mother's movements slowly wove their way into her steps and gestures.

Other men—the single men who stood around the room—stepped in front of Paul. They did not dance among themselves the way the men danced in her mother's village. They waited alone for a chance to dance with her or other girls, and Paul didn't seem to mind that they pushed him out of the way. There was only one boy who didn't dance. He stood against the wall and looked away from her every time she looked at him. He seemed lonely and shy, almost afraid. He smiled when other boys teased him for not dancing, but the teasing didn't move him from the wall. She wished she could ask him to dance, but she was afraid, too. She was afraid that he would say no. She was afraid that if she stopped even for a moment, she would forget the stories her mother told through her dancing.

Paul was never alone, but he never danced with anyone else. He waited his turn for her, and she was always happy when he came back. Her new boots, however, were killing her.

Chapter 8

It was ten after four on Friday afternoon, and the empty office was so quiet that Anne heard the hum of the fluorescent lights above her. She envied everybody who had someplace to go. Even those who stopped at the Greek's for one drink, one drink that stretched into the night, had someplace.

Years ago—God, how long ago was it?—Vivien had given her a cat. It was right after Vivien broke her arm and was still wearing the cast. She must have been ten or eleven. On her own initiative Vivien had gone to the pet store, bought a kitty that she fell in love with, and brought her to Aunt Anne on the bus because she thought Aunt Anne needed somebody to play with. To Vivien, the cat was somebody. How could she tell her niece with a broken arm and a big grin that she didn't want the kitty that her niece already loved? Turning away the cat would be like turning away the child who brought it. So the cat stayed, but no matter how hard she tried she could not endear herself or become endeared to that animal. In the end Vivien got the cat and the litter box, the cat food, and the scratching tree. Everyone was happy with the arrangement except Vivien's mother. Now Vivien had a baby herself, and she still gave her aunt coffee mugs with cats on them.

Anne sipped coffee from the Cheshire cat mug Vivien had given her and read the arrest report one more time. The night before, a patrol officer had stopped the suspect for a traffic violation in the North End. Just as the officer was finishing the ticket, an attempted assault in a library parking lot five blocks from the traffic stop was broadcast on the radio. The traffic violator matched the description of the suspect.

Anne had a case of a rape two weeks earlier in Madison Park with the same MO and with a suspect who matched the description of the suspect in the North End. The earlier rape was the reason that Anne waited at her desk as the minute hand slowly moved around the face of the clock. The first victim, Marcella, had been in a library, too. Marcella was a schoolteacher who liked to walk to the library on Wednesday evenings, the one night that it was open until eight o'clock. On her way home a man emerged from the passenger's side of a car parked on the street. There was no one in the driver's seat. Instinctively, Marcella knew that he had been waiting for her. Perhaps it was the concentration of his eyes upon her, or the swiftness with which he covered the ground between them, as predator to prey. He put a knife to her throat and dragged her into a wooded area where she often walked at dusk to listen to the Swainson's thrush that built a nest there every spring. The thrush was the last bird in the woods to sing before dark, Marcella said, and its song lifted the heart of everyone who heard it. The man forced her deep into the woods with the knife pressed against her throat. He didn't have to tell her to be quiet, although he may have said it. Marcella cried to herself, pleaded with him to let her go, and begged God not to abandon her in the dead leaves below the trees where the thrush sang.

He tied her hands behind her back with twine. Then he turned her over and before raping her made two deep cuts on her face, one on each cheek. Why? Marcella wanted to know. To show how sharp the knife was? To frighten her? She was already so frightened that she had no strength to cry out even if she had dared. She felt the knife blade deep in her flesh, but she didn't remember any pain. Was there pain that followed the blade? Why did he cut her? Why did he cut her twice? Did he want to leave his mark so that each time she looked at herself in the mirror she would remember, so that she could no longer bear to look, so that she would see the horror on the faces of everyone who stared at her? The doctor said he could erase the scars with surgery. She would see them and feel them even after they were gone.

The arrest close to the library in the North End was a stroke of luck. Unlike Marcella, the woman screamed when she saw the knife. A neighbor walking by the library shouted for somebody to call the police, and the suspect ran. He got into his car and drove through a red light five blocks away. The officer who had been waiting at the light was in no hurry to write the ticket. The officer was still waiting for Radio to come back with his record check when the assault call came out. Now they had a rape suspect and his knife—a hunting knife with a long curved blade.

They also had found a coil of twine in the suspect's apartment. It was a thousand yards bundled neatly into a coil no bigger than a flower pot. The amount of twine recovered, one piece from Marcella and another from the suspect's pocket, totaled a few yards. There was enough twine in the coil for a thousand rapes. Maybe there was enough twine to hang him.

Anne waited for the minute hand to arch down the face of the clock before she called Marcella. Marcella had just gone back to work, and Anne didn't want to call her at her school. She wanted to wait until Marcella was home. That was how she would want it herself. She wouldn't want to be called at work and have everyone pretend not to hear. She needed Marcella to identify the rape suspect Monday morning in a lineup. Anne would tell Marcella that the suspect would not be able to see her, but it wouldn't matter. He never saw her the first time. He had left his mark on her as if he were carving his initials into one of the fallen trees deep in the woods.

Anne had been thinking about Lucy Means, too—the young woman who said she was waiting for the bus. Lucy thought the man with the rope was tall, but maybe he just looked tall sitting in the car. The age of the two suspects was different, the build was different, the rope was different. Lucy said it was yellow rope and as thick around as her little finger. Yellow versus brown, thick versus thin, tall versus short. There had been too many differences to link the two cases. Nevertheless, there was a rope with each, and it might be a good idea to talk to Lucy again. Sometimes a photograph made all the difference. Sometimes the victim was wrong about all the physical characteristics, but she remembered the face of the suspect. She remembered it forever.

Her telephone rang, and Anne picked up the receiver. "Sex Crimes, Detective Smith," she said. There was no response, and the telephone rang again. She saw that the wrong button was pushed, and she punched the one that was flashing.

"Smith," she said a second time, describing herself in truncated form.

"Anne, it's Irene from Spokane. I've been out of the office all day and didn't get your message until just a minute ago. What the hell are you calling me about this time?"

Anne smiled and rocked back in her chair.

"I want to know why you don't take care of your creeps over there instead of sending them over to us."

"Seattle is where they belong," Irene said. "Spokane is a nice quiet town. What do you have?"

"Alexander Davis, white male, thirty-five years old, short, stocky build. Assault, attempted rape. We think we've got him on another rape a couple weeks ago where he slashed the victim's face just for the hell of it. He's got a driver's license with a Spokane address. He's rented an apartment here for two months. His record shows that he's done time in Walla Walla for rape."

Anne gave Irene the Spokane address from the driver's license and heard Irene breathing into the telephone as she wrote down the information.

"Slashed her, you say?"

"Yeah. One cut on each side of the face. All the way down both her cheeks. Tied her hands behind her back with twine and left her in a wooded area."

"Did he kill her or is she still alive?"

"Alive, mostly," Anne said.

"Yeah, I know what you mean. I'll check it out from here. And I'll see if we've got any active cases with a suspect matching this guy. I'll check the old case files, too."

"How about rope? Got anybody tying women up over there?"

"Morley, but he doesn't count."

Over the telephone she heard Irene's laugh. Morley was a short plump accountant who adored Irene. Anne could see it with every look he gave her. They had been married seven years—her third marriage, his first. Find yourself a man who works all day with numbers was Irene's advice. Any woman with flesh and blood looks good to him.

"How is Morley?" Anne asked.

"Same as always, but I'm getting worried. He's going to the gym after work to lose a few pounds. How are you doing? Long time, no see."

"I'm fine. I haven't found that accountant yet."

"No? Well, look, if you get desperate, come over here and we'll make it a threesome. I'll tell Morley tonight, and he'll head right back to the gym."

They both laughed. What else could they do?

"How are the new women working out in your department?" Anne asked.

"Good. Of course we've got some cowboys who can't

stand the idea, but so far so good. If I were ten years younger, I'd go out on the street myself."

"Ten years? Ten years, Irene? You liar. Ten years wouldn't make a damn bit of difference and you know it."

"Don't tell Morley. He still thinks I'm thirty-five."

"Good old Morley. Give him my best. Call me if you find some rope, will you?"

"Will do. Take care of yourself, Anne."

"You, too."

Anne looked at the clock. It was after four thirty. Marcella said she usually got home from school by four thirty. Anne opened the file and found Marcella's telephone number. Anne doubted she had ever heard a thrush. For sure she hadn't if she had to go into the woods to hear it. She wondered if Marcella would ever hear its song again.

Anne closed up the file. It wasn't that far to Madison Park—just up the hill and down to Lake Washington. She could just as well stop before going home. The traffic might not be so bad if she started now, and while she was at it, she might just stop and talk to Lucy once more. Maybe she could convince the girl to come to the lineup as well. It would take a few extra minutes to stop and talk to Lucy, but so what. It wasn't like she had anything else to do on a Friday night. At least she didn't have to worry about that damn cat anymore.

Chapter 9

He hated small towns. They were all like the island he remembered with its perfect yards and everybody knowing everybody else's business, where he had to cross the bridge to get to where nobody knew him. There was a bridge in this town, too, but there was nothing on the other side—a few warehouses, an abandoned gas station and nightclub, farms. He wasn't looking for a farm.

He crossed back over the bridge and drove downtown, but there was nothing there, not even a black neighborhood where there might be a whore who wouldn't know him.

The whores made it easy, beckoning to him from the shadows of dark streets. They always promised to please. When the air was choked from them, they begged to please.

He parked on a dark narrow street close to the university for a moment to clear his mind. For a moment, that was all. When his mind cleared, he would go back to his room. He could go back. He should go back. This town was too much like the one where everybody knew everybody. He would never come here again.

A light mist was falling, but none came through the open car window. He heard party music from a big house on the corner. Cars came and went; shouts disappeared into the mist. Partygoers passed without noticing the shadow in the car. A single girl staggered toward him. He wasn't sure if she was drunk or if it was the sidewalk broken by the roots of the enormous trees that caused her to stagger. He waited until she was beside his window before he opened the car door. With the light from the open door, he saw her dull unsuspicious eyes. He smiled the perfect smile he had practiced while growing up on his perfect island.

Someone shouted a name, and the girl looked back toward the house. Somebody ran toward her and shouted her name again.

Still smiling, he sat back in the car and closed the door. He started the engine and slowly pulled away from the curb. He looked nowhere but at the street ahead of him. He didn't turn his head as he passed the house with the party. He wouldn't look anywhere else in this town, and he would never come back again.

Chapter 10

Her mother's room was on the sixth floor of University Hospital. From there Grace could see much of the campus. Earlier in the evening the lights of the football stadium had glowed brightly before the dark void of the lake. Her father thought the team was practicing late. Now the stadium lights were off. Her father and Evangeline had left for the night.

The plan was for each of them to take a shift by the hospital bed, but each was reluctant to leave and the shifts overlapped. Her father had been at the hospital since her mother's surgery the morning before, and Grace had come immediately after her classes rather than waiting until the evening.

"Go home," her mother had said. "All of you."

Perhaps for the first time in her life Grace had ignored her mother's instructions.

Her mother's eyes were closed, but Grace didn't think she was asleep. Before leaving, Evangeline had brushed her hair, and it shone against the pillow behind her head. Perhaps the pain had eased. Her mother's face looked tranquil. Her father had told her how difficult the first night had been, but her mother had not and would not complain. From her chair beside the bed Grace looked over her open book and studied her mother's face for a sign. Was the cancer gone, or were the malignant cells gathering somewhere else in her body?

The surgeon told them that they had caught the cancer early, and it had not spread into the lymph nodes. Nevertheless, the oncologist recommended radiation and chemotherapy. Difficult days were ahead, he said. Yet, they were lucky: They had caught it early.

Yes, Grace thought as she studied her mother's face. We are lucky.

Grace remembered walking into Grandmother Bess's kitchen and seeing her mother and Grandmother Bess sitting across from each other at the old kitchen table where the linoleum beneath her grandmother's feet had been worn through to the wood. The two women were leaning toward each other, and Grandmother Bess's hands covered her mother's on top of the kitchen table. Her mother had tears in her eyes, and Grandmother Bess's calloused gentle hands gently and soothingly patted the white hands of her mother. Grace never knew what they were talking about. They did not pull away from each other the way people usually do when they are interrupted at an embarrassing or earnest moment. The two women kept their hands together on the center of the table even as Grace wiggled beneath one of Grandmother Bess's arms and onto her lap. Grace put her hands between her mother's and grandmother's hands. It felt so natural. She couldn't imagine, then, how rare the moment was, how rare the two women were, how rare, especially, was her mother.

Grace leaned forward and slipped her hand beneath her mother's hand that lay on top of the hospital sheet. I'm here, Grace said with her hand. Her mother smiled as serenely as Grandmother Bess had smiled at the table in her kitchen. Without opening her eyes, her mother gently squeezed Grace's hand. I'm here, too, her mother replied.

"I love you, Mama," Grace whispered.

Her mother opened her eyes and turned her head on the pillow to look at Grace.

"I know you do."

A curtain separated her bed from the one closer to the door. The curtain was like a cocoon that shielded them from the outside world. Silent and secure, they looked at one another within their protective cocoon.

The curtain parted, and Rigmor stood in the opening with a shopping bag in her hand.

"I didn't hear you coming," her mother said.

"So how are you doing, dear?" Rigmor asked.

"Terrific," her mother said.

"*Ja,* I'll bet, but I know you're tough."

The curtain ballooned behind Rigmor as she walked in the confined space between it and the bed. She took the patient's other hand and kissed her on the cheek. Her mother pushed a button that raised the head of the bed so that she was almost upright.

"I don't like to see you here," Rigmor said.

"I won't be here long," her mother said.

"I believe that. Are they taking good care of you?"

"Yes, they are."

"Well, they better or Grace and I will go down the hall right now and talk to that doctor."

Her mother shifted her body to Grace's side of the bed.

"Is there room for you to sit down?"

Rigmor looked doubtfully at the offered space.

"No *ja,* I'm not so sure about that. I think my butt is too big to sit there."

"Come to this side, Rigmor," Grace said. "You can have this chair. My butt will fit."

"*Ja,* but you just wait until you're so old as me, and then we'll see if you have anything to brag about. Of course I will never see that, but you remember what I said."

"I always remember what you say."

"*Ja*, I believe you do."

Grace pushed back her padded chair and stood on the opposite side. Rigmor pushed the curtain out of the way again as she made her way around the bed.

"As much as these rooms cost, you would think that they could make them big enough to have a few guests," Rigmor said as she sat in the chair. "Maybe they don't want us to get too comfortable, *hvad*?"

She reached into the bag at her feet and pulled out a tall clear vase filled with red roses. "These are from Arne," she said, "and they need some water. I just have a wet paper towel around the stems right now."

Grace took the vase from Rigmor's hand and carried it to the sink.

"And look at these pretty flowers," Rigmor said, indicating the bouquet on the nightstand. "Where did these come from?"

"From Katherine," her mother said, touching a large yellow chrysanthemum that bowed its head toward her. "Aren't they beautiful?"

"They are," Rigmor said. "She would send flowers, wouldn't she? I tell you I feel pretty lucky to have these two girls in Ballard. I miss it now every time they have the day off. Oh, and here is the card from Arne. It's probably not so sweet as they used to be, *hvad*?"

Grace watched the knowing looks exchanged between Rigmor and her mother. Her mother looked at her before raising the card to cover her smile. Grace was about to question that smile when, like a magician, Rigmor produced a wooden box from her bag.

"This here is from Al. In it you can put all your diamonds."

Rigmor handed her the box.

"It's lovely." Her mother opened the lid carefully and looked inside.

"That it is. He hasn't made anything so nice for me, and I can tell you that I'm a little jealous. Anyway you can see that we haven't forgotten you on Ballard Avenue. And here," Rigmor said, producing a round red canister, "I've made you some *kringler,* but don't open the lid until you're ready to eat them. And a little Norwegian chocolate." She raised two square bars wrapped in silver foil. "A little chocolate can never hurt, *hvad*?"

Rigmor placed the canister and chocolate bars beside Katherine's flowers. Grace squeezed between Rigmor's chair and the window and found a place for the roses in the midst of the bounty. In one hand her mother held the card from Arne and in the other the jewelry box from Al. She had no hand free to wipe away the tear that fell.

"Thank you, Rigmor," her mother said. She laid the card and box on the bed and extended her hand. Rigmor took it in both of hers and placed it against her cheek. "We've been through a lot together, so this is nothing."

Grace picked up the box and card from the bed and found room for them, too. She peeked at Arne's card. It said nothing beyond what she expected. There was no hint of the secret shared by the two women who had been through a lot together. Grace squeezed behind Rigmor again and sat down on the bed.

"If it wasn't for your mother," Rigmor said to Grace, "I wouldn't have the store in Ballard."

"That's not true, Rigmor," her mother said.

"Yes, it is."

Grace knew the story, and she knew Rigmor was going to tell it again—not to her mother but to her. It was the only way her mother would listen to a compliment.

"Your mother came to work in the store after my husband left me and the boys and went back to Denmark. It was a tough time, and business wasn't so good. The Danes didn't come to my store, and the Norwegians thought I didn't make food the right way, and the other people on Ballard Avenue didn't want to come in either. Your mother brought them in."

Her mother waved her hand as if to send them away, but they weren't leaving.

"You see how she is," Rigmor said, addressing Grace. "She won't take credit for anything. Me, I take it whenever it comes. It was her idea to make the sandwiches and have something for people to eat at lunch. Until then I just made the food and put it in the cooler and waited for them to come. And use two slices of bread, she said. That was a little hard to take since we don't do that in Denmark.

"Your mother made sandwiches: roast beef with remoulade, ham with *Italiensk salat,* even *frikadeller* with red cabbage. She took free sandwiches to the butchers, to the auto mechanics, to all the stores on Ballard Avenue and then up to Market Street, and soon we had all the lunch business we could wish for. Then these people bought a little cheese, and a jar of this and a jar of that. Of course some of them came in just to see your mother. Such a smile she had. So beautiful she was, inside and out. And look at her. She hasn't changed."

Grace looked at her mother and saw beauty, if not the same as Rigmor. She had heard many times Rigmor's story about her mother's sandwiches—not, however, about the customers who came into the store just to see her mother. Who were they? she wondered. Arne? Was that the reason for the secret smiles?

"Rigmor tells only half the story," her mother said. "I wasn't so good for business when I came back from Europe."

"*Ja,* but that was a long time ago," Rigmor said. "Grace doesn't want to hear about that."

"About what?" Grace asked.

"About how the customers stopped coming when I returned to the store after I came back from France married to your father."

"They didn't all stop," Rigmor said.

"Enough did."

"Well, I wasn't so sure myself, to tell you the truth. It's one thing to believe how we are all the same, but it's another matter when you have to face it. But what did I know about such things? I married a Danish man, and look what happened to that."

"I was so sure that I was right that I didn't think about anything else, but it would have been better for your business if you had fired me."

"But it wouldn't have been better for me. Besides, can you imagine me firing you?"

"No," her mother said, "and I'm glad you didn't because we needed that job. Martin was in college on the GI bill, but it didn't pay enough to cover the rent, and it didn't pay for babies."

"I didn't pay so much either, but I got to see these beautiful children grow up. Of course my hand itched around Evangeline sometimes, I can tell you that. But this one— I knew from the first day. Who could look into those brown eyes that came from heaven and not love her?"

Not these two women with eyes so blue that they looked like the sky had been brought down to earth.

"I'm ready to open the can of *kringler*," her mother said. "If Martin sees it, I'll be lucky to get any."

"Then we shall do that," Rigmor said. "I don't suppose a shot of cognac sounds good."

"Did you bring some?"

"Just a small bottle."

Mischievous lightning flickered across the blue sky of her mother's eyes.

"Grace," she said, "see if you can find three glasses."

Grace knew better than to object to any scheme of these two women. She walked to the nurse's station at the end of the hall and waited for the nurse to bring her three medicine glasses.

"Don't come into Mom's room for a little while," she told the nurse.

The tin of cookies was on the bed beside her mother, and there was already an open space in the circle of *kringler,* which were so light and delicate that to eat one was like taking a bite of cloud. Grace held the glasses as Rigmor poured the cognac. She gave the first to her mother.

"Happy birthday," Rigmor said, her toast for every occasion. She raised her glass to Lisa.

"Happy birthday," her mother said and raised hers in return.

"*Skål,* dear," Rigmor said to her.

"*Skål,* Rigmor."

The three glasses touched, and each woman took a sip of the fine cognac Rigmor had brought. As was the custom, they looked into each other's eyes until each lowered her glass to her heart.

Chapter 11

"My company flies into New Orleans. I can get you a ticket for almost nothing," Evangeline said.

From the middle cushion of the couch Lady looked up at Grace, and Grace petted the Shetland sheepdog and scratched her in the pleasure zone behind her ears. Lady cocked her head and closed her eyes. At the opposite end of the couch, sitting with her feet curled inside her nightgown, Evangeline sipped from a glass of white wine.

"I'll think about it," Grace said.

Evangeline was staying the night so that Grace could take her to the airport early in the morning. Grace felt disappointed that Evangeline had come for a week but had chosen to stay with her only one night and then mostly for convenience. Grace had been fixing up her house for the past year, and she was secretly proud of the work she had done. She told Evangeline about a corroded steel pipe that led her farther and farther into the walls and through the floor joists in the basement until she had replaced every steel pipe in the house with copper. For weeks she had flushed the toilet with buckets of water that she filled from the hose outside. Evangeline listened, but she wasn't interested in the plumbing story. Evangeline was interested only in the story she had discovered in their parents' attic.

"Yes, you think about that, Sister Etienne, but don't think too much. We could meet at the airport and rent a car. I already checked the map. It's not far to St. Martinville. This is like *Roots*. Who knows what we'll find there? Do you remember Grandpa Joseph saying, 'It didn't take no old Civil War to set us free. We were already free.' Do you remember that?"

Grace remembered.

"I wonder how much he knew, why he didn't tell us more."

Grandpa Joseph could fix any machine, Grace remembered. His garage in Omaha had been filled with mysterious machine parts and the smell of gasoline and oil. The neighbors brought him their cars and motorcycles and lawn mowers, any machine that stopped working, and he would fix it. "You just listen to what it says," he told her once, "and if it won't talk, then you start talking to it." Like his father, Richard, who had moved from Chicago to Omaha, Grandpa Joseph worked in the meat packing plant, but he didn't stay long on the slaughter line. He could fix any machine they had, he said, but he couldn't fix the business. When the packing plant closed, he moved to the brewery with his skills. They had machines, too, but then people began to buy the beer they saw on television commercials even if it had no taste. When the brewery closed, he went home and opened his garage. He was old enough to retire, but he had no intention of spending his days sitting on the porch in a rocking chair.

"I made copies of the land deed," Evangeline said. "I can't believe it's been stuck away all this time and nobody knew about it. There had to be a reason why Dad learned French in a place like Omaha and why he named me Evangeline."

"He knew our people came from there," Grace said, the second child, the child with the single simple syllable in her name. "Grandpa Joseph said so."

"But why did they move? They were free people before the war, and they had land. The deed shows that. So why did they move, and why did they change the name?"

"You can't be sure that Emile Etienne was anybody in our family."

"He has to be. I'll bet he was Richard's father, our great-great-grandfather, or at least somebody related to us. Why would they keep somebody else's land deed? Etienne is Steven in French. Even I know that. Richard or Emile must have changed the name in Chicago. But why? Don't you want to know? Wouldn't you rather be Etienne than Stevens?"

Grace didn't understand what difference the name made, and she didn't understand why Evangeline had been digging around the attic in her parents' house when she could have been doing something useful to help their mother. The day before, Evangeline had spent the whole morning at the downtown library looking for books about Louisiana history while Grace cleaned the house, bought fresh flowers, and washed the sheets on her mother's bed. Nothing felt as nice as freshly laundered sheets.

Now Evangeline wanted a French name. She hadn't learned French at home when the language was given to her, declaring pompously that learning French was like hiding from the real world. How could you hide by learning a language? Their mother stopped speaking Norwegian when Evangeline was present, but their father continued to speak French. At the table he would ask Evangeline, *"Faites passer les pommes de terre"* or *"Faites passer le sel,"* and she would stare at her plate as if she didn't understand. Grace would hand her father the potatoes or the salt even if she had to stretch across the table for them. During the time when Evangeline was forgetting her French, no one enjoyed potatoes or anything else at the table. Evangeline took Spanish for her required foreign language in high school and studied diligently every night so that she would be at the top of her class. Grace learned both French and Norwegian at home and cruised through the foreign language classes in school. And yet, her father admired Evangeline's stubbornness and began to substitute his limited Spanish for the French words he knew so well.

"What difference does the name make?" Grace asked.

"I don't know. It might make a lot of difference. Aren't you even a little curious?"

"Of course, but I'm more worried about Mom right now than some name you found in the attic."

There, she had said it. Evangeline could get angry, and she could put down the wine that Grace had given her and walk away as she used to do on those rare times when Grace challenged her. She wouldn't be able to walk far in her nightgown.

"I am worried about Mom," Evangeline said, her voice low and cautious, her brow wrinkled into a frown. "That's why I came."

"It doesn't seem like it. It never has."

"Be careful, sister. Be sure you know where you're going."

Maybe Evangeline was right. They could hide behind language as well as anything else. They could leave words unsaid or skirted, repeat phrases that meant one thing or another but nothing if left alone. What was the point as long as her sister sat on one end of the couch and she on the other? They might as well be as far from each other as they would be tomorrow after Evangeline flew back to Los Angeles.

Somehow they had separated from each other growing up. It shouldn't have happened. Evangeline and she were the two who were the same but different from everybody else—from everyone in the family, from everyone in school, from everyone in the neighborhood. They were the only ones with a mix of black and white and who knew what else, but whatever it was it was the same; and it should have brought them closer together, not pushed them apart. When they walked up the hill to the park from their grandparents' house, they should have held hands to show that at least there were two of them. But they never did.

Evangeline had always been the angry child. Because Evangeline was older, she went first to everything—first to grade school, first to high school, first even to the soccer team. Each first brought Evangeline new anger. Sometimes Grace wanted to be angry, too, but Evangeline had used so much of it that Grace felt there wasn't any left for her.

"You were always mad at me for learning French and Norwegian at home," Grace said, "especially Norwegian. You refused to say the simplest words, even though it would have pleased Mother. It would have pleased *Mormor* and *Morfar,* too."

"Do you think it pleased them to hear you speak their language?" Evangeline asked.

"Sometimes."

"If it pleased them so much to hear you, why did they move to Poulsbo as soon as Grandfather could sell his business? And then to the desert in California? I'll bet they were shaking in their shoes when they heard I moved to Los Angeles, so close to them. If Grandfather hadn't died, they probably would have moved all the way back to the homeland."

"*Mormor* needed the dry air. She had bad lungs."

"Do you believe that?"

"I don't know. It would have pleased Mom, too."

"She understood."

"She understood that you rejected everything that made her. You still do."

"That's not true."

"It is true."

"All right, so what if it is? Those people rejected me and you, if you would ever admit it. But instead you buy a house in the same neighborhood and mow the grass so that the neighbors won't complain. Dad made us do that. I'll never cut another blade of grass in my life."

"He liked a neat yard. It wasn't because of the neighbors."

"Our grass always had to be shorter. He mowed the grass or made us do it when it was so wet that you couldn't push the lawn mower through it. He even mowed the grass one Christmas morning."

The neighbors' opinion had played some part in her father's mowed yard, but the other part was that her father liked a neat yard for himself. How do you separate the two and say this one is true and that one is not? Why isn't it possible to accept both sides?

"It was warm that year," Grace said. "The grass was still growing at Christmas."

"I suppose you mow your grass in the rain, too."

"I don't like to mow the grass. I hire the neighbor boy to do it."

"Well, that's a start. That's a start. Wouldn't it be more interesting to dig for information about your own people than it is for Indian tribes that lived up the coast a thousand years ago? That's what you're doing, isn't it? What about your own family? What about you?"

"What about me?"

Lady raised her head and stared intently at Grace. Always alert to the slightest change in tone, Lady pricked her ears and stuck her long expressive snout beneath Grace's hand. Her mother had given her the puppy to keep her company when Evangeline left home for college, and Lady had always been good company. Grace petted the dog on the top of the head, smoothing down her ears.

"Sometimes I wonder about you, sister," Evangeline said. "I used to think that you wanted to be white, but now I'm not so sure. Everybody else sees color, but I wonder what you see."

Lady inched forward and rested her head on Grace's lap. Lady's hair was mostly black, but she had patches of brown and white on her shoulders and, more recently, graying above her eyes.

Grace remembered the first time Evangeline accused her of wanting to be white. It was the twentieth of May, and Grace was seven years old. She knew the precise day because it was three days after the Seventeenth of May, Norway's Constitution Day. On that day the Norwegians held a parade in Ballard, rain or shine. Usually it rained. In the year in which Grace was seven, their mother had made Norwegian dresses for both girls—beautiful ankle-length red and black dresses with white lace that billowed into a dizzy circle when she twirled. On the day of the parade Evangeline announced that she wasn't going. At first her father tried to reason with her, tried to find out why she wouldn't go to the parade, but Evangeline wouldn't talk. Then their father became angry, and Evangeline became defiantly silent. Their mother had spent days making the dresses, and her father insisted that Evangeline was going to the parade. As always in these matters their mother intervened. She was the one who had made the dresses. Evangeline could stay home.

Grace, herself, felt divided about what to do. She could be loyal to her sister and stay home with her, or she could go to the parade wearing the dress that her mother had made with such great care. Grace knew that there would never be another dress like it.

Grace went to the parade and stood on Market Street at the corner where the parade turned south toward Ballard Avenue. The king of Norway was the grand marshal that year, which was the reason her mother had spent so much time making the dresses. All of Ballard was there, all of Poulsbo, every Norwegian within a hundred miles—probably two hundred, probably more. She stood at the curb in front of the crowd that filled the wide sidewalk. When the king came, she raised her small Norwegian flag and waved it back and forth like everyone else. The king wandered the wide street from curb to curb, greeting his expatriate citizens. When he came toward her, people surged out from the sidewalk, and she was surrounded by the crowd. She thought she was lost, but the people parted like the Red Sea in the Bible story, and the king stood before her as if he had been searching for her. In English he told her that she had a lovely dress, but she responded in Norwegian to the Norwegian king. She told him that he looked pretty good, too. She saw the surprise in his face. Maybe it was even pleasure. He said a few words in Norwegian, and she answered back in the same language. Then he knelt beside her, and she talked to the king of Norway while the entire parade, which stretched all the way down Market Street and around the corner and up 24th Avenue for blocks and blocks, stopped and marched in place. He was the king. He could do whatever he wanted.

For Evangeline it was bad enough that Grace had gone to the parade. When Grace's picture with the king appeared in the newspaper the next morning, Evangeline refused to even talk to her. For three days she wouldn't talk. Grace told herself that she didn't care, although she and Evangeline shared a bedroom and always talked to each other before they went to sleep. They might not talk to each other all day, but it was different at night when the lights were out and they were alone. They would play spelling games or Evangeline would make up ghost stories until their father told them to be quiet. For three days Evangeline said nothing even at night. Finally, in the dark she asked Grace about the picture.

"Do you remember seeing anybody like you in the picture?"

Grace had almost become used to the silence, and she considered that it might be good to maintain it. She had looked at the picture many times and could see it even in the dark. She knew what Evangeline was getting at, and she didn't want to talk about it.

"Do you?" Evangeline had been insistent.

"There's another girl beside me," Grace had said.

"She's not like you."

"We're wearing the same kind of dress."

"You want to be white like her, don't you?"

It wasn't true. She knew that the girl had light skin and blond hair. Anybody could see that even in the black-and-white picture. Grace's was the only black face in the picture. Anybody could see that, too. If Evangeline had been there, there would have been a progression—light, medium, dark. In the summer some of the kids in their neighborhood became nearly as dark as Evangeline, but it didn't matter. There was never a right color.

With pride her father and Aunt Margaret believed that there was Cherokee blood mixed into theirs—a Cherokee wife somewhere among the obscure stories of Grandmother Bess's family line. She had heard the same pride of Indian blood from other families—white and black—not too much, just enough to add intrigue and mystery, a background hue. In a hundred years, in two hundred years, would the family talk with pride about the mingling of the African and Norwegian? Would one or the other become so diluted that it was finally safe to talk about it? When would such talk become absurd? Blood was a deep red no matter where it came from. Over the last few years she had seen enough to know.

"I see colors," Grace said, smoothing the gray spots above Lady's eyes. The dog trusted her even when her fingers came close to the eyes. "I've never wanted to change mine. Why would I? That would be completely illogical. If I am not this color or this height or this person, then I am not me and I am nothing. To wish to change something like that is a death wish. I don't wish to change, and I do think about color. But sometimes I look in the mirror, and I think, 'Well, that's me.'

I don't say to myself, 'Oh, there's a black woman in the mirror.' Sometimes I live an entire fifteen minutes without thinking about the color of my skin or anybody else's."

"Is that why you still live here, in this neighborhood?" Evangeline asked. It was a question in the present tense, although such questions never remained there. "Did you make that decision during one of your fifteen-minute lapses?"

Evangeline smiled. When they were girls, Evangeline had never smiled when she pushed Grace for answers. The smile was a concession to propriety, but it didn't reduce her insistence, and it didn't change her sense of certainty that she already knew the answer. Other kids had tried to resist Evangeline's will, and sometimes they succeeded if they formed a collective resistance, but Grace seldom resisted. What would be the point? Evangeline wouldn't change.

"I looked at houses in other places," Grace said. "I liked this one."

When she was looking at the house with the real estate agent, the neighbor boy wandered into the backyard where she was standing. Billy, who was four years old, asked her, "Do you have any kids?" He was disappointed that she had no kids, but she told him that she had a dog. "Can I play with him if you move here?" "The dog is a lady," she said. "That's her name." The lady dog would do, Billy decided, and he came regularly to play. Other kids came, too, and their parents, once they got to know her. Evangeline had no children who came to her apartment in Los Angeles. Grace knew. She had visited there one time shortly after Evangeline's divorce.

Enough, Grace decided.

"Why do you say things like that? It hurts, Evangeline. All these years I've wanted to be your friend, but you never let me. I think you look at Mom and resent that she's white. You think white people won't accept you because you're too dark, but you're afraid that you're not black enough either. Isn't that why you dyed your hair? Isn't that why you want to go to Louisiana and find your roots? Isn't that why you want me to go with you—me, the black sister who wants to be white?"

Instead of the anger Grace expected, instead of the sharp reply—Evangeline was a master of the sharp reply—her sister's expression softened, and she gave Grace a curious smile. Evangeline finished her wine and placed the empty glass on the coffee table.

"Well, sister," Evangeline said, "finally we're getting somewhere."

Chapter 12

He watched her work alone—tall shiny boots, tight pink skirt that rose up her legs when she walked or posed for a passing car. Black-Asian mix—something new. He watched her pump herself up when a car slowed down and watched the deflation after it passed. There was nothing real about her. She was like the robot his father had given him for Christmas when he was a boy. Turn on the switch, move the lever forward, and the robot walked. Turn off the switch and it froze. Just like the whore, just like the rest of them. There was no difference.

He tasted the night air, felt the heat and smog burning his eyes.

He had almost stayed inside the room and was finally driven out by ritual more than the other thing. How far would his indifference carry him? Past the whore in black boots? Past the black asphalt street still hot from the day? Past the night into the morning?

He wore his father's coat—a blue blazer with a gold sailing insignia. In a twisted reversal of roles his father was proud that the son, strong and young, could wear his clothes—not the trousers, but the suit coats and sport coats that he borrowed.

His father had taught him all about disguise. The father

thought that the son wouldn't see, but the son could imagine the father's women well enough. There was the housekeeper who wore long dangling gold earrings, the secretary at the Christmas party who forgot to hide her smiles, and others he imagined through the brief telephone conversations he overheard. He imagined them from the tone of his father's voice—all of them.

If the father had known of the son's disguise, he would have had lost all pleasure in the loaned clothes. He shouldn't be surprised, thought the son. The son had grown up in disguise. Nothing was ever as it seemed.

He understood why his father didn't want to touch his mother. He didn't want to touch her either. There was something wrong with her voice, something wrong when she pleaded for love and tried to hold him. "Don't you love me?" she asked, and he learned to disguise his distaste so that he could get away. It was the alcohol she loved, not him—alcohol and the pills for pain that never went away. Like the robot his father had given him, she could stand still and straight when his father came home or move forward at his father's command. His father could switch her on and off. She could become sober for a day or a night or half a day. When his father came home, she would be in pain and would not beg the son for love.

The son was thinking that indifference would take him back to his room when the whore saw him. Slowly, so slowly that he barely noticed the difference himself, he straightened his back and felt the muscles tense in his legs. The whore moved cautiously along the sidewalk until she was directly across the street from him. The tension spread to his shoulders and from there into his arms.

"Why are you parked over there?" she asked from across the street.

"Because I want to," he said.

A car passed between them, and she watched it until it turned the corner.

"How come I didn't see you?"

"You tell me."

"You a cop?"

As if a cop would tell the truth.

"A schoolteacher," he said. He pushed his heavy glasses higher onto his nose.

They were on a side street, a block off the main commercial thoroughfare where most of the whores traded. He preferred the darker streets where there was always someone working out of the limelight.

"You looking for a good time?" she asked.

"I don't know."

The whore edged closer to the street and looked both ways as if she was going to cross. And then she did. He reached across the seat and pulled the door handle on the passenger's side. The door swung open, and the whore came around the front of the car and slid into the seat. He smelled the cheap perfume that disguised her scent.

"What's your name?" she asked.

"Iago."

"What kind of name is that?"

"Italian."

"I haven't seen you before."

"I'm here for a teachers' convention. I'm from Pocatello."

"Where's that?"

"Idaho."

"So, Mr. Yago from Idaho, what are you interested in tonight?"

He followed her directions onto even darker streets until they were behind a large metal warehouse. They passed over a gravel parking lot into a weeded recess with garbage scattered about. On one side was a tall wire fence with barbwire at the top, and on the other side and at the front was the warped metal of the building. He heard a dog barking; he couldn't tell where. There were no other sounds. It was a different city, a different street, a different whore, but they were all the same.

The whore reached for his zipper and tried to persuade him to add another twenty to the forty he had given her. She promised greater pleasure with every twenty he would add. In the dark he smiled to himself. She knew nothing about pleasure.

"Afterward," he promised.

As her head lowered to his crotch he reached down to the floor for the length of rope he had hidden. Before she knew what the schoolteacher was doing, he slipped the rope around her neck. She squealed and tried to grab it. They all made the same mistake. The rope was too tight to grab, and he twisted it tighter as he used his weight to force her down to the floor. She gurgled for air as the rope restricted her windpipe, but it was the absence of blood that stopped her struggle. No blood to the brain, no oxygen to continue the struggle. Simple science. Any schoolteacher would know it.

Light illuminated the garbage-strewn lot briefly as he pulled her from the car. Darkness returned when he closed the door—near darkness. He draped her over an overturned barrel and ripped away her skirt and underwear. She lay exposed beneath him. He removed his belt and hit her as hard as he could. She made no sound. He hit her again and again with the same unrestrained violence with which he had learned to play; then he uncurled the rope from her neck. As her breathing resumed in ragged gasps, he released his sperm on top of her. When he finished, he withdrew his wallet from his pants pocket and took out another twenty. He opened her hand and squeezed it around the money. Then he left her, just as she began to whimper, just as she began to feel again—as much as any of them could.

Chapter 13

Maria turned off the coffee burners and divided the last of the coffee between Silve and her father, who sat together at the counter listening to the football game on the radio. Silve had turned up the volume after the last lunch customers had left. He had taken off his chef's hat, and a ring from the hat circled his hair like a departed halo. From what she understood, it was halftime at the football game.

"Your boyfriend is playing good today," Silve said. Humor, subtly hidden, peeked out from the old man's tired eyes. Her father looked up from his coffee cup and grinned, but said nothing. He must have told Silve about the football player, knowing that she could never be angry with Silve. They all knew that.

"Which boyfriend?" she asked.

Silve cackled toward the ceiling and spilled coffee from his newly filled cup as he lifted it to drink. The new stain joined the others on the front of his chef's coat.

"The one who is the big star. You should bring him here, and we'll see if he likes your adobo."

"It's your adobo, Silve. What has he done today that's so great?"

"Aren't you listening, daughter? Almost a hundred yards in the first half," Silve said.

"A hundred yards doing what?" she asked.

"Running with the football. Don't you know what he does?"

"Sometimes he throws it," Maria said. "A hundred yards doesn't seem like much. Anybody can run a hundred yards. You and I can run a hundred yards. I'm not so sure about Dad."

She carried the empty coffeepot away from her father, who continued to grin, and away from Silve, who continued to laugh at the ceiling. She had tried to listen to the game on the kitchen radio as she carried plates of food from the kitchen into the dining room, but it was like a radio program in a foreign language. She heard Paul Renzlau's name often, sometimes in conversation between two announcers, sometimes in shouted excitement. Then she might listen more carefully for a moment to try to understand the noise. Everyone else seemed to understand.

She could not reconcile the descriptions of Paul from the excited radio announcers with the soft-voiced man who shared an hour with her each day in class and an hour afterward in the cafeteria. Nor could she reconcile the stares she received because of him with the way he looked at her. Since the party a little more than a week earlier, he had taken her to a Shakespeare play on the campus, of which she could not remember a single line after he took her hand and smothered it within his huge fist. At the door of her house after the play, Paul had kissed her, and now she could not think about him without thinking about the kiss.

She placed the coffeepot upside down in the dish tub that was on the rack of the dishwashing machine. Henry was scrubbing the first of the cooking pans in the triple sink. He looked up from the dirty water in the center compartment and smiled at her. There was sweat beaded on his forehead. Two days earlier he had told her not to get too close to him because he had a sore throat and didn't want to give her his bug.

Today he had switched from ice water to a glass of ice cubes to cool his burning throat.

"You should go to the doctor," she said. "Have him look at your throat. Maybe he can give you some medicine."

"Sure. I might do that," he said.

She knew he wouldn't.

She swiveled the long neck of the faucet into the right compartment of the triple sink and turned on the hot water. She squirted dish soap into the compartment. Henry raised his eyebrows questioningly.

"I've finished the dining room," she said. "I'll help with the pans."

"No need for that," Henry said. "You'll cut into my wages. Besides, your father is waiting for you."

She looked back at her father.

"He's listening to the football game," she said.

"Are we winning?" Henry asked.

"I guess we are," she said.

Maria gathered the rest of the pans from Silve's stove and submerged them into the soapy water. She picked up a steel scrubbing pad from the sink counter and reached into the water for the first pan.

"You won't tease me about the football player, will you?"

"Which football player?" he asked.

He grinned, and she saw the gap in his teeth from his years of hard living, as he called them, which she understood to be most of them. She stood beside the little man with more hard years than good and thought how little she knew about him, how little she knew about any of them—even her father—the one she knew best and who, therefore, puzzled her most. She knew that Henry left in the afternoon when the last pot was clean and went back to a small room in the Lutheran mission where he had lived since he quit drinking. And these were the good times.

Her father told her that Henry had probably saved her life

because he had sat in the rain one afternoon two years earlier and had watched the alley behind First Avenue when any sensible person would have left, but not Henry. Henry had agreed to do a surveillance job for her father, and he didn't leave despite the rain because her father had given him a pair of shoes the week before when he was down on his luck and nobody else was giving him anything. She understood how Henry must have felt. She had taken the job at the Donut Shop, not knowing its reputation as a hub of evil, because she knew she would see her father there on his beat, even if he wouldn't see her—not her, as his daughter at least. Henry had seen her lured into the basement behind the Donut Shop and had reported it to her father. By then she knew the reputation of the Donut Shop. She knew, even as she allowed herself to be lured to the alley behind the Donut Shop and into the basement beneath it, that she should stop, turn around, leave, but she went anyway.

What was she supposed to do knowing that Henry had saved her life? Was it enough to help Henry with the last of the dirty pans? When she had tried to thank him—it was difficult to know how to do it—Henry said that it was her father who had given him the shoes that made him stay in the alley in the first place. Without that act of generosity, Henry told her, he would have left the alley and walked down to the first bar he could find for shelter. Henry said that it was her father who had saved her life. But her father said that it wasn't he. Before she came, her father told her, it was Silve who had made it worthwhile for him to get up every morning. Without Silve in his restaurant, her father said, he would have left First Avenue long before. But Silve asked what else would he do if he didn't have the restaurant? Without his restaurant, Silve asked, where could he go?

Was it enough, she wondered, to be in their company, to be included in their jokes, in their acts of kindness? What did it mean when Silve called her daughter? Was it a slip of the tongue, or did he mean that she was his daughter in some broad sense? Or was he simply addressing his friend Sam's daughter?

How long would it take for four people to know enough about one another that each of them could say, "Yes, I know him. Yes, I knew she would think that." She didn't even know what Silve's apartment looked like—how many rooms were there, what color were the walls. What did he do on Sundays when the restaurant was closed? Did he write letters back to the Philippines, or was no one there any more to receive them?

This morning her father told her she could take the car to work instead of getting up with him, but she had gotten up anyway and paddled with him. When they arrived at the restaurant, her father stood at the stove beside Silve who was preparing the adobo. Together he and Silve looked out the windows toward the Olympic Mountains. "Maria," her father said, "look at the mountains. The sun is coming up."

She stood beside him and Silve and looked west at the first pink rays of sun reflected from the new snow of the tallest peaks. Only a few times a year would the first reflected light come when they were all together. The rest of the time the sun came too late or too early or was hidden in clouds. But this morning the three of them stopped for a moment and looked out Silve's window in the Pike Place Market and watched the sunrise reflected from the western peaks—each thinking his own thoughts, each translating the morning and the moment in her own light. She would have missed it if she had stayed in bed. Her father and Silve would have seen the sunrise without her. That thought was hard for her to bear.

Later in the afternoon as they walked downhill through the canyon of redbrick walls of Post Alley, her father put his arm on her shoulder.

"Sorry I blabbed to Silve about Paul."

She looked at him and saw that he was sorry.

For the first months after she had come, perhaps for the

first year, they had lived in an emotional eggshell. She feared that the first harsh word, the first flash of anger, would break the shell and as in the nursery rhyme, never let them come back together. For months there had not been a hint of anger, but the angry words finally came. She had left his tools outside in the rain—a handsaw, a box of nails, and his hammer. She had been building a cedar planter box for the deck where she could plant geraniums. Her mother had loved the red of the geraniums. She didn't think it would rain. It did.

The next morning when her father was getting the kayak ready for their paddle to work, he had found the tools outside. He brought them in and wiped them dry with an oily rag. If she used his tools, he told her harshly, he expected her to take care of them. His anger startled her, and she didn't know what to do except silently accept it. A short while later when they were in the kayak headed for work, he turned in the front cockpit and told her that his mother had given him the hammer when he was a boy. That was the reason he had been upset. Someday, he said, when he was too old to swing it anymore, she could have the hammer.

She hadn't known about the hammer, not that her ignorance was an excuse to be careless with his tools, but she hadn't known. When he resumed paddling, she cried silent tears as she paddled in rhythm to his strokes—not because of the hammer or his anger or her carelessness, but because she knew she could stay.

"You're forgiven," she said now and hugged him around the waist as they walked down the rough cobblestone alley.

It was a seven-block walk to Jefferson Pier at the foot of Washington Street where they secured the kayak each morning. Her father unlocked the padlock that tied it fast to a steel cable on the pier. Together they turned the kayak over. She removed the rear hatch cover, reached into the compartment, and pulled out her life jacket, spray skirt, and paddle. Her father removed his equipment from the front hatch.

She had been looking forward to their afternoon paddle. It had none of the reservations and doubts of morning when she had to leave her warm bed while it was still dark. In the winter there would be rain as well as darkness to add to her doubts, and she would be cold until the exertion of her strokes warmed her and woke her up at the same time. It was tolerable once they got going, but the first strokes were always a challenge. Not so in the afternoon, especially in warm weather when she didn't even need her jacket.

They lowered the kayak into the water, and her father sat on the pier and swung his feet into the forward cockpit. He held on to the pier as he slid in the rest of the way. While he stretched his spray skirt over the combing of the cockpit, she snapped her paddle together and zipped her life jacket over her spray skirt. Then she swung her feet into the rear cockpit and eased herself into the boat as her father held the kayak steady against the pier.

Their strokes merged together into a single motion. She no longer had trouble keeping up with him as she had in the beginning, and she used the foot pedals sparingly to move the rudder. They now changed course subtly and quietly by tilting the kayak or sweeping wider with their paddles.

On Sundays when Silve closed his restaurant and she stayed home, her father paddled to work alone in *Gloria,* the single kayak he had bought and named years before her arrival. *Gloria* was her mother's name. Sometimes he took *Gloria* out on his days off while she was in school. She knew because of the wet spray skirt that he draped over the kayak. She wondered what he thought about on those days. Was he thinking about her mother, or did he simply want to be alone? Was anything ever simple?

She looked past him and saw that the way was clear. A ferry was at the terminal, but it was still loading cars. Another was approaching from the west, but their kayak would pass well ahead of it. The tourist season had ended, and there were only two sightseeing boats at the terminal beside the Chowder House. Neither of the sightseeing boats was seeing any sights today. There were no freighters pointed toward the grain terminal farther north on the Sound and none that were bringing cars from Japan into the terminal beyond the grain elevators. It was clear sailing, and she settled into the familiar rhythm of the kayak.

She heard her father humming one of the three or four songs that he knew. It meant that he was comfortable with their course, that he was comfortable with the water, that he was comfortable with their pace. Swells lifted the kayak a few feet, then lowered it as the line of the wave moved past them toward the shore.

A few times she had crossed the Sound with him when the swells were higher and not gentle. When they knew the water would be rough, they drove to work in the car or, if the water changed during the day, they left the kayak on the pier and took the bus home. Once, despite her silent reluctance, they set off from the pier in marginal water that got much worse as they crossed. The swells broke sharply over them, and the bow of the kayak crashed heavily into the bottom of the waves. "Are you okay?" her father had asked repeatedly over his shoulder. She said that she was, but the waves frightened her. The waves came from all directions, from the open part of the Sound and from shore as they ricocheted back, and tossed them around as if they were a toy on the water. He shouted instructions—rudder right, rudder left, paddle hard, stop paddling—and she followed them as well as she could even when they didn't make sense. A final wave dropped them onto their beach, and he jumped out of the cockpit and pulled them to higher ground while she was still in the boat. Her fear resolved into a silent anger as they carried the kayak up the beach to their house, but at whom, at what? Her father, the water, herself?

Today, the water was easy and smooth. Today, they would paddle again to the west side of Magnolia Bluff to a small beach made inaccessible from land by steep bluffs that rose from each side. Her father had taken her there last weekend because she wanted to see if she could use it for an intertidal field study for her oceanography class. Her plan was to map the beach and note the plant and animal life for four successive weeks. During that time the tide would run though a complete cycle, and she could observe changes in a restricted environment.

She wondered if the beach was one of the places he went when he paddled alone in *Gloria*.

"I could take *Gloria* by myself if you want to go home and finish listening to the football game," she said.

Her father stopped paddling and turned in the cockpit.

"You can take *Gloria* when you learn how to paddle."

"I know how to paddle. I've taken her out before."

"Not out of my sight, you haven't."

That was true. He had stood on the beach as she paddled back and forth within his view. It was also true that *Gloria* was a different type of boat—sleek and responsive, requiring stability from the paddler. The double kayak provided its own stability. It was like a bathtub, her father said.

"How will you know when I'm a good enough paddler?" she asked.

He turned to her, then looked down at the water as if the answer were there.

"When you can Eskimo roll five times in a row without a mistake, I'll know you're good enough."

Maria looked down at the same dark water. Even in summer it was cold from the Alaska Current that entered the Sound. The thought of tipping over into the water, of suspending herself upside down beneath the kayak, sent a chill through her spine. She stared into the water, which was dark and impenetrable a few feet below the surface. She couldn't see what was down there any more than she could see into the depths of her father, or Henry, or Silve, or anyone else.

Chapter 14

After passing all the temptations along the way, Grace helped herself to a cup of coffee from the large stainless-steel vat at the end of the cafeteria food line in the Student Union. Any other day she would have been studying in the library, but on this day she needed a cup of coffee. She carried her cup from the line and looked for a quiet place to sit. Sunlight pulled her through glass doors and onto a flat stone patio with a view south toward the Montlake Bridge. At that moment the bridge was open and had its arms extended above the trees in supplication to the sun that was passing over in its autumn migration.

A dream had awakened her at four in the morning, and she hadn't been able to go back to sleep. In the dream her mother died when their house burned down. All that was left of their home was a field of red geraniums. The chief of police, whom she saw leaving the poker party at Rigmor's apartment, sent Grace on a mission to kill another mother in retribution. Grace didn't want to go; she wanted her mother back; she wanted the house to stand. She didn't want to kill anybody.

It was a dream that lingered, and she tried to shape and finish it while she lay in bed half awake, half asleep. No, her mother wasn't dead. No, she wouldn't kill another mother for retribution. The chief of police could go back to his poker party and leave her alone.

When she woke completely, she understood how the dream had formed. The dream should have left her then, but she continued to think about it. It disturbed her that her mind could twist people and events so cruelly in her sleep. It disturbed her that her mind could make up such a horrible story while she slept, a story that had seemed so real that she still ached from the illusory loss of her mother. God, how she would ache if it were true.

On the previous evening she had visited her parents after getting off work, which was her usual Sunday routine. She hadn't stayed long because her mother was tired. Before the cancer surgery, her mother had always stayed up late reading. Her father was the one who went to bed early. Now their roles had reversed. Her mother had lines in her face that Grace had not seen before—lines from the physical shock of the surgery, lines from pain and fatigue. Her mother had always been as strong as a horse, which were her mother's common words to describe her health. She was fond of telling the story of Grace's birth. She and Grace both slept through their first night as if each was so comfortable with the other that there was no reason to stir and fret. Her mother took her home from the hospital the next day, and while Grace lay in the playpen in the living room her mother went outside and planted geraniums in the window box. Her mother said she would always carry a vision of watching Grace through the blooming red flowers.

So that was how her mother entered the dream with red flowers.

The burning and retribution came, Grace was certain, from her study of the Kwakiutl, a native tribe from the inner coast of Vancouver Island. Their culture fascinated her, and she was focusing her study more on them all the time. According to Ruth Benedict, who formed her theories from the observations of Boaz, rivalry was the central feature of Kwakiutl culture. The tribal members accumulated wealth, which most Western cultures could well understand, then they destroyed it. Perhaps that could also be understood. Boaz wrote about a chief who gathered his people and rivals at a great potlatch and bragged about his wealth and power. The women sang about him, about his ancestors. No one, they sang, could better their great throw-away chief. Inside the potlatch lodge, the great throw-away chief stacked a thousand blankets and burned them at the feet of his rivals. He destroyed one canoe after another to show how insignificant the canoes were to his wealth and power. He brought in slaves and killed them before the other chiefs. Finally he broke apart etched copper pieces that were worth ten thousand blankets and challenged his rivals to match him.

The rivals pretended that the destruction was nothing. Even when the blankets burned so hot that the flames burned their feet, the rival chiefs feigned nonchalance. At one potlatch, Boaz reported, the lodge caught on fire, yet the chiefs sat immobile while the walls burned down around them. So there was the fire in her dream.

She knew where the retribution came from, also. For the Kwakiutl, rivalry and revenge had an unusual manifestation in death. If a chief's son died, the chief was shamed and overcame the shame by killing the son of a chief of equal stature. In that way the tears would be wiped away from the chief's clan and given to another. In her dream Grace had not wanted to wipe away her tears. She couldn't understand how killing another mother would do that, but still, against her will, she had searched for a mother to kill until the anguish woke her. And now she remembered the final detail: It was Katherine's mother she was looking for. God, she thought, how could these dreams form?

Grace took a sip of coffee and watched the Montlake Bridge begin to drop.

It couldn't have been me inside that dream.

She was not to judge, Benedict said. A scientist's job was to observe and record. Each society formed its own patterns of culture, and each proceeded more or less successfully. Not all scientists agreed with Benedict's interpretation of the Kwakiutl culture. Even fewer agreed to withhold judgment. Grace wasn't sure that she could either.

From her canvas backpack she removed a stapled set of papers copied from *The Anthropology Review* and flipped to the third page where she had underlined a paragraph she wanted to think about. The entire article was about the collapse of a society that depended upon the cod fishing industry off Newfoundland. What if, asked the writer, the collapse was not a matter of economic and political factors as most scientists thought but was instead a matter of the environment, radically changed by fishing technology? From that question, Grace had begun forming a similar question about the Kwakiutl. What would have happened to them if the salmon, which was their primary food, had been decimated? Would they have chosen a different pattern of culture if more time had been required for sustenance, making less time available for the accumulation of ancillary wealth?

She shielded her eyes from the midmorning sun and saw Mt. Rainier above the tops of the trees. Rainier, or Takhoma as the native tribes called it, seemed much closer than it was. It was a hundred miles away, Grace knew, and yet it looked close enough to reach in an afternoon's walk. Below her the campus street curved around the Student Union and dropped sharply toward Pacific Street and Lake Washington. On the trees that followed the curve the leaves were beginning to change. If good weather lasted another week or two, the leaves would become magically colored—gold, yellow, and red. What were the scientific odds that Indian summer would hold off the rain that drowned the leaves in a soggy mush every year?

As if in answer an Indian girl stood before her in the Indian summer sunshine. Grace moved her head and squinted at the girl's face.

"You're Grace, aren't you?" the girl asked.

"Yes."

"I'm Maria," the girl said. "We met this summer at Katherine's apartment. It was just for a few minutes. Katherine told me that you were going back to school."

"I remember," Grace said. "Katherine told me how you became friends when you met her during that investigation on First Avenue. You're a policeman's daughter."

When she saw the girl's expression, Grace wished that she had used a different description of her memory of that afternoon. Katherine had told her much more about the girl than who her father was. Maria should have a description of her own and not one based on her father.

"Katherine tells me how well you're doing in school. Would you like to sit down? I have some questions for a marine biologist."

The girl walked around the table and sat in a chair so that she faced away from Rainier and toward the Student Union. She placed her book bag at her feet and rested her empty hands on top of the table.

"How could you pass all that food without buying something?" Grace asked.

"I bring a lunch with me. I was looking for somebody."

"But not me," Grace said.

The girl returned her smile. She had strong features. The strength showed in her face and in her straight upright posture. The girl needed strength, Grace thought, strength and courage. Katherine had told her how the girl left Alaska on her own to find a father who knew nothing about her. Grace wondered if she would have the courage to make that journey.

"Katherine has told me quite a bit about you."

"Does she ever talk about my father?"

"Sure."

"I mean about the two of them."

"Is there something to talk about?"

"There was, or there might have been. I think I got in the way."

"I doubt that," Grace said.

"Is she seeing anybody?"

"We kind of keep that to ourselves."

Maria nodded that she understood, but what she understood made her sad.

"There was somebody a while back," Grace said. "A doctor. But he moved to California to finish whatever they do, and I don't think there's anybody now."

"For my father either."

"Do you want me to tell her?"

The girl's face brightened, and Grace saw beauty in her face in addition to the strength. At first Grace had seen only what she would call handsome features, but Maria's shy smile brought out the beauty.

"I'll tell her," Grace said, smiling herself.

The patio began to fill with students holding large soft drink cups all bearing the same scripted logo. The cups made her Styrofoam coffee cup seem small and plain. The high voices of the girls and the newly acquired bass tones of the boys on the patio made her feel old. At least in the main reading room of the library, she had found students her age. Perhaps she should retreat back to the library.

Maria smiled as she looked past Grace, and Grace turned toward the door and saw a tall man approaching them. He, too, looked older than the other students, but it may have been his size that made him appear so. It was more than that, she decided. He walked with unusual confidence. Did she recognize him? She couldn't be sure. He stopped at their table.

"Hi," he said to Maria.

"Hi," Maria said, projecting in the single syllable both pleasure and uncertainty. "Grace, this is Paul."

He extended his hand to Grace across the table and looked into her eyes. He acted as if he knew her, or as if for one moment there were no one else in the world except the two of them, not even the young girl who had presented him to her. She had seen him somewhere. He brought no books, notebooks, paper—nothing. He sat down empty-handed next to Maria, who had a backpack stuffed full.

"We have an oceanography class together," Maria said, "whenever Paul decides to come."

"I couldn't make it this morning," he said to Maria.

His voice was low and intimate. Grace saw the effect it had on the girl—a shifting of her head, her body, a slight but perceptible movement toward the voice.

"Why?" she asked softly.

"A little ding on the knee," he said, as if the knee belonged to somebody else and had nothing to do with him. "Nothing serious, but I had to go in and see the trainer this morning. So what did I miss?"

"A lecture about seaweed."

"Oh, no, not the one about seaweed."

Grace remembered where she had seen this man. He was a football player, and she had seen his picture somewhere. Perhaps she had even seen him on television.

"Would you like a Coke?" he asked Maria. "Is that coffee? Can I get you another cup?" he asked Grace.

"No thanks," Grace said. "I need to go."

He looked at Maria.

"A small one," she said.

He pushed back his chair and stood. "It was nice to meet you," he said to Grace.

"Likewise," she said.

She watched Maria watch him leave, then turned in her

chair to watch him pass through the door into the cafeteria. He was favoring a knee, but so slightly that a person would have to pay close attention to notice.

"Whew, Maria," she said as she placed her anthropology review back into her bag. "How did you find this Adonis?"

"Adonis?" the girl asked. "What's that?"

"A beautiful man. And famous, this one. He's a football player, isn't he?"

"I guess so."

"You guess?"

"We met in class. We don't talk about football."

"Good for you."

Grace pushed her chair back and was about to get up when she noticed another girl coming toward them, one timid step at a time, the only other black girl on the patio. Grace had noticed her earlier sitting in the far corner of the patio— how could she not? Grace had no doubt that the girl was coming to her. If she didn't quickly escape, the segregation of the patio would be complete. Then there would be three people at the table when Adonis returned with Maria's Coke. She was certain that Maria would not appreciate that.

Grace stood and picked up her coffee and backpack with the intention of meeting the other girl halfway, of diverting her from Maria's table, when she saw the fear in the girl's dark eyes. Grace froze under the stare and wondered what could give the girl such cold fear on this sunny patio.

"Is he coming back?" the girl asked.

"What?" Grace asked, not understanding the girl's question.

"Is he coming back?" the girl asked again, looking toward the door where the Adonis had gone.

"Yes," Grace said.

"Are you with him?" the girl asked.

"Why are you asking?"

"Are you with him?"

Again the girl looked toward the door. It remained closed.

"No," Grace said. "I was just leaving. My friend is with him." Grace tilted her head toward Maria and looked at the young woman who had radiated beauty just a moment before. Maria may not have seen fear like this, but Grace had—too many times.

"Be careful," the girl whispered to Maria. "He's not what you think."

From the corner of her eye Grace saw the door open. The girl saw it, too, and stepped back as if someone had shouted at her. No one had said a word, not even a whisper, but the girl took one more step back, bumped the table behind her, and whirled around. She was gone before Grace could think about stopping her. The girl hurried down the steps of the patio to the sidewalk below as Paul arrived with the Cokes—one big and one small. His Adonis face was ashen, as if he had seen a ghost.

"What the hell was that about?" Grace asked, as much to herself as to anyone else.

Paul placed the small Coke in front of Maria and looked away from them toward the steps where the girl had run. When he turned back, his face had regained its color. It was a remarkable transformation.

"I thought I recognized her," Paul said. "Did she say something?"

Maria looked at Grace for the answer, but Grace had none to give.

"She told us to be careful," Maria said.

"Then that must be her," Paul said.

"Who?" Maria asked.

"A girl that used to hang around the team. I'm afraid there are a few guys who take advantage of that."

"Why?" Maria asked.

"I don't know," Paul said.

Grace heard voices from other tables. To the students at

those tables, nothing had happened. The girl and her fear had not existed. Their voices and laughter went on unbroken. Maria looked at the tall beautiful man standing next to Grace and waited for him to explain more, to explain everything.

"I've got to go," Grace said to Maria. "I'll see you again."

With those quick words she was gone—down the steps where the girl had fled to the sidewalk. The girl was gone. There was no sign of her in any direction: She had disappeared like a ghost.

Chapter 15

Grace pulled the shoelace tight across the top of her foot.
The string snapped, leaving the short piece in her hand.
"Ah," she muttered in disgust. There was no one in the locker
room to hear her.

She stood on her toes and dug through the junk on the top
shelf of her locker. A box of Kleenex, lipstick, as if she ever
used it, cold tablets, an extra set of keys, two stacks of pocket
notebooks, each rubber-banded together, rubber bands, an
empty tampon box that she threw at the garbage can beside
the door just as Katherine walked in, but no shoelaces.

"Cleaning house?" Katherine asked as she walked to her
locker, three lockers away from Grace's.

"I ought to."

Grace gave up trying to find a shoelace and sat on the
bench. She bent down to her shoe and tied the broken ends of
the lace together. Carefully she tightened it again. It would
last until she could buy new ones.

"Need a shoelace?" Katherine asked.

Grace looked up at her partner, whose locker was always
neat and clean.

"Got any?"

Katherine reached to the top shelf of her locker and removed a small gray card file. She raised the hinged lid, rum-

maged through the contents with her finger, and pulled out a package of black laces. She handed them to Grace.

"See if they're long enough."

"What else do you have in there?" Grace asked.

Katherine smiled as she snapped the lid shut.

"Secrets," she said.

Grace smiled, too, as she reached down and pulled the broken lace from her shoe. At the beginning of their partnership five months earlier, Katherine would have told her everything that was inside the box.

"I ran into your friend Maria today," Grace said.

"On campus?" Katherine asked as she stuck the pin of her badge through the narrow slit on her police shirt that she had hung on her locker door.

"Yes."

"How's she doing?"

"I think she has a boyfriend."

Katherine closed the metal latch over her badge pin and cocked her head toward Grace.

"Did you meet him?"

"Yes. He's a football player."

In silence Katherine slipped her bulletproof vest over her white T-shirt.

"What's he like?" Katherine finally asked. From the tone of her voice Grace could tell that Katherine was already prepared to dislike him.

Grace began with her first impression of the Adonis. By the time she finished telling Katherine about the girl who had run away, her partner was sitting beside her on the bench. Grace had still not tied her shoes.

"His face, the way it changed," she said. "I don't know if Maria saw it. It was strange. It was beyond strange. Maybe I'm seeing too much in this. Maybe that girl hung around the team like he said and got more than she wanted, but I don't think so."

"We'd better check him out," Katherine said. "What's his last name?"

"I don't know, but I've seen his picture, either on television or in the newspapers. You'll probably recognize him."

"Probably not," Katherine said. "I don't pay any attention to it. I hate football."

"I know what you mean," Grace said. "I don't understand football either, but even my father likes it. There must be some reason everybody else gets excited about it."

"No, there isn't," Katherine said.

Katherine rose from the bench, pulled off her shoes, and tossed them into the bottom of her locker. Then she pulled off her jeans and tossed them after her shoes. She looked at Grace who remained on the bench and watched her partner's uncharacteristic behavior. Unlike the mask of the Adonis, her partner's face was easy to read.

In the break room Grace found remnants of the Sunday paper scattered across the table. On the first page of the sports section, she saw Paul Renzlau's picture. He was in his uniform, shaking the hand of a small frail boy wearing a Washington team cap. Even with the cap covering the top of the boy's head, it was clear that the boy had no hair. Renzlau had befriended Jimmy McIntyre at Children's Hospital in Seattle, the story said, and had organized supporters to fly the boy to Los Angeles for the football game. In the photograph Renzlau was giving the game ball to the boy. Afterward, she read, Jimmy McIntyre was going to Disneyland.

She remembered a different image, not the face captured and preserved in the photograph beside the adoring boy. She had seen the ashen face of the Adonis as it transformed before her.

"Here's our guy," she said to Katherine, who had followed her into the break room. Grace gave her the newspaper and pointed to the picture. "He doesn't look like much of a threat here."

Katherine scanned the article and gave the paper back to Grace. She took out her pocket notebook and flipped to the first empty page.

"How did they spell that football player's last name?"

Grace put her finger at the name below the photograph and raised it to Katherine's sight.

"Poor kid," Katherine said as she wrote down Renzlau's name. "I'll call Records and see if they have anything."

Katherine walked over to the telephone on the counter beside an ancient refrigerator and dialed the last four numbers of the Records Bureau. She identified herself and gave her serial number. Then she pronounced the name, Paul Renzlau, spelling Renzlau for the clerk.

Katherine lowered the telephone mouthpiece as she waited. "How old is he?" she asked.

"I'd guess twenty-one or twenty-two," Grace said, "but he looks older."

Katherine returned her attention to the telephone.

"Nothing, huh? Okay, thanks."

She broke the connection but didn't cradle the receiver.

"No arrests," she said. "I'll check Moving Violations just for the hell of it."

She punched in four more numbers and repeated the process. This time she began writing in her notebook. Grace saw the words: *stop sign – reg.—taillight.*

"Nothing else?" Katherine asked the clerk.

"Who was the officer?" Grace asked softly.

"What is the officer's name and serial number who issued the ticket?" *Christopherson – 3506,* she wrote. "Okay, thanks."

Katherine hung up the telephone. "A traffic ticket last month, but no arrests. Just the one ticket."

"He must have pissed Christopherson off," Grace said. "Nobody gets a ticket for a taillight."

"Do you know the officer?" Katherine asked.

"He works Third Watch in the U-District. I've never heard of him getting mad at anybody. The college kids must finally be getting to him. I'll call him after roll call. He should be up by then."

Word was out that Captain Reimers planned to hold a surprise inspection at roll call. There were a half-dozen officers at the shoeshine bench and several more cleaning their revolvers. Grace pulled out her gun, too, and opened the cylinder. She blew off a few specks of lint and holstered her gun. When a shoe brush became free she swiped each of her shoes with a few quick strokes. There was enough polish on the brush to shine the toes and to give at least the illusion of care. The captain's inspections were no more than that anyway.

For Captain Reimers it was Monday, and he was in a freshly pressed uniform with sharp creases and no stains. For Katherine and her it was the end of the week after six days in a row wearing the same shirt and pants. Her shirt and pants were ready for the cleaners, but the captain didn't look closely enough to notice as he moved down their row. He looked like an unhealthy man. He had a splotchy red face, and the bulge above his gun belt was not due to a bulletproof vest as it was for many in the line. He didn't wear one. Grace wondered why he didn't retire. He was never a happy man.

When Captain Reimers came to Murphy, he asked her to present her revolver. Katherine pulled it from her holster, flipped open the cylinder, and held the frame for him to take. Grace knew that the captain wouldn't find any dust in Katherine's service revolver. Katherine was probably the best marksman in the squad, and she took excellent care of her revolver—not that the captain would know. She doubted he even knew how close Katherine had come to using that revolver two weeks earlier. He hadn't said a word about the arrest or about the indentation from the firing pin on the cartridge. Nobody had, except the detective who sent them a form notifying them that the man had been charged with a gross misdemeanor—not a felony. If Katherine had pulled the trigger, someone would have said something.

The captain passed Grace with a brief acknowledgment. He didn't even look at her shoes.

After roll call Grace called Christopherson at home. She imagined his cheerful face at the kitchen table. Although she had never worked with him, he had been one of the few officers in the beginning who had made her feel that she might belong. He reminded her more of the repairman who came to fix her washing machine than a cop. Maybe that was why she liked him, that and the friendly waves he gave her when they passed in the parking lot.

No, he didn't mind that she called him at home, he said. "What's up?"

"Do you remember a ticket you wrote to Paul Renzlau about a month ago?"

"The football player? Yeah, I remember that turkey. Why? You got him on something?"

"No. I was just curious about what happened that night."

"Sure you are. Don't tell me he showed up on Ballard Avenue with all you Norskies?"

"No. I ran into him on the campus. He was with a cop's daughter."

"Not good," Christopherson said.

"Why? What do you know about him?"

"Only what I saw."

"And what was that?"

"He blew through this stop sign on frat row, and I pulled him over. When I went up to the car, he just sat there like I was supposed to know him. I told him to get out his license, and he had this smirk on his face like he was the governor or something. So I made him get out of the car and put his hands up on the roof and frisked him. He wasn't so smart after that."

"Did you know who he was?"

"Sure I did, but I wasn't going to let him know. The turkey. He couldn't find the registration either, but he knew the name of the owner, and that's who the car came back to. I wrote him a ticket for the stop sign and kicked him loose."

"You wrote him up for the registration and a broken tail-light, too."

"Did I?"

She heard Christopherson's chuckle.

"It wasn't just that he thought he was God's gift to the world. There was something else about the guy I didn't like. I never turned my back on him, if you know what I mean."

"We never turn our backs on anybody," Grace said.

"You got that right. I had half a mind to call the coach and report him. Coach Bourne wouldn't put up with that kind of crap."

Through the window facing the parking lot, Grace watched the stream of blue cars heading toward the street. Some would continue east toward the University District; some would turn west where she and Katherine would go unless they found something more suspicious than a frightened girl and a traffic ticket.

"Why do you think the coach would care about a stop sign?" she asked.

"It was three in the morning, for chrissake," Christopherson said. "Saturday morning. They had a game that afternoon. What? These players are such big shots they don't have curfew anymore?"

"Did you ask him?"

"Nah. I didn't want to give him the satisfaction. Hey, I told my daughter about you and Murphy working together, and she's decided that she wants to be a police officer, too, since she won't have to work with an icky boy like her brother. But now she doesn't want to take piano lessons. 'Police officers don't play the piano,' she says. I don't suppose you play the piano?"

"Never did. Sorry."

"How about Murphy?"

Grace lifted the receiver up from her mouth but didn't cover the telephone.

"Did you ever play the piano?" she asked Katherine. "Christopherson needs to know. His daughter wants to be a police officer, and she wants to stop taking piano lessons. She thinks police officers don't have to play the piano."

"I used to play," Katherine said. "He can tell his daughter that the torture of piano lessons is good practice for this job."

"Did you get that?" Grace asked Christopherson.

"Got it," Christopherson said. He was laughing again and thinking about his daughter, not the football player he had stopped at three in the morning. In his mind the two were as far apart as his daughter's wish to be a police officer and his for piano lessons. That was how Grace left him.

"So what would this guy be up to at three in the morning?" Katherine asked after Grace gave her a summary of Christopherson's traffic stop.

"A party, a date, it could be anything," Grace said.

"Some date."

"Not much to go on," Grace said. "Still, I saw something in Renzlau that bothered me. So did Christopherson."

"I wonder if Maria saw it, too," Katherine said. "She's a pretty smart kid."

"I don't know. It looked like he was doing a good job of smoothing things over when I left. Maybe you should talk to her father."

Katherine looked out to the parking lot, but Grace was quite certain that she wasn't watching the departing patrol cars.

"I can do that," Katherine said.

"I forgot to tell you. Maria wanted you to know that her father wasn't seeing anybody, whatever that means. I'm sure I don't know."

Katherine looked sideways and turned her head just enough that Grace could see the slightest smile beneath the more evident lines of the frown showing in her forehead and eyebrows.

"Have you checked the FIR file yet?" Katherine asked.

"Not yet."

Katherine's eyebrows rose from their frown.

"But I will," Grace said.

There was no Field Interview Report for Paul Renzlau in the ancient wooden file cabinet. The new FIRs were carbonless, but the old forms had required carbon paper to make copies. Grace's fingers became smudged from the carbon on the backs of the thin forms that were no bigger than traffic tickets. Many of the old FIRs were so smudged that they were barely legible. In the academy they had been instructed to write FIRs for suspicious people when there was nothing else to write. The FIRs were then sorted and filed, but hardly anyone ever bothered looking at them. She wondered if they were even worth the effort.

"Nothing here," Grace said as Katherine returned with the keys to the patrol car.

"Want to check downtown?" Katherine asked.

Grace's stomach growled from hunger. It was Monday, and Rigmor made *skipperslabskovs* every Monday—sailor's stew flavored with beer. The stew would simmer on the stove through the afternoon, but it was never as good later in the day as it was at noon before the beer evaporated.

"Be careful," the girl had said. "He's not what you think." Nobody is who we think they are. But why such fear? She thought the girl's face would become less distinct as the hours passed, but the opposite was true. She was beginning to see the face more clearly as time passed. And Maria, the policeman's daughter and Katherine's friend, what was she getting into? The sailor's stew would have to wait even if all the beer evaporated.

Grace sat on the bench seat with her knees touching the dashboard as they merged with the freeway traffic and headed downtown. In their first weeks together Katherine had positioned the seat farther back, so far that she had to stretch uncomfortably to reach the gas pedal and brake. She was apologetic even then, but Grace told her to move the seat forward. They didn't spend enough time in the car to make any difference.

From the freeway bridge at the ship canal Grace could see a huge skyscraper that was under construction next to police headquarters. The skyscraper was supposed to be the tallest building west of the Mississippi or north of San Francisco or somewhere of someplace. Compared to Mt. Rainier farther east, the skyscraper had a cold arrogant face. She had heard that the skyscraper developer was a clever man who had manipulated zoning rules to build higher than anyone anticipated. Some said the skyscraper was so tall that at the right time of year it would cast a shadow all the way to Mercer Island. All the money that went into the skyscraper didn't soften its appearance.

"So why do you hate football?" Grace asked as they reached the end of the freeway bridge.

"What?" Katherine asked. She rolled up her window and turned the fan higher on the air-conditioner that was just beginning to pump out cool air. The air smelled stale.

"Football," Grace said. "In the locker room you said you hate football. Why?"

"Did you ever watch a game?"

"Sure."

"So why are you asking, then? Don't you see what they do to each other?"

"It's kind of rough. I agree with that."

"Rough? I think football players should just line up in two rows and beat each other over the head with baseball bats. Last guy standing wins. That would be faster and simpler than the way they play the game. God, it takes forever for one of those games to end."

"You don't like the violence," Grace said.

"I don't like the violence," Katherine said. "I think we have enough of that without teaching it to a bunch of brainwashed boys. Girls don't play, you know, even if there were any girls who were dumb enough to want to. It's the last reserve of male dominion, and they're not going to give it up. Girls get to jump around on the sidelines like a bunch of idiots."

Grace laughed at Katherine's description of the game. It was one of the characteristics she liked best about her partner—her unambiguous descriptions. Katherine laughed, too, but Grace doubted they were laughing about the same thing.

"All the cheerleaders can't be idiots," Grace said. She wanted to hear more descriptions from her partner.

"I was one. I ought to know," Katherine said.

"You?" Grace asked, this time with surprise and not with the intention of spurring on her partner.

Katherine nodded as she watched the traffic in front of them.

"In high school," Katherine said.

"Do you remember any cheers? I never could understand them when I was in school."

"Here's one," Katherine said. She straightened her back in the car seat and took a deep breath. "Take the ball and stuff it, stuff it. Waaaay in!"

Grace slapped the dashboard beside the shotgun barrel and laughed again.

"Try it," Katherine said. She removed her right hand from the steering wheel and led Grace in the cheer.

For Grace it was the first football cheer that she ever understood, and she chanted the cheer with Katherine as they reached the northern slope of Capitol Hill. There was no applause after their last cheer died away.

"You're telling me those are the reasons you hate it? Violence and mindless cheerleaders?"

Katherine looked sideways at Grace.

"I thought so," Grace said. "Was he the big star, too?"

"He thought he was. What I was thinking about is beyond me now. I wasn't thinking. I was all hormones and no brains. I found out that he told his buddies in the locker room about us, and they told everybody else. Except he wasn't talking so much when I missed my period. He ran home crying to mommy then. He wouldn't even call me."

"What happened?"

"It came next month right on schedule."

"I mean, what happened with him?"

"Nothing. Nothing happened with him. He's probably still home with mommy and daddy."

"He sounds like a fireman I met when I got out of the academy," Grace said.

She was surprised to hear her own words. She had told no one about the fireman, about the disappointment anyway. Katherine's honesty had disarmed her. It didn't feel so bad to be disarmed.

"I knew firemen had strange hours, but his were really strange. Then I met him and his wife and two little kids at the Northgate Mall Christmas shopping."

"And you didn't know?"

"No."

"That must have been an interesting meeting. What did he get you for Christmas?" Katherine asked.

"A lump of coal," Grace said.

Grace turned away and looked out the window of the police car. Her joke wasn't funny after all. For three months she had a beautiful man in her life, someone who made her laugh, who made her cry with pleasure, who made her smile when she was alone, and then he was gone. It was worse than that. He had never been. She was a cop, she had told herself.

She wasn't supposed to be fooled. He was better looking than the Adonis she had seen in the morning, his dark body supple and alive to her touch, but he was only a mirage.

Katherine turned into the police garage and parked at the far end of the car deck. Somewhere back on the freeway their cheer had lost its humor. Grace wasn't sure just where that had been. Perhaps it was at the point where the volcano Takhoma disappeared from their sight and the cold giant tower became the singular landmark.

Together they walked through the double doors of the garage into the third floor hallway. They stopped at the locked door of the Crime Analysis Division.

"They must be at lunch," Katherine said.

It didn't matter. Katherine used her police master key to unlock the door. The Crime Analysis room was divided into cubicles with six-foot maps of the hourglass-shaped city. There was a map for each classification of crime, and each map was dotted with different colored pins—blue for crimes that occurred during the First Watch, green for the Second Watch, red for the Third. In some areas the pins were so thick that Grace couldn't see the map under them.

"Look at this," Katherine said, pointing to a row of green pins that formed a distinct pattern above Golden Gardens. Grace looked at the map title and saw that it was for sexual assault. Katherine removed the long-spindled Second Watch clipboard from its hook and began flipping through the pages.

"It's some guy exposing to little girls on their way home from school. I didn't know the incidents were so close together. Maybe we should spend a little time up there."

"And everywhere else," Grace said, waving across the face of the brightly dotted map. "Where are the FIRs?"

She hadn't driven downtown to look for exposers. Of course, once you began looking for something there was no telling what you would find. Her studies of the Kwakiutl were proving that.

Katherine hung the clipboard back in place. "Up here," she said. She walked to the front of the room to a metal file cabinet and opened the drawer marked *R*.

"Jeez," Grace said.

The drawer was packed so tightly it appeared that any attempt to withdraw a single FIR would cause the entire mass to spring free. Katherine tried to separate the slips of paper enough to read the names, but she finally gave up and pulled out a handful from the front of the drawer. The remaining mass expanded to fill the void. She handed the stack of FIRs to Grace and prevented further escape with her other hand.

Grace placed the stack on top of the desk and began flipping through them. They were arranged alphabetically, more or less, the *RE*s following soon after the last *RA*.

"I'll be damned," Grace said when she found a FIR with the last name of Renzlau. It was a new form and largely free of ink smudges. She pulled it out and laid it aside so that Katherine could read it. She explored further into the stack, but there were no more for him.

" '14th and Yesler,' " Katherine read. " '0230 Hours.' " She flipped to the back of the FIR. "'*Individual made two separate contacts with suspected prostitutes. Stated he was looking for someone. Officer advised individual to leave known area of prostitution.*' This was written a year ago, November fifteenth. They're still playing football in November, aren't they?"

"They play through Thanksgiving," Grace said. "I'll make a copy of this. Let's go up to Records and see if he's ever been listed as a witness or a suspect. And maybe they have an old calendar lying around so that we can see what day of the week this is. Wouldn't it be interesting if this was a Saturday morning, too?"

While they waited at the Records counter, Grace heard

sharp-heeled taps on the floor that produced a sound unlike the dull thud of all the other shoes, and she turned to see Anne Smith walking toward them.

"Are you ladies lost?" she asked.

"Not yet," Grace said, "but we're working on it."

The records clerk brought back the photocopy of the FIR and laid it on the counter in front of them.

"We don't have him anywhere," she said. "Anything else you want me to check?"

"No thanks," Katherine told her.

Anne picked up the copy and held it at arms length. It still wasn't far enough away, and she put on the glasses that hung from her neck from a gold chain."

"Don't tell me you're back working with Vice," Anne said.

"No. I met this guy on the campus today," Grace said.

"I hope you're not checking him out for yourself."

"Not for me. He was with another cop's daughter."

"Ah," Anne said, looking back at the paper before removing her glasses. "Where have I heard this name before?"

"He's a football player," Grace said.

"That's where I heard it. Well, what they say about football players getting all the girls must not be true or he wouldn't be down at 14th and Yesler, would he?"

"Do you have any old calendars lying around?" Grace asked. "We'd like to see what day of the week this was."

"Everything I have is old. Come on. I'll bet you two would like a fresh cup of coffee."

Chapter 16

Katherine crossed the Ballard Bridge, which she expected might rise as an omen and block her passage. It did not, and she reminded herself that she didn't believe in omens from bridges or anything else. She remembered the way to his house although she had not been there for a long time. Take the last bridge that crossed the tide flats and follow the street to the top of the hill. Curve back down through the ravine to the narrow road where only one car could pass at a time. Once there it was hard to turn around and go back.

She had called ahead, and they were expecting her. On the steep road that followed the ravine to the bottom of the bluff, she rehearsed what she would say to Maria and her father. The words didn't come easily. She had never been very good at talking to herself.

Maria answered the door. There was a lightness about the girl, a freedom of movement that had been missing when Katherine first met her. Katherine stood in the doorway for a moment admiring the girl. Finally, she had to say it.

"Maria, you're becoming beautiful."

The girl blushed into a deeper color and hugged Katherine. The girl was strong. There was no doubt about that. The kayak trips were giving her powerful shoulders like her father's. Was there a resemblance beyond that? Something in her eyes, the shape of her mouth?

The walk? No, it wasn't the walk. Maria led her into the kitchen where Sam sat at the table with a pair of reading glasses perched low on his nose.

"I'm reading Maria's research paper," he said. "The first installment anyway. I would never have imagined that there would be so much to find on a little piece of beach. I just look for a place to land, but Maria can find all kinds of stuff. How are you doing, Kat?"

"Fine," she said. He was the only one who ever called her by that name.

"Sit down. I hope you're bringing good news."

Katherine sat in the chair across the table from him, and Maria sat beside her. Sam folded his glasses, gathered the papers he had been reading into a neat stack, and placed them off to the side.

"It's not good news," she said. "It's about Paul Renzlau."

Maria's smile faded. The girl sat perfectly still and focused on Katherine. Her eyes didn't seem to blink.

"When Grace came to work today, she told me about meeting you and Paul Renzlau at the Student Union. She told me about the girl who came up to your table. Did you tell your father about it?"

Maria moved her head slowly from side to side. "I didn't know what to say."

"Grace said that when Renzlau went to get Cokes for you and him, this girl came up to the table. The girl looked scared. She asked Grace if she was with Renzlau. Grace told her that you were the one who was with him. Then the girl told you to be careful. Did you hear that?"

"Yes," Maria said. Her voice was barely loud enough to reach Katherine.

"When this girl saw Renzlau coming back, she took off

like she was afraid of him, really afraid. That's what Grace saw. Is that what you saw, too?"

"Paul explained that to us. He said that she used to hang around the team and maybe something happened. I didn't know what to think. I've never met any of the other players. He never talks about football."

"I see," Katherine said, but she was having difficulty seeing Maria with this man. She had difficulty imagining that he didn't talk about football. The player she had known, the boy from her hometown whom she had cheered without knowing what she was doing, had talked about little else.

"He's smart, Katherine. He already has enough hours to graduate. He wants to go on to law school, and he's already been accepted at Stanford. We're just friends. I don't know why, but we are."

The girl was growing restless. She shifted in her chair and glanced out the window. Sam looked at Maria, grimaced, and turned to Katherine.

"What else did you find out?" he asked. He would know that she wasn't finished, that she had dug deeper. He might have been wishing that he had done the same thing, but it was clear that he hadn't.

"Grace and I ran his name. He got a traffic ticket last month for running a stop sign at three in the morning, which seemed a little strange since it was the morning of a football game. We went downtown and checked the FIR files. Renzlau was stopped a year ago at 14th and Yesler. The officer who wrote the FIR said that Renzlau was observed making several contacts there and was told to leave the area."

She had spoken the last words directly to Sam. She knew he would understand the meaning beneath her vagueness. Sam's face became more troubled, but he didn't say anything.

"What does that mean?" Maria asked.

Katherine hoped that Sam would explain the meaning to

the girl. Instead he gestured with his hand. The interpretation was up to her.

"Fourteenth and Yesler," Katherine said, addressing Maria, "is an area where prostitutes walk the streets and pick up customers. According to the officer, Renzlau talked to two prostitutes. One or two more contacts and he could have been arrested for soliciting a prostitute. This was also early on a Saturday morning during football season. Maybe the timing of the two incidents could just be coincidental, but it doesn't look like it.

"A couple weeks ago about two o'clock on a Saturday morning, a man picked up a young woman on 14th and Jefferson Street in the Central District. This is a few blocks away from 14th and Yesler where Renzlau was stopped before. The young woman denies she's a prostitute. She said that she was waiting for a bus. After she got into the man's car, he drove up to Beacon Hill and parked. This wasn't where she told him to go, and she got scared. She saw him reach below the seat and pull out a yellow rope. The young woman jumped out of the car and ran before he could do anything. She flagged down a police car a block or two away. The officers looked for the car, but they couldn't find it. They filed a report.

"That report went to Detective Smith from Sex Crimes. She's somebody Grace and I know, and we met her today when we were waiting at the Records counter to see if Renzlau had ever been listed as a suspect or witness in a crime. He hasn't, by the way. We told Detective Smith about Paul Renzlau. The suspect on 12th Avenue was described as being a little older and smaller than Renzlau, but he was wearing large black glasses. That's what made Detective Smith curious."

"Paul doesn't wear glasses," Maria said.

"He was wearing them on the night he was stopped and FIRed on Yesler Street," Katherine said. "His driver's license doesn't require that he wear glasses, but he was wearing glasses that night, that morning, I mean."

Maria's lower lip began to quiver. It wasn't fair, Katherine thought. She knew what it was like to see a dream, a fantasy, crumble with the truth, whatever truth was. Maria bit hard on her lip and stopped its trembling.

"Detective Smith called us late this afternoon. She had cut out about twenty pictures from a program they sell at football games, just the faces, and taped them to a sheet of paper. She showed the paper to the young woman who filed the report. The woman picked out Renzlau's picture. She wasn't one hundred percent certain because he wasn't wearing glasses, but she thought it was the man who picked her up that night on 12th Avenue. Anne said that the young woman isn't very cooperative, but she did pick out his picture.

"We don't have proof that he committed any crime. We don't have proof that anybody committed a crime, but there are too many things here not to pay attention. I don't want you to get hurt, Maria."

She reached for Maria's hands, which the girl was holding motionless in her lap, squeezed them with her single hand, and smiled what she knew was the same reassuring smile that she had hated to receive when she was a girl. A tear dropped from Maria's eye, and the girl quickly pulled her hand free and brushed it away.

"Sam," Katherine said, "may I speak to Maria alone?"

"Sure." He stood abruptly but halted in front of his pushed-back chair as if he were going to say something. Katherine and Maria waited. His chair screeched on the floor as he pushed it back to the table, but he left the kitchen noise-lessly.

"No," Maria said after her father left, "we haven't done anything, if that's what you want to know."

"Well, that part was easy enough. Have you gone out with him?"

"Yes," Maria said. "He took me to a party at his fraternity, and we went to a play on the campus, but we're just friends. He kissed me once, but that's all."

"Do you like him?"

"What you said doesn't sound like the same person."

"How do you know what a person is like?"

"How do you?" the girl asked.

"I don't know, Maria."

Maria's hair was pulled tight into a ponytail. She wore a plaid flannel shirt and blue jeans. Sam claimed that she dressed like a lumberjack. The girl's appearance could not have been more different from the women on Yesler.

"What happened after Grace left? What did you and Renzlau talk about?"

"He didn't stay very long. He got hurt in the last game and had to go back to the training room for some kind of treatment."

"Did you talk about the girl?"

Maria nodded at the question, but she wasn't looking at Katherine. She was looking back, not forward.

"A little bit," she said. "He thought there must be something wrong with her."

"Is that what you thought?"

"Yes," Maria said. "There was something wrong."

"I don't think you should go out with him again until we find out what's going on. We'll find the girl who came up to your table and talk to her, or at least Detective Smith will. Then we'll see what happens."

"What do you think he was doing at night at those places?" Maria asked.

"We don't know for sure. We can only guess."

The guess sent a shudder through the strong shoulders of the young woman. Maria was strong, but her strength wouldn't be nearly enough to match Renzlau. Maria tightened her jaw and frowned.

"Do you want me to find out who she is?"

"From Renzlau?"

Maria nodded.

"No," Katherine said. "I want you to stay out of this. We don't want him to suspect anything, and I don't want you to get hurt. Does he know that Grace is a police officer?"

"No."

"That's good."

"What am I supposed to do tomorrow when I see him in class?"

"It's hard to imagine that he would do anything to you knowing that your father is a cop. That's probably the only advantage you get from having a cop as a father. Even so, you shouldn't go anywhere with Renzlau alone. You might just want to stay away from him completely."

For a moment Katherine couldn't understand the change in Maria's expression, but when she imagined herself in the young woman's shoes, it became clearer. Not that Maria's boots would fit her. They were several sizes larger than any she would wear.

"He doesn't know, does he?" Katherine asked. "What did you tell him about Sam?"

Maria hesitated a moment.

"I told him my father was a poet."

Katherine covered her mouth with her hand. A poet. If only she could have used that line about her father. Maria covered her mouth, too, but when the girl lowered her hand, there was no trace of the smile or the laugh she might have covered. There was no trace, either, of the youthful lightness Katherine had first seen in the girl. Or was she still a girl? When, Katherine asked herself, do you cross that line so that you can never go back?

Chapter 17

Maria didn't want to see him. When Katherine told her about the man with the yellow rope, she didn't know who it was. She couldn't imagine that it was the same man who sat beside her in class, spoke softly and seldom about himself, whose softest touch had begun to probe through her skin into deeper territory. She believed Katherine. How could she not? But how could the two men be one?

Overnight the two had merged. She had dreamed of him wearing a yellow shirt with a large number across the front. He took her hand, and the sleeve of his yellow shirt stretched like a long thin rope and coiled around her. It bound her arms tightly to her body. The binding was strong, and she could not break free. He laughed and pretended he didn't notice the sleeve that wound around and around, and his laugh stayed after all else blurred away.

She had considered skipping class, but she had chosen the desk first and now sat in it waiting for the class to begin. Perhaps, just as the day before, he would not come. Then she would meet Grace after class as planned. Her father wanted her to have nothing more to do with Paul, to break off any contact even if she couldn't tell him the real reason why. Her father wanted to sit with her in class, take the man aside, and pass along words of wisdom to the football star.

No, she said. No. No.

The professor walked in and strode to the front of the room. He deposited his worn briefcase on top of his desk and looked up to meet the two, then three students who approached with papers in hand and excuses for why they were turning them in late. He was accepting none of it. They would lose ten points just as he had promised on the first day of class. His sunburned face made him look more like one of the captains from the fishing boats that she used to see on summer trips to her mother's village in Alaska than a pale-faced professor who seldom saw the light. When he lectured, he stomped around the front of the classroom as if he were in his high boots wading through tide waters on a field excursion.

After dismissing the students with late papers, he made his way to her and placed her proposal for her research paper on her desk.

"I read this over the weekend," he said. "Nobody in this class has ever proposed such thorough research. From a kayak, no less. I think the beach you found is perfectly and uniquely suited to the observations you plan to conduct. If you would like to continue the research after the quarter ends, I'll help you publish the paper."

It was a day that she had hoped for—her work singled out, the prospect of working independently with her professor, the first clear sign that her effort was paying off. She could stop worrying that she wouldn't succeed with her studies. At least she could worry less. But instead of feeling pleased, she dreaded what would happen in the class.

She had known that something was wrong even before Katherine had come. There was something heavy, something oppressive looming. She had felt it from the time she first saw the fear in the girl's face when Paul limped out of the cafeteria. The fear had lingered after the girl fled, and she had seen its effect on Grace—and Paul, too, now that she thought about it. There had been a moment when she hadn't recognized him, when his face had clouded with an expression completely new and strange.

Everything had been going too well. Something was bound to happen, just as it did in the Trickster stories her mother had told her. The Trickster lived in the forest outside their village. He might come to the village as an animal or a lost relative. When people began thinking that they were gifted with a special life, the Trickster would come and remind them how easily life could change. It was cancer, not the Trickster, that had taken her mother, but Maria had tried to live with great care anyway—never setting herself apart. She had been careful never to feel too much, never to love too much. Perhaps she had let her guard down since finding her father. She had begun to feel safe in her father's house, feeling it was beyond the reach of the Trickster. There were mornings now when she tarried in bed instead of rising with the first ring of the alarm, when she thought about letting her father paddle alone to work so that she could sleep another hour beneath her warm covers. After all, Silve would still be at the stove when she arrived an hour or two later. Henry would come and take his place at the dishwasher. Her father would still sit at the counter and drink coffee with Silve, or he would retreat to a booth in the dining room and write words that grew to poems that he stuck away in his pocket. Each of them had a place—Silve, Henry, her father, and herself. Even the words, she had begun to think, had a place beyond the reach of the Trickster.

Now the old fear was returning. What if you could never get beyond his reach?

The tall man entered the room, no longer limping. Adonis, Grace called him, but he was as quiet and agile as the Trickster in her mother's stories.

Chapter 18

Grace sat on a bench in the empty bleachers high above the artificially green field. Where she sat, straight wood planks were etched with lines and numbers—one butt per number, she supposed. In passive defiance she straddled two numbers and extended her legs over the plank below her. On the north side of the stadium the sun warmed the purple and gold bleachers, but it was cool in the shadows where she sat.

Below her a hundred or more boys and men on the too-green field were divided into groups that crashed into each other. She smiled when she thought about Katherine's idea for the game, to line up the boys and give them bats to hit each other on the head. Older men clutching clipboards shouted instructions to the players in helmets and uniforms. Occasionally a clipboard dropped to the ground, and the older man demonstrated with both hands what he could not communicate with words. On a platform high above the center of the field, a single man walked in circles within the boundaries of protective railings and scanned the field like Ahab in search of the great white whale.

There was water to the east, an inlet from Lake Washington that reached toward the open end of the stadium, but the solitary man on top of the scaffold did not look to the water. His gaze seldom rose from the field, and much of his atten-

tion was focused on the sub-group closest to his platform.
Within this group she recognized Renzlau. She had come to
watch him, too, although she wasn't sure why.

His helmet covered his face; therefore, it wasn't facial features she recognized. It was the rhythm of his gait, his sure
stride as he glided untouched through the colliding lines.
There was an unmistakable similarity to the Adonis she had
watched moving untouched through the throngs of students
in the Student Union.

Below her a man passed through a gate into the seating
area. She suspected that it was no coincidence that he was
climbing the stairs in the empty stadium toward her. He wore
a white shirt and a tie a few shades lighter than his sleek gray
suit. He raised his arm and waved. He had a pleasant smile,
but she didn't trust it and didn't smile back.

"I saw you and was wondering what you're doing up here
all by yourself."

"I'm watching the practice," Grace said. "What are you
doing?"

"The same as you, I guess. Are you waiting for somebody?"

Grace looked around the empty seats for her answer. She
wasn't sure why she felt like being rude.

"Do you mean waiting for one of them?" Grace asked,
looking past the man toward the football field. "One of the
boys running around, or one of the fat old men yelling at
them?"

He looked down at the field and chuckled. "They're not all
fat," he said. He extended his hand toward her. "Bobby Flowers. I didn't mean to offend you by coming up here. I can
head back down if you want."

"Suit yourself," Grace said as she shook his hand without
changing her position.

"And you are . . . "

"Grace Stevens."

"Grace Stevens," he repeated. "I was just curious how you got in here. This is supposed to be a closed practice."

"Through the front door or whatever they call that gate on Pacific. Why? Are you the football police?"

"Not me. I'm with the *Seattle Tribune*. I used to be one of those guys, so they trust me. Maybe you remember our team. Rose Bowl champions five years ago. Bobby Flowers, a hundred forty-two yards rushing, player of the game." He spread his hands, palms up, as if he had just finished singing a song and was waiting for the applause. He was smiling, too, to show that he wasn't serious about the applause.

"I don't follow football very closely," she said.

"Then why are you here?" he asked.

"I'm not sure yet," she said. "Why do those two players wear green shirts and nobody else?"

She pointed to the group closest to the steel-ribbed scaffold in the middle of the field.

Bobby Flowers looked down to the field. "Nobody is supposed to hit them," he said. "They wear the green pullovers to remind the other players."

"I thought everybody got hit in football."

"Not in practice. You don't want to get the quarterback hurt in practice."

"And the other guy?"

"Renzlau," Bobby Flowers said. "He got a knee strain last game, and he's just getting over it. Coach doesn't want to take any chances on him getting hurt again."

"I thought nobody was tackling him because he was too good."

"Nobody is that good."

"Not even Bobby Flowers in the Rose Bowl game?"

"They got to me a few times," Bobby Flowers said. He smiled again and sat on a bench number a few digits from hers. "You say you don't know why you're here?"

That was what she had said. It was her day off from work,

and she should have been in the library reading the single fragile copy of Hansen's *Life Among the Inuit*. She was interested in finding a connection between the pre-European era cultures of the northern Alaskan tribes and those who lived along the more hospitable southeast coast. The young woman, Maria, was from the southern people. Perhaps that was the reason she was here. For the last two days she had met Maria in the Oceanography Building lounge after the young woman's morning class in an effort to appease the father who wanted his daughter to break off contact with Renzlau immediately. Or he could do it for her, he said.

The arrangement wouldn't last long. Maria wouldn't be able to sit beside Renzlau in class for long without running out of excuses why she couldn't join him after class, or why she couldn't go out with him at night. The girl would surely give away her secret, one way or another.

Then there was the other girl whose ancestors, probably like her own, had been dragged from their homes in West Africa and enslaved in the West Indies and America. Perhaps the fear she had seen in that young woman's face was the reason she watched the football practice—the fear that was the same for any woman, no matter from which tribe she was dragged.

"Do you write stories about Renzlau?" she asked.

"He's our star, isn't he? Oh, that's right. You wouldn't know."

"What do you say in your stories?"

"I say that Paul Renzlau is the best thing to happen to our football program since white bread."

She could have laughed at his clever remark. Neither of them were white bread, he was saying. He, Bobby Flowers, and she, Grace Stevens, could share this clever remark because they were on the same side of the racial divide. She could have joined him and made it easy. Instead she raised her eyebrows without acknowledging the divide. "Is he?" she asked.

"Now, don't repeat that to somebody and get me in trouble," Flowers said.

"So you don't think he's that good."

"He's good. Last year he led the nation in combined yards."

"What does that mean? Which yards are combined?"

Flowers looked perplexed for a moment; perhaps he was considering if she was worth the effort it would take to answer.

"It's like this," he said. "Some guys are good at running with the football, some are good at passing, and some are good at catching the ball. Renzlau isn't the best in any one category, but he's pretty good at all of them. If he stays healthy, he might go over a thousand yards in both rushing and receiving this year."

"And that would be good," Grace said.

"If he does it, he'll probably win the Heisman Trophy."

"Also good, I suppose."

"Also good," Flowers said. "For a football player winning the Heisman is like an actor winning the Oscar. The hype is already building. We've got a big story coming out Sunday."

"Why do you do that?"

"Because it sells newspapers."

"Not the paper—you. Why do you write about football?"

"I hope you don't mind me saying this, but you sound like my father. 'Four years of college,'" Flowers said with an artificially low voice to imitate his father, "'and still playing games.'"

"Did you write the story about Renzlau and the boy with cancer?"

"Should have, but that was somebody else." The smile that had survived the imitation of his father faltered now.

Competition, resentment—something else took the place of the smile. "I thought you didn't follow football."

"I read that story."

"Is that why you're here?"

It was the third time with the same question, but this time the tone was more insistent. Grace looked away from Flowers and back to the field where she saw Renzlau in his green shirt behind the quarterback. For a moment every player was perfectly still. Then the lines exploded, and the quarterback tossed the ball to Renzlau, who ran toward the edge of the field with his smooth sure strides. When it looked as if another player was going to tackle him despite the green shirt, Renzlau threw the ball far down the field in an arc so true that it could have been the end of a pencil tracing a rainbow. Another player, the quarterback in green and all alone, caught the ball. A deep-throated cheer rose from the field through the piercing sound of whistles. She turned toward Flowers, who had missed the entire play.

"I met Paul Renzlau on the campus a few days ago. He was with somebody I know, another student. The three of us were sitting on the patio of the Student Union, and Renzlau went inside to buy Cokes for my friend and himself. I was getting ready to leave when a young woman, a girl really, approached my friend and me. This girl was afraid, not of me or my friend, but of Renzlau. She told us to be careful. Then the girl took off. It was strange how frightened she was. You're a reporter, Mr. Flowers. You must know a lot about Renzlau and the team. Why would the girl be so afraid?"

"Why didn't you ask him?"

"I did. He said some girls hang around the team and get more attention than they want. I suppose I know what he meant."

"I suppose you do," Bobby Flowers said.

"Perhaps you thought I was one of those girls when you came up here."

"I wasn't thinking that at all," Bobby Flowers said.

"No?"

"No."

Flowers stood and moved back onto the steps he had climbed earlier. He was no longer smiling pleasantly as he had been when he arrived.

"I'll let you have this spot to yourself again," he said. "It's been interesting talking to you."

He nodded and started down the steps. Grace pulled back her feet from the lower bleacher seat and sat upright on the bench. Now that he was leaving, she didn't want him to go. Or did she? What did she expect him to do? She had already let the girl go without trying to stop her. She regretted that now. If she had stopped the girl she might have had her questions answered, and she wouldn't have to waste her time watching a football practice that would provide no answers at all.

"Mr. Flowers," she said.

Grace picked up her backpack and started down the steps after Bobby Flowers. Renzlau, she reminded herself, was the man on the football field in the green jersey. Bobby Flowers was the one who stopped on the steps right in front of her. He didn't have a speck of green in his clothing. She shouldn't have to remind herself about such things.

"I'm sorry I said that," Grace said. "I had no right to be rude."

"You have the right to be anything you want," he said.

For some reason Flowers had made her uncomfortable from the moment he had passed through the gate. She didn't like feeling uncomfortable. But the reason she had come to the stadium had nothing to do with Flowers, and it had nothing to do with her. She shouldn't have to remind herself about that either.

"Can you keep a secret, Mr. Flowers?"

"I guess I can."

Grace unzipped the outer pocket of her backpack and removed her black leather badge case. She opened the leather wallet and showed the badge to Flowers. He reached for it, and contrary to her training and instincts, she let him take it. He held the case with both hands and rubbed a finger over the shiny silver surface.

"Whoa, now," he said. "Is this why you were asking me if I was the football police? You got a gun in that bag, too?"

"Perhaps. And books."

"Books?"

"I'm a graduate student."

"But that's not why you're here," he said. "You didn't come here to study. Do you have some big investigation going on?"

"Nothing big," she said. It was growing, however.

He handed the badge back to her.

"Big or not, I hope you know what you're getting yourself into," Flowers said. "Renzlau isn't some brother on the corner, you know."

"I didn't say that we're investigating Renzlau, but if we are, he's no different than anybody else."

"You're sure about that? You know the song, 'His daddy's rich, and his mama's good looking'? That's Renzlau and a lot more. Just look around you. On Saturday all these seats will be full, and half of them will be here to watch their fair-haired boy. You mess with that, and you're going to have a lot of people mad at you."

Grace didn't bother to look around. She had already seen all that she needed to see. "You mean because he's white."

"Nobody will say it, but that's what they'll be thinking."

"You're exaggerating, Mr. Flowers."

"Am I? Look down there."

This time he pointed and didn't drop his arm until she looked down to the field.

"Do you see that squad over there to the left? All the way

down in the end zone. That's the second offensive unit. Look at the running backs, the guys behind the quarterback. What do you see?"

"Two guys in uniforms like everybody else," she said.

"They're black," he said. "Now look over there on the thirty-yard line. That's the third string. Look at the running backs. What do you see?"

"You want me to see two more black men."

"That's what you do see. It's that way everywhere, at least in the big football schools. You'll find a white blocking back here and there, but the running backs are black, except some white guy three deep on the chart."

"So most of them are black," Grace said. "What of it?"

"All of them," Flowers said, "except Renzlau. Nearly all of them. He was recruited as a quarterback, but he switched to running back after the first year. He told the coach he would transfer to another school if they tried to move him back to quarterback. We all thought he was crazy. Everybody wants to be quarterback, but not him. Now I'm thinking he was crazy like a fox. He's not the fastest guy on the team, and he doesn't have the best moves, but he gets his yards. The offensive line works a little harder for him. After every touchdown he gives one of them the ball, and he shakes every one of their hands. As a receiver he's a big target with good hands, and the quarterback looks for him, especially now. I wanted to write a story about that, about why he's successful when no other white backs are, but my boss wouldn't let me. It was okay to write about black quarterbacks when there were just one or two, or black head coaches, but not white running backs. The paper wants stories about Saint Paul and the kid who is dying from cancer."

"Saint Paul?"

"It's what we call him sometimes."

"I can't imagine that it would matter if Renzlau were

black or white or green. All athletes get special treatment, don't they?"

"Donations to the athletic department are up twenty-five percent this year," Flowers said. "Over there in the press box there's a special section for university bigwigs."

Flowers nodded across the football field, and Grace was now paying attention to his stadium directions. She looked at the giant edifice that loomed over the north bleachers like a misshapen skull balanced on a skinny steel neck.

"The athletic director holds court there at every football game like she is the queen of the ball. She's got so many people wanting to give her money that she has to ration the time in the box. The governor drops by every game, too. How often does he drop by to any of your classes?"

"He hasn't made it so far this year."

"Or any year," Flowers said.

"Or any year," she repeated.

"It's the money. They get millions of dollars when they fill this stadium, more from television, radio, endorsements, boosters. The more you pay, the better your seat. Pay enough and you get into the press box and shake the governor's hand. Coach is the highest paid employee at the university, the highest paid state employee anywhere, and that's only what we know about. You can bet there's a lot more from side contracts. The lowest paid coach out there makes more than any professor you'll ever have. You fool with their fair-haired boy, their cash machine, you'd better get ready for a whole lot of trouble."

"I just came to watch the practice," Grace said. "Besides, Saint Paul has dark hair. There's nothing fair about it."

Bobby Flowers looked at her with a neutral expression that matched her own. She wasn't sure but that hers would change first. Then she heard the soft laughter in his gut. It didn't rise to a louder tone, but it was loud enough to hear above the warlike cries that suddenly rose from the football players below. She looked down to the artificial grass and saw them running in straight lines from one end of the field to the other. They charged forward on the field, line after line, shouting and growling so loudly that they were surely unable to hear anything else.

"Wind sprints," Bobby Flowers said. "That's one thing I don't miss. Practice is over."

"How well do you know Renzlau?" Grace asked.

"As well as I know any of these guys," he said. "I see him in the locker room, on the road, at the banquets. This summer, I followed him around for a day. It was his father's idea so that I could see what his kid was really like. What he really wanted was a Saint Paul story in the newspaper."

"Did you write the story?"

"Sure, and my boss loved it. It was the beginning of the Heisman push—me, the former running back, writing about the new star. They put my picture in the story, too. Of course we wouldn't know why they did that."

"Have you ever met any of his friends?"

"What is it that you really want to ask me?"

"Did you ever see Renzlau with a black girl?" Grace asked.

"A black girl? Why are you asking?"

"I can't tell you."

"What's her name?"

"I don't know. She's tall and thin, dark skin like mine."

Grace touched the dark skin on her face. Flowers watched her hand rise to her face, but he didn't watch the hand as she dropped it back to her side.

"I met one black girl," Flowers said. "He introduced me to her this summer when I was writing the story about him. I guess he thought I would be impressed with his open mind."

"Were you?"

"No. It seemed phony to me. The girl liked him all right, but she was way out of her league. You can't be interested in

Renzlau, as a police officer I mean, because he went out with a black girl. There's no law against that, you know. You must have something else. Could this be the girl who came up to you at the Student Union?"

"Your father is right," Grace said. "You're wasting your talent writing about football players."

A line creased his forehead. "We might be able to help each other," Flowers said. "I get information for you, you do the same for me."

"I'm not sure I can do that," Grace said.

"You can do whatever you want to do."

"Do you know people who are close to Renzlau? Teammates, for example. Could you help me meet them?"

"Sure, as many as you want."

"What about the girl? Where can I find her?"

"In church."

"What?"

"Her father is a preacher. Go figure that."

"Which church?"

"Why don't I take you there," he said. "I could pick you up Sunday morning if you're free."

"I need to talk to her alone."

"You can talk to her alone. I won't get in the way."

"I can find out who she is without your help," Grace said.

"Suit yourself," Bobby Flowers said, repeating the words she had spoken to him.

Chapter 19

"So, Officer Murphy," Anne asked, "why are we sitting here in front of a pancake house instead of Rigmor's kitchen in Ballard? Another football player?"

Katherine turned sideways in the front passenger seat of the police car and looked at Anne in the backseat. A man wearing a brown tweed jacket passed Anne's window riding a bicycle. His tie fluttered over his shoulder, and he had a leather briefcase strapped to the rack over the bicycle's rear tire.

"You have to ask Grace about that. I'm just along for the ride."

"It's the fullback, Jerome Johnson," Grace said. "He rooms with Renzlau. Mr. Flowers thinks that Johnson might know something about the girls Renzlau has dated, or he might know something about Renzlau's activities before the football games."

Katherine watched the man in the brown jacket pedal down Roosevelt and coast toward the last exit before the University Bridge. She wondered what he had in the briefcase.

"Maybe we should just ask Renzlau," Katherine said.

"We've thought about that," Anne said. "It's too early. We don't have any victims yet. We're not sure there are any."

"You don't believe that," Katherine said.

"No."

"If he knows we're after him, he might stop whatever he's doing. We might prevent something else from happening."

"We might," Anne said, "or he might just make it harder for us to find out."

Katherine was thinking about Sam and Maria. It wasn't working for Maria to remain silent and cover up what she was feeling. Maria and Grace were meeting every day after class, supposedly to work together on some sort of fish theory that Grace had about a coastal native tribe. She couldn't imagine that Renzlau wouldn't see through the story. He was still getting treatment for his leg or knee or whatever it was that the paper wrote about every day, but that wouldn't last either.

Then there was Sam. He had already had enough. He took Maria to class each day in his police car and waited until she was inside the building. He remained there and watched her walk to the Oceanography Building after class to meet Grace. Maria didn't want him to wait, but he did, and there was growing friction from that.

"They're going into the restaurant now," Grace said. "Flowers and Johnson. Shall we go in or shall we sit out here and continue this discussion about crime prevention?"

Katherine looked at her partner. For the first time there was friction between them, too—not much, but just enough to sharpen words that had never been sharp before.

Grace was thinking mostly about the girl she had seen for one moment with Maria. And now there was this washed-up football player in the picture who was going to bring on the next revelation. They could find enough trouble in Ballard without spreading themselves all over the city. The woman with the broken television was already back. She was in the Smoke Shop getting drunk every afternoon and telling everyone how much she missed her Johnny.

As they crossed Roosevelt Avenue toward the pancake

house, Katherine thought about Maria, whose beauty was just beginning to flower. She thought about the drunken woman, whose beauty had long since wilted. And she knew that Grace was thinking about the other girl. Everything was more complicated than it ought to be. All she knew for certain was that she wasn't interested in meeting any football players.

She followed Grace through the door into the restaurant and down an aisle with booths on one side and tables on the other. The two men were easy to spot. They were the only black people in the restaurant. One man, the older of the two, wore a gray suit and the other a white T-shirt that stretched tightly across his chest. Grace stopped at the booth, and the man in the suit slid out from the table and stood beside her.

"Officer Stevens," he said, "nice to see you again."

The meeting was supposed to be a surprise, but Katherine didn't think the younger man looked fooled. Grace introduced Anne and her to Flowers.

"Why don't you join us," Flowers said.

The younger man became trapped as Grace slid into the booth beside him. Flowers directed Katherine and Anne into the seat where he had been, and he pulled over a chair from a neighboring table and sat at the end of their table, blocking the aisle. They were at the back of the restaurant. Nobody would pass them.

A waitress came, and the three women ordered coffee. Katherine slid Flowers's cup over to him. The young fullback had a large glass of soda. Bubbles of carbonation were still working their way up through the ice cubes and freeing themselves at the surface.

The young man was eighteen or nineteen at the most. His smooth face seemed at odds with the enormous strength of his body. He was nervous or shy and wasn't comfortable looking at Katherine or at any of his new booth companions. He wet his lower lip repeatedly with his tongue.

"Jerome here," Flowers said, "will be our tailback next year. He'll make us all forget about Paul Renzlau."

"Have to see about that," Jerome said. "Have to get my weight down first."

"Jerome put on weight this year to be a better blocker," Flowers said, "but he's still one of the fastest men on the team."

"You put on weight intentionally," Anne asked, "and then you plan to just get rid of it?"

"Yes, ma'am. It won't take long, I expect."

"How much weight will you lose?"

"Twenty pounds. That puts me at two-ten. That's where I work the best."

"Twenty pounds, just like that," Anne said. "What's the secret of your diet?"

"I cut back some at the table," Jerome said, "and run a little more."

"I knew there was a catch. These young officers could do that, but my running days are over."

"Yes, ma'am."

"I wish you wouldn't agree so fast, Mr. Johnson."

"Yes, ma'am."

"We have some questions we would like to ask you," Grace said to the fullback. "It's not an accident that we're here. Mr. Flowers and I set this up."

"I was beginning to figure that."

"Our questions are not about you, but we thought it would be better if we met here rather than at the crew house or at football practice."

"I suppose I appreciate that."

Katherine smiled at him. She hadn't expected his politeness. It was only a few years since she had been at the university, but he made her feel that it was much longer.

"Where are you from, Mr. Johnson?" Katherine asked.

"Arkansas. A little town just south of Little Rock."

"Don't they play football in Arkansas?"

"Yes, ma'am. They sure play football there."

"Why did you come all the way up here, then?"

"I went to junior college my first year, and my coach sent out information about me. Washington offered me a scholarship. I figured I could play here."

"And you are."

"Yes, ma'am."

"And playing well, too," Flowers said.

With that Flowers stood and pushed his chair away from the table. He slid it over into its original place. Jerome watched every move that he made.

"These officers want to talk to you alone," Flowers said. "You'll be okay. Just don't let them pay for your soda. We don't want to break any NCAA rules here. Isn't that right?"

"Yes, sir."

"I'm still doing that story, Jerome. I wasn't fooling you about that."

"Appreciate it," Jerome said.

"It's been a pleasure meeting you," Flowers said, looking at Anne and Katherine. "Sunday?" he asked, turning away from Katherine and looking at the other side of the table where Grace and Jerome sat.

"Sunday," Grace said.

Flowers smiled as if he were getting away with something. Katherine was sure that she saw that something change in Grace's face, too—a widening of her eyes, a smile that aimed at indifference but hit Flowers instead.

"Do you really have rules about somebody buying you a soda?" Anne asked the young fullback.

"Probably," Jerome said. "There are rules about most everything."

"It's the same with us," Katherine said. "We're not allowed to take free drinks either."

"Is that right?" He looked surprised that there would be rules for them, too.

"Of course," Anne said, "some people always seem to be above those rules. Do you agree, Mr. Johnson?"

"Could be, I suppose."

"We were wondering if Paul Renzlau was like that," Grace said.

The young football player had difficulty keeping up with the voices that surrounded him at the table, but the mention of Renzlau made him focus on the last one he heard.

"You're asking me about Paul? I don't know anything about him."

"You room together," Grace said. "You must talk. You must know a little bit about him."

"We talk, sure, but it's like 'how you doing, how you feeling?' Stuff like that. Or we talk about the game. He gives me pointers. He knows what the other guys will be doing. We don't go into much else."

"How about girls?" Grace asked. "You must talk about girls now and then."

"Nothing like that," Johnson said. "Nothing you'd care about."

"Tell us even if we wouldn't care."

"No, ma'am, there's nothing to mention. We're not friends or anything."

"Did you ever meet any of his girlfriends?"

"That's none of my business. I don't get into any of that."

"Any of what, Mr. Johnson?"

"None of it, that's all. He takes care of his business; I take care of mine."

"Perfect harmony, then," Grace said.

"There's nothing perfect," Jerome said. "I expect you know that."

Grace was quiet for a moment, but it wasn't the sort of quiet that invited anyone to interrupt.

"Mr. Flowers said that Renzlau chose you to be his roommate," Grace said. "Why do you suppose he did that?"

Under Grace's steady gaze Jerome fidgeted with his sweating glass.

"Maybe it's because lots of times I'm the last blocker he's got. If I miss, he doesn't get any yards."

"And if he doesn't get yards, what happens to you?"

"I'll be watching from the bench."

"And somebody else will be his roommate."

"I suppose so."

"Maybe he chose you because you're such a quiet young man—somebody who minds his own business. Do you suppose that might be true?"

"You'll have to ask Paul about that."

Katherine recognized a different look from Grace. Jerome was stiffening his back against the seat, against Grace's questions, and it was time for them to come from another direction.

"Jerome, how often do you get to see your family?" Katherine asked.

The young man was slow to look toward her and even slower to acknowledge her question. From Renzlau to family. It was a big jump.

Katherine remembered what it was like her first year at the university. Everything was different, foreign. There was no place to find the solitude that she had always found on her family's farm. She hadn't thought she would miss the treeless land, the quiet, but she had. She still did. She could only imagine what Jerome Johnson would be missing.

"I'll be seeing my folks come a week from Saturday," he said.

"Are they coming up here to a game?"

"We're going down there. Close enough anyway. We play Louisiana State, and they're all driving over to Baton Rouge to see me play—everybody who can get in the car and then some, maybe."

Katherine smiled along with Jerome as he thought of his family and the coming reunion. She could understand how he would look forward to that reunion, and she didn't want to be the one who ruined that thought. What was the point anyway? He already made it clear that he wasn't going to tell them anything about Renzlau.

"What are you studying, Jerome?" Katherine asked.

"Ma'am?" he asked.

"What's your major?"

"I started in Physical Education, but I'm thinking I would like to switch over to Education. Elementary Education, maybe. I'm thinking about being a teacher. I think my folks would like that."

"I'll bet they would," Katherine said.

"Have you ever met Paul Renzlau's family?" Grace asked.

Jerome reluctantly looked to his left where Grace sat. Katherine could appreciate his reluctance.

"A few times. They go to every game, no matter where it is."

"What are they like?"

"I expect you'll have to talk to them to find out. I don't worry myself about that sort of thing."

"Oh, I expect you're a pretty good observer, Jerome. On the football field you see the tackler coming up behind you, don't you?"

"Yes, ma'am. I make it a point to see him."

"On the night before a game do you have a time when you're supposed to be in? A curfew?"

"Coach wants us in by eleven o'clock."

"Is it a rule?"

"Yes, ma'am. It's a rule."

"So at eleven, you and Mr. Renzlau tuck yourselves in and go to sleep?

"We might watch TV or listen to some music a little past."

"But then you go to sleep?"

"Yes, ma'am. I sure do."

"And Mr. Renzlau? Does he do the same?"

Jerome paused, and Katherine imagined him looking over his shoulder as he might on the football field to spot the tackler coming up behind him. Except this time there was somebody in front—two tacklers and both pressing toward him.

"He doesn't sleep so good. They're talking Heisman about him. I might not sleep either if they talked that about me."

"What does he do when he can't sleep?"

"I expect you ought to ask him about that."

"I'm asking you, Jerome, and you have to tell me what you know. It's another one of those rules."

Jerome looked across the table at Katherine to see if she might be offering a different opinion. She wasn't.

"He leaves for a time," Jerome said. "When we're traveling, I expect he goes to his folks' room. They stay in the same hotel as us, and they always have a big room."

"Do you ever ask him where he goes?"

"No, ma'am."

"So he leaves the room both here at home and when you're on the road?"

"It won't do me any good if I cause him trouble. My folks are counting on me to finish what I started up here. I'm the first ever to go to college. I don't want to be letting them down."

He looked at all of them in turn. Surely someone would understand that.

"We understand," Grace said, "and we'll keep this to ourselves as much as we can. We can't promise you more than that. You said that when you travel you thought he went to his parents' room. There's no harm in that, is there? That can't be against the rules."

"No, ma'am. No rule about that."

"And he did that all three times when you traveled to other towns this year?"

"Yes, ma'am."

"About how long was he gone?"

"A couple hours, I expect, but I wasn't keeping track of the time."

"Did he say anything when he came back to the room?"

"No, ma'am. I acted like I was asleep. I wish I had been, too."

"I'll bet you do," Grace said. "We appreciate your help. We can't tell you why we're asking these questions, but we wouldn't be asking them if we didn't have to."

"Yes, ma'am."

Katherine hadn't expected that she would like this football player. There was more than his extreme politeness, although that didn't hurt. It wasn't fair to put him in the middle, any more than it was to put Maria there. It wasn't fair, but there they were.

"Mr. Johnson," Anne said, "we would like to keep this conversation to ourselves. Nobody else needs to know about it, especially any of the other players on the team. I don't imagine you have any trouble with that."

"No, ma'am."

"That's good, because if word got out, we'd have to come down to the football field and start asking questions there."

"They won't hear anything about this business from me."

"I see you've finished your drink," Anne said. "We should probably let you get back to your studies."

Grace slid out of the booth. Jerome moved to the edge and was about to get up when Katherine reached out and touched his arm. She had something else she wanted to say.

"I'm sure you'll play especially well when your folks are watching you," she said. "They're going to be proud of you."

"Thank you, ma'am," Jerome said as he finally escaped the booth. "I'll take care of my drink up at the register."

Grace slid back into the seat when the polite fullback left. In the absence of his massive presence, Katherine felt like the small girl on the teeter-totter hitting the ground after the big kid got off the other end.

"I didn't even consider other cities," Anne said. "As soon as I get back to the office, I'll get a football schedule and start calling."

"You might check last year's schedule, too," Grace said.

"Right. I've been intending to call Vice and ask them to show Renzlau's picture around to some of the girls. Maybe we can get them to stake out his room this weekend. I'll call Sergeant Parker. He owes us one."

Grace sat up straighter on the bench and looked over their heads. It was a signal to the other two at the table. A moment later Jerome Johnson stood before them again.

"Pardon me," he said with an uncertainty that he would never show on the football field. "I just wanted to tell you that Bobby paid for my Coke."

"Don't worry," Grace said. "We won't say anything."

Katherine could feel the same smile in herself that her partner was holding back.

"He paid for your coffee, too."

Chapter 20

Lady paced the floor as if she were the one waiting for Bobby Flowers. The dog sensed Grace's nervous anticipation and sniffed her way from the front door to the back and back again to the front, stopping each time at the couch for Grace to pat her on the head.

"I know you," Grace said. "As soon as he comes, you'll hide in the bedroom."

Grace had long before given up any illusion that the dog would protect her. Lady barked when a stranger came to the door and then ran for cover.

The house was so neat that Lady might not have recognized it. The rawhide bone, the album covers that always leaned against the stereo, and the coffee cup on top of the newspapers had all been put away in their proper places. Sitting on the couch, Grace was as neatly dressed and organized as the strange house that the dog continued to explore. She listened to Pia Zadora on the stereo, a Sunday morning custom she had brought from her parents' home to hers. The singer's plaintive voice reminded her parents of happy Sunday mornings in Paris when they were young lovers and nothing else mattered. For Grace the singer's voice invoked a different feeling than it did for her parents. She imagined that one day she, too, would have Sunday morning memories from a faraway place to preserve.

She didn't understand why she had cleaned the entire house. She could and likely would meet Bobby Flowers at the door and not bring him inside, but once she started cleaning at ten o'clock the night before, she didn't stop. She, who had lived with exposed wood studs around her bathtub for three months while replacing the plumbing and the crumbling plaster, scrubbed away the last stain inside the bathtub and everywhere else. She hadn't finished until midnight.

There had been no reason for her to clean the entire house, no reason to listen to the old recording that brought good memories to her parents on Sunday mornings, no reason, even, for Bobby Flowers to come. For the time it took to clean the bathroom, she could have called every black minister in Seattle and inquired about a certain young woman, nineteen years old or thereabouts, tall and thin, and inexplicably frightened. She need not and probably should not have waited for Sunday to find this girl, to wait for Bobby Flowers to take her. She wasn't sure that she even liked him. He made her nervous, and she didn't like to feel nervous. Why, then, was she waiting?

Grace looked again at the full-color photograph on the front page of the neatly stacked newspaper. The photograph captured Renzlau diving into the end zone, with the football crossing the chalked line within the firm grasp of his extended hands. It was an amazingly clear photograph, the only color photograph on the page. She could see the focus in his eyes, the muscles in his forearms, and the distended veins in his hands. Above the photograph in large bold letters the caption shouted, "TOUCHDOWN!"

Parker's men had lost him the night before the game. "On the Montlake Bridge, if you can believe that," Anne had said on the telephone. "Two fifteen in the morning and the damn bridge goes up." Renzlau crossed just ahead of the cross arm, but Parker's men got stuck behind it. The Vice officers searched Pike Street and Yesler for his car but never found it. They went out to Aurora before heading back to the crew house to wait for his return. They waited until three thirty when their shift ended. "They're not sure if he ever came back," Anne said.

He came back. The story that began on the front page continued into the sports section. It described every important play of their star player. Several pages deep inside the sports section was a story Bobby Flowers had written about the details that made the Renzlau machine click—a fake by Jerome Johnson the fullback, an alert read by the quarterback, wide receivers running patterns that confused the defense, linemen holding their blocks an extra second—little of which made any sense to her. She did understand the final paragraphs in which he described the small town in Arkansas where Johnson lived and the pride the whole town had in their native son. Through Flowers's words she saw again the polite young man she had met in the pancake house. The paragraphs about Jerome Johnson were sincere and revealing— three quiet paragraphs buried in page after page of bluster.

She inserted the sports section back into the neatly folded newspaper. Lady followed her to the bathroom and stood in the doorway with her head cocked to the side while Grace washed the ink from her hands.

"Are you trying to understand what I'm doing?" she asked the dog.

Lady took a few steps forward and stopped again.

"Let me know if you find out."

Bobby Flowers arrived at exactly nine thirty. He must have waited around the corner to be so precise. Lady barked once when she heard his feet on the steps and took off for the bedroom. Grace waited for the knock before rising from the couch and opening the door.

"Come in, Mr. Flowers," she said.

He was wearing a conservative black suit and a bright white shirt. It was a suit that the preacher at her grandmother's funeral might have worn or the undertaker who stood beside the casket.

"You look fine this morning," he said.

Was he talking about her or her dress? She had worn the white dress once on an unsuccessful Vice detail. A Vice officer had told her she looked like a schoolteacher and not a prostitute. She didn't think he had meant it as a compliment.

"Thank you," she said. "You're right on time."

"My mama told me never be late for church."

Lady peeked around the corner from the plaster archway that divided the living room from the dining room, prepared to run if the situation looked unpromising. Flowers's voice had not scared her yet, which was surprising. His expressive voice filled the room around his substantial presence. When Flowers saw the dog, he squatted to make himself smaller and held out his hand to the dog. He expected her to come.

"Hey there, little friend," he said, softening his voice as he might to a child. "Come here. Come here." He made a clicking noise with his tongue on the roof of his mouth, and to Grace's surprise Lady walked cautiously forward.

"Careful," Grace said. "She's my ferocious guard dog."

The dog sniffed Flowers's hand, and he held it steady until Lady rubbed her head against it. He scratched behind her ear and then found the sweet spot on her belly. Lady closed her eyes and leaned into his touch.

"Hmmm," Grace murmured softly to herself.

The church where Flowers took her was a small, well-preserved wood building on a single lot on 23rd Avenue. There was no parking lot, but there were plenty of empty parking spaces on the opposite side of the street. The church was painted white like her dress and the dresses of several older women Grace saw walking up the steps to the front door. Every man wore a dark suit and white shirt as did the friendly greeter inside the door who gave them a church bulletin and instructed Brother John to seat them.

By the time she realized that Brother John was ushering them to the front, they were well down the center aisle between the two rows of pews. Grace saw an opening and indicated with her hands her preference to sit there. Brother John acceded to her request. Four pews ahead, in the front row, a young woman turned around. Grace saw the surprise and dismay in the young woman's eyes. She had hoped to avoid detection until the service was over, not wishing to deprive the young woman one more hour of peace.

Bobby Flowers nudged her arm after the young woman turned her face back to the front. Grace nodded but didn't look at Flowers. She realized that the young woman, a girl really, may have recognized both her and Flowers and might now be trying to understand what they were doing in her church. What would she think if she were in the same place as the girl?

The music began with a gospel song that brought all to their feet and stirred in Grace a faint memory. She wasn't certain if it was the song or the singing that did the stirring. The singing was loud enough so that if she closed her eyes the church would seem full, but it wasn't. Many pews had been empty when they arrived, and few additional people had arrived after them. The church could hold four times the number of people who now filled it with song.

Bobby Flowers sang, too, and she heard his voice clearly above all the rest. It rose and fell with the notes she saw in the hymnbook. He offered to share the hymnbook with her. She took the bottom corner of the open book and read the words that he sang. Soon she understood the source of the congregation's volume. The choir walked up the aisle, two by two in flowing robes. She was certain that their number exceeded the rest of the congregation. They took their places behind the organ.

When the song ended, Bobby Flowers took the hymnbook back, and they sat down in unison with the choir and congregation. He smiled at her as if he had thought of something funny, or was he mocking the clumsiness with which she had passed back the hymnal? Or was it because she didn't sing— surely, the only one in the whole church who hadn't? Even the girl in the front row sang despite what she might be thinking about the two who stood behind her. Beside the girl was an older woman, her mother probably, and beside the mother were two boys, one seven or eight and the other not yet a teenager but getting close.

With her family Grace used to attend the big Baptist church close to the freeway at the bottom of Capitol Hill. She had noticed it again as Flowers drove up the hill on Madison. *Attend* was the word they used in that church. It was an open-minded church, her father claimed, and mixed, which meant that she and Evangeline weren't the only dark-skinned children in the Sunday school classes. At one time there were three others. In the big church, religion was something to understand. It seldom made her uncomfortable. Religion in the big church had a theoretical base that allowed a person to think freely and safely. The senior minister was an intelligent man who preached intelligent sermons as he smiled benignly at all of them sitting below his pulpit. She thought for sure that he was smiling at her.

Since childhood she had felt that the day would come when she would find something in her religion that she could hold on to. In the big church at the bottom of the hill, she had recited their beliefs at the appropriate time with everyone else, and the collective recitation was like a powerful force. But the recitation was not from her heart, nor was it like the expression of belief that originated deep inside Grandmother Bess in the small church in Omaha. Grace had felt that expression. On their summer visits to Omaha, there was at least one Sunday in church, and Grace remembered sitting on her grandmother's lap, leaning back against her when she got tired, and closing her eyes to the words of the preacher. She sat enclosed within her grandmother's arms and listened to her. "Um-hmm," her grandmother would say in response to the preacher, and Grace believed her.

Members of this congregation voiced approval of their preacher, too—voiced it more loudly and more heartily than Grandmother Bess had. Grace wondered if the intelligent senior minister was still preaching in the big church at the bottom of the hill. No one voiced approval there. Everyone sat silently and listened and thought. Some would even disagree with a point of view that the minister expressed and might tell him so, given that it was such an open-minded church.

Bobby Flowers reached for the hymnbook. It wasn't time to sing. The reverend hadn't finished his sermon about the prodigal son. He was coming to the point in the parable, where having wasted all that he was given, the prodigal son returned home. There was more to the story.

Flowers placed the church bulletin Brother John had given him on top of the hymnbook and removed a ballpoint pen from his coat pocket. He wrote on the bulletin and handed it to her. He had underlined words at the top, THE REVEREND JAMES SINCLAIR. Below this line he had written Alice Sinclair.

Grace glanced at Flowers and nodded furtively with the acknowledgment of a trespasser. She had been listening to the sermon, the cadence of which was rising to a conclusion. What had Bobby Flowers been doing? Thinking of the story he would write, of controversy, of fame? She had been listening to the preacher, and if she did not sway in rhythm to the preacher's words as did the woman at the end of their pew, she had at least felt its effect on her equilibrium.

It didn't seem fair that the wasteful son should be allowed to come back and resume his former standing and position. He ought to have to work a bit, this wasteful child, to prove himself before he dressed again in fine clothes and sat beside his father at the banquet table's place of honor. What about the sons who had stayed behind and had not wasted their fortunes? At night in the privacy of darkness, wouldn't the prodigal son laugh at them? He had his memories of wild times that mocked the staidness of his brothers. What if they had all left instead of just the one? Would the father take them all back, or would the loss of wealth quell his generous spirit? And what about the daughters? Was this a family only of sons? Would he take back the prodigal daughter, too?

The bass sounds of male approval echoed inside the walls drowning out for the moment the higher tones of the women. Grace stared above the preacher's head and imagined sitting on her grandmother's lap with her ear pressed against her grandmother's bosom as she had in the church in Omaha. Her grandmother's arms were around her shoulders so that if she fell asleep she would not fall. She wasn't asleep. She was listening. Did she hear the faint sound of approval and feel the hum of it pass into her body? Or was her grandmother withholding her approval because of experience and practicality?

She had sat on her grandmother's lap even when her legs were so long that they nearly reached the floor. On their last visit before the one for the funeral, her father told her that she was too big to sit there, but her grandmother reached for her anyway and brought her in. There had never been and never would be a more comfortable place.

The singing began again, and she found herself standing with Bobby Flowers. It was a song she knew by heart. She closed her eyes and hummed softly to herself and Grandmother Bess below the voices of the choir. She had had to get off her grandmother's lap when the singing began—the solace being that the service was almost over. With the beginning of the second stanza she took the corner of the hymnbook that Bobby Flowers offered again. No one in the choir had a songbook open. Everyone knew the words. Flowers had a good voice, but she could never carry a tune for more than a few bars without losing her way. Nevertheless she found the words on the page and sang louder: *I once was lost but now am found.*

Strange, she thought, to be singing words in a black church written by the white captain of a slave ship. Such beautiful words. For some time during her childhood Grace had thought the song was about her—especially when Grandmother Bess sang it.

There was joy when the service was over and the last song began. It was a moving song, a marching song, and the choir marched down the aisle followed by the Reverend Sinclair. The choir gathered in the back and cast their voices forward until the last word had been sung. The congregation remained standing, but no one moved until the two men who had greeted them in the beginning orchestrated the departure.

Beginning at the front the ushers dismissed the first pew. Alice looked away as she passed where Grace stood with Flowers, waiting their turn to follow. Grace worried that the girl would leave before she and Flowers could get out, that once again she would lose the girl. She considered slipping into the aisle before their turn, but when she looked around and saw the alert eyes of everyone who waited and watched, she became convinced that there would be no slipping through in this church.

The Reverend Sinclair shook the hands of all as they departed. He was particularly pleased to see new faces, and there was no way to slip past him. The reverend recognized Bobby Flowers, and he had a few words about Saturday's football game. He also had a few words about Flowers's column, which he read every Sunday morning even if it was the day for the Lord's work.

Grace stood beside Flowers, held by the invisible bonds of decorum. Flowers introduced her to the reverend even though she had already shaken his hand without the need of introduction. A friend, Flowers explained to the Reverend Sinclair so that the reverend, she supposed, would have no misconception about them.

Outside, the girl stood alone on the sidewalk some distance from the church, far enough away that she was beyond the friendly clamor that spread out from the church door. If she had kept walking, Grace would have lost her again. Grace sensed that the girl was waiting for her. If so, it was with none of the joy of the last song or grace from the one before. Flowers stayed on the church steps as Grace walked toward the girl. Alice Sinclair looked down as if she couldn't bear to watch Grace approach.

"Alice?"

Alice looked up in surprise.

"You know who I am?" she asked.

"Yes."

"Did you know I would be here?"

"Yes, I knew," Grace said. "I appreciated that you warned me about Renzlau. I wanted to thank you."

"Is that all you want?"

"No, it's not. I'm a Seattle police officer. I would like to talk to you about Paul Renzlau. Do you want to see my badge and identification?"

No, the girl said with a slow movement of her head. No, she didn't want to see the badge, and she didn't want to see a police officer standing in front of her either. In the girl's face Grace saw the same expression of fear that had preoccupied her for days. Grace had considered the possibility that she had misread the girl's fear after their first brief improbable meeting, but she had not. If anything she had underesti-

mated its depth. There was something else, too, something
that held the girl on the sidewalk when she could have
walked away and disappeared. Was it need, or was it something beyond that—some invisible and unknowable bond
that had stretched over the chaotic assortment of tables,
chairs, voices, and people on the outdoor patio of the Student
Union? If so it was more than color, more than race—something which Grace could not understand but surely wished to.

"Is there some place we can talk?" Grace asked.

The empty church was behind them, but they couldn't go
there. They would have to pass the members of the congregation who lingered outside and would see the girl's distress.
Inside the church would be the ghostly voices of the choir
and the girl's father, and perhaps even the divine voices of the
Three in One that the Reverend had called upon during
the service—none of which had yet removed the fear from
the girl. More likely all the voices had increased it.

23rd Avenue was a busy four-lane street with little space
between the sidewalk and the car lanes. The street had been
widened, but the overall space had not. The expansion had
taken away most of the planting strip separating it from the
sidewalk, and it had taken, as well, the buffer of parked cars
on their side of the street. Grace felt the gusts created by each
car that passed, too fast and too close for comfort.

Alice looked around her, but she couldn't seem to focus
on any one place. She seemed to be stricken with the idea
that Grace wasn't the woman she had seen across the tables,
but was now somebody else, some additional threat rather
than someone who should be warned. It had taken courage to
walk through the tables in the Student Union. Maybe it had
taken all the courage she had.

"This way," Alice said at last.

They passed small houses as they walked south on the
sidewalk. Some were well-maintained; others were rotting
from without if not from within. Several of the best main-

tained houses had bars on the windows. The houses had been on the street long before it had become a major four-lane thoroughfare, long before it supported the rush of indifferent trespassers that trapped those still behind the barred windows.

The girl changed direction at the first intersection and headed down the steep hill that crested on the busy street behind them. Soon they were below the direct sound of the cars. The sidewalk was broken by roots from trees planted in the planting strip, but it was a peaceful walk with the rays of the late-morning sun in their eyes.

The girl didn't talk but proceeded with the pace of a person who finally knew where she was going. A block and a half below the crest of the hill she turned into a dirt alley with houses and yards on both sides. Some of the yards had wood or wire fences enclosing their boundaries; others were open to the back of the houses. On each property there was a small garage. On the west side of the alley garages were dug into the hill, and the foundations rose to meet the ground. On the east the foundations rose above the ground to create a flat single-spaced plateau barely large enough for any but the smallest of cars.

"This is where I live," Alice said. "My family won't be coming for a while."

She pointed to the roof of a single-story house with bright green asphalt shingles. It was one of the houses without fences. Alice led her down winding steps to a small flat level of grass terraced into the steeply sloping backyard. The terrace was little wider than the two heavy lawn chairs that occupied it. More in resignation than invitation Alice motioned for Grace to sit.

"I don't know what to tell you," Alice said. She stood in front of the second chair but couldn't seem to force herself down.

"Why did you tell us to be careful?" Grace said, looking up at the girl. "What did you mean?"

"Did he say anything after I left?"

"He said that you used to hang around the football team, and maybe some of the players took advantage of you."

"That's a lie," Alice said. She looked angrily at Grace, and Grace wasn't sure if the anger was for her or for the football player.

"I know it is. That's why I came here to find you."

"How did you know about my father's church?"

"Bobby Flowers told me. He met you once last summer. You might not remember."

"I remember."

Alice sat down and stared at the grass beneath her feet. Her hair had been straightened and pulled tightly into a bun that seemed to draw back the skin on her face as well as her hair.

"There was more than him . . . "

Alice looked at Grace, and tears began flowing down her face. The girl gave no other sign of emotion. There were only the tears and the silence that followed them. Alice tilted her head back as if she could hold them in, but the tears continued to flow and ran down her face like rain on a windowpane. Except there was no seeing through this glass.

Grace slid forward in her chair. She needed to help the girl. She knew that she had caused the immediate pain, but the real source of pain was somewhere else. Grace reached for Alice's hands, which lay useless in the girl's lap, and squeezed them as tightly as she dared. Alice's body shook once, and a moan rose from so deeply within the girl that it didn't sound like it came from her at all. Alice's muscles collapsed and her head dropped back onto the arched top of the chair. Had she been standing, she would have fallen to the ground.

At first Grace thought that Alice had fainted, but she

hadn't. Her muscles had simply stopped trying to hold her erect. Her body shook with sobs of grief, of pain, of loss, and Grace held the girl's hands more tightly, no longer worried that she might hurt her.

"Alice," she whispered. "It's all right. It's all right."

It wasn't true, and the girl probably didn't hear her anyway. So to whom was she speaking, whom was she comforting? Grace moved forward in her chair and pulled Alice toward her until their knees were touching. She released Alice's hands and reached behind Alice's unsupported head, lifted it, and brought it forward onto her shoulder. The girl grabbed Grace's arms, and for a moment Grace didn't know if the girl meant to push her away or hold on. She held on.

"It's all right," Grace whispered again and again, feeling the heat of the girl's skin against hers. This time she was sure that Alice could hear her even if the words made no sense. They were just words anyway, a sound, a form of communication; it didn't matter what they were.

Maybe it did matter, and someone who knew what to say should be saying them. But there was no one else, and there hadn't been. Grace was sure of that. This girl would not weep like this more than once. No one could. She had cried, certainly, and there was no end in sight for the times she would again, but never again like this.

There was no one else. Is that why the girl had come to her the first time? Is that why she had looked across the tables even before Maria came, before the football player? Grace had looked away once when the girl's look had projected such need across the empty space. She hadn't recognized it or hadn't wanted to, hadn't known how desperate the girl must have been. Alice probably didn't know. Grace had been able to brush aside the girl's look, had been able to turn away from it as if she had not seen it, but still the girl came up to them and warned them, warned her. Grace could have gone after her right away after the girl fled. She could have willed herself up from the chair instead of letting shock and bewilderment hold her. The girl was gone by the time Grace walked down the steps to look for her. Of course she was gone.

Grace felt the easing of Alice's grip and heard the rhythm of normal breathing coming back to Alice through her spent sobs. "More than him," she had said. How long had she kept this inside?

"Alice, are you with me, girl? Are you breathing now? Take a deep breath."

The girl took a deep breath and trembled, but she trembled less with each breath until she finally pulled back on her own and released Grace's arms.

"I'm sorry," Alice said. "I got your outfit all wet."

Alice smoothed the shoulder of Grace's dress.

"That's all right," Grace said. "Have you told anybody about this?"

"No."

"Do you want to tell me?"

"You as you, or you as the police?"

"Either one."

"I don't want my father to find out. I don't want anybody to know."

"It might not be as bad as you think."

Alice closed her eyes and shook her head.

"No," she said. "Nobody else."

"All right. Nobody else."

"I don't want anybody else hurt, but I don't want anybody else to know. You have to promise me that."

"I promise," Grace said. "I'll have to tell some other people, but I won't tell anybody it's you."

"Nobody," Alice said.

"Nobody," Grace affirmed.

The girl took another deep breath.

"We were in this class together during the summer quarter," she said.

Grace leaned forward. The girl's voice was so distant that she could barely hear it.

"It was a lecture hall with hundreds of students, one of those classes where you sit and listen and take notes, and maybe two guys in the front row ask all the questions. He looked at me, you know, and I looked at him, and after a few days he sat down beside me.

"I didn't know who he was, but one of my friends asked me, 'Don't you know who he is?' No, I didn't know, but everybody else did, and they gave me some trouble about that. But he was nice. We'd walk together a bit after class, and he would ask me what I thought about something, and I'd give him an answer that wouldn't offend him. I thought it was nice that he would ask, that he would ask me."

"Why? What was the class?"

"Race Relations."

Despite everything, the girl's lips formed a rueful smile.

"Did you ever take the class?" Alice asked.

"No," Grace said. "How are the relations?"

"Not so good."

"But this Paul Renzlau, he was going to make them better?"

"I thought so. We dated a few times. My father didn't like the idea. Somebody famous. A football player. A rich white boy. He didn't like any of it, but Paul came to the house to meet him, and he mostly changed his mind. Anyway he kept quiet after that. He'd just sort of wonder, you know, 'Why would that famous white boy want to go out with you?' A father can't say that to his only girl child, even if that's what he's thinking. Can he?"

"I don't know. My father had two girls."

"You have a sister?"

Again Grace saw the want in the girl's eyes and heard it in the question, which was suspended in the air like an impossible wish—a sister to confide in, a sister who would understand, share the grief, lead her out of this deep dark pit back into the light. Most times, Grace remembered, Evangeline was too busy to ever listen.

"Yes, I have a sister," Grace said. "What about your mother? Can't you talk to her?"

Alice shook her head again, less vigorously than when asked about the father, but decisively enough.

"She would have to tell my father, and he'd think it was my fault. And it was. I shouldn't have been there. My father was right."

Grace worried that the girl would lose her composure again. She considered touching the girl's hand again, to bring her away from the then and forward to the now, but she feared that the touch might be more than the girl could stand.

She moved closer to Alice so that their faces were not more than a few inches apart. There was something that had to be said. It had to be said even if the girl would break again. It was time. It was long past time.

"Alice, it wasn't your fault. Do you hear me? It wasn't your fault."

"You don't know what happened yet."

"I know enough. I know more than you think, and whatever happened, it wasn't your fault. You're not the first, not by a long ways, and you're not alone in this."

The girl did not break. Her eyes misted, but beneath the mist Grace saw the first glimmer of optimism, of hope—something she hadn't seen on the patio outside the Student Union and not today, until now. Hope sprang briefly into the girl's consciousness, surprised her, then fled just as the girl herself had fled down the steps when Renzlau walked through the door.

"Let's go back a little," Grace said, trying to hold the girl together. "Tell me what it was like in the beginning."

Alice nodded. She nodded for a long time, biting her lip and hugging her slender arms around herself and squeezing with all the strength she had. There wasn't much strength in her arms.

"He was so polite. He would open the door for me wherever we went. He gave me a book of poetry by Langston Hughes and took me to a play at a theater just off the campus. It was *Anthony and Cleopatra,* and afterward we went to a restaurant and had coffee and talked about the play. I didn't think I knew anything about Shakespeare, but I did. With him I did. He didn't even try to kiss me the first three times he took me home. I was beginning to think he never would, but finally he did."

"And that was okay with you?"

"Yes, it was okay with me. It was on the front porch just like in the old movies. I must have been an idiot not to see what he was. You can't turn into a monster without showing something before. You can't, can you?"

"I don't know," Grace said. "I think maybe you can."

"I didn't see anything. He made me want to get close."

"Did you have sex with him?"

"Before that night?"

"Yes, before that night."

"No," the girl said softly, "but I dreamed about it. I'd never had sex with anybody before."

There should be somebody else talking to this girl, Grace thought—somebody who knew what she was doing. It frightened her to think of the girl's needs and how poorly qualified she was to meet them. She had come to hear the girl's story, to set in motion an investigation of the football player. That was what she understood. Get the facts, put them down on paper, gather evidence if there was any, step back and analyze. If there was probable cause, they would make the arrest. If there wasn't, they would file the report and move on. Probable cause? What was probable in any of this?

Once she had Alice's story, she or some other cop or prosecutor might coerce the girl into cooperating, but she wasn't going to do that. She wasn't going to even try to persuade Alice, to appeal to her guilt, or her decency, or her responsibility to prevent it from happening again. Alice had come forward once on her own, had overcome immeasurable fear for just one instant and was already paying the price for that. And now she was talking about secret dreams, destroyed and corrupted, and looking across the empty space above the well-groomed grass into Grace's eyes. Grace had been prepared to ask the questions, but what about the girl's questions—the questions that the girl couldn't ask but was asking in silence anyway?

"That wasn't sex," Grace said. "I don't know what it was, but it wasn't sex."

"I won't ever have sex again."

"You didn't have it that time."

"I wanted to. It's the same thing."

"No, it's not," Grace said. "Believe me, it's not. I can help you find someone, a counselor, somebody who can help you. I'm a police officer. My job is to find out what happened, to do something if I can, but you need to talk to somebody who knows how to help you. You need to see a doctor, Alice. He might have given you a venereal disease. Is there any chance that you're pregnant?"

"I'm not pregnant."

"Have you had a period since then?"

"Yes."

"But you should still talk to somebody. A counselor, a doctor, somebody. There are a lot of people who will help if you give them the chance."

The girl shook her head emphatically. Nobody else. Now, with you, but not again. Not with anybody else.

"All right," Grace said because she didn't know what else to say. "All right. What happened that night?"

Alice closed her eyes as if doing so would make her see

less in her mind. She kept her eyes closed. Maybe it was better for both of them.

"There was a party at his fraternity house. There weren't many people living in the house because it was after the summer quarter ended and before the fall quarter began. He wasn't living there either. He was staying with the football team. They have their own place to live during the season, but he still had a room at the fraternity."

"Do you know when it was? The exact date?"

The girl shook her head. "Sometime in early September."

"Was it a Friday night before a game?"

Alice opened her eyes. "Yes."

"Keep going, Alice. You're almost there."

Alice looked at her intently for a moment before closing her eyes again.

"We were dancing," she said. "There was only one other girl and four or five guys, including him. Two of them were from the football team. They were good dancers, even though they were big. They were huge men, but they could dance. I drank too much. I don't usually drink at all, but they kept bringing me more. We were laughing and dancing. He would dance with me, and then one of the other guys would take his place. I could tell that he liked watching me dance. Then he came back, and we began dancing closer and closer. I kind of lost control of my body. Everything went by in a blur.

"Then everybody was gone except Paul and me, and he kissed me, and touched me, and I wanted to be touched. I knew I shouldn't, but I wanted to be touched. We went to his room, and he pulled my dress over my head. I didn't look. I just let it go. And then he took off his clothes, and I could feel his skin. I wanted, I wanted, I just let it go, and then something happened. Something happened to him. Somebody else took his place. It was that monster that I never saw. He hit me. I was so shocked that I didn't even say anything. And then he hit me again. I told him to stop. He did it again and shoved my face into the pillow, and then he hit me until he pushed inside me. It hurt so bad and I screamed, but he held my face in the pillow, and he kept hurting me until he finally stopped.

"He told me that I wanted it. I couldn't talk. I was shaking so bad that I couldn't talk. He got up and got dressed, but I couldn't move. I couldn't move anything, except I was shaking so bad that my whole body was moving. He went out of the room, and I was alone and I didn't know what to do. I finally started to get dressed in the dark and the door opened again. I couldn't see anything, but it had to be him. I told him I wanted to go home. I wanted to go home. But it wasn't him. It was one of the others, and he grabbed me, and then, and then . . ."

The girl began shaking, and she hugged herself with her slender arms, but they weren't strong enough to stop the shaking. Grace's arms were much stronger, but they couldn't stop it either, nor the moan, the original, universal, involuntary female lament.

Grace thought that surely the girl's parents would come, but Alice must have known that they wouldn't. If they had, they would see their daughter, and they would have to be told. Alice must have known this, too, and she began to compose herself. She looked so thin, even thinner than the girl Grace had seen in church, but that couldn't be. It was something else that Grace saw, something within the girl herself.

Grace walked back up the hill alone. She did not look up from the broken concrete of the sidewalk. Alice's story wouldn't let her, wouldn't release her concentration so that she could see anything else. It was what she had expected, more or less. First had come the fear in the girl's eyes, unmistakable in retrospection, then the hints of perversity in Renzlau's record—the rope the one girl had seen, the information from the other football player about Renzlau's nighttime behavior, then Bobby Flowers's description of the money and influence and the fair-haired star who was not fair-haired at all. Step one, step two, three, four. Alice's story was what she should have expected, more or less, and there wasn't much she could do about it. She should have expected that, too.

So what next? Let it go? Put on the uniform in the station, listen to the sergeant call out their assignments, walk the quiet Sunday afternoon beat on Ballard Avenue where she could avoid all the cracks in the concrete sidewalk just as she did as a child? Here, on the hillside rising from Alice's house, there were too many cracks to avoid. If she had worn her blue uniform to interview the girl, it might have been different. Probably the girl wouldn't have talked to her. Grace wouldn't have heard the story of the prodigal son, and she wouldn't have heard Grandmother Bess's heartfelt murmur. If she had worn the uniform, she might not have reached out to Alice and held her as tightly as she dared, and Alice would not have held on in return. Certainly the girl would not have held on. Grace still felt the girl's grip.

But what next? Alice had come to her, to warn her, to tell her, "Be careful. He's not what you think." From that simple, fearful, generous impulse, a series of actions had unfolded that the girl could have never imagined. When Grace thought of Renzlau and the two giants, the two men who were faceless to her but not to Alice, her muscles tightened reflexively as if she were going to act, react, do something, but what? For what purpose was her anger growing and deepening? Where would this anger go? It had to go somewhere, or it would be as futile as the anguish that Alice made clear would never be expressed again.

Grace didn't look up until she reached the busy street where the last few remaining churchgoers prepared to leave. Across the street Bobby Flowers stood outside his car watching her. He was waiting to hear the girl's story, but she couldn't tell it. Maybe he was waiting for more than the story. Maybe he was waiting for her. She now wished he wasn't there, but there he was.

Chapter 21

Edith sat at a table outside Rigmor's store eating soup from a large Styrofoam cup. She ignored the two police officers who approached her, ignored them even when Grace sat in the chair across the table from her. Grace smelled the split pea soup that Rigmor made—soup such as no one else ever made, with vinegar to balance the richness of the cream and the wholesome blandness of the peas. There was also the less pleasant odor of the large-boned woman who ignored her. Katherine stood a short distance upwind.

Doug from the hardware store and Michael, the sheet metal artist, walked toward them on the sidewalk. Edith's grocery cart blocked the sidewalk and forced them onto the pavement of Ballard Avenue. Doug waved as he passed, unperturbed by the obstacle. Rigmor may have lost his business, however, as he and Michael crossed the street and headed in the direction of Vera's Cafe.

"I called your daughter, Edith," Grace said. "She's very upset that you left the group home."

Edith scraped the side of her cup with a plastic spoon, circling in a downward spiral to capture every drop of Rigmor's soup, the improbable combination of cream and vinegar.

"Elizabeth is worried about you. She would like to come,

but she can't get off work again right now. Your daughter asked me to tell you that she loves you, Edith."

Edith looked at Grace with cold suspicious eyes, with no trace of love returned in response to the loving words of her daughter. Grace had heard the daughter's voice, but Edith had not. Edith only heard Grace's translation. Grace wondered if it would make any difference whose voice Edith heard. Her mother's cancer was a fearful burden, but Edith's disease would be even harder to bear. Grace found it impossible to imagine what it would be like to lose her mother's love.

A bell rang with a rich peaceful tone, and Grace looked toward the triangle where Ballard Avenue and 22nd Avenue intersected. Arne, the youngest of the aging brothers at Johansen Brothers Meats, pulled the mechanical lever at the base of the tower. People stopped on the sidewalk and didn't move even after the bell stopped ringing. Grace knew why. She was waiting, too.

"Ask not for whom the bell tolls," Edith said as she stood.

Edith's words were not directed at Grace, nor at Katherine, nor anyone on the street. Her words drifted into the air like the languorous peals of the bell. Edith packed the plastic container and spoon among her possessions in the grocery cart. As she pushed the cart away, the butcher began singing beneath the arches of the Bell Tower. Grace had heard the song many times and knew it by heart, although it was a century old and the language Italian.

Who, then, could say that Edith was crazy? Not the people who stopped on the street to listen to the butcher's song, not the singer who stopped them, not she who was somewhere between Arne in his stained white coat and Edith in her moveable abode. So what if Edith heard voices? Everyone heard voices of some sort. Some called the voices the devil, some called them God. To Arne they were voices of lovers expressed through music. The lovers always died in Arne's songs.

What would possess a man to sing on the street corner?

Rigmor came outside to listen and stood in the doorway of her store. Arne closed his eyes as he came to the conclusion of his song. He didn't see the street; he didn't see the men in their work clothes listening or the line of cars stopped at the stop sign, the drivers waiting for the final words of the song. He saw none of that. Like a shaman, like Edith, he saw a vision all his own.

"So beautiful," Rigmor said as applause followed the last beautiful note of Arne's vision. "I wish I could understand what he sings."

"He wants the night to be over," Grace said.

"Is that right? I feel that way myself sometimes. Are you hungry, Katrin? I've made some nice soup today."

"I know," Katherine said. "It smells wonderful."

"So come in and try a little. I think the music show is all done."

"Edith was sitting out here when we came," Grace said.

"I know," Rigmor said. "Poor soul. A little food is the least we can do. That can't hurt anything. *Hvad*?"

"No, it can't hurt anything, except you lost a few customers when Doug and Michael saw that she was here."

"Ah, they'll come back if they're hungry."

"I was hoping she would get better."

"I know. Poor soul."

A dull green compact car scraped its wheels against the curb and parked behind the blue and white police car. Anne waved to the trio at Rigmor's door.

"I hope I'm not late," Anne said when she got out of the car. "I got stuck behind a bunch of cars at that stop sign. Nobody was moving. I didn't think Ballard had traffic jams."

"They were listening to the opera," Rigmor said.

"Opera?"

"*Ja,*" Rigmor said. "Sometimes our butcher sings after he rings the bell. You should come early sometime and listen. I can't understand what he says, but Grace knows the words. She can explain."

Anne, Katherine, and Grace sat around the small table in Rigmor's back room eating split pea soup and thin slices of buttered rye bread. As Edith had done, they scraped the sides of their bowls for the last drops of the creamy pungent soup.

"Delicious," Anne said. "Whoever thought peas could taste like this? This soup might even be better than the meatballs we had last time. It's a good thing you ladies walk as much as you do. I bought one of those treadmills where you walk yourself to death and never get anywhere, but God, they're boring. Did you ever try one?"

"Not me," Grace said.

Katherine smiled as she rested her spoon inside her bowl.

"Well, don't bother. I use mine for a trellis. The clematis loves it. In another year I won't even be able to see the machine for all the leaves and vines. Anyway that's not why we're here, is it? You found the girl."

Yes, she had found the girl.

Grace had already told Alice's story to Katherine the day before when she had gone to work after church. They had sat on the bench in the locker room and were joined by the two other women who worked the Second Watch. She told the story without telling them who the girl was. It was a long story, longer than she had intended it to be, but no one looked at the clock or left the locker room until she had finished. Roll call began in the assembly room like the old days when the men had the place all to themselves.

She told the story to Anne just as she told it to Katherine and the women officers in the locker room, again without the girl's name. Grace wondered if she told the story often enough, would the girl's fear and shame disappear in the redundancy of the telling? The girl's fear would surely disappear if her story were ever to be told in the dry technical language of justice.

"Can you at least get her to identify the other two men in a photo lineup?" Anne asked.

"I don't know," Grace said. "The room was dark. She didn't see their faces."

"But she knew who they were," Anne said. "She saw them when they were dancing with her."

"I don't think she will want to see them again, not even their pictures."

"Could you get her to talk to me?"

"I promised that I wouldn't tell anybody who she was."

"I know. You said that, but even the reporter knows who she is."

"Yes, but I didn't tell him what happened. I promised the girl."

"For chrissake, somebody has to be willing to testify or we'll never get anywhere."

Grace understood Anne's frustration. She felt it, too.

"Grace is doing everything she can," Katherine said. "If Grace can't get this girl to cooperate, nobody can and nobody should."

Grace looked at her partner who was standing up for her although Katherine had not risen from the chair that separated Grace from Anne Smith. Grace appreciated her partner's support more than she could say. Something had happened and was happening to her. She wasn't sure what it was. She only knew that she would take one step and another, but she didn't know where the steps would lead her. Wherever it was, it was comforting to think Katherine would be there. It was a sudden illumination of something she had known for some time, but the articulation of it was still a surprise. She was glad it was Katherine who sat beside her in Rigmor's back room and not Wes Mickelsen, not anyone else.

"I'm going to Louisiana," Grace said to Katherine and

Anne, deciding finally what she had been contemplating for a day and a night and a morning, knowing that it was a place where Katherine could not join her. Her sister, Evangeline, could, and Evangeline was already making plans. Grace had only to give the word.

"I'm wondering if you could call the Sex Crimes division in Baton Rouge and sort of prepare the way," Grace said to Anne.

"Prepare for what?" Anne asked.

"The football team plays in Baton Rouge this Saturday. He's going to go out again the night before the game. I know it. We all know it. Maybe he'll be careless and make a mistake. If you can get the Baton Rouge department to work with me, we might be able to catch him trying to assault a woman down there."

"Our department will never pay for a surveillance trip. Can you imagine how much that would cost? Sorry, they won't do it."

"They don't have to pay anything," Grace said. "My sister works for an airline that flies into New Orleans. She's getting me a ticket. She and I have family down there who we've been planning to visit. I think this would be as good a time as any to do it."

Anne was silent for a moment. She looked first at Grace, then at Katherine, who showed no change in her expression despite the surprise she must have felt at Grace's announcement.

"When are you leaving?" Anne asked.

"Wednesday. I'll use a couple of vacation days."

"You don't fool around, do you?" Anne asked. "All right, I'll see what I can do. I'll have to run it through Captain Lowery. He's in charge of the Sex Crimes division. But don't worry. He'll support us. He's not like some of these guys who are afraid of their shadows. He actually likes to see a little work done. He might call your captain if he thinks it's necessary, but I won't encourage him. If he has any doubts, I'll remind him of the good old days when he was a hard-charging young cop on the street. He likes to remember those days. It works every time."

"Rigmor has made a fresh pot of coffee," Grace said. "I'll get us some."

Grace gathered the plates and bowls and carried them into the front part of the store where Rigmor stood at her register. A customer was leaving, and the small bell chimed as he opened the door. Outside on the sidewalk Edith walked by again, pushing her cart, looking up to the sky, talking to somebody or some thing. The customer stood in the door until Edith passed. He walked away in the opposite direction.

"Poor soul," Rigmor said.

Chapter 22

Is that why you came?" Evangeline asked.

Grace and Evangeline sat in rocking chairs outside their room on the second-floor balcony of the old hotel next to the Evangeline Oak, sipping wine provided by the hostess. The story Grace had told pressed as heavily upon them as the warm humid air that gave life to the Spanish moss in the giant oak tree. It wasn't really the Evangeline Oak, Miss Peggy had told them. The Evangeline Oak was a much older tree down the bayou, but this one was on city property. When tourists came to see the Evangeline Oak tree, it didn't matter which tree they saw. It was the story that mattered. Beyond the oak tree that anchored the Boulevard d' Evangeline, the green, barely moving, murky water of the Bayou Teche glimmered with the last angular light of the setting sun. Evangeline, radiant since the moment they had crossed the Atchafalaya River, looked at her with less radiance than any time that day, than any time since they had met in the New Orleans airport and had begun their journey in the rented car.

"I don't know," Grace said. "It had something to do with the timing, I guess."

"Yes, I guess so."

"You can't tell anybody else this story, Evangeline. I

promised the girl that I wouldn't let anybody know who she was. I can tell you about her, but not who she is."

"Does the newspaper reporter know? Does Bobby Flowers know about this?"

"No. I showed him the police report about the young woman who saw the rope, and he knows that this girl I just told you about warned me to be careful. But he doesn't know her story. I suppose he has his suspicions, but he doesn't know. And he won't. I promised the girl."

"I'm going with you to Baton Rouge," Evangeline said.

"You don't have to. I'll get another car."

"I'm going with you. Don't even think about anything else."

"It's probably a wild-goose chase, a waste of time."

"You coming all this way to waste your time? I don't think so."

It would be another two days before they began that particular chase.

In the meantime they had another, beginning with the copy of the land deed handwritten in French and dated March 1, 1858, that recorded the sale of one hundred fifty arpents of land to Emile Etienne for $450 and two of the buyer's mules, with the seller selecting.

Grace had sensed a change in the air when they crossed the Atchafalaya Basin, the wet heavy air for which Evangeline had declared her immediate approval. It was the end of October, and the temperature still reached eighty-five degrees. The heat was tolerable in the evening with the breeze, Grace thought, but add another ten degrees and take away the breeze and it would be enough to stifle the life of any moving creature.

Evangeline could imagine those ten degrees, too, but there was something about this place, she said, something so right that she wouldn't think about ten degrees. Even the story about Alice and the football players didn't dampen her spirit

for long. It was no match for the warm moist air that gave life
to the Spanish moss hanging from the Evangeline Oak.

From the balcony the sisters watched the occasional car
pass on the street below them. Across the tree-lined boulevard were the two steeples of St. Martin de Lourdes, the
larger tower at the front and the small steeple at the back,
both rising above the trees that stood between them and the
church. Beyond the Evangeline Oak was the silent water of
the Bayou Teche, flowing slowly, imperceptibly toward the
Gulf. Their chairs were closer together than they would be in
Seattle where the cool air acted like a barrier between them
or in Los Angeles where the brightness of the day made their
reflections sharp and harsh. They spoke softly to each other,
hardly above a murmur.

It was worth coming just for this, Grace realized, to sit beside her sister, who was certain that something was right as it
had never been before. Just think of the names, Evangeline
had said. It couldn't be a coincidence. Her name, Evangeline,
on the oak tree and the very street where they were staying;
their father's name, Martin, the name of the parish, the town,
the church, the saint who was the namesake of all. "Your
name," she said to Grace with the new soft voice of a sister,
"hangs over this town. It's in the air like the sound of the
church bells. There is a sense of grace here. I feel it."

Grace hoped Evangeline was right, that the deeper explo-
ration that would begin in the morning would confirm what
they saw on the surface. For Evangeline's sake and for her
own, she hoped so, but she wondered why they knew so little about this place. Nothing was known, really. "From the
South" was all they ever heard about their family roots until
Evangeline found the paper in the attic. From free people, not
slaves, Grandpa Joseph always said, but little more than
that—little more than that and the few French expressions
that he liked to use but never said exactly where they came
from. Somewhere down there, was all he had said. Did the

few French expressions encourage his son to learn the language and make a living teaching it to indifferent high school students? Maybe bits of the language, buried in their genes and waiting for the right light and the right air and the right voices to come forth again, had seeped unconsciously into the family. If so, what other languages would come forth?

On the balcony above the Boulevard d' Evangeline, Evangeline began recalling the French phrases of her father and grandfather that she wouldn't repeat as a girl. As a girl she wouldn't even acknowledge that she understood them, but on the balcony in the moist air that she felt was just right she began to form sentences and express thoughts from the abandoned language.

The evening turned to night, and an owl across the bayou began speaking in its plaintive native tongue. "Who, who, who." For the owl it wasn't a question, but it was for Grace. *Who is this sister now beside me with a softer voice than before? Who am I who listens with a sister to the bells of grace? Who? Who?*

Later that night they lay together in the huge four-poster bed in their hotel room. None of the rooms in the old refurbished hotel had more than one bed, and they hadn't wanted to bear the cost of two rooms. It was more than that. From the very beginning there had been an unspoken agreement that neither wanted to be apart from the other on this trip. Grace remembered the smaller bed they shared whenever they visited Grandmother Bess and Grandpa Joseph in Omaha. She remembered how she and Evangeline could whisper to each other so softly in their shared bed that even their father could not hear them. They could talk as long into the night as they wanted. When they returned to Seattle, Grace sometimes wished for one bed instead of two. A few feet was all that separated their Seattle beds, but the distance was great enough that no matter how far she reached during the night she could not touch Evangeline the way she could in Omaha.

The bells of grace rang in the darkness. It was midnight in St. Martinville.

"Are you asleep?" Evangeline whispered.

"No."

"If he hurt you like that girl, I would come and we would get your gun and we would find him and shoot him."

Grace turned over on her side so that she was facing her sister. She couldn't see her, but she knew where she was. She reached out and put her hand on Evangeline's shoulder. Her sister was exactly where she thought she would be.

"If he hurt you like that, I would come and we would find him and we would get a big knife and start cutting him away."

"I know where I would start cutting," Evangeline said.

Chapter 23

At eight o'clock Grace and Evangeline were in Miss Peggy's breakfast room surrounded by photographs of the graduating classes of Our Lady of Mercy High School. Grace sat in the corner chair beneath the oldest photograph from 1919. Four young women in heavy wool skirts, each with a sash across her chest and a four-square mortar board on her head, stood before a large outstretched American flag. The girl on the left held the staff, but there was no visible support for the other end of the flag as it disappeared off the photograph. There were no names for the girls, only the date. The photograph below the 1919 graduating class had names but no date. It took several years for the two concepts to merge.

The faces of the girls—there were only girls in the photographs—disoriented her. Each girl was fixed in time, youthful and hopeful in Grace's imagination. Some were now old, Grace knew, and some were probably dead. She had trouble imagining that.

The hotel, Miss Peggy explained when she brought in the breakfast, had been used as the girls' high school for St. Martin's de Lourdes Catholic Church until the new school was built. When she bought the building to return it to its original use, she found the school photographs left behind. She hung them up, and the girls came and stayed in the hotel for class reunions. On those occasions the halls echoed with voices from the past. She heard the voices sometimes when the hotel was empty.

"Beignet, French toast, fresh eggs, bacon," Miss Peggy said as she pointed to each item on Evangeline's plate. "You might want to try some of our syrup. It's a little strong, but we like it here. Now is there anything else you would like?"

How could they want anything else?

The syrup was too strong, Grace decided. It had a flavor like extra-dark molasses. A little of the flavor was good in the wafer-thin cookies Rigmor made at Christmas, but its undiluted form was too strong for her on French toast. She raised her eyebrows to Evangeline as a signal to use caution. Evangeline poured a few drops of the syrup on a corner of one piece of her French toast and tasted it. She, too, raised her eyebrows, but she signaled pleasure and covered the rest of her French toast in the rich dark syrup.

Two more guests entered the breakfast room, a couple with the white-haired intimacy of age, who greeted them with good mornings before sitting at a table nearby. On the second floor a door closed with the reluctance of old hardware. Grace wondered if the girls, who seemed to be watching them from the walls, had learned to walk quietly on the wood floors. It would be difficult to sneak around in this old building, to avoid the squeak in the final step of the staircase as they descended for a surreptitious purpose. Or had they nothing to hide from the nuns, who taught them civics and chemistry, typing, proper posture and behavior?

Grace walked as properly as she could to the coffeepots that were on a stand beneath a display of more recent photographs. One of the pots held regular coffee, but the other was a Cajun version of café au lait with dark coffee, milk, and caramelized sugar. The photographs above the coffeepots remained black-and-white until the class of 1976. That photograph and the next several color photographs had faded so completely that they looked like old-fashioned sepia photographs instead of color. In more recent years, the color improved.

Grace mixed the café au lait with black coffee to cut the sweetness. Evangeline joined her and poured café au lait alone into her cup. Together they scanned the faces in the rows of class photographs. Grace knew that they were looking for the same face. Through the '20s, '30s, '40s, and '50s, every face in the black-and-white photographs on the walls was white, a shade of white at least, or at least white as far as they knew. But what did they know? They were strangers in the room, interpreting faces without hearing the voices Miss Peggy heard at night during the slow season when no one was staying at the hotel.

1972. Celeste François. She was the first black graduate. The sisters stopped at the same photograph but said nothing to each other.

Celeste François did not look unhappy. Her smile was not quite complete, but that could have been the timing of the shutter. Grace interpreted the smile through her own experiences and from her imperfect imagining of the voices in the hall. 1972 was the end, the graduation, not the beginning. It was the beginning about which Grace wondered.

"The class pictures at Ballard wouldn't look any different," Evangeline said. They were walking to the courthouse in the middle of the one-lane street beside the bayou. There was no sidewalk, no need for one. Evangeline didn't have to explain what she meant.

In the fourth grade in Ballard another black girl had joined Grace's class. Her name was Rosalie. The teacher put Rosalie close to Grace but not so close that it would be obvious that she was pairing them. It was obvious to everybody. Almost from the first day they didn't like each other. Although not as tall as Grace, Rosalie was heavier and stronger and picked on kids at recess. The boys played their own games away from the girls, especially after Rosalie came, but she would catch up with them when they formed lines to go inside. She punched them in the back if they irritated her. Rosalie was often irritated.

Grace tried to stay away from her and never once invited Rosalie to her house after school. None of the girls did, and after Rosalie joined the class fewer of the girls invited Grace.

The fourth grade was the only time she got into a fight at school. Evangeline often got into fights, and their mother had to go to the school office and listen to the most recent episode.

The fight with Rosalie wasn't really a fight. It was a burst of anger that had been building since Rosalie joined the class and probably long before a clear target emerged. It was over so quickly that Grace hardly knew what happened. The immediate cause was a home run that Grace kicked in a game of kickball at recess. Rosalie was the pitcher on the other team. As Grace rounded third base on her way to home plate, as her teammates clapped and cheered the home run, Rosalie yelled out above the cheers that Grace's mother was a white whore. She yelled loud enough so that all of them heard.

Without knowing what she was going to do except that somehow she was going to hurt the girl who was taunting her, and without knowing the exact method until she arrived at the streak of chalk on the asphalt that marked the pitcher's mound, she hit Rosalie in the face with her fist as hard as she could. The bigger girl didn't fall down, but she didn't laugh anymore. Grace hit her a second time with her other fist. Rosalie fell to the ground and curled into a ball for protection. She cried for help, and help came quickly from the playground teacher.

Grace was marched to the principal's office by the teacher who held her arm so tightly that Grace thought she would cry, but she didn't cry until her mother came and took her home. Grace never told her mother what Rosalie had said, although her mother eventually found out. Everyone did. For weeks afterward, for weeks and weeks, Grace walked home from school alone. For weeks and weeks she played on the swings by herself instead of playing kickball with the other girls. Rosalie moved away before the school year ended.

"My God," Evangeline said, "look at that tree. That must be the real oak that Miss Peggy was talking about."

For certain it was a real oak tree, the biggest tree Grace had ever seen. If Evangeline had not stopped her, she might have walked past it looking at the ground and thinking about the girl, Rosalie. The tree was so large, so magnificent that it seemed impossible to miss, and yet she would have missed it because of a memory that seemed ancient to her. Compared to the tree, the incident was but a moment ago. Grace wondered why the memory was returning to her now.

At the base of the tree a huge mass of gnarled burls had grown on top of one another and pushed out from the main trunk. Altogether the diameter of the base must have been fifteen feet through. The burls were like old arthritic joints and gave the tree a sense of agony as well as majesty, a sense of misery along with hope, shouts of joy, moans of pain and moans of another kind, which may have been pain, too, during steamy nights along the bayou.

"It was here before us," Evangeline said. "Before our people came."

"A long time before us."

"Would you even dare to climb that tree?" Evangeline asked. "It would be disrespectful, like climbing on top of somebody's tombstone."

Evangeline raised the twice-folded sheets of legal paper, which she had held in her hand since leaving the hotel headed toward for the courthouse, and brought the quartered

copies of the handwritten legal document to her chest and
took a deep nervous breath.

"I want to do this. I've wanted to do this ever since I was
a little girl even though I didn't know what it was that I
wanted to do, but it almost scares me now that we're here. It's
one thing to have this paper, to know that somebody named
Emile Etienne bought land here in 1858, but it almost scares
me what else we'll find. Maybe there won't be anything.
Maybe we've come all this way and there will be just this one
piece of paper or maybe not even that. Maybe the courthouse
burned down a hundred years ago and all the records are
gone. Didn't the Union troops burn down the courthouses
during the Civil War? Somewhere they did. But maybe we'll
find something else, and that's what scares me most. Maybe
the Etiennes in the phone book don't have anything to do
with us. Or maybe they do and we don't want to know. Or
they don't. Doesn't it scare you at all to think about it?"

All the while she spoke, Evangeline faced the great oak
tree, talking to the tree as if some answer would come from
it, but she turned to Grace with the last question and looked
up at her, meaning that the last question was for her, if not
only for her.

Grace thought for a moment before answering. No, Grace
decided. This didn't frighten her. She had been frightened
that her mother would be angry after she hit Rosalie. She
had been frightened that her mother would be more hurt than
the girl she had hit in the playground. She had been frightened when she heard about the cancer that attacked her
mother just when everything was going so well. She had
been frightened when the man pointed the gun at Katherine,
and afterward when she realized she had not grabbed the
gun in time after all. Those were the things that frightened
her, but not this, not the paper Evangeline carried.

"You're not scared of anything," Grace told her sister.

On the street in front of the giant oak tree Evangeline

hugged Grace around the waist, crushing the folded paper with the title State of Louisiana, Parish of St. Martin into her back, pinning Grace's arms at her side and brushing rows of braided hair into Grace's cheek. Before Grace could respond, before her surprise subsided and she could free her arms of Evangeline's embrace to reciprocate, Evangeline released her and laughed.

"Let's go," she said.

They passed three-foot-thick concrete columns into the courthouse, which surely would never burn no matter how many Union torches there may have been. The assessor's office was the first office inside the courthouse. Behind the front counter a woman sat at a desk and looked over her reading glasses at the two women in front of her. Evangeline opened the copy of the land deed and smoothed out the wrinkles that it had received since leaving the hotel. The clerk rose from her desk, removed her glasses, and left them dangling about her neck by a gold chain.

"We would like to know if we can find this record here," Evangeline said, turning the document around so that the woman could read it.

The clerk put on her glasses and scanned the document.

"Sure, but it looks like you already found it," she said. "Somebody did anyway."

"The original of this was in the attic of my father's house. We'd like to see if we could find a document here that matches it."

"Oh, this isn't ours, is it?" the clerk said to herself. She picked up the wrinkled copy of the land deed and held it closer to her eyes.

"Our records are stamped with a page number and a conveyance number so that they're easier to read. These handwritten numbers are difficult to make out sometimes. Your father must have had the original from the notary. Back then, of course, they copied them all by hand. Go back there." The woman laid the paper on the counter and pointed toward the back of the building. "You'll see ledgers with numbers on the covers. Look for the one that has this number." Her finger moved to the handwritten number at the top of the document—2233. "That's an old one. It'll be in one of the books on top, but you'll see it. Just down the hall. Come back here if you have any questions."

Grace and Evangeline walked past open steel doors into a large vault where there were hundreds of green volumes, each labeled with a beginning and an ending transaction number. The volumes were squeezed together on wood shelves ten feet high. The sisters stared up at Volume 25, 1938 – 2401, but neither reached for it. It was on the second shelf from the top, and Evangeline had no hope of stretching that high. Grace wasn't sure she could reach it either, or if she could, whether she could support so large a book at the extent of her reach. It wasn't the physical difficulty alone that restrained her. She felt like a stranger about to peer into the affairs of people she didn't know. If she reached for the volume, someone would surely shout for her to stop. There were plenty of people in the room who could shout, but they were all busy with their own work and paid no attention to the two strangers seeking Volume 25.

Evangeline found a wheeled stepstool at the end of the counter, pushed it into place, and climbed the three steps to the top. She pulled out Volume 25, handed it to Grace, and climbed back down. She took the book from Grace's hands and laid it on a sloping counter on the opposite side of the aisle. Before opening the volume she looked at Grace.

"Here we go," she said.

Evangeline flipped through the pages toward the back, not stopping until she came to the number 2233. She laid her copy of the deed that she had found in the attic in Seattle beside the page in the book with the same transaction number. Grace stood beside her and watched her sister's finger move down the page a line at a time. Evangeline turned the page in the book to expose the back and laid her second sheet of paper beside it.

"They're the same," she said at last, her voice hushed as if they were in a church. "Every line is the same. It's the same paper that Daddy had in the attic. The handwriting is a little different, but it's the same document. Who would have thought that it would be this easy?"

"We found the record anyway."

"You're right. It's just paper, but from this there has to be a way to trace what happened to the land. At least we can drive out there and see it. That will help. That might be enough. If we see the land, we'll know something about them. Is it farm ground or just some swamp where they lived? We can see that at least. And maybe we can find out who owned the land after him. If we're able to trace it far enough ahead, maybe we can find somebody who will know something, anything. Maybe somebody will know if any of the Etiennes in the phone book are from our family."

"That's why we came," Grace said.

"That's why I came."

"That's why we both came," Grace said.

And it was true. Without the land deed, she wouldn't have come. Evangeline wouldn't have gotten the airplane tickets; they wouldn't have sat together on the balcony of the old hotel or shared a bed as they had not done since they were children in Omaha.

Evangeline carried the open volume back to the counter in the office, and the woman removed her glasses again and rose from her chair.

"So you found it," she said.

"It's the same as our copy," Evangeline said.

"Of course it is."

"We were wondering if there is a way to trace what happened to the land after this man, after Emile Etienne bought it."

"Sure, that's what all those people are doing in there, except they're going the other direction. They're going back and you want to go forward. All you have to do is look in the vendor book under his name, Emile Etienne. If he sold the land, you can find who bought it. Then you can go to the conveyance records and make sure that you have the right transaction. And then you find who sold the land after him, but that could take a long time for something this old, a long time. What are you trying to find out?"

"We're just trying to find somebody who might know about these people. We think this man may have been a relative of ours," Evangeline said.

The woman looked at them with a curiosity that made Grace feel like a stranger again.

"You're not from these parts, are you?"

"I'm from Los Angeles," Evangeline said. "My sister is from Seattle."

"Sisters. I see," she said, although Grace was not certain that she did. Most people didn't. "There are still Etiennes out toward Catahoula. Look here," the woman said, pointing to the description of land written in the book. "This land that you're talking about is in Section Twenty-seven—one hundred fifty arpents. An arpent is an old form of measurement, about eight-tenths of an acre. There are Etiennes who own lots of land out that way. Come in here and I'll show you."

Grace followed Evangeline behind the counter. The clerk walked over to a huge map of St. Martin's Parish that was hung on the wall behind her desk. She moved her finger across the map.

"Here," she said. "This map is some twenty years old now, but this is Section Twenty-seven, and this is where they are. Do you see the names?"

Evangeline, and after her, Grace, edged closer to the names inscribed in tiny handwritten letters in the oddly shaped angles of land in the upper-right corner of the map.

There were a number of parcels that the clerk's finger circled, and there were a number of first names within the circle, but all ended the same.

Etienne.

Chapter 24

Grace turned right at the first intersection after the church, following the directions that Evangeline read from notes she had written on a piece of paper at the courthouse, and drove on the road toward Catahoula where there were one hundred fifty arpents of land that had once belonged to an Etienne and still did as far as they knew. The worst that could happen, she told herself, would be that the woman at the courthouse was wrong and the land was empty and would give no clues to the Emile Etienne on the deed of sale. If so, if the worst happened, they would turn away and go home without learning more about him. Already they had discovered more than they had hoped, more than she had hoped anyway. Evangeline had seen her tree, and they had heard the bells while lying so close to each other that each knew what the other was thinking.

No, she decided, the worst would be if they found someone who didn't want to be found or didn't care and turned them away with indifference, but even that wouldn't change what they had already found.

They passed field after field of sugarcane, some fields so tall and thick that they looked as impenetrable as a forest in a primitive wilderness, except that the cane grew in rows so straight that only a machine could have imposed such precision. Man or woman alone could not plant such straight rows. In her experience men or women always left a mess behind their actions—curves and false leads and dead ends.

Some fields were immature, with leaves reaching out to touch their neighbors, before the desire for sun drove them higher and left the lower leaves wilted and useless. There were also fields of new growth—delicate fragile stalks no more than a foot above the deep black soil. In field after field stood the sugarcane, to sweeten what was sour, to satisfy cravings that would be satisfied no matter the effort.

Now and then they passed a grouping of homes, some with small black children playing in the yards and some with white. Those with black children were usually smaller, less prosperous, with abandoned houses among them, but not always. Sometimes there would be a new brick home and a black child on a tricycle on a newly paved driveway.

Evangeline's face never turned from the window where the fields of sugarcane passed by in a blurred panorama. They didn't talk, except for Evangeline giving directions and Grace acknowledging them.

"I think we're almost there," Evangeline said.

She looked at Grace to see if she agreed, and Grace nodded her head in solemn agreement. Evangeline was looking for more than agreement. Evangeline, who had been afraid of nothing as far back as Grace could remember, who would stick her face into the face of the biggest boy on the block or at least as close to it as she could reach and make him back away with her undivided fury, looked to Grace for more than agreement as she announced their imminent arrival—just this once, let it be right.

Grace assessed the assembly of farm buildings they were approaching as she would assess a house in Ballard where the husband was supposed to have a gun or one of the fishermen's taverns where a fight had broken out or soon would. First, she looked for movement and then something out of place—scared faces, rigid postures. As she slowed the car on the highway and prepared to turn, she saw a truck loaded with sugarcane moving toward them from the driveway of the farm. A black man was driving. There was no fear on his face. He waved to them as he turned onto the highway where Grace had come to a complete stop with her blinker ticking away in expectation of her turn.

"Hang on, sister," Grace said. "We're going in."

Evangeline placed her hand on the dashboard as the car hit a deep rut on the white crushed rock road that led into the farmstead. On their right was a field of new cane rising from mounds of deeply grooved soil. A Posted No Trespassing sign greeted them from the edge of the field, and Grace wasn't sure if the sign was intended for the field or the road. On the left side of the road was a field of mature cane, and the cane soared above their car.

There were four houses in the farmstead, and the road split in front of them like the delta of a river. In a direct line with the road was the smallest house, which was enveloped by huge oak trees that spread their green canopies over the roof. It was the oldest house. Its well-tended wood siding was painted white and the shutters green. A screened porch stretched across the entire front of the house. The house to the right was larger but had the same well–preserved siding. On either side of the white houses were brick homes, one with trees beginning to mature and the other so new that the trees were but saplings in ground only recently retrieved from the field of mature cane that formed the outer boundary of the lawn.

Another truck was leaving the assembly of equipment beyond the older of the two brick homes. It moved slowly as it approached their car and rolled to a stop without the need for brakes, even as Grace pulled to the side of the delta drive so that it could pass. Grace set the transmission in park and left the motor running as she got out of the car. She approached the open window of the cab where the driver leaned out and pushed back the bill of his baseball cap.

"We're looking for the Etienne farm," she said.

"This is one," he said.

"Are you Mr. Etienne?"

"No, ma'am. He's over yonder. I just work here sometimes."

She looked over yonder where the man pointed. A hundred feet away three men stood in front of a huge machine that would cut the rows of sugarcane. All three men were looking at them. Grace observed their clothing, which wasn't much different from man to man—blue denim work pants, work shirts, billed caps to shield their eyes from the sun. Two of the men were black, deep black as the soil of the newly plowed fields, and the other was the color of the mature stalks that were shielded from the sun. His face was deeply tanned but otherwise would have been much lighter.

"Which one?" Grace asked, although she was already beginning to know. The worst thing, she realized, was that they would find their people and it would not be them.

"Why, he's the white man, ma'am," said the black man from behind the steering wheel of the truck. "That's Mr. Etienne."

Mr. Etienne was walking toward them, and the driver eased his truck into a low gear and moved slowly away. Evangeline got out of the car and joined Grace on the crushed rock roadway.

"Good morning," the man said, stopping a few feet away from them.

It was a friendly enough greeting as far as Grace could tell.

"Good morning," Grace said back to him. "Are you Mr. Etienne?"

"I'm Ronnie Etienne. Which one you looking for?"

Grace glanced at Evangeline, who for the first time looked as if something was not and would not be just right.

"We don't know," Grace said. "I think we made a mistake."

"How's that?"

"My sister found an old deed in our father's papers for land in this county, this parish I mean, dated 1858. At the courthouse they said the land was out here somewhere. They said that Etiennes still live here."

"We do. These Etiennes do anyway." He pointed with his thumb over his shoulder to the houses that stood behind him. "What was the name on the deed?"

"Emile Etienne," Grace said.

"Is he some relation of yours?"

"We think so."

"And what are your names, if you don't mind me asking?"

"I'm Grace Stevens and this is my sister, Evangeline Stevens."

"He changed the name," Ronnie Etienne said.

"Somebody did."

Ronnie Etienne smiled, but it was a cautious smile that formed only as he crossed his tanned arms over his stomach.

"You're not from here, are you?"

It was the second time they had been asked that question.

"I'm from Los Angeles," Evangeline said, stepping forward to be closer to Ronnie Etienne. "My sister, Grace, is from Seattle. That's where our mother and father live. His name is Martin."

"Martin and Evangeline," the man said. "You sure have the right names for this area. Do you have that land deed with you?"

"It's in the car," Evangeline said. "It's in French."

"Yes, it would be," he said.

The three moved toward the car. The motor had remained running in idle since Grace had parked to talk to the truck driver. That had been only a few moments ago, but Grace felt the time slip away into the new growth of sugarcane and back into the rich black soil, which held secrets that they would never know. Evangeline opened the passenger's door and set off the warning chimes inside the car.

"You can turn the car off if you want," Ronnie Etienne said to Grace.

What did she want, Grace asked herself. Not that it mattered what she wanted, not that it ever mattered, but if Evangeline had hoped for something to be just right she had hoped just once for simplicity—a simple straight line without all the mess of humankind, a line so straight and true that she wouldn't be able to tell the difference between it and the new rows of cane laid down by the planting machines.

Grace turned off the ignition, and the three claiming an Etienne name or a variation of it gathered at the front of the car where Ronnie Etienne spread the two copied pages of the land deed over the heated hood. He began translating the French words from more than a century and a quarter earlier.

"My French isn't as good as it ought to be, but it's good enough to know that you found the right place," he said, standing straight with his hands holding down the papers so that they would not blow away in the breeze. "Over there where those trees are, we still call that the Breaux Section." He pointed across the main road. "This Emile Etienne bought the land from Maurice Breaux. And beyond this field is the Castille land that we bought thirty years ago. I was just a kid, but I remember that. The deed you have says the land is between those properties. It's Miss Felicia's land now, or it was before we bought it from her."

"Who is Miss Felicia?" Evangeline asked.

"My great-aunt. She lives in the old house. This was her land, right here, this land that's on your deed. My mama and daddy live beside her, and my brother and I live in the houses on the outside."

"Did she ever say anything about an Emile Etienne?" Evangeline asked.

"No, I don't think so. Maybe you should tell me why you came. Do you think this paper will give you some claim to this land? I'm pretty sure it won't. I sure hope it won't."

"That's not why we came," Evangeline said. She pointed to a line on the first page of the land deed that Ronnie Etienne still held down with his deeply tanned hand, a working hand with scrapes across his knuckles and dirt beneath his fingernails. "It says here that Emile Etienne was a person of color, a free person of color, *'homme de coleur libro.'* That's who we thought we would find."

"One drop was the rule back then. One drop of black blood and you could never be white. You could have blond hair and blue eyes, but it didn't matter if you had that one drop of colored blood. So you found who you were looking for, only it wasn't who you were expecting, and we weren't exactly expecting you either. Me, I don't mind. My wife and my daughter know all about this, and it doesn't bother them, but my brother might not want to be reminded. I know his wife won't."

"We'll leave," Evangeline said, pulling the papers from beneath Ronnie Etienne's hand. "We didn't come here to cause trouble for your family."

"No," Ronnie Etienne said, his green eyes squinting in the morning sun, "you had better come in and visit with Miss Felicia a bit. She would never forgive me if I didn't bring you in."

"Don't tell her we came," Evangeline said. She, too, had a hint of green in her eyes. Grace always thought that the color was from their mother's family, but now she wasn't sure.

"I don't think I could prevent myself from doing that," Ronnie said.

He had a face, Grace decided, on which there was always

a grin waiting to come forth. One almost came as he spoke to Evangeline, but Evangeline didn't see it. She had been looking for someone much different, a face more deeply colored than that of this white man despite his drop of colored blood. A man of color, the deed said, a tract of land, a sum of money—words of legal standing intended to pass land from seller to buyer, nothing else, and yet the words would be read, interpreted, and misunderstood for a hundred twenty-five years and who knew how much longer.

"I think we should go," Evangeline said.

Evangeline looked away from them and didn't see the expression changing in Ronnie Etienne's face, a sadness coming on to replace the humor that had been there only a moment before. Evangeline hadn't seen either expression because she was looking beyond him to her own expectations, which she had lost somewhere out in the field of new cane.

"If anyone knows anything about Emile Etienne, it will be Miss Felicia. I imagine she's the last one who will know," Ronnie said.

"Let's talk to her, Evangeline," Grace said. "We've come this far."

Even when they were girls, Grace had a keen sense of direction and Evangeline did not. Evangeline often got lost in strange places, but she would never admit it. Evangeline insisted upon leading even when she didn't know where she was going. If Evangeline got too far off course, Grace became disgusted with her sister's stubbornness. She would then set off in the right direction on her own. Evangeline usually followed some distance behind so that she could say she wasn't following at all, then she would sprint ahead when she finally reached a familiar landmark. There were no familiar landmarks in this country out toward Catahoula, and Evangeline turned away from the sugarcane field where she would surely get lost and looked at Grace.

"You're right," Evangeline said. "We've come this far."

Ronnie Etienne led them across the crushed white rock to the door of Miss Felicia's screened porch.

"Miss Felicia," he called as he opened the door. He led them across a painted wood floor to a second screen door. "Miss Felicia," he called again.

"Don't slam that door, Ronnie," came a voice of indeterminate age from within.

"No, ma'am," Ronnie said. He turned back to Grace and Evangeline. The humor had returned to his face.

An old lady, Miss Felicia, Grace supposed, sat in a rocking chair before a window facing the screened porch and the driveway where they had met and talked with Ronnie Etienne. Grace supposed, also, that Miss Felicia had been watching them, had been waiting for them to come, and Ronnie would have had to explain who they were even if they had not come inside. The old lady turned her head sideways to them, as if she were listening to their arrival instead of watching, as if she didn't want to see them directly.

"Miss Felicia, I've brought some folks in to see you. They have come all the way from Los Angeles and Seattle, Washington. Their family may have once owned this land."

"Who was that?" Miss Felicia asked.

The old lady cocked her small head as if she were a bird listening intently to the ground for the stirring of worms. Even though it was warm in the room, warm and humid from the outside air, Miss Felicia wore a sweater over a long-sleeve blouse buttoned tightly around her neck. Ronnie Etienne nodded to Grace. It was now up to her to explain.

"Emile Etienne," Grace said.

"Emile?" Miss Felicia asked sharply. "Come closer so that I can see you better."

"Miss Felicia's eyesight is failing her," Ronnie said.

"I see all I want to see," Miss Felicia said. "More than I want, sometimes."

She extended a shaky hand toward Grace. The half dozen

steps to reach Miss Felicia were more than Grace wanted to cross by herself, and she took Evangeline's hand and pulled her along. The old lady's extended hand was warm and soft, and Miss Felicia directed her to a place in the sunlight beside her rocking chair. She turned away from them and looked at the two sisters with the peripheral vision that remained to her.

"I see now. What are your names?"

"I'm Grace Stevens, and this is my sister, Evangeline."

Miss Felicia released Grace's hand and studied the two women who stood in the light. She would not have seen them when they were outside talking to Ronnie.

"Did you two have the same mama and daddy?"

"Yes," Grace said.

"How come you're so much darker?"

It was a question that nobody asked out loud, but many surely wondered. Grace knew that the question was for her, but the peculiarity of Miss Felicia's vision made it seem as if the old lady's eyes were focused on Evangeline, and since she had long ago given up trying to answer that question even for herself, she turned to her sister for help.

"She just got lucky," Evangeline said.

Grace could hear the sound of heavy machinery. There was work proceeding outside, but inside Miss Felicia's house everything had stopped, except a mechanical clock somewhere in the room that ticked out seconds that never stopped. Then the old lady smiled, and Grace thought she heard a wheeze of laughter from deep within Miss Felicia's chest.

"How is Emile Etienne related to you?" Miss Felicia asked.

"We're not sure," Evangeline said. "We guess that he might have been our great-great-grandfather."

"Guess? Is that what we've come to? Guesses. Who is the oldest one you know? Of these Stevens, what is the oldest name you know something about?"

"We know that our great-grandfather was Richard

Stevens," Evangeline said, "and he lived for a time in Chicago."

"Ah, yes, Ricard," Miss Felicia said. "Ronnie, bring us all a glass of sherry. Girls, pull some chairs over here. Put them in the light so I can see you."

They gathered around Miss Felicia's rocking chair, Ronnie in shadow and the two sisters in the sunlight of the east window, with Miss Felicia looking into the void between them but seeing everyone.

"I'll tell you about Emile," she said.

Miss Felicia looked up and closed her eyes so that she didn't see to either side but somewhere back into the memory that held the last story of Emile Etienne. Evangeline pressed forward, leaning toward the old lady. Grace sat upright in her chair, holding the fragile crystal glass of sherry with both hands.

"Our people," Miss Felicia began—our and not my people, Grace understood her to say, "came from the island of Haiti in the early 1700s after the slave uprising. We were planters there, sugarcane just like now. Yes, for three hundred years and more we have planted the same crop, changing methods with the times, I suppose, but the same crop. We have either absolute persistence or a complete lack of imagination. We left Haiti with the French and came here and tried to live exactly as we had lived on that island. But we were not French, not purely French no matter how much we wanted or claimed to be. On that island the mixing of the blood began, but no matter how diluted it became the black blood controlled who we were until this boy's grandfather went north and found a woman who didn't understand this, or maybe didn't care, and their father did the same thing, only he didn't have to go quite as far north, and now these boys think that the black blood that's still there was a mistake not to be taken seriously, a mistake like the fling of a young man made so long ago that it's not worth mentioning. Isn't that right, Ronnie?"

"Ma'am?"

"But now you're here," Miss Felicia said, ignoring the question in Ronnie's reply and turning so that the blind and useless parts of her eyes faced the two sisters who sat in the sunshine, "and I'll tell you about Emile."

"But first tell me. Which one is light," Miss Felicia asked, "your mama or your daddy?"

Her question was one that only an innocent child would ask, if any child were innocent. It was a question that startled Grace like the one from her best friend when she was eight asking whether she was adopted or born. "I was born," Grace answered, not realizing that adopted children were also born. "My mom says you must be adopted," her friend told her. For weeks Grace had believed her friend, as if she had never heard the stories of her birth or seen the pictures with her mother in the hospital, as if all of that had been a lie and her friend's mother's offhand statement the truth. She accepted her friend's mother's version of her, and it helped her understand why her father laughed more at Evangeline's stories than hers and why her mother treated her with more kindness than she deserved. She was adopted and not born.

"Our mother is white," Grace said.

"Is she white or just light colored?"

"I guess she's white."

"I thought so," Miss Felicia said. "It happened back then, too. Every so often the dark child would come, and there would be a hush in the house as if the child or the mother had died, and there would be meetings late into the night, and sometimes the child would be taken from the mother and sent far away to live with black folks somewhere else. Think of that—every birth the mother looking first for the color of the child.

"Ronnie's brother's children won't come to visit me. They live a house away, and they don't come."

"Now, Miss Felicia, that's not true," Ronnie said.

"They won't come alone. They are not permitted to come alone. Their mother fears that they will leave here with stories about black babies. Now, that's true, Ronnie. You can't deny it."

"No, ma'am."

"I might just change my mind someday about selling this land," she said.

"You've already sold the land, Miss Felicia. We don't want to go back that way again."

"But not the house. I could give this house to these young women, and nobody could do anything to stop it."

"No, ma'am," Ronnie said. "You can do whatever you want with this house."

The old lady raised her head in triumph or vindication, and Grace felt the warmth of the sun as she froze within the sideways stare of Miss Felicia. Evangeline was less frozen than she, and she leaned toward Miss Felicia as she had done when she waited for Miss Felicia to begin the story.

"We didn't come here to cause trouble, Miss Felicia," Evangeline said.

"No, you came to learn about Emile Etienne. You want to know who he was."

"Yes, ma'am," Evangeline said. "That's why we came."

"I can tell you about him," Miss Felicia said. "Ronnie, will you pour us another glass of sherry? These young women have come a long way to hear this. Your shoes aren't muddy, are they?"

"No, ma'am. They're clean," Ronnie said, bringing the bottle of sherry from the dining room table.

"Ruth just cleaned the house yesterday."

"Yes, ma'am. I know she did."

"Tell Ruth that we have guests for lunch. I think we should eat here, don't you?"

"I think that's a good idea."

Ronnie tipped the bottle over the edge of the glass that Grace held out to him. Either the glass or the bottle was shaking, or both, and Ronnie took the glass from her. Miss Felicia supervised the service with her sideways vision and nodded her approval.

"What about your brother and father?" she asked.

"They're in Lafayette today," Ronnie said.

"They leave the farm to go to Lafayette in the middle of harvest?"

"It's only twenty-five miles away, Miss Felicia."

"But in the middle of the harvest?"

"We'll be cutting cane for three more months."

"Well, then, it will be just you and Ruth who will join us."

"And Maddy," Ronnie said.

"Yes, and Maddy," Miss Felicia said. "She's not old enough to understand these stories yet."

"She's as old as I was when you started telling them to me."

"And you didn't sneak away like your brother."

"No, ma'am. I stayed and listened."

"And you didn't go north to find a woman to marry either."

"No, Miss Felicia," Ronnie said. "Ruth lived just down the road—a mile east of here."

Ronnie smiled as he handed Grace the refreshed glass of sherry and winked at her as she took it from him. Something calmed her—the sherry or the signal from Ronnie or his large calloused hands that looked out of place holding the fragile glass. It calmed her to know that Ronnie had listened to Miss Felicia since he was a little boy and was listening now instead of excusing himself to return to the sugarcane fields. It calmed her to think of a little girl coming for lunch who wouldn't know and likely wouldn't care yet who the strange women were in Miss Felicia's house.

Miss Felicia rocked back in her chair and waited for all the glasses to be filled, including her own. She took a small sip of the sherry and lifted her head so that the tawny liquid slipped gently down her throat.

"We had our own society," Miss Felicia said. "You have to understand that first. It was simple and yet so very complicated. We called ourselves Creoles of color. We associated within our own kind, married our own kind, and buried ourselves in our cemeteries. Of course, this was before the war. Mostly. But some of it lasted long afterward. Some of it still exists, I suppose. No, it still exists.

"In Louisiana we could buy and sell property even before the war. Now, I'm talking about the war with the North, you understand. We could own businesses and prosper, but we couldn't vote and we couldn't send our children to school. Some, like the Lemelles, sent their children to France to be educated. That was acceptable, but they couldn't go to school here. We could be as white as the French and the Spanish, whiter even, but the history of the blood made the difference. Even so it was all very comfortable as long as everyone knew his place. We lived in this illusion of calmness, politeness, civility, and it worked as long as everyone accepted his place. If you understand that, I can tell you about Emile Etienne."

"We understand, Miss Felicia," Evangeline said.

Miss Felicia turned toward the voice, and Grace had the feeling that Miss Felicia could see into Evangeline's eyes, could see even deeper perhaps without the use of her eyes.

"I wonder if you do," Miss Felicia said. "I don't think I understand, not all of it, maybe not the important parts. Are you married, child?" she asked Evangeline, or at least it was still Evangeline who was the focus of her unseeing eyes.

"No," Evangeline said. "Not anymore."

"I'm glad I never married," Miss Felicia said. "When you

have children, one of them sits and listens and one sneaks away at the first opportunity. All that we learn or don't learn is for nothing, and the children, even those who listen, must start again. God has not planned this very well. Ruth told me that God might be a woman. I don't think so. If God were a woman, a mother, she would have planned this better.

"No, I'm glad I didn't marry. It's difficult enough for yourself to grow old and die, but then to add children is almost too much. And why would I need a husband to tell me what to do? There are plenty of other people who want to do that. And Ronnie is wrong about this land. I can take it back whenever I want. I have a clause in the deed that says I can buy the land back if I choose to do so. Paragraph Twelve. You haven't forgotten that paragraph, have you, Ronnie?"

"No, ma'am. I haven't forgotten."

"A man would never have gotten that paragraph in there, would he, Ronnie? He wouldn't have even thought about putting it in."

"It's unusual. That's certain, Miss Felicia."

"God should put in a paragraph like that." Miss Felicia said, "But then, he's not a woman. Oh, yes, I can tell you about Emile, but first you have to understand the woman, the slave girl he married. I can tell you about Emile, but you have to understand the slave girl first."

Chapter 25

H e rented his wife," Evangeline said.
   The sisters sat in the dark on the balcony above the front door of the hotel. Grace looked down the street toward the bridge that crossed the Bayou Teche, which they had crossed again upon their return some hours earlier. On the drive back to town they had exchanged few words. There had already been more words than either could absorb. In the dark, however, their conversation returned to the story Miss Felicia had told them.

"He bought her before the war was over when he could have waited another year and she would have gotten her freedom for nothing," Grace said.

"It wasn't certain yet who would win. It was likely, Miss Felicia said, but it wasn't certain."

"She could have run off with the Union troops earlier when most of the slaves did, but she didn't. That says something, too."

"I know," Evangeline said. "I know it says something. But he rented her first, and no matter what happened later, it doesn't change that."

"No, it doesn't. Whatever happened later doesn't change anything. What a day, sister."

Had it been just one day? In the morning they had a piece

of paper, two pieces of paper: copies of a land deed that Evangeline had found in the attic digging through old books and documents in their grandparents' chest when she should have been cleaning their parents' house. If Evangeline had helped as Grace had thought proper, the paper would still be in the attic. They would not be on the porch of the old hotel in St. Martinville trying to understand the story, trying to place themselves and their forebears, and those who would bear after, in the history they had heard that day.

Grace believed that she would never have come to this place herself. She would not have come only because of the football player. Nor would she have come only for the land deed. She had come because of the combination of the two searches for truth and because the girl had warned her on the University campus and had waited for her after church, waited with resignation, despair, and maybe even, before she knew who Grace was, with hope against all chance of hope. Grace had come to St. Martinville, believing they wouldn't find anything or anybody here. So far, she had been wrong about everything.

"Nobody even knows her name," Evangeline said.

A slave girl was all that Miss Felicia knew about her. Emile rented her to take care of his house, not hired but rented as he would an extra piece of land that he couldn't afford to buy and didn't own or didn't want to own. The money went back to her owners as a return on their investment. "We owned no slaves ourselves," Miss Felicia said, "although we could have and did when our people were in Haiti. The law allowed it just as it allowed us to own other property. We hired help for the fields, and sometimes we paid the Negro slaves directly if it was Sunday work, and sometimes we paid the owners for the labor, but we didn't own slaves ourselves as some of them did."

It was the word *we* that affected them, the two young women who sat beside Miss Felicia and listened to her story.

It wasn't a *we* they ever expected to join, but Miss Felicia included them with the word. While they were with her, there was no getting away from it. Grace doubted that they ever would.

Miss Felicia talked about the child who had come but not the getting of that child, and it was the getting that Grace was trying to understand. He was a male child with the French name Ricard. Richard was the name that had passed through Grandpa Joseph to Martin to them. Richard, their great-grandfather, son of Emile and the slave girl. One child was all that any of them knew about, but it seemed unlikely that there would be only one child. Even Jesus had brothers and sisters, Miss Felicia said, although he wouldn't have if God were a woman like Ruth said he was. Maybe the others were girls and nobody knew their names either.

"He must have loved her," Grace said, "or he wouldn't have gone into the fire after her."

"Maybe he went after the son."

"She had already thrown the baby through the window and was trying to get to the money that was hidden beneath the floorboards."

"He might not have known that," Evangeline said, "or maybe he went after the money, too."

"He carried her out of the house and got water from the well while the house burned. He poured the water over her to cool the burns on her skin while the house burned to the ground. That says something."

"I know it does, but he still rented her like a piece of property. She's the only innocent one. All these years we've heard that we were free people before the war, that it didn't take the war to free us, and somehow we were all proud of that as if we had something to do with it or if that freedom had something to do with us. But she wasn't free, and nobody even knows her name. She is the only one without blame."

So that was it. Her sister had come looking for innocence,

and the innocence she found had no name and was now so remote and diluted by guilt and blame that the whole story was
corrupted. Who could say that the slave girl herself was innocent? She could have left with the others when the Union
army retreated south, leaving the land and fields and houses
barren of black labor and blood. She could have left and
found freedom with the others instead of remaining shackled
to the house by love or whatever else it was that shackled her.

Her hands remained scarred after the fire. They knew that
even if they knew nothing else about her. The house burned
around her as she tried to get to the money beneath the floor.
One brother came to help, Miss Felicia said—her grandfather, Eduard, the only brother of five who came to help. He,
too, fetched water from the well and poured it over the slave
woman while the house burned to the ground. No one else
came.

A bird called out into the night from the row of cypress
and oak trees along the bayou. It was different than any call
Grace had ever heard, and she turned toward the call as if that
would help locate the bird or recognize its voice. Her eyes
were no more capable of seeing through the dark than Miss
Felicia's were at seeing anything directly in front of her.

She wasn't a slave by then, Miss Felicia said. Emile had
bought her by that time, and if he hadn't freed her, the war or
the amendment that followed the war would have freed her,
but she was no freer than when Emile had rented her. Maybe
she was. If she had not been free, she might have carried the
baby out the window herself instead of breaking the glass
and throwing him as far from the burning flames as she could
so that she could get to the money beneath the floorboards.
They needed the money to start again. She understood
money. Money was the medium of both bondage and freedom.

It wasn't that he rented the woman or that he slept with
her that bothered the family. It wasn't even that he fathered

the child because that happened often enough. It was because he wanted to keep the woman, to marry her, and had found a priest who performed the rite that nobody accepted as legitimate. For that reason only one brother had come to help when he saw the flames. None had come before that, shunning Emile and the black-skinned woman who was no longer a slave and who could no longer be explained without shame.

After the fire Emile sold the land to Eduard, Miss Felicia's grandfather, the one brother who had come to help. He sold the land and everything else that would not fit into a few cloth bags, and left the farm with the woman's hands still wrapped in bandages and still so tender that she could not hold the child to nurse. Emile had to hold the child to the mother's breast, Miss Felicia said—the baby, Ricard, who was black as coal.

That was the end as far as they knew, Miss Felicia said, because they never heard from Emile again, not even the brother, her grandfather, who had bought the land and animals and tools and whatever else they couldn't take with them. Her grandfather paid all he could, and it would have been more if Emile had agreed to a contract, but Emile wanted only cash as if he didn't want to have anything more to do with any of them. That was the end as far as they knew until the two sisters came and filled in, with their sparse knowledge, the migration to Chicago, to Omaha, to Seattle and Los Angeles, and finally back to the sugarcane fields in St. Martin Parish, Louisiana. So that was it, Grace thought. Evangeline would have to look somewhere else for innocence, if that was what she was seeking.

"Don't you wonder how that fire started?" Evangeline asked. "Miss Felicia said that Emile was driving the team of mules home when he saw the flames, and by the time he got there the house was all on fire. His woman, the wife with no name, was making his supper in the fireplace, and maybe a spark from the fireplace started the fire. If she used cypress wood for anything more than kindling, it could spit sparks out into the room. That's what Miss Felicia said. It must have been the story that was passed down. But how would anybody know what kind of wood she used? Wouldn't she know about cypress wood, this slave girl who tended Emile's house long before he ever married her? Maybe they made up the story after she was gone and couldn't defend herself, if she would dare defend herself anyway, or if any of them would listen."

"What are you saying?"

"I'm saying that I wonder how the fire started. I'm saying that one brother came and helped throw water on the woman, but nobody else came. Where were the others? Wouldn't they at least be curious about the fire? Wouldn't they at least come and watch it burn? And don't forget. Emile sold the farm after that and left. Was the fire the final straw? Was that when he realized that they would never accept him and his wife? Maybe he knew it was the beginning of a new level of rejection, of violence toward him and the woman, when shunning alone was no longer sufficient, because he had tolerated that. The shunning didn't start with the fire. It had already been going on. Maybe that's what he saw and the woman, too, and that's why she went after the money—so that they could leave. Anyway, they left after the fire and didn't want any more to do with any of them. And never did until we came. I wonder what Emile would think about us being here. I wonder what the woman would think, our great-great-grandmother."

"They kept the land deed, not the sale but the purchase. Why would they do that?"

"They?" Evangeline asked. "Did they keep it, or was it just him? What choice did she have? What choice did she ever have?"

"We came here looking for the wrong person," Grace said. "We had Emile's name on the paper, but we found her instead, our great-great-grandmother, even if we don't know her name. Miss Felicia said the girl was burned so badly that she couldn't hold her child to her breast. She pulled away the burning floorboards with her bare hands so that she could get to the money. It was her," Grace said. "Think about it. She threw the baby to safety first, far enough from the house that he would have a chance to survive, and then went back. The floor was already on fire. She got the money, but she got the land deed, too. Maybe that was what she was after. Maybe she didn't know that it was only a copy, that the original document was in the courthouse. Maybe she thought they would lose everything if she didn't get it. She was the one who kept it. After they left, even before they left, Emile wanted nothing more to do with these people or with this place, but she was the one who kept that piece of paper. Maybe she knew that someday you would find it."

The motion of their rocking chairs slowed and stopped, if not simultaneously, nearly so, and their movement was suspended as if the heavy moist air that provided life to the moss in the Evangeline Oak had finally pressed down upon them tightly enough to stop them. The bird call that neither had heard before and neither recognized continued along the bayou. It was hard to place, hard to mark its exact source or to even imagine the size and shape of the bird that produced it. It was a ghostly sound, now in front, now in back, surrounding them in the same way they felt the very air they breathed, the same way the memory of the slave girl haunted them.

Once again they lay together in the big four-poster bed. Although there was a sign posted on the balcony door reminding them to keep it closed, they had agreed to break the rules because neither wanted the false climate of the air conditioner. Through the open door came the call of the strange bird in the trees along the bayou and the warm, unbelievably moist air. They lay in the dark on the bed without even the sheet for cover.

"I want to go to the courthouse tomorrow morning before I go to Baton Rouge," Grace said. "I want to see if we can find her name."

"I do, too," Evangeline said.

"I won't have much time. I'm meeting with a detective in Baton Rouge in the morning."

"I know."

"You don't have to come with me. I can get another car."

"I know. Do you suppose Emile was as light-skinned as Ronnie is now or the little girl, Maddy? You can't see any trace of Africa in her, can you? It's all gone."

"I think he was more like Miss Felicia," Grace said, "with that faint gray or green stain that might be French or Spanish, or it might be something else, too. That's what I think he looked like, but the woman was all Africa."

"Yes, I believe she was," Evangeline said.

"This has been going on a long time, hasn't it?" Grace asked. "I mean I know it has, but I've never felt the time like this before. Hundreds of years that we know about. Maybe you've known all the time. Maybe that's what you were trying to tell me when we were girls. I knew then, too, but not like this. Maybe you did."

"No," Evangeline said. "Not like this."

"I wonder if Alice knows what this feels like. Somehow, I don't know why, but somehow she's a part of all this."

"You're going to follow him tomorrow night even if they won't help, aren't you?"

"I don't know," Grace said, staring at the shadows cast upon the ceiling from the street lamp outside. "He might not even leave the hotel. We're not sure that he does."

"But if he leaves, you're going to follow him."

"Yes."

She felt her sister turning in the bed and felt her sister's eyes looking at her, even though the most Evangeline could see would be some faint outline distorted by the dim glow of the light outside. Then she felt her sister's hand squeezing her arm, a hand that was even warmer than the moist night air that penetrated the room through the open door.

"He had better not try to hurt you," Evangeline whispered fiercely. There were centuries of memories in her voice.

Chapter 26

Mile after mile concrete pillars rose from the swamp and supported the elevated and divided freeways, one headed east and one west. Grace drove on the eastbound section toward Baton Rouge. Below the raised roadways the trees had been cleared away and had not yet returned, new channels were met by older cross channels. Twice there were enormous bridges that took them high above navigable waterways. The second bridge crossed the Atchafalaya River, with its distributary link to the Mississippi somewhere to the north. The Atchafalaya offered an alternative route to the sea, a shorter route; nevertheless, the river continued its ancient winding path to Baton Rouge, New Orleans, and finally the Gulf of Mexico.

The sisters had said little to each other since leaving the courthouse in St. Martinville. Grace was trying to assimilate what they had found there so that she could mentally move on to the appointment ahead. The concurrence of their historical investigation behind them with the police investigation that lay ahead was too much to reconcile with so little time. She knew she was heading eastward at sixty-five miles an hour, but her thoughts had not moved from the courthouse behind them. For this reason she had been quiet, as had Evangeline. Evangeline finally spoke after they crossed the second tall bridge on their way to Baton Rouge.

"She was the one who changed the name," Evangeline said. "It wasn't Emile or Richard like we thought."

That was true. It wasn't what they thought.

They had waited on the courthouse steps for the heavy doors to be unlocked at eight o'clock and were the first to enter the giant vault where the books of commercial conveyance stood side-by-side from the early days of the parish to the present. They had not been able to find documentation for the slave girl's purchase in records listed for Emile Etienne, their great-great-grandfather, and had resorted to looking through the transaction records one at a time. Grace chose to look forward through the book of documents that began in February 1865, and Evangeline looked backward from the preceding book. Evangeline found her—June 15, 1864.

"Her name is Rosalie," Evangeline had whispered at the sloping counter in the courthouse while pointing to the name. Not was, but is Rosalie, and not only Rosalie—*a certain slave named Rosalie, who calls herself Rosalie Stevens, a negro woman age about twenty-one years.*

"We found her, sister. She's not who we came looking for, but she's the one we found."

Her emancipation payment, in a combination of gold, Union dollars, and Confederate scrip, was worth more than Emile received for the land he sold to his brother, Eduard, four years later. They found the record for that, too.

Nothing, so far, had been as they thought. They had to continually adjust and reshape their story with each new revelation.

Rosalie. How that name haunted Grace. The memory of the school girl, Rosalie—the girl who had mocked Grace's mother on the playground—had appeared like a vision to Grace on the way to the same courthouse where they had gone to find the name of Emile Etienne but ended up finding the name of another. Perhaps it was a coincidence. Perhaps it was the spirit of the slave girl following them.

Just as the slave girl had named herself, she had purchased her own freedom with help from Emile who cosigned the note for the remaining debt, which was to be paid in French currency. The woman at the counter told them that it wasn't unusual for slaves to earn money for themselves, although most that she knew about were men. They would hire themselves out on Sundays and holidays, but normally it would take a long time to earn enough money to buy freedom. Maybe the war changed that, she said, like it changed everything else, like it changed the form of payment, which was most unusual. From the document it was clear that Rosalie had paid mostly in Union dollars.

"Maybe her emancipation document was the reason she went back into that burning house," Evangeline said. "Maybe she didn't trust that the war was over or that slavery wouldn't come back. Maybe she wanted that paper just in case."

"Maybe," Grace said. "I guess you won't change your name to Etienne now."

"No," Evangeline said. "I'll never change it. How about you?"

"I'll never change it."

"I wonder why we never heard about her," Evangeline said. "Grandpa Joseph always said that our people weren't slaves, but she was. I wonder why we never heard about that."

"I wonder," Grace said.

They drove through a terrain different from any Grace had ever seen or imagined. Although the main waterway, the Mississippi, veered southeast toward New Orleans, a tremendous amount of water seeped through the land directly south toward the Gulf. The rumor had been and maybe still was, Miss

Felicia said, that outlaws and men who hated the colored lived in the swamps beyond Catahoula. Few slaves had ever tried to escape there. Some did, however, and were never heard from again.

The freeway finally reached solid ground, and Grace looked ahead toward the giant suspension bridge that crossed the Mississippi. They had crossed it once already on their way from New Orleans to St. Martinville two days earlier, but that was a distant memory. Baton Rouge was just beyond the bridge: Baton Rouge and police work and the football team. It was coming too fast. She had not had enough time to put into perspective the story of the slave girl, but already the car was climbing toward the highest point of the bridge. In a moment they would begin to descend.

She felt as if she were on the Ferris wheel at the Seattle Center that she and Evangeline had ridden together as children. There was always that one moment, she remembered, when she didn't know what would happen next, when her mind knew but her senses told her something else. There was that one moment at the peak that made her stomach jump, the time and place where anything might happen no matter how many revolutions they made. They had sat apart then, just as now, she on one side of the Ferris wheel seat and Evangeline on the other—both pretending that they were not afraid. Grace wished she had taken Evangeline's hand before they reached the top. What might have happened with that one single act?

They began their descent on the bridge, and Grace spotted the solid wing of the exit that Evangeline told her to take. Evangeline had opened the Louisiana map and had placed her finger on the paper just as she had done on the emancipation document earlier that morning. Grace turned on her signal and slowed to make the turn. It had come too fast. The freeway over the swamp had not given her enough time to make the transition in her mind from the slave girl to the police investigation, which were so different but somehow inextricably linked.

"We follow the road along the river," Evangeline said. "That will take us downtown."

Evangeline navigated their route, turn after turn, until they arrived at the police building. Grace had expected it to be about the same as police headquarters in Seattle. She should have known better. Nothing had been the same since they arrived.

Anne Smith had warned Grace that the Baton Rouge Police Department wasn't exactly waiting for her with open arms. Without discussing specifics, without needing to, Evangeline agreed to wait by the car so as not to make Grace's appearance any more of a surprise than it probably would be. "It's the South," Anne had told her on the telephone, as if that were a code word that they could use to talk among themselves. It was like the number 220 from their blue incident card. "He's 220," they would say to each other to warn of a crazy person. They had no such code number for the South or for the North.

Her Seattle Police badge cleared the path to the Sex Crimes unit where a stocky detective in a white shirt led her to Detective Roman Beauregard, who was expecting her. She sensed that all those who watched had been expecting her—not her, perhaps, but a police officer from up North with a story about a football player who needed his ass pinned to the wall, as the stocky detective had described her mission.

Detective Roman Beauregard regarded her in silence for a moment, not with hostility and not with warmth but with the impenetrable police expression that she knew well enough to return. She wished, although she knew there was little room between them for wishing, they could dispense with the sizing up and the staring down. She wished she could tell him about Evangeline who was waiting for her down by the car. She wished she could tell Beauregard about the girl back in

Seattle in such a way that he would understand why she had come. She even wished she could tell Beauregard about the burned hands of her great-great-grandmother just across the Atchafalaya Basin. He looked like a man who might listen to such stories. He didn't have a hard face despite an expression that gave nothing away. He reminded her a little of her old partner, Wes Mickelsen, and he reminded her a little of Ronnie Etienne.

Beauregard rose from his desk and extended his hand. She took it.

"Beauregard," he said.

"Stevens."

His hand was gone much too fast.

"Sit down." He gestured to a padded steel chair on the opposite side of his desk.

Grace removed her badge case, opened it, and placed it on Detective Beauregard's desk so that he could read it from there or pick it up and examine it if he chose. He looked at it, folded the leather wallet back together without saying anything, and pushed it across the desk a foot closer to her.

"You-all must have more money than you know what to do with if you can follow this boy of yours all the way down here."

Detective Beauregard was a strongly built man softening around his midsection as he entered what she thought must be his mid-forties. He had the skin coloring of Miss Felicia, but Grace refrained from asking about that. She doubted that it would be a helpful question. Besides, she had his question to answer although he hadn't actually asked one. It was a comment that could lead in several directions.

"I imagine Detective Smith explained to you why I'm here," she said as she stuck the badge case back into the rear pocket of her khaki pants.

"You might say that," he replied. "She said you have this football player who doesn't like to stay home at night, but you don't know for sure what he's doing, or at least you don't have anybody who will stand up and testify about it. It's a long way to come just for that. Who is this guy anyway?"

Beauregard pushed a game program over to her. On the cover was a girl in a skin-tight golden body suit. She had long golden hair that matched the gold letters on the cover spelling out LSU'S GOLDEN GIRLS.

"It's hot off the press," he said.

"I see that," Grace said. "Detective Smith probably told you that we don't want to mention his name just yet. I'm sure you understand. If we can't get the victims to testify, or if somehow we make a mistake and this gets out, none of us are going to look very good."

"That's about what Detective Smith told us, but we're glad you said it, too, because that's just what we're thinking down here," Beauregard said. "My lieutenant wants you to call up your coach and tell him to keep his boys in the hotel. We don't want any of our girls assaulted, although I hear he's probably conducting most of his extra activity in those areas of town where the girls don't ever talk to us much anyway. I guess we can understand that. So you call the coach, or we can do it for you, because we don't want any interference with this game. Your coach is a good Christian man, as I understand, and he will take the appropriate measures to avoid any problems.

"We plan on whipping you-all anyway. Come the fourth quarter your boys are going to start wilting. They won't be able to breathe and they're going to lose all their fight, and we're going to whip you-all then. We don't want your people claiming that we didn't do it fair and square. Besides all that, your team comes down here with all the newspaper reporters from up North, and if we arrest one of your players, it might turn into some big racial incident for all we know, and we're not going to have that. That's all. We're not going to let that happen."

Grace listened to Detective Beauregard and gradually began to understand what he was saying. Sometimes, she thought, we forget to ask the first question first, the simplest question, or else we can't ask it the way Miss Felicia could. People expect cops to know everything and to have experienced everything so that nothing is ever new, and sometimes, Grace thought, we believe it ourselves and forget to ask the simplest question first. Maybe it wasn't a simple question. Maybe the words were simple, but the question was part of those hundred and more years since Emile Etienne left the burned-out house with his wife whose name they hadn't known. Emile intended to never return, although his wife had kept the land deed that brought Grace and Evangeline back. That was becoming clearer to them all the time. It was the slave girl who had kept the paper.

Detective Roman Beauregard waited for her to agree or not, but she did neither. She thought instead about the simplest question, the one that he had not yet asked because maybe it wasn't a simple question to him. Or maybe he thought he knew the answer like they always were supposed to know, even when they didn't.

"You probably don't like what I just said," Beauregard said. "I can't blame you. Maybe if it was up to me we could at least watch and see what happened, but it's not up to me. It's way beyond me. You know how that works. The lieutenant has to think about what he'll read in the newspaper, while you and I might not care about that. If it was up to me, I'd help you all I could. I know you don't trust me enough to even tell me his name, but I'd still help if I could."

She knew she could remain silent even longer, and he would probably go on talking. She was tempted to remain silent.

"You think he's a black player, don't you?" she asked. "Maybe there was something that Detective Smith said that made you think that, or maybe it was me." Or maybe it was something hidden way back in the swamp somewhere east of Catahoula or farther back, but Grace didn't mention that.

Beauregard's impenetrable mask cracked a little, and she watched an eyebrow rise. The movement was barely perceptible as he stared at her from within his own newfound silence.

Grace knew that she might begin to talk, too, so that Detective Beauregard would not think that she was judging him by any different standard than he would judge himself. There was a great temptation to bridge the space between them with words. It would take a lot of words.

"He's not," she said. "At least as far as we know. Since coming here, I've learned that we don't always know these things for certain."

Beauregard smiled faintly, re-forming his composure with the practice of a dozen years and probably more as a cop. Her old partner could do that. Katherine's face was still an expression of herself, but Wes Mickelsen could recover with the best of them.

"Is this fellow any good?" Beauregard asked.

"He's one of the best players on the team."

"And you think we've got a chance to do some good police work here?"

"We've got a chance."

"Well, why didn't you tell us he was white? Nobody can accuse us of anything for going after a white player. You wait here," he said. He stood up behind his desk and tightened the loose tie around his neck. "This might take a little time."

Evangeline was outside the car, pacing the sidewalk from Cajun Bonding in the middle of the block to Wilshire Associates, Attorneys at Law, at the corner. Grace caught up with her just as she turned to retrace her steps to the bonding company.

"I thought I was going to have to come in and find you," Evangeline said. "What took so long?"

Drops of perspiration had gathered in a perfect row on Evangeline's forehead beneath her tightly braided hair. For the first time Grace recognized what was different this time about Evangeline. Evangeline continually experimented with her hair, so that was not unusual. What was different this time was that Evangeline had always worn her hair so that it covered the freckles on her forehead no matter how long or short her hair might be.

Grace placed her fingers on Evangeline's forehead. "Warm," she said.

"Hot," Evangeline said. "What happened in there?"

"Like everything else on this trip, it's been an education."

Chapter 27

Grace and Evangeline waited for Bobby Flowers in the rear courtyard of a restaurant two blocks from the hotel where the football team was staying. Evangeline fanned herself with the program Grace had brought from Detective Beauregard's desk. The golden girl flapped upside down in the breeze. Grace felt something cool and moist on her foot, and she looked beneath the table to see what it was. Condensation from her tall glass of sweet iced tea had dropped through the grillwork of the outdoor table.

The tea was so sweet that Grace wondered how the sugar remained dissolved within the liquid. It surely had reached the saturation point. At least she knew where one row of sugarcane had gone. She couldn't decide whether she liked the sweet tea or not, whether the taste was pleasant or overwhelming.

"He's bringing you a gun?" Evangeline asked.

"A gun and a police commission," Grace said. "I'll officially be a Baton Rouge police officer tonight."

"I don't know if I like this," Evangeline said.

"Stop worrying. Nothing ever happens with these things. We make a bunch of plans and pretend that we're going to do something and nothing happens."

"That's not true."

"It's true most of the time."

"I don't see why he can't make me a police officer, too, and take me along if there's no more to it than that." Evangeline smiled, showing that she wasn't serious. "But don't you worry. I'll keep Bobby Flowers company while you're working. Tell me more about him. Is he as handsome as he is in the pictures?"

"I wouldn't know. I've never seen a picture of him."

"Never? You've never seen a picture of Bobby Flowers? Come on, you must have peeked in the paper just once when you were in school. Rose Bowl? Your second year in college? You must have seen one little picture of him."

"If I did I don't remember."

"Grace, girl, I wonder about you sometimes. You spend too much time looking at old bones. You should look at some young ones now and then. Someplace other than church."

Evangeline took a sip of sweet tea through the candy-striped straw. Grace had never confided in Evangeline where or when she had looked for young bones, as Evangeline called them, and Evangeline had never told her much either, only enough to know that there had never been a shortage of them. Grace could see why. Although the temperature must be ninety degrees, Evangeline looked as fresh in her light summer dress as she would if she had just gotten out of the shower. Evangeline had seen the dress in the window of the department store next to their hotel and had bought it off the rack. It was on sale and fit her perfectly. The freckles on her bare arms matched those on her forehead. Grace could try on a hundred dresses and not one would fit the way this dress fit Evangeline. That wasn't true. She would give up long before reaching the hundredth dress.

Grace saw Bobby Flowers at the courtyard entrance talking to the hostess, then giving her his picture-perfect smile as he came to their table. He pulled out the chair between them and introduced himself to Evangeline without any help from

Grace. Grace expected that he would prolong the conversation, which would allow him to look longer at Evangeline, or that Evangeline would—she was good at that. She was good at finding summer dresses and lingering a moment in conversation with someone worth lingering with. Bobby Flowers turned to Grace, who had never acquired the talent to linger, and gave her a slip of paper with decipherable but hastily written numbers and letters.

"This is his license number," he said. "It's a white Lincoln Continental. The old man travels in style."

Grace leaned forward in her chair and picked up the scrap of paper, which was the remnant of an airline ticket.

"How did you get this so soon?"

Bobby Flowers smiled and delayed his answer an extra moment with obvious pleasure.

"He gave me a ride over here from our hotel."

"What?"

"That's right. Mr. Renzlau gave me a ride. He's thinking this is a big weekend for his boy, and he's hoping we write something special that the wires will pick up. The game is televised here and on the West Coast, but not on the East Coast. Mr. Renzlau is hoping that we fill in the gaps."

"He said that?"

"No. He's way too slick to do that, but that's what he meant. He told me that his boy was watching film of me to improve his defensive reads, and he was learning more all the time. His boy's not learning anything from me, but that's how they work, you see. They're smart, too smart this time. I told him I was heading over here to talk to some local reporters, and he offered me a ride. The man is just trying to be helpful. If there's anything else I need, all I have to do is ask."

"Ask him why his son carries a rope around with him in the car. Ask him—" She stopped abruptly, but she had said enough to remove all the pleasure from Bobby Flowers's eyes. Her words were a rebuke to him as much as they were to Renzlau's father. It wouldn't have hurt anybody to let him have a moment of pride in his detective work.

"I'm sorry. I didn't mean to pop off like that."

"No. You were right," Bobby Flowers said. "I was thinking too much about the story and not enough about what Renzlau might have done to that girl if he had gotten a chance to use the rope. I'm sorry."

"No, I'm sorry," Grace said. "It just popped out. I'm thinking about this way too much."

"Come on, you guys. Everybody is sorry. Let's move on."

Grace looked across the table at Evangeline. She had almost forgotten that Evangeline was there. She had forgotten, if only for a moment, and so had Bobby Flowers. It was funny, Grace decided. Nobody ever forgot about Evangeline.

Chapter 28

A rock band played somewhere, and discordant chords floated through the open windows of their unmarked police car, a car so intentionally plain and nondescript that it would draw no attention except to those who knew what to look for. Grace hoped Renzlau wasn't one who knew. Detective Beauregard chewed on the tapered end of a long cigar but didn't light it.

"Lights are going out," he said.

Flowers told her that most of the team was staying on the fifth floor of the hotel with a few on the fourth, including all the coaches. Already several of the rooms on the fifth floor had gone dark. They watched specifically a room toward the west end of the fifth floor.

"There," Beauregard said, pointing with his unlit cigar toward the darkness that had just replaced the glow behind the curtains of the third to the last room. "Now we wait."

They had already been waiting for a half hour behind a travel trailer with a Washington license plate at the far edge of the hotel parking lot. As far as they could tell, no one was in the trailer.

From their vantage point they could see the upper floors of the hotel and the hood of the white Lincoln Continental but not the front door of the hotel or any other door. They weren't sure he would leave, and if he left, they weren't sure he would take his father's rental car. But it was as good as any guess. What else would he take? Flowers had learned from the father that Renzlau didn't go to his parents' room as Johnson had suggested. "Oh, no," the father said, "he never leaves the team."

Flowers had also provided her with the team schedule that she had given to Detective Beauregard on the telephone. The team meal was at six. After eating, the team would be driven to the stadium in two buses and would work out for an hour in sweat clothes to become accustomed to the artificial turf— no contact, no full-speed running, just an hour of easy work to get acquainted with the stadium and to keep their minds on the game. They would return to the hotel at nine thirty, with lights out at eleven.

It was eleven thirty when the last light went out on the fifth floor. There were still lights burning on the floor below. Grace had yet to recognize a single song from the rock band.

"Jesus, those guys are terrible," Beauregard said. They had been blasted by a loud finale, and there was silence at last.

Grace knew that Bobby Flowers and Evangeline could hear the music, too. They were in the parking lot or some-where nearby or within a block of it, listening to the same music and watching the same lights go out. She had been waiting for the right moment to tell Beauregard about them.

Without Flowers she might not have found the girl in Seattle or talked to the fullback. She might not have gotten the license number of the father's car or the schedule or the location of the room. Without the information Flowers had given her, she and Beauregard would not be waiting in the parking lot watching the lights go out in the third room to the end on the fifth floor.

Flowers was waiting with Evangeline to follow the story that he was eager to write, but he didn't even begin to know half of it. Just as she and Evangeline had found someone they didn't expect in their search for a name and a piece of land, Flowers might find something much different from the story he expected. The deal between Flowers and her, spoken and unspoken, was that Flowers could follow the investigation as long as he didn't get in the way. What he would find was up to him. She would have to explain all of that to Beauregard as soon as the right moment came along.

In the silence after the last song, Beauregard turned down the volume on the police radio. This might be the time, she decided. She looked around the lot to see if she could spot Flowers's rental car. She told Bobby Flowers that Beauregard would almost certainly not appreciate his and Evangeline's company, but nobody could do anything about it if his car couldn't be found. What was the color anyway? Was it blue or a shade of aquamarine?

"Aw, shit," Beauregard said as the band started up again. Rather than turning up the volume on their police radio so that they could hear it above the music, he turned it off in disgust. "They play the same music up where you live?"

"I haven't been able to figure out what they're playing."

"It's not country, I can tell you that. I hear it rains a lot up there."

"I thought so until I came down here. I'm not sure how you tell whether it's raining or not. It feels like it's raining all the time."

"When it comes, you can tell," Detective Beauregard said. "Don't worry about that."

She wasn't worried about rain. Jerome Johnson wasn't sure what time Renzlau left the room, but his activity in Seattle, what they knew about, had always taken place late at night. It might be another two or three hours before he left his room, if he left at all. What could she and Beauregard talk about for three hours? Rain?

"Detective Smith said you might have some family around here that you were looking for."

More like ghosts, Grace thought. It was no wonder that the air felt so heavy, that even breathing was an effort. The ghosts hovered in the air, waiting for discovery or hiding from it.

"My sister found a land deed in my father's papers in Seattle. My great-great-grandfather bought land in St. Martin Parish in 1858."

"Before the war," Beauregard said. "That's not so unusual. There were a number of free blacks around here who owned land."

"They were colored people," Grace said. "That's what they called themselves—free people of color. My sister and I didn't know about all the possible variations of that word."

"Did you find any of these people?"

"We did."

"Were they glad to see you?"

"Those we met seemed pleased enough."

"And those you didn't meet?"

"They weren't eager to see us."

Beauregard chuckled through the cigar clenched in his teeth.

"Welcome to Louisiana."

"It's more complicated than I thought."

"I'll bet it is. Oh, yeah, I'll bet it is. Now you take Ellis you for example."

"Who?" Grace asked.

"The school. The place where you-all are all playing tomorrow."

"Right," Grace said. "LSU."

"Now you got it. Who do you think the first president of the school might be? I'll tell you because you'll never guess. William Tecumseh Sherman. That's right. The Yankee general who destroyed the South. He was the first president of

LSU. He resigned when the war started and went up North to reenlist. You won't find any buildings on the campus named after him, but there's one or two for General Beauregard. I guess he's some family of ours and my daddy has it all figured out, but don't ask me why. Sherman knew how to wage war, but near as I can tell, Beauregard was a political hack who didn't know a division from a platoon, but there's a building over there with his name on it. Now I can understand why there's not a Sherman Building, but why they have one for Beauregard strains the imagination.

"We've got a detective in our unit who won't carry a five-dollar bill," Beauregard said, "and when a clerk gives him change, he'll tell the clerk to keep the pennies. He doesn't want them."

"Lincoln," Grace said.

"You got it."

"Does he tell the clerk to keep the five-dollar bill, too?"

"No. He gets Washington dollar bills instead."

"The war has been over a long time."

"Maybe, maybe not. The South would have freed the slaves on its own. The writing was on the wall for that. It was a dying system before the war ever started. Twenty years ago there wasn't a black player on the football team, but we finally got tired of getting our asses whipped. It took a while, but we have as many black players now as you do."

"It seems to me it took a long while."

"I'll bet it does. Are you going to tell me that everything is perfect up where you live?"

"No," Grace said. "I'm not going to tell you that. Do you think it's going to rain tonight or not?"

"There's a good chance," Beauregard said. "There's always a chance."

Beauregard turned the police radio back on. The police calls weren't much different than what she would have heard had she been in Seattle. The dialects were different and so were the codes, but the problems were the same. Fear, anger, greed. Hunger, thirst, revenge. Predators, abettors, prey. Cruelty, misunderstanding, hopelessness. And every now and then, out of the heavy, pressing, rain-promising air, a hint of goodwill, a gesture of kindness, a ray of hope.

The band finally gave up disturbing the peace, the radio became quieter, and Beauregard threw his wasted cigar out the window onto the asphalt of the parking lot. He rubbed his face with his hands, and she heard the scratch of new whisker stubble over the sound of his weary sigh. There was a flash of light.

"Did you see that?" Grace asked.

"What?" Beauregard asked.

"The dome light of the Lincoln. He's in the car."

"Jesus, I missed it." He sat upright behind the steering wheel and peered across the illuminated parking lot toward the Lincoln Continental.

There was no way to miss it leaving. No other car was moving in the lot. None had for the last hour. Beauregard didn't start his car until the Lincoln entered the adjacent street, and he left the headlights off until the Lincoln turned and disappeared from sight. Then he sped up to the end of the block, braking sharply before the corner in order to make a turn that would seem normal to anyone looking in the Lincoln's rearview mirror. Grace looked over her shoulder and saw the green rental car make the same turn. Beauregard saw it, too, in the rearview mirror.

"It's my sister and the reporter," Grace said. "I told them to stay back, to keep out of the way."

"You're damn right they're going to stay out of the way. You should have told me they were planning on following us."

"I should have. I wanted them to stay at the hotel, but my sister never listens to me."

"I'll get her to listen." He picked up the microphone and began looking for a street sign.

"The football player is Paul Renzlau," Grace said. "He's turning again."

"Jesus," Beauregard said, glancing toward her before speeding up as the taillights of the Lincoln disappeared around the corner. "The guy is an all-American."

"I told you he was one of our best players."

"I know, but I was thinking it might be a linebacker or one of those big fellas in the offensive line. Renzlau. Holy shit. This might be more complicated than I thought."

He still had the microphone poised in his hand, but Renzlau had entered a freeway on-ramp and was gathering speed. Beauregard looked at her one more time and slammed the microphone back into its holder.

"Keep your eyes on that car," he said. "I don't want to lose him now."

"I'm watching."

After a few miles Renzlau signaled and left the freeway. Grace sneaked a look behind them and saw the green car still following.

Streets passed in a blur. Her focus remained on the big white car ahead of them. Sometimes Beauregard moved closer to it; sometimes he eased away and hid behind other cars. She knew he had to do it, a risk he had to take, but more than once they got stuck behind a car in a single lane of traffic and fell dangerously far behind.

She saw a traffic light changing to yellow. The Lincoln passed through before it turned red, but there was no chance for them. She heard Beauregard swearing to himself as he pulled over to the parking lane and turned off his lights. He turned right at the intersection and made a fast U-turn in the middle of the street ahead of a delivery truck approaching much too fast on the passenger's side of the car. She held on to the door and swore to herself as Beauregard turned once more onto the trail of the Lincoln Continental.

"Where are we?" Grace asked.

"Catfish Town," Beauregard said. "That boy of yours is sniffing around like an old hound dog. Just keep on going, Paul boy. Just keep on going."

They came to a dimly lit neighborhood of small houses and abandoned cars. On a corner, before a lighted doorway, a group of men and boys, all black, watched them pass. They faded into the shadows as soon as they recognized the unmarked police car. There were more lights ahead and music that oozed through the doorways like Miss Peggy's thick syrup, insinuating itself into the rhythm of the street and the groups of hangers-on. Beauregard turned off his lights and coasted to the edge of the narrow street as the brake lights of the Continental announced a stop. The Continental moved forward again, creeping as slowly as the car a half block behind it.

"He's found him something," Beauregard said.

A single woman walked into the street. She remained there a moment even after the Lincoln departed. Then she moved back out of their view into a secluded spot where little light reached her. When Beauregard arrived at the spot where the Continental had slowed, the woman took one step toward them before realizing her mistake and turning away. Grace heard a short whistle behind her, and she turned to look. There was no clear source for the noise. It originated from and evaporated into the pressing night air.

Grace pushed back her unneeded jacket to touch the .38-caliber revolver that Beauregard had loaned her. The gun rode high in its holster and pressed against her side. She looked over her shoulder to see if she could spot a green car behind them. There were cars, but she couldn't make out any color or any shape, and none that seemed to be following.

Maybe they had lost Bobby and Evangeline. If so, she hoped that they had lost them before they got this far.

"I'm glad we're fooling him," Beauregard said, "because we ain't fooling anybody else."

Farther ahead another woman entered the street. Again the Continental stopped before moving on.

"Picky bastard, isn't he?"

Grace saw that the way was clearing in front of them. Some word, some signal, the whistle perhaps, was traveling faster than they, and men and boys went into the bars and the women disappeared from the street. If whatever signal, whatever communication caught up with the Continental now almost a full block ahead, their night would be over.

Brake lights again, and this time the car did not move on. The black woman who walked to Renzlau's window bent low to peer into the car and then straightened to look up and down on the street. No signal reached her, no communication except that from inside the car, which was sufficiently compelling to make her walk before the illumination of the headlights around to the passenger's side. The dome light came on for an instant and disappeared as did the red glow of the brake lights.

"Bingo," Beauregard said.

The Lincoln cautiously moved away from the Friday night street of blues and laughter and turned onto another less populated with curious strollers. They passed a brightly lit all-night laundry with condensation so thick on the windows that she couldn't see inside. They passed a gas station and a pawn shop, and the Lincoln continued its course another block. Suddenly, there was a change in speed as the Lincoln braked sharply and turned.

"I got to keep going," Beauregard said. "He might be dumb, but I'll bet she isn't. Don't lose them now."

Beauregard did not slow down as they passed the driveway the Lincoln had entered. Grace saw an unlit painted sign advertising rooms for rent, and there was a row of tiny cottages in a semicircle around an unpaved drive. Beauregard took his foot off the gas but didn't brake. He looked in the rearview mirror. Grace turned completely around in the seat. She saw a car behind them, but it wasn't the white Lincoln. As the car passed beneath a streetlight she thought she saw a tint of green.

"Is he coming out?" Beauregard asked.

"Not yet.

"I'll turn around up here. Keep an eye on that place as long as you can."

Grace kept both eyes on the driveway until Beauregard turned right at the next corner. The street wasn't wide enough to make a U-turn. He swerved sharply toward a dirt ditch and backed up so quickly that his back tires squealed on the narrow strip of asphalt that composed the street. He turned off his lights and headed back toward the street they had left. A green car passed slowly in front of them, and Grace could see Evangeline's silhouette in the window.

"That your sister?" Beauregard asked. He was looking toward the driveway and not at the green car that continued down the street.

"It is."

"They better not jinx us now."

"They kept going."

"What kind of car is that down there? Does it look like a Lincoln to you?"

Grace leaned forward so that she could see past Beauregard. The taillights of a car were moving away from them far down the street.

"I'm not sure."

"Me neither."

Beauregard turned on his headlights and entered the street.

"When we drive by where he turned in, look and see if his car is there. If not we'll go after that one up there."

Ahead of them the car was turning. She didn't think Renzlau could have turned around quickly enough in the driveway to get back onto the street ahead of them, but he might have. He had been successfully getting away from them for some time, for years maybe. Who could say how quickly he could turn around?

Beauregard raced down the block, slowing only when the driveway was near. The Lincoln wasn't there. There was an old pickup truck and a black car beside it, but otherwise the half-circle drive was empty.

"Shit," Beauregard hissed.

Grace turned in her seat as Beauregard accelerated. She saw a gleam of white at the far left curve of the semicircle.

"I see it," she said, but by then she could not.

"What?" Beauregard asked, his voice sharp even though he turned the question away from her and looked back toward the driveway.

"I saw the car."

"Are you sure?" he asked. In his voice was the disbelief of someone used to following his own observations and nobody else's.

"Turn around," Grace said. "He's back there."

Beauregard swerved into the next driveway and quickly turned around again. He stopped with the front of the car not quite in the street. Grace looked back toward where she had seen the gleam of white metal. The other car they had been following would now be long gone.

"I hope that's what I saw," she said. "It was almost hidden by the last cottage."

"We'll leave the car here," he said.

He looked over his shoulder and backed up until he was well off the street. They got out together. From the car seat he picked up a little plastic flashlight that didn't look power-

ful enough to see itself. She should have brought her own.
Even during the day she carried a flashlight that was bright
enough to blind any hard-drinking fisherman on Ballard
Avenue.

They walked back toward the cottages. Cottage was a
generous description for such decrepit buildings. They were
more like abandoned shacks that had once been a motel or
auto court of some sort, but that had been a long time ago. In
the yard behind the first cottage was a refrigerator dumped
on its side and reflecting white from the streetlight across the
street. The reflection gave her a frigid chill although this was
not the white paint she had seen. That flash of white was farther on, behind the cottages that formed the opposite curve of
the semicircle.

There, she said to herself with great relief—the white reflection from the curved trunk of the car in the space between
two of the cottages. She put her hand on Beauregard's arm,
but she didn't need to. He saw the car, too. They huddled beside the first cottage they came to. It had shattered windows
facing the street; the glass was on the ground at their feet.

"You want me to bring in some backup?" Beauregard
asked.

"That's up to you," Grace said, "but I wouldn't mind holding off until we get up next to the building so that we can hear
if she's in any trouble. I don't see back doors to any of these
places."

"Me neither. That boy of yours must be hard up or one
sick bastard to go into a place like that."

"He's not the one I'm worried about."

"Understood," Beauregard said. "You make the call.
When you want to go in, we go. Too early and we got a
whore turning a trick. Too late . . . Well, you know your boy
better than me."

Grace wasn't sure that she knew anything. Somewhere,
somehow, sometime this story had gotten away from her. She

hadn't thought it through to this point: outside a run-down, desolated, used-up shack, listening through walls and glass and playing god with another woman's torment. How much should she endure, not herself but the woman inside the shack, so that someone else would not have to endure the same? Was that what God did—listen outside the walls and decide when enough was enough?

She should have known that this was where she would end up when she first got on the airplane with the ticket Evangeline had given her. This is not what we do, she thought. This is not what cops are supposed to do. We stumble into problems and react, or people call us, cry for us, scream for us, and we go in and put an end to it. Or we assemble the pieces, construct a story from the fragments we're given, and say that's justice. We don't stand outside and listen, waiting for enough cruelty to do something but not so much that we won't be able to look at ourselves in the mirror and wonder what we've become.

To Beauregard it was the whore and the sick bastard inside the shack. Is that how God could stand and listen, saying to himself that it was a whore and nothing more? Miss Felicia was right. God wasn't a woman after all, because it wasn't a whore Grace imagined. It was the girl back in Seattle, whose eyes drifted off into some other world that she couldn't believe she had seen and yet believed she would never see anything else. Maybe the woman inside went all the way back to the rented slave girl who, until today—no, yesterday—had been without a name. Was it really only yesterday? Miss Felicia was right. God was not a woman.

Grace pressed her ear close to the window glass that was covered within by an ancient but heavy curtain and tried to understand the voices inside. She could hear sounds but nothing clearly. It sounded like a radio being played in the last room of a long corridor with words bouncing from wall to wall and only a few faint echoes reaching listeners at the end of the hallway. It was a radio, she decided, played low to cover the voices and sounds she needed to hear to make a choice. She closed her eyes so that she would not see Beauregard looking at her from where he stood at the other side of the window, to close out the past as well, to listen only for the woman inside.

Grace heard a cry rise above the background noise. The cry was cut off before it reached full voice, then came a thud she felt against the outside wall. She opened her eyes. Whether it was the right time or not, she couldn't wait any longer.

"Let's go," she told Beauregard and pulled out her gun as she scrambled past him to the door.

She tried the doorknob, but it remained frozen in her grasp. She took a step back, made sure that Beauregard was with her, and kicked in the door with the heel of her foot.

"Police!" she shouted as she blocked the ricocheting door with her shoulder.

Renzlau had the woman pinned against the wall with both hands on her throat. His hands seemed unable to move even as he stared at the gun that Grace kept in front of her as she approached. The woman was the one who moved, who broke from his grasp and stumbled away. She backed away from Renzlau, from Grace, from all of them.

"Turn around," she told Renzlau. "Put your hands on the wall."

He seemed to have a vague recognition of her but nothing more. He reluctantly turned around but didn't place his hands on the wall.

"Baton Rouge Police," Beauregard said, stepping ahead of Grace. "You're under arrest, son. Put your hands on the wall like the officer said."

Renzlau put his hands on the wall. Beauregard pulled them away, one at a time, and placed handcuffs on them. When Renzlau was safely restrained, Grace turned toward the woman who was still clutching her throat. She was still trying to remove the hands that wouldn't let her breathe even though the hands were now handcuffed behind Renzlau's back. She gasped for air, opening her mouth and grabbing air in gulps. Grace holstered her revolver, removed her Seattle badge from her back pocket, and raised it so that the woman would see it as she approached.

"Police officer," she said. "You're safe now. You're safe."

The woman didn't believe her, or if she did, was still afraid. She backed away until her back was against the wall. When it became clear that she could go no farther, she looked for an escape past Renzlau and Grace and Beauregard. There wasn't one.

Grace took a quick look over her shoulder and saw her sister in the doorway. She had forgotten about Evangeline and Flowers. She raised her hand to Evangeline, telling her to stay where she was, and slowly moved the hand toward the frightened woman.

She could hear Renzlau talking, telling Beauregard how the woman had tried to steal his money. She heard him adding detail after detail to his story and Beauregard telling him that he might want to hold off talking until he could read him his legal rights. Renzlau had a story that would make all that unnecessary, and he kept on with the story until something made him stop in mid-sentence. Grace looked back again and saw Bobby Flowers standing behind Evangeline.

"You-all just want to stay back now," Beauregard told them. "I'm taking this fella out to the car. You gonna be all right there, Officer Stevens?"

"I'll be all right," she said.

"I'll get us another car to take him to the station."

Recognition crept into Renzlau's eyes. Maybe it was even fear. If so it was a new experience for him. Evangeline and Flowers stepped out of the way as Beauregard led Renzlau past them. Before going out the door Renzlau looked back at her to make sure that he wasn't mistaken. There was no mistake.

"What's your name?" Grace asked the woman.

With Renzlau out of the room the young woman was able to get her breath. She eased away from the wall and looked suspiciously at Evangeline and Flowers who remained close to the door.

"Who those people?" she asked.

"They're with me," Grace said without looking away from the young woman. "We followed this man all the way from Seattle, Washington. I'm a police officer there. He's hurt women there, too."

"He hurt people there, why don't you do something instead of letting him come down here and bother us?"

"We didn't have enough proof to stop him. He was going to hurt you a lot worse. He was just getting started."

"He wasn't starting nothing with me."

"Let's sit down," Grace said. "We'll help you with this."

"I ain't sitting anywhere. I want to leave. You gonna stop me?"

"Yes. I'll stop you. Do you have any identification?"

"They all know me here. What do I want with identification?"

"I don't know who you are. What's your name?"

The young woman looked at Grace as if to size her up. Grace stood still for the sizing and didn't try to pretend that she was anybody else except the one who was blocking the exit. The young woman was not large. With his hands around her neck Renzlau had been able to lift her off the floor.

The young woman took a deep breath, and the tight knit blouse that zipped up the front and molded around her breasts expanded with the intake of air. She had a ragged scar that started beside her eye and disappeared into her straight black hair.

"Stephanie Baptiste," she said.

"What he did to you, Stephanie, nobody should get away with. Detective Beauregard and I both saw him strangling you. We'll testify to that. You won't have to do it alone. This is about more than what he did to you. It's what he did before and what he'll do again unless we stop him."

"You stop him, then. Leave me out of it."

"Sit down, Stephanie," Grace said, motioning toward the unmade bed. The bed was the only place to sit in the room, but from the looks of the room and the bed, no one did much sitting.

Stephanie reluctantly sat down where Grace directed. While Beauregard waited outside for the squad to arrive and transport Renzlau to the police station, Grace tried to examine Stephanie Baptiste's neck, to make some physical contact with the young woman that would demonstrate her concern. Stephanie didn't want to be touched. She didn't want Grace's concern and didn't believe it existed. Repeatedly and suspiciously the young woman glanced at the open door of the cottage where Evangeline stood just beyond the threshold.

Evangeline backed away when Beauregard returned to the cottage. He carried a rope with a small roll of gray duct tape dangling from the outside loop. He dropped the rope and duct tape on the side of the bed closest to Stephanie Baptiste.

"Looks like you were fortunate to bring him inside," Beauregard said. "If you had stayed in the car, he might have used this stuff. Of course he might have gotten around to using them anyway if this officer hadn't stopped him. She came a long way to help you, Miss Baptiste."

"Didn't nobody come from anyplace to help me," Stephanie Baptiste said.

On the way back to the station, Grace sat in the backseat with Stephanie Baptiste and took turns with Beauregard trying to convince Miss Baptiste to cooperate, to become a good citizen, to look after herself, to think of other women, and finally to stay out of jail. It came down to that—Beauregard leaning over the backseat at the last traffic signal outside the police station and giving Stephanie Baptiste the final persuasive element of their ineffective logic.

"You want to go to jail instead of him? He says you're a prostitute who tried to take his money. You want us to believe him and you go to jail, that's okay with us."

"I been there before," she said. "Do what you're going to do."

They walked down the hallway with Stephanie Baptiste between them. She was wearing shoes with thick high heels and a complicated stringed wrapping that went halfway up her legs. Cops stared at her as she passed, and she exaggerated the movement of her hips in mockery or because she enjoyed the attention. The zipped knit blouse could come off in an instant, but it would take forever to undo her shoes.

They placed their victim in a room heavy with graffiti that was just like the one where they held Renzlau. Grace knew that the writing was already on the wall. What did she expect? If she couldn't get a minister's daughter to talk in Seattle, what chance would she have with a prostitute in Baton Rouge?

"Good arrest, but a can of worms," Beauregard said. "It kind of makes you wish you would have waited another ten minutes, doesn't it?"

"I don't know."

"You want to talk to your boy, or do you want me to do it? Maybe he'll say something stupid."

"You go ahead. I haven't been very persuasive so far."

"Not true, Officer Stevens. You persuaded me, didn't you?"

"You talk," Grace said. "I'll listen."

Beauregard opened the door to the holding room. At most it was eight foot square. Renzlau sat on a flat bench bracketed to the far wall, his hands still cuffed behind him.

"Stand up, son. I'll take those off."

Renzlau stood up and faced them.

"Turn around. I can't take them off from the front."

Renzlau turned around, and Beauregard released the handcuffs from his wrists. When he was free, Renzlau turned back toward them, rubbing the raised welts on his wrists.

"Sit down," Beauregard said.

"I want to call my father," Renzlau said.

"We'll get to that," Beauregard said.

"I have a right to make a phone call."

"Here we haven't even gotten acquainted and you start telling me what your rights are. Sit down on that bench, son. You're making me uneasy."

Renzlau sat down on the bench and continued to rub his wrists until a wide patch of skin was red, not just the narrow marks left by the steel cuffs. Beauregard sat down, too, leaving a space between them. Grace closed the door to the holding room and stood with her back against it.

Renzlau looked at her, ignoring Beauregard. He was no longer afraid, as far as she could see. He wasn't exactly smiling. His lips didn't rise into a smile, but they came close to it. It bothered her that they hadn't, at the very least, made him afraid.

"I told you your rights, and you knew them without me telling you, but you notice none of them says anything about you having the right to lie to us. You're in trouble now. We saw you strangling that young woman, and we found a rope and some tape out in your car. What on earth were you going to do with that?"

"I want to call my father," Renzlau said.

"I had a case a year or two ago where there was a roll of Scotch tape. Do you know that little roll of tape had a long number on it, and we found out it was made in Georgia and then shipped to Miami for sale? Can you imagine that we can find all that out from a little roll of tape? Now, maybe you were planning on fixing something. I have a fishing cabin out in the basin, and I always keep a little duct tape around. I could understand that."

"Do you catch any fish out there?" Renzlau asked.

"Now and then," Beauregard said.

"Do you go fishing, too, Officer Stevens? Is that why you're here with Bobby Flowers?"

"I think you should answer Detective Beauregard's question."

"Beauregard," Renzlau said, switching his focus to the detective on the bench. "Wasn't he a general or something in the Civil War?"

"That's what the books say," Beauregard said. "Are you a student of history, Mr. Renzlau?"

"No, but I've read enough to know that you lost."

Chapter 29

They walked out of police headquarters together, Grace between Bobby Flowers and Evangeline. Renzlau had left a half hour earlier with his father and the football coach, the good Christian man, as Beauregard had earlier described him.

There wasn't a serial number on the roll of duct tape. Not that it mattered. There would be no assault charge without the help of Stephanie Baptiste, and that wasn't coming and never would. The young woman had two outstanding warrants, one for soliciting an act of prostitution and another for assault, so she was the only one who went to jail.

"At least we got somebody," Beauregard had said.

But not for long. A lawyer friend of Renzlau's father from Baton Rouge, who had helped smooth the release of the football player, took up the cause of the incarcerated woman. As a gentleman, he explained, it was the least he could do. They all knew, including the gentleman, that he didn't care a Lincoln penny about the welfare of Stephanie Baptiste. As Renzlau's lawyer he wanted Stephanie Baptiste as far from the jailhouse as he could get her—at least for now. While Grace walked between Evangeline and Bobby Flowers to the rental car, the gentleman lawyer was arranging bail for

Stephanie Baptiste and offering his help to the unfortunate woman in her time of need.

"But you saw him choking her," Evangeline said.

"He claims he was defending himself."

Rather, the lawyer made the claim for Renzlau, and it wasn't hard to imagine, he said, given the unfortunate woman's history. Certainly the boy shouldn't have left the hotel, and the coach would have to deal with the breach of team rules. But boys will be boys, he said.

"Coach Bourne won't put up with that," Flowers said. "He didn't look like a happy man."

"He didn't look happy to see you," Evangeline said. "That's what I saw."

Flowers unlocked the car door, and Grace got into the backseat by herself. She felt more numb than tired, as if she hadn't slept for so long that she had forgotten how to do it. In the east the sky was becoming golden, but above them it was still night.

"He'll understand when he knows the whole story," Bobby Flowers said.

"You can't tell him, Bobby. Not yet."

Evangeline looked over the seat at her, turning her body around and holding on to the back of the seat with her hand. Her eyes had the same unblinking wide-eyed look of concern or wonder that they had the first moments inside the shabby cottage. Bobby Flowers also turned to look, and Grace realized that she had called him by his first name without any preface in her address or without the adjunct of his last name even in her mind.

"I won't," he said, "but I'm going to write up what happened tonight. We'll at least get that out."

Grace nodded, although she wasn't thinking about the story he would write.

"I was sure we would lose you when we were following him. How did you keep up with us?"

"Your sister would have killed me if I lost you."

He laughed softly and looked at Evangeline, who neither laughed nor smiled. Grace looked at her, too, at her unblinking gaze, and then beyond her where the beginning golden arc of morning shone above the gradual incline of the east-running street.

Chapter 30

The game had begun early for many of the fans wearing purple and gold attire, with purple being the dominant one of the Washington team colors. Grace and Evangeline passed the colorfully dressed team admirers on their way through the hotel lobby to the bar to find Bobby Flowers. On the telephone Bobby had told Grace that she needed to see it through, and he had gotten them press passes for the game from an unsuspecting LSU press relations officer. Grace suspected that Bobby was right. But more than seeing it through, she wanted to see it over.

When Bobby saw them, he weaved his way through the already celebrating groups who raised their glasses to interrupt his progress. He shielded himself from those who knew him and called out his name. When he reached them, he guided them toward an empty table at the back of the bar away from the celebration.

"The team left for the stadium an hour ago," he said. "Renzlau was with them. I couldn't get any of the coaches to talk to me."

"Hey, Bobby, big game tonight," a man called out from several tables away. "We might need you to suit up."

Bobby flashed an automatic grin in the direction of the voice. In addition to the voices inside the bar, there was noise from a half-dozen televisions sets scattered around the room blaring cheers and frenzied narrations of faraway games. The fans from Seattle, those who had not already left for the stadium, shouted to one another over their drinks and increased the uproar. Bobby leaned toward Grace, Evangeline moved closer, and they formed a huddle in the midst of the tumult.

"There's a rumor that Renzlau has an injury and might not be able to play," Bobby said.

"Injury," Evangeline said with disgust. "What happened? Did he hurt his hand strangling that girl?"

"I imagine they'll explain it some other way if the rumor is true," Bobby said. "I faxed my editor the story about what happened last night. He doesn't know what he's going to do with it yet."

"What?" Evangeline asked. Evangeline was not enjoying any part of the celebration.

"He wants verification from the Baton Rouge Police Department or from Seattle. It's Saturday. There's nobody in the press office either here or in Seattle. So then he wants me to get a response from Renzlau or Coach Bourne."

"They won't say anything," Grace said.

"No. Bourne wouldn't even talk to me this morning. Marshall asked him what happened last night, and Bourne told him that there was a team rule violation that they were looking into."

"Who's Marshall?" Grace asked.

"He's the other Tribune reporter down here. I thought Marshall was a decent guy, but he acts like I'm a Judas or something."

"But you were there," Evangeline said. "You saw what happened. We all did."

"I know, and Marshall and my editor have questions about that, too. How come I know about this and nobody else? They already think I hold back on the guy because I'm jealous or something. So maybe I am a little jealous. He rushes for a thousand yards, and everybody thinks that's a big deal. I rushed for eleven hundred yards when I was a sophomore, and nobody was writing about anything except the yards I got on Saturday. You see what I'm getting at?"

Grace could see well enough.

"Anyway, this is way beyond that now. What I'm trying to figure out is how this guy can be Saint Paul visiting kids at the hospital in the afternoon and a sadist at night. It doesn't make sense."

"Maybe there's something twisted in his mind," Evangeline said.

"You got that right."

On a winding route beneath overhanging branches of enormous oak trees, Grace, Evangeline, and Bobby Flowers rode the bus to the stadium with many of the celebrators who had been in the bar. Grace and Evangeline shared one seat at the front of the bus, and Bobby sat alone across the aisle— three people of color, as the recorded land deed had said, four including the bus driver immediately ahead of them. There was plenty of color behind them, too—mostly the purple clothing of the team followers.

No one else on the bus seemed concerned about color, and Grace wondered why she was thinking so much about it now after diligently ignoring it for so long. Was it the increasingly-evident similarity in the color of the football player's known victims that increased her awareness, or was it the demarcation set forth in the old pieces of paper that should have been ancient history by now but had become much less ancient in Miss Felicia's retelling? Grace wondered about herself, too. Was she learning a new truth, or was she sinking back into a destructive system that her mother and father had stood against, that her great-great-grandfather Emile and great-great-grandmother Rosalie had stood against or had at least decided that there was something more important?

Love. It was one word that could explain what they did, that explained at least the willingness to defy custom, risk banishment, and forget the future as well as the past. If that was what it was, there had to be something more, some urge to defy an illogical system, some instinctual sense of ultimate survival that exceeded the norms of the species but had to exceed eventually if the species were to survive. Such was her anthropological view anyway, but maybe she was wrong. It was possible, she supposed, that the species would survive or fail without regard to logic.

The bus might have slipped quietly past the followers of the home team whose colors were the same purple and gold as the visitors', except that somebody had fastened a banner on the side of the bus urging the Washington team to GO. The GO banner provoked a moving reaction among some of the home team followers, who turned toward them and shouted unwelcomingly as the bus passed. Some home team fans who lacked Southern hospitality pointed their thumbs down like Roman rulers in a match of gladiators or their fingers up in a more modern accompaniment to their jeers although there was little difference between those on the sidewalk and those in the bus. The colors of the team followers were the same inside and outside the bus—purple, gold, and white. Only the names were different—Washington, Louisiana.

The bus entered a huge paved parking lot, but the parking lot wasn't used for parking. It was the site of a vast party with open tents set up on one side and row after row of recreational vehicles on the other. Everywhere smoke rose from grills, laughter from circles of lawn chairs, music and crowd noise from television sets showing football games being played hundreds, even thousands, of miles away.

"I've never seen so many tailgaters at a football game," Bobby said as he leaned toward the bus driver, who was slowly and carefully driving them through the crowd.

"There's lots of them, that's for sure," the driver said, "and they all pay to be here, just like you-all."

"I work for a newspaper," Bobby said. "They pay me to come."

"That right? Well, not these people," he said, sweeping his hand across the front window of the bus. "They all pay. Them that pay the most get up front. Helps the football team, I guess. Always plenty of money for the football team."

"I get the impression you're not a big fan," Bobby said.

"I drive the bus, sir. I'm here because they pay me, just like you."

He parked the bus by the side of the stadium where there was a line of trucks, most with satellite dishes mounted on top. The sun was almost gone, but it still reflected brightly from the light poles that rose a hundred feet or more into the air. The field lights were lit although there was still daylight above the towers.

Grace felt the heat and moisture in the shaded air as soon as she stepped off the air-conditioned bus. The air wasn't like the furnace of summer heat in Omaha. This air felt as if it were an accumulation of hundreds of years of sighs and groans and would press her into the ground. WELCOME TO DEATH VALLEY said a sign above one of the stadium gates.

The land was as flat as the water of Puget Sound, and she guessed that the valley was either of the mind or of a very different perspective. The Washington followers set off in a line to the south end of the stadium. She and Evangeline followed Bobby to a gate marked PRESS ONLY. Like Bobby Flowers, each hung her press credentials on a cord around her neck.

Pressed inside an elevator with a dozen men and Evangeline, Grace rose in silence from the valley of death. When the elevator doors opened, she heard a deep hum that came from the core of the stadium. Bobby took them to a walled-off, multi-tiered platform that reached out over the seats below. From there she could see the entire field far below her. For-

mations of players, toy-like in size when viewed from her
high platform, were already performing warm-ups.

She and Evangeline sat on chairs on either side of Bobby
Flowers. Cool air blew from the electric fans at the back of
the press box. Grace couldn't determine if the air was condi-
tioned like the air in the bus, or if the breeze felt cool only because it passed over the sweat on her skin. A radio was on,
and two announcers were talking about the upcoming game.
Grace couldn't imagine that anyone would be listening already.

As the stadium filled, the underlying hum became louder.
Another radio with different voices began a broadcast, then
television joined in from two screens on either side of the
press box. The Louisiana band, seated below them in a section of the stadium, played loud raucous songs that echoed
throughout the structure. It became impossible for her to separate one noise from another.

Cheerleaders in short skirts and tight tops danced in front
of the band. A reporter in the row of press seats below them
pointed his binoculars at the dancing girls and adjusted the
focus. His notebook lay open and the page was blank.

Grace had watched football games on television with her
father, at least parts of them. She had even taken him to two
games at the University of Washington with tickets she
bought from other students with her own money. When he
cheered, she cheered; when he booed the referee, she booed;
when he laughed, she laughed. Her father laughed often at
the two games they attended together. While she had not enjoyed the games, she had enjoyed spending time with him
and listening to his laughter.

This game was different. She wouldn't be able to laugh re-
gardless of who laughed beside her. Renzlau, last year's all-
American and certain to repeat, Bobby said, was somewhere
on the field. So were two other men who had raped Alice. All

she knew of them was what Alice had told her. They were two of the huge men in the line who protected Renzlau.

Grace felt alone as she looked at the spectacle below her. It was different than when she had been in the midst of the crowd with her father. Even the dancing girls disgusted her. They looked like they were in a mating dance, gyrating their hips, throwing back their long hair, demonstrating their health and agility to their potential mates. But who were the mates? The football players didn't even look at them. They had formed into groups and were charging up and down the field unopposed. Maybe the potential mates were the men in the bleachers or those all the way up in the press box, the men who watched approvingly with binoculars.

"Renzlau is on the sideline with the coaches," Bobby whispered to Grace. "He's not starting the game."

He gave the binoculars to Grace, and she found Renzlau's number 32. He had his hands on his hips and was watching the field. The chinstrap hung loosely from his helmet. She tried to see the expression on his face, but the helmet concealed it.

"Hey, anybody know why Renzlau is on the sidelines?" asked a reporter from the center of the room.

Immediately everyone within the press box became focused on number 32. Grace handed the binoculars back to Bobby, who passed them along to Evangeline. The radio voices soon joined the chorus of speculation, and on and on the questions went.

When Grace was a child, she had often wished she could blend in with the other children in school. Sometimes she wished she were not so tall or not so colored; sometimes she even wished she were not so smart. She often felt that she was out of place with the other students. When she looked at the thousands of people below her, she knew that she was out of place again—the one who didn't understand, the one who didn't belong.

The two teams lined up against each other, and the nubile dancing girls raised signs that said NOISE. And there was noise, a fearful noise as the spectators stood and screamed. A player from Washington kicked the ball to a player from Louisiana at the opposite end of the field. The two lines crushed into each other, and the player who caught the ball was knocked to the ground.

Grace watched as the fury enveloped the entire stadium. When she had been with her father, the game hadn't seemed threatening or frightening, but it did now as she watched the spectacle from high above in the press box. On the radio, voices spoke approvingly of the primitive behavior on the field: punishing blows, crushing tackles, brutal blocks. The crowd became quiet only when a player lay still and unmoving on the field, but the cheering resumed when he was carried away and replaced by another.

The object of the struggle, as any anthropologist could see, was simple enough—to carry the ball past the last line on the field. In doing so the competitors fought one another with an elemental fury. In an increasing frenzy the crowd in the stadium urged the players to fight harder. The crowd, more like a mob, reminded Grace of children who surrounded a playground fight and would not let the fighters part. Except the scale of the circle was different. The scale here was thousands of times greater than with the circlers in the schoolyard.

On it went below her. From her view in the press box she watched the players hitting each other, hurting each other, the cheerleaders dancing with seductive pleasure, the crowd chanting, cheering, jeering over the oblong ball that was not even gold or silver like a true prize.

Halfway through the game the players retreated from the field, and the hundred-strong marching band from LSU pranced out from the stands to replace them. A long straight line of girls with golden hair and skin-tight golden suits, the same girls who were on the cover of the game program, followed the band onto the field. The girls performed in unison: raised their arms together, threw back their golden hair, stretched and turned and writhed so that all in the stadium might see the golden delights. Within the glow of the stadium lights, within the radiant golden island of the warm Louisiana night, rose a murmur of appreciation. The same murmur came from the reporters in the press box, a murmur of longing as they watched, some through binoculars and others with their naked eyes.

Bobby Flowers looked at her, resisting the enticements from the field, which were not for him anyway. He leaned closer.

"Now we'll see what Bourne is thinking." Bobby's voice was no more than a whisper, and it disappeared into a blare of trumpets.

"What do you mean?" Grace whispered back.

"We're behind twenty to nothing. Washington is behind," he said, correcting his first statement.

Grace knew that she wasn't part of the "we" of his first statement, but she wasn't sure if he had made the correction for her or if the correction included him as well. She suspected it was to accommodate her. After all, he had been part of the spectacle below not so long ago. In an earlier day he might have shared in the delights, too.

"If Bourne puts Renzlau into the game in the second half, it means he buys Renzlau's story, or at least doesn't care what happened. If he keeps Renzlau out, Renzlau is in trouble, as far as football is concerned."

"What do you think will happen?" Grace asked.

"He's suited up," Bobby said. "I think he'll play."

The voices on the radio asked the same question. No one knew why he hadn't played in the first half, and the radio voices pressed on with guesses and speculation. The speculation went on inside the walls of the reporters' booth and probably throughout the entire stadium during the golden intermission. The only certainty was that the Washington team was in a desperate position as the second half began.

Suddenly from the small wedge of the stadium behind the goalposts where the unwelcome visitors sat, the entire mass transplanted from Washington stood and cheered. Their united voices carried all the way up to the press box as Renzlau ran onto the field and number 32 joined the other ten members of the team. The Washington fans cheered, Grace believed, because they saw their champion, their all-American on the football field, not because they knew anything about him. They wouldn't cheer if they could hear the strangled screams of the woman the night before or Alice all the way back in Seattle. Yet the cheers continued from the wedge of fans behind the south goalposts, and they became louder to her than the combined cheers of all the rest of the stadium.

Grace thought once more about the games she had shared with her father. This game was different. They would all be different from now on. She doubted that she would ever be able to cheer that unknowing innocent cheer with him again.

With Renzlau in the game the tide turned for the Washington football team, one of the radio voices said, or perhaps it was one of the faces on the television screen. Washington's team scored a touchdown early in the second half and scored again as the game progressed to the fourth and final quarter. The tide had turned and was turning even though the ocean was a hundred miles away, or thousands if they meant the ocean tide back in Seattle. The tide had turned, and the cheers from the small sea of Washington purple continued unabated. Grace wished she had stayed away. She wished she hadn't come to see it through as Bobby said she should. It was already over as far as she was concerned. For Evangeline, too. The two of them sat back in their chairs, leaning away from the crowds and the fierce contest below them. They looked at each other behind Bobby's back, two sisters who whispered in the closeness of a shared bed who couldn't hear each other above the noise of this game.

"This is it!" she heard a voice shout. She looked at the television screen and saw that it was not the announcer there who had shouted, but she heard the voice again louder than all the rest. It came from one of the radios. "It's third and forever!"

Forever would end soon, and she could leave with Evangeline into the forever night away from these forever screams. Anywhere, she thought, but this place with its forever noise, which now was so painful that she covered her ears.

She looked down to the field and saw the number 32 running away from her. With the ball in his hands Renzlau was running to the opposite side of the field, and nearly all the players from both teams were running along with him. Soon he would have no place to go, and forever would arrive. Then number 32 stopped and Renzlau threw the ball back across the field. The screams from the general mass of the stadium faded as the football reached its highest point, and the screams died nearly completely as it dropped into the hands of a player running alone. All was silent except for the small sea of Washington fans behind the goalposts. Their cries, like screaming seagulls, rose in waves that echoed to the far reaches of the stadium and beyond. She feared that they would drown out the strangled screams of the two women. She feared that the cheers would continue even without ignorance, without innocence. She feared there was no innocence.

Grace rose from her chair and communicated to Flowers with hand gestures that she was leaving. He had his job to do, but hers was over. She would listen no more to the screams from the field or the shouts of the reporters or the excited voices of the radio announcers. She would listen no more. She turned and walked up the steps toward the exit from the press booth. Evangeline followed close behind her. They stopped when they reached the top of the stairway. Detective Beauregard was standing there. He had a strange smile on his face.

"It looks like your boy saved us a lot of trouble tonight," he said. "Won't anybody around here be celebrating much now. You-all need a ride back to the hotel?"

Chapter 31

Beauregard had parked his car away from the stadium to avoid the traffic congestion around it, and Grace and Evangeline walked with him across the campus grounds littered with plastic beer cups and empty bottles. Beauregard had been right. The celebration was over, although party tents still lined the campus street. The tent caretakers who had not gone to the stadium were packing up in silence beneath the moss-covered trees.

"What are you going to do now?" Beauregard asked.

They had stopped at the curb of an intersection for a red light, and Grace felt the pressure of the people who had left the stadium. They accumulated behind her, surrounded her, and pressed forward in anticipation of the change to green. She should have left earlier. She didn't want to be in the crowd any longer.

Beauregard's question was simple enough, and she could give him an answer that would satisfy him, but for herself she could not see ahead to the next morning or the one after that. It was simply impossible. She would fly back to Seattle, but she could not see herself there. There, were Rigmor's grocery and the alternating design in the concrete sidewalk. There, were the university fountain that sprayed water into the air and the volcano Takhoma looming on the horizon. There, were the rhododendron bushes in front of her parents' house, her father on the porch waiting for her to come in, and her mother reading at the kitchen table just as she had before the cancer attacked her body. There, was her own house with Lady waiting, but there she could not see herself.

Somewhere behind her, among the crowd who pressed against her, or farther back to the voice shouting that it was third and forever, or among those who cheered for a champion who could throw an oddly shaped ball all the way across the desperate field into another's hands; or farther back to the oak tree where she and Evangeline had sat in the warm moist air; or farther back, farther back to the slave girl, Rosalie, who had thrown the crying child out the window of a burning house—somewhere back there she had lost the image of herself so that whoever stood on Rigmor's sidewalk or passed the bedding plants that her father brought inside for the winter or looked at the volcano from the university would not be anyone she had known before. She could answer Beauregard's question about what she would do as long as she didn't have to answer who would do it.

"I don't know," she said.

As the light changed to green, Evangeline took her hand. Evangeline's hand was sweaty from the moist night air and from the heat of the crowd that surged around them. Evangeline did not drop her hand once they reached the opposite curb, and Grace didn't pull hers away. Instead she squeezed Evangeline's hand so that her sister would know that she was there.

"I wish we could have put that boy of yours away before he hurts somebody else," Beauregard said as they continued walking on the sidewalk away from the stadium. "Maybe he'll stop now that he knows you're on to him."

"He won't stop," Grace said.

"No, I don't suppose he will."

"I should have waited longer," Grace said. "He would

have choked her unconscious. We would have that and maybe an attempted rape if I had waited long enough. Then we'd have a felony with or without the girl's help, and he would be in jail right now. Would you have waited, Detective Beauregard?"

"That might have been a little hard to explain, wouldn't it?"

"We could have explained," Grace said. She stopped on the sidewalk and sidestepped onto the grass with Evangeline so that the surging crowd from the stadium could pass. "There's always some way to explain, isn't there?"

In the light that filtered through the ancient fingers of the oak trees she saw a smile forming slowly and cautiously on Beauregard's face.

"If you ever need my help up North with this fellow, Officer Stevens, you give me a call. You hear?"

"I will. Tell me something, Detective Beauregard. If I ask you for change right here, right now, for a twenty-dollar bill, what will you give me?"

The smile spread a little farther, but there was something in it, something way back that she wasn't sure she could or ever would understand.

"Right now, I don't know for sure what's in my wallet," he said. "It's been a while since I last checked."

Chapter 32

Silence was all Grace heard. The sound of a chair scraping the floor, muffled footsteps passing behind her, and whispered voices were all drowned in the ocean of silence in the massive reading room. Here she did not hear the screams from the football stadium across this campus or the one thousands of miles away, or the strangled woman gasping for air, or the child crying outside the broken window of the burning house. The woman within the burning house would not cry. She would in desperate silence pull away the boards to reveal the hiding place in the floor to get the money and the deed of land and maybe the emancipation document: all of which she must have thought were more important than her very life.

Grace added another line in her notebook, another shred of evidence to link the life cycles of three species of salmon to the life cycles of the tribes who gathered along the riverbanks from southern Alaska all the way to the Strait of Juan de Fuca. When she closed her eyes she could smell the alder fires burning within the smokehouses. She wondered how long they lasted—the smokehouses they built—but her question had more to do with the people than their structures. When do a people, when do people change? At some point they must move on, physically and intellectually, or disappear. Would their knowledge of food preservation be sufficient to sustain them through the bad years when the salmon did not come or too few came? Where was the evidence?

Outside the wind blew hard and splattered raindrops flat against the tall southwest windows of the library. Inside she was protected, warm and dry. She imagined the sound of a fall storm as it passed through enormous first-growth Douglas fir trees outside sturdy lodges, the people inside also warm and protected. The last of the salmon catch would be drying on wood racks before going into the smokehouses, the women would be weaving baskets, and the old men telling stories to the children. She wondered if Maria had heard any of those stories.

How strange that Maria had traveled from Alaska to Seattle looking for ancestors, while Grace studied the salmon in Alaska, which probably had some link to them. It would have been more logical for Maria to study marine life in Alaska instead of here, where the salmon were almost gone and not likely to return. While she was considering logic, she couldn't deny that it would have been more logical for her to study her own ancestors and not somebody else's. That was the reason Evangeline was still in Louisiana talking to Miss Felicia. Grace wondered if Evangeline would ever follow the story to Chicago and Omaha and then on to France where their parents met. Would Evangeline ever follow the family history back to Norway, or would she follow only one of the trails? Maybe it didn't matter which story any of them followed. In some ways the stories were all the same. In one way or another they were all waiting for the fish to dry and hoping that the salmon would return again next year.

Without any sound of footsteps, without any echo of them swallowed by the somber volumes, the girl stood before Grace's table, her hands folded as if she were praying—only prayer would not bring such an appearance of foreboding into the girl's face.

"You said I could find you here," she whispered.

Grace closed the book that prompted images of alder fires and stories by the elders and pushed it aside with her notes. She gestured for Alice to sit down in the chair beside her.

Alice sat forward on the chair, spread a wet newspaper before Grace, and placed her finger on the paper.

"Did you see this?" she whispered.

Grace pulled the newspaper toward her and saw the largest headline on the page—JUSTICE IN LOUISIANA. The by-line read, Harold R. Flowers, Jr. He had published the story after all, the one he said his newspaper wouldn't print. It was all the same to her, she had told him in Louisiana, and so were football writers and football talkers and fans. She had known even then that what she said wasn't true, but she had told him anyway when he had called her hotel room after the game. No, she was tired, she had said. She didn't want to meet for a drink. She had a flight early in the morning and was through with football.

This wasn't his newspaper. His newspaper had multiple sections even in the small Wednesday edition, and the sports section was somewhere inside. This newspaper had one section and mixed everything together. Bobby had taken the story to *The Voice*. She knew about *The Voice,* the small neighborhood paper from the Central District that her father subscribed to. She read it at her parents' home when there was nothing else to read. *The Voice* always carried news about preachers and churches in the Central District. There might be a story, too, about a police arrest that stirred the community or about a new business, the dream of which would likely collapse under the bills. Some dreams lasted longer than others and advertised on the back pages of the paper.

Harold. She smiled secretly to herself. He had never told her his name was Harold.

Harold Flowers reported all that had happened that night in Louisiana: the pick-up of the woman in the car rented by

Renzlau's father, the distance to the motor cottage, the time of night, the police response, and the strangled woman. He reported the football coach's words at the police station, the appearance of Renzlau's father and the lawyer who got Renzlau released. He reported the jailing of the woman for prostitution warrants and the posting of her bail. Briefly and without substantial detail he reported the investigation in Seattle that had led to Louisiana. A young woman was picked up at 12th Avenue E and East Jefferson Street and fled when she saw a rope that was similar to the rope found in Renzlau's car in Baton Rouge. More fully he explained how the actions of an unnamed female police officer from Seattle, who had traveled to Louisiana on her own time and money, had saved the young woman from a more serious injury and assault. Harold Flowers's report took up most of the front page.

"Did you go down there?" Alice asked.

She had waited until Grace looked up from the story.

"Yes, I went down there. We arrested him, but as you can see it didn't turn out very well."

"At least you arrested him. That's important. And you saved that other girl. That's important, too."

"A lot of people won't think so."

"I do," Alice said. "I know what would have happened to her. I told my father and mother what happened to me."

Those were good words to hear. They were words that lifted the burden a little or at least shared it, both for the girl and herself.

"I'm glad you did, Alice."

"I want to tell you everything that happened so that you can do something if you can. I don't want him to hurt anybody else."

Do something, the girl was saying.

Grace thought she heard a muffled cheer coming from the entrance, from outside, and she looked toward the door of the reading room. The door remained closed, the reading room silent. The sound must have been in her imagination, a flash-back to the football stadium in Louisiana. There had been only a few thousand Washington fans there. What would it be like with many times that number, with a whole stadium, a whole city of them? The girl had heard only her own cry, and maybe not even that. She couldn't possibly understand the screams that Grace had heard.

"I can try," Grace said, "but it will be very difficult. He'll lie about what happened. He'll say terrible things about you. A lot of people will believe him and not you."

"But you believe me."

"Yes, I believe you, but that's not enough. It's not nearly enough."

"I know I waited too long. I know it's probably too late, but I believe I should try."

"It's not too late," Grace said. "Whenever you're ready we can meet at the police station and begin. I think it would be best if your mother and father came with you."

"They're outside," Alice said. "I wanted to come in here by myself, but they're waiting outside."

Grace looked past the girl to the high southwest windows and saw that the storm continued unabated. The salmon would never dry in this weather.

Chapter 33

W e have probable cause," Captain Niels Lowery said. "That's not the problem."

Anne looked at the cops gathered around the captain's desk in the Sex Crimes division. There were as many opinions as there were cops; there always were. She was pushing for an immediate arrest with probable cause as were the two young officers who stood behind her chair. Murphy was the only one in the captain's small office who was in uniform, having come directly from the North Precinct. Her blue shirt and silver badge stood out distinctly in the midst of the somber colors of the detectives' plain clothing. Katherine had been quiet so far, but that might not last. After reading Alice's full statement, she had been ready to drag Renzlau off the practice field by herself, never mind the giant linemen who were supposed to protect him.

Officer Stevens was more deliberate, but there was no question where she stood. She had taken the statement from the girl while the parents sat on the oak bench in the hallway so that they would not have to hear every detail. They had heard enough already. It was the second time Grace had heard the girl's story, except this time the description and details were more specific. They had to be. The written statement was now part of the official record detailing one

specific act after another, which would in turn justify from
the police one specific action after another. But which action
would they choose? To Anne the choice was clear, but there
were other choices. Each choice had its consequences, and
each choice could be fine-tuned with any number of options.

Sergeant McHenry was ready to choose any option the
captain wanted. If the captain decided to steer the case
through the prosecutor's office and get an arrest warrant,
McHenry would agree. If the captain decided to act now, he
would agree with that, too.

Lieutenant Fletcher was the obstacle. Lieutenant Harry
Fletcher was the voice of restraint. Harry Fletcher was always the voice of restraint. If Harry had his way, they would
be so restrained that they wouldn't move until hell froze over.
If he had his way, they would all be waiting in hell for that
day. The case was old, he argued—fifty-fifty at best.

The captain nodded. He knew the odds as well as any of
them.

"You mean it's fifty-fifty if we arrest them now, don't you,
Lieutenant?" Anne asked. "It will be even less if we wait for
the prosecutor's blessing. If we do that, it will end up on
Janklow's desk, and Janklow and Murdock will sit there and
hold each other's hands and worry about how this will affect
the election. Maybe they won't say so, but that's what they'll
be thinking. They might decide, independent of all political
consideration of course, that there isn't enough evidence to
make an arrest and that they shouldn't put the poor girl
through the trauma. That will be the excuse. Janklow doesn't
have the black vote anyway. I can hear him now: 'There is no
point in ruining the reputation of these young men for nothing, especially considering the extraordinary contribution
they have made to the state of Washington,' and blah, blah,
blah. That's what will happen, and we shouldn't kid ourselves. Stiles is already in the loop from the prosecutor's office. He's writing up the search warrant now. We can give

him a heads-up that we're going to make the arrest. I know Stiles. He'll be fine with that. Janklow won't be able to say that we blindsided him with this."

"She can't even identify with certainty two of the suspects," the lieutenant said. "She thinks they're the same guys who were at the party, but it was dark in the bedroom, and she can't be sure. What are we supposed to do, Anne? Just overlook that minor fact?"

She could give him a few suggestions where to look.

"We have the boy from the fraternity, Harry. He took the girl home after she was raped. He can testify how scared she was even if she didn't tell him what happened. Jane got his statement. He's scared, too, but he'll testify. My God, there was a police officer's daughter who almost fell into Renzlau's trap. This boy saw the two men go into Renzlau's room at the fraternity house. He watched them leave. These guys are two hundred eighty pounds or more. Isn't that what the boy said? And she's what, a hundred pounds? One guy holds her down and the other guy rapes her. And then they switch. She knows who they are."

Red crept up the lieutenant's neck and shone on top of his bald head. She hoped that the captain would not get promoted any time soon. If the lieutenant took over the captain's job, she would probably be assigned to Auto Theft and spend the rest of her career crawling through junkyards.

"Does anyone think that these men didn't rape Alice?"

The voice came from behind her, and Anne turned to Officer Stevens, who still held the girl's sworn statement. It was five pages long—five pages of experiences that the lieutenant would never have to endure. The young officer flipped a page and began reading.

" 'Then it was like something exploded inside him, and he slapped me across the face. He hit me again, and I tried to scream, but he pushed a pillow into my face. I told him that I couldn't breathe, but he didn't say anything. He grabbed me by the hair and pushed me onto the floor and hit me with something across the legs. It must have been his belt. The buckle tore my skin. He shoved my face into the pillow again and kept hitting me. I couldn't breathe. After a while I couldn't do anything.' "

The young officer flipped to another page and no one told her to stop although they all knew what was coming. The room became still. The only movement came from outside as raindrops struck the windowpanes of the captain's office with such force that the water ran sideways across the glass.

The girl was with her parents in the hall—three hurt and confused souls sitting on the bench with the reporter, Flowers, close by and all refusing to leave until they heard what the law would do. The father refused anyway. The mother had her arm around the girl the last time Anne had seen them, and the mother and daughter were holding each other upright on the bench. Across town three football players were finishing practice, if anybody practiced for a game in such weather. It was already getting dark outside.

" 'I thought it was him coming back,' " Officer Stevens read in a voice so flat and mechanical that the girl's words had to do all the work. " 'It was dark in the room, and I couldn't see anything. I hurt everywhere. I had never had sex before. I thought it was him coming back, but it wasn't.' "

"Okay," the captain said with more expression in his voice than Officer Stevens, "we've all read the statement. We believe what she said."

"We can believe her all we want," the lieutenant said, "but the jury won't care what we believe. They'll want to know why she went into that guy's room in the first place. The kid says he heard someone crying inside Renzlau's room. They can say she was screaming with pleasure. Who knows what they'll say?"

"She still has marks on the back of her legs and on her

buttocks, for chrissake," Anne said. "The boy said she hurt so much she could hardly bear to sit down in his car."

"Fine. Any marks or scarring will get reported in the medical examination. Let's have a doctor tell us first how long they've been there or what caused them. Maybe she fell in the parking lot. Jesus, Niels, you pull these guys out of the locker room, and we'll be in every newspaper in the country tomorrow."

The captain raised his eyebrows as he considered the lieutenant's warning. It didn't have the effect the lieutenant wanted.

"I hadn't thought about the locker room, Harry," the captain said, "but that might not be a bad idea. If we grab them in the team house, we could have a hell of a mess. It might take half the department to get them out of there if they decide they don't want to come with us. But if the coaches are around, they'll be a lot more under control, not so likely to do something stupid. And it will shock the hell out of them. Maybe one of them will say something. It would really be nice if we could get an admission from one of them. God knows we might need it. Anybody know how to find the locker room?"

"Mr. Flowers can tell us where it is."

Anne turned around to look at Officer Stevens again. The young woman had not moved an inch since the last time she spoke. Anne heard a hissing sound from the lieutenant as he exhaled his exasperation about the thickheaded cops who weren't listening to him. Of course, he might be right. They could wait another day or two. The girl had waited two months before telling them. Anne couldn't imagine what those two months must have been like. That wasn't exactly true. She could imagine if she had to.

The captain looked up at the tall young officer behind Anne rather than at the exasperated lieutenant. Anne knew the captain well enough to know that he had made his decision, and she knew from his expression what it would be.

"Officer Stevens, do you want to take the victim up to Harborview Hospital or do you want to go out with us when we make the arrest?" the captain asked.

The tall young officer straightened her back even more.

"I'll make the arrest," she said.

"Murphy?" the captain asked.

"I'm staying with Grace."

"Jane can take the girl and her family up to Harborview," Anne said. "She's itching to help."

She knew of a half-dozen other detectives who had remained in the office after the four o'clock rush. Each of them had found some case that needed a little more work. Jane wasn't the only one itching to help.

"All right. Harry, I want you to drive out to the University Police Headquarters. Find their chief and tell him what we're doing. We'll have their dispatcher send a university officer over to the practice field to meet us, but I don't want their chief to get wind of this until we're done. So don't hurry. Their station is hard to find. I've been out there a couple of times, and I always get lost. Do you understand what I'm saying? I don't want him showing up until we've already made the arrests. He'll just get in the way with all of his university sensibilities. He reports to the Regents, you know, and I don't imagine they're going to like this.

"We'll get a few extra patrol cars to go in with us and have others ready to come in if we need help. But I don't think we'll need them. We'll just keep this nice and low key. Officer Stevens, you will arrest Renzlau and lead him out. Murphy, you pick one of the other two suspects and arrest him. Maybe pick the biggest guy. Make sure he has his pants on. And, Anne, you take the other one. All in all, I think that will make an appropriate statement, don't you?"

"It will, Niels," Anne said. "I always knew you were smart, but I didn't know you were a poet, too."

"We'll see how poetic I am when I tell the major what we're going to do. You still have your handcuffs, don't you, Anne?" the captain asked.

"I'll find them somewhere."

Chapter 34

Grace walked out of the Sex Crimes office and down the hall to where Alice waited with her parents and Bobby Flowers. Reverend Sinclair stood and faced her as she approached. Bobby Flowers was already standing. Grace nodded to Alice's father, but she wanted her message to go straight to the girl. Alice looked up at her, and Grace thought she saw something in the girl's expressive eyes that she had not seen before. If it wasn't hope it was at least relief that she wasn't carrying her burden alone anymore. So that was good, Grace thought. She might have felt the same relief if she didn't know what was to follow.

"Alice," Grace said, "the captain has decided that we will arrest Renzlau and the other two suspects immediately. I'm going with the captain and others out to the university to make the arrest. Another detective will take you to the hospital for an examination. You don't have to be afraid," she said hurriedly as another emotion replaced the hope or whatever it was that had shown through the girl's expressive brown eyes. "Your parents will go with you. It's important that you do this. It's important for the investigation, but it's also important for you."

Alice's mother nodded in agreement, but Grace continued

to focus on the girl until Alice nodded in approximate duplication of her mother.

"Will you put them in jail?" Alice asked.

"Yes, but they won't stay there long. They will appear before a judge as soon as the prosecutor files formal charges. Then the judge will set bail. They'll be out of jail soon, but you don't have to be afraid of them. If they even try to come close to you, we'll arrest them again. They will know that.

"The arrest is only the first step. We have a long way to go after that. I wish it didn't take so long, but you have your mother and father with you now. You'll have help from doctors and counselors, too. It won't be easy, but you're not alone anymore. Detective Smith will handle your case after we make the arrests, but you can call me anytime. I mean that, Alice. Call me anytime. Do you have any questions before you go to the hospital?"

"No," Alice said.

Grace looked at the mother and father. They had no questions for her either.

"Someday, Alice," Grace said, "I want to tell you what else I found when my sister and I were in Louisiana, something that had nothing to do with Renzlau and the girl he attacked in Baton Rouge. Or maybe it did. I want to tell you because it's something I think you'll understand. Someday I'll tell you about it."

Grace walked away from the girl, who she hoped would be thinking of someday and not today and especially not a day two months earlier. That was too much to hope. All she could hope was that Alice would find something she didn't expect, something within herself that would surprise her.

Grace stopped beside Bobby Flowers, who was there at the Reverend Sinclair's request. She asked Bobby Flowers to walk with her down the hall and around the corner so that they were out of sight as well as earshot of the girl and her parents.

She hadn't seen him or talked to him since returning from Louisiana early Sunday morning, although he had left two messages on her telephone answering machine, one on Sunday night and one on Monday. If he had left a message about the story he had written or had intended to write, she might have called him back. He said only that he would like her to call him. She almost did Monday night but, after picking up the phone, decided she didn't know what to say to him. In her mind he had become mixed up with her thoughts about the football team and the coach and the screaming crowd.

He looked tired, more tired even than he had looked after staying awake all night in Baton Rouge. He was more solemn, too, and more formal in the distance he stood from her.

"Why did you give your story to *The Voice*?" she asked.

"It wasn't my story," he said. "It belonged to the girl in Louisiana, and this girl here, and maybe even to you."

"All right, but why did you give it to *The Voice*?"

"The *Tribune* wouldn't print it. They wanted to take out everything that was important."

"They can't be very happy with you."

"I don't know what they are. I quit."

"Why? You didn't even know about Alice then. Were you that upset about the prostitute in Baton Rouge?"

"No."

"Then why would you quit? Why would you publish that story despite what they said?"

"I decided my father was right. You probably don't remember, but I told you that he thought it was time I stopped playing games or writing about them."

"I remember," Grace said.

"Did you read the story?"

"Of course."

"What did you think?"

"I thought, 'Who do I call? Bobby Flowers or Harold Flowers, Jr.?'"

"Either one would have been fine with me."

"I'm sorry I didn't call you back."

"I think I understand. Evangeline called me and told me about your family in Louisiana, about the slave girl. She told me a lot about you."

"Busy woman, that Evangeline. She must be running up some big telephone bills."

With the first break of his solemn face, Bobby, or Harold Flowers as his byline was printed in *The Voice,* smiled at her. She wasn't sure who he was. It would take time before she could think of him as Harold.

"The captain asked me to ask you if you will draw a map of where the locker room is. He wants to arrest Renzlau and the other two guys there."

"I can do better than that. I can ride along and show you where it is. It would give me a chance to pay my respects to the coach."

"Do you think he'll talk to you?"

"No. None of them will talk to me, but I don't care. I could show you where the locker room is and point out the two linemen when we get there."

"You would do that? You would go into the locker room and point out these guys?"

"I would do that."

"The captain just wants a map. You'll have to pay your respects another time."

"Are you sure you'll be able to recognize the other two guys?" he asked.

"We have their descriptions, and we have photographs from a football program. Alice recognized them from the photographs. I guess we'll be able to pick them out, too."

"Maybe, but there will be fifty big white guys in the

locker room. And you know how it is. They all look the same."

Bobby Flowers sat with Anne Smith in the backseat of their patrol car as Katherine navigated the freeway through rush-hour traffic. The captain had decided that it wouldn't hurt to take Bobby Flowers along so that he could show them where the locker room was and point out the two linemen, if that became necessary.

Close behind their car were the captain and the sergeant in two patrol cars, and behind them were two detectives from the Sex Crimes unit in an unmarked car. Grace remembered one of their names. It was John. The other was longer and hadn't planted itself in her memory. Two more patrol cars from the North End would be waiting for them in the first parking lot across the Montlake Bridge along with the sergeant from the Union sector and an unsuspecting officer from the University Police Department.

Bobby Flowers was explaining to Anne Smith how Renzlau was not just a star; he was *the* star. His picture had been on the cover of *Sports Illustrated,* and he was a finalist for the Heisman Trophy. He had a good chance of winning it, too, and that meant more exposure for the football program. There was talk of a shoe endorsement for the team, and with that money they could build an indoor practice facility. But it wasn't only football that would benefit. Money would flow into the athletic department, and there would be more money for all the athletic programs. There were plans for a new rowing facility so that they could compete with the Ivy League schools, which the athletic director believed would give prestige to the athletic program and the university. New rowing facilities cost money, and the rowing team generated little money. The money came from football.

"And they'll get it because of this guy?" Anne asked.

"It takes the whole program, but he's the star right now and the money is flowing."

"Well," Anne said, looking out the back window of the police car, which was stuck in the rain-delayed traffic on the freeway, "there won't be any stars tonight. We probably won't see any for months."

Anne smiled at Bobby Flowers. She had a smile, Grace decided, that would turn any man's head. Grace herself smiled as she turned back toward the front where the line of cars ahead of them seemed endless. She caught a glimpse, just a glimpse, of the smile Bobby returned to Anne.

"They'll be gone before we get there," Katherine said. "We should have taken Madison to 23rd."

"The captain wanted us to stay together," Grace said.

"I'm going to use the emergency lane. Tell the others to get in behind me."

Grace picked up the microphone as Katherine flipped on the yellow flashers. The flashers warned other drivers that they were coming but not to pull over so they wouldn't get in the way. The blue lights would make a mess that they would never get through.

Soon the four cars were moving purposefully in a tight formation beside the right guard rail of the freeway. The only slowdowns came when a lane merged from the right. Well before they reached those points, Katherine flipped the toggle and gave the merging traffic a flash of blue—just enough to part the sea of cars so that their procession could slip through unhindered.

Katherine turned off the flashers when they left the freeway, and the two patrol cars behind did the same. When they passed beneath the lighted bridge-tender's hut on the Montlake Bridge, the traffic flow was heavier in the other direction. The university was emptying for the night. The road ahead was clear.

Grace saw the unmistakable blue and silver insignia of the

waiting patrol cars in the parking lot. There were three police cars in a row, with those on the outside pointing in the opposite direction. The middle car with its two officers served as the bridge for the conversation that flowed through their half-opened windows. Katherine drove next to one of the outside cars.

"We can't all line up," Grace said, but she saw that she was wrong. There was room in the lot for all of them. The officer in the car next to them reached across the seat and lowered the window nearest Katherine. Grace leaned forward and recognized Ritter who worked the Laurelhurst car. Nothing ever happened in Laurelhurst.

"Hey, Murphy," he said, checking out the passengers in the backseat. "What's going on?"

"We're cleaning up your district."

"This isn't mine. It belongs to our university brothers."

The captain got out into the rain and walked over to the car on the far side of the lineup where the Union sector sergeant was smoking a cigar and sending out puffs of smoke into the rain like soggy smoke signals. The captain got into the sergeant's car.

"We're arresting three university football players for rape," Katherine said to Ritter. "We need you to cover the back doors of the locker room."

"Who are they?"

Katherine pulled her notebook out of her pocket and held it up so that the light from one of the giant poles that illuminated the parking lot shown on her paper as well.

"There's a David Kennedy and a Craig Reed. They're both linemen. And then there's Paul Renzlau," she said, no longer reading from her notebook. "He's a runner."

"Jesus," Ritter said. "How did you guys get into this?"

"It was Grace. I didn't have anything to do with it."

A marked patrol car from the University Police entered the parking lot, and the single officer inside the car stepped out into the rain. He scanned the array of Seattle Police cars, which may have numbered as many as all of the cars in his department.

The captain passed in front of their car and motioned for Katherine to move forward. She eased the car ahead and stopped abreast of him. He leaned down to her window.

"We're ready. I'll talk to the university officer. Have Mr. Flowers get us as close to the outside door as possible. We'll be right behind you. Remember, we want to keep this low-key."

"Sure," Katherine muttered as she drove forward. "We're going to arrest their big star, and he wants to keep it low-key."

Bobby Flowers directed them to follow a narrow road that circled to the back of the football stadium. Beyond the reach of the headlights lay the darkness of the lake with a few lights from the far shore twinkling through the rain. Beside them loomed the massive lurking shadow of the stadium.

Hours ago in the university library she had been thinking about food preservation, the drying and smoking of salmon, when the girl appeared before her like a vision from one of the tribes. Now she was back at the university, but as far from the library as she could imagine. Alice would be at the hospital, and Grace imagined her having to explain once more what had happened. There were no medicine men there who could purge her torment.

In a thousand years when the archaeologists discovered the foundation of the stadium, they might sift through the ruins for clues of a culture. They would know nothing about the girl or the great football star. Maybe they would conclude they had found another Roman colosseum without understanding how far the culture had evolved from that era since it no longer demanded the deaths of the losers. Or maybe, given the direction she saw them proceeding, the culture would have re-evolved so that it once again demanded death to the loser. Then again, it was likely that the whole structure would be underwater as the polar ice melted and inundated the coastal areas. The stadium ruins would be underwater, and all the screams of the spectators would rise to nothing and leave nothing behind.

"Right up there," Bobby Flowers said, extending his hand over the back of the front seat and pointing toward a lighted building north of the stadium. Beyond the building the lights of the practice field were still shining brightly.

"They're done with practice," he said. "I'm surprised they used the grass practice field in this rain. This is probably as close as you can get."

Katherine drove over the curb onto a wide sidewalk that got them closer.

"Well, maybe it's not," Bobby said.

Several people in yellow rain slickers and pants were carrying purple coolers from the practice field toward the open doors of the building. They stopped when they saw the procession of blue and white police cars coming toward them on the wide concrete walkway. Soon a small semicircle of yellow slickers and purple coolers formed a colorful arc around the police cars.

Observers also appeared in the doorway as the police cars emptied, but none of them said anything. Grace looked for Renzlau although she didn't expect to find him. She didn't see anyone in a football uniform. He must already be inside.

The captain led them to the doorway. The police procession entered a massive hallway where the concrete floor was wet and muddy. Grace walked behind the captain with Anne on one side of her and Bobby Flowers on the other. Katherine was in front with the other uniformed patrol officers.

There were loud noises from a doorway where more young assistants gathered. There were assistants everywhere. On her soccer team in high school they had one girl who had volunteered to help. The soccer players carried their own water coolers and practice balls and everything else they needed. Here, it seemed, the players carried nothing. The noise inside the locker room became louder as they approached the door, but the moving wedge of police brought with them a wake of silence from the spectators outside it.

The locker room smelled the way she remembered—steam, sweat, dirt, adhesive tape, balms for bruises and sore muscles. A partition screened most of the locker room from her view, but not all of it. An older man wearing sweat clothes in the university's colors approached them warily.

"Is there something I can do for you?" he asked.

"I'm Captain Lowery," the captain said. "Seattle Police Department. Who are you?"

"I'm the equipment manager."

"What is your name?"

"Jim Meyers."

"We have police business here, Mr. Meyers. Where is Coach Bourne?"

"He's in his office."

"Would you please call him? It's quite important that he come immediately."

The equipment manager hurried into his office and picked up the telephone. The police formed a line that nobody crossed, either to come in or to go out. Soon, the noise inside the locker room subsided just as it had done among those in the hallway. The general uproar they had heard upon arriving turned into individual voices and distinct laughter. The last laugh faded as the football coach and a host of assistants strode into the locker room.

"What's going on here?" the coach asked.

His voice was tense and demanding. His face was flushed a deep red.

"I'm Captain Lowery of the Seattle Police Department," the captain said in a steady voice. "We are here to arrest three of your players for suspicion of rape. We'll make the arrests quietly and leave. We expect your full cooperation."

Bourne looked around at his other coaches as if consulting them as he would when making a decision at a critical point in the game. None of the coaches offered a suggestion.

"You didn't have to come here. You could have waited until later. You have no right to come in here."

"Oh, but we do, Mr. Bourne. We certainly do have that right. Rape is a very serious matter, at least to us."

Grace didn't believe that Bourne's face could become redder than when he first walked in, but she saw that she was wrong. The red deepened on the skin above his royal purple sweatshirt.

"Who are they?" Bourne asked.

"You will see that soon enough," the captain told the football coach. "We will have women officers entering the locker room. Can you tell us what the proper procedure is for that?"

Bourne looked at the three women who were in the police line that blocked him from his locker room but reserved the final look for Grace. She thought it was the same look he had given her in the police station in Baton Rouge. It wasn't the benign expression of the good Christian man Beauregard had described, but Grace didn't care how he looked at her.

"Get Joanna over here," Bourne barked out to one of his coaches.

"Who is Joanna?" Captain Lowery asked.

"Director of athletics," Bourne said. "You can talk to her about going in there."

Bourne nodded his head toward the partition that divided the silent locker room from them as the assistant coach hurried away in the opposite direction.

"Mr. Flowers," Lowery said, "what is the procedure for women entering the locker room?"

"All you have to do is shout, 'Women coming in,'" Bobby said. "They're used to it."

Captain Lowery turned away from the coach and moved into the opening of the partition that separated them from the main locker room. All the police officers moved with him, but Grace stopped short of the divider that blocked her view of the football players inside. Katherine and Anne stopped with her as did Bobby Flowers. Bourne had a special look for Bobby Flowers, too.

"Gentlemen," the captain said in a voice that was not a shout but would carry far into the silence, "I'm Captain Lowery of the Seattle Police Department. We have a job to do in here, and we'll do it as fast as we can and leave. Coach Bourne and I expect your complete cooperation. Women officers will be coming into the locker room."

Grace looked back to the doors through which they had entered. More yellow-and-purple-clad watchers had gathered there, girls as well as boys.

"Mr. Flowers, would you come up here?" Captain Lowery said. "I would like you to tell me if you see Kennedy and Reed in this room."

Bobby edged through the blue uniforms until he was beside the captain. He studied the room for a minute and then spoke softly to the captain. The captain nodded, asked a question, and nodded again when the answer came.

"I want Murphy, Smith, and Stevens to come with me. Sergeant, I want everybody else to stay here. Nobody comes in, nobody leaves. Anne, did you find your handcuffs?"

Anne dug into her purse and produced the cuffs.

"Officer Stevens, I imagine you will recognize our main suspect."

"I will," Grace said.

"All right, officers, let's go."

Grace moved to the front with Anne and Katherine and for the first time saw the entire length of the locker room. It may have smelled like the locker room where her high school soccer team showered, and it was warm and steamy, but nothing else was the same. The main room was huge, and instead of narrow metal lockers there were wire cages replicating each other for a hundred feet or more. The men who filled the huge room were standing beside the cages. From the silence and stares she received, she felt as if she had entered a sacred sweat lodge and had interrupted secret rituals.

The captain stopped before two of the largest men Grace had ever seen. Although they were sitting on a bench, they appeared to be as tall as Katherine. The longer Grace looked at them, the more they appeared to be merely overgrown boys. She recognized their faces from the pictures in the game program. Bobby Flowers had been wrong. They didn't look alike after all. They didn't look like anyone else in the room.

Katherine separated herself from the trio of women and took a step toward the two young men. Both of them were dressed in jeans and T-shirts. Both had their shoes on.

"David Kennedy," Katherine said to the larger of the two, "you're under arrest for suspicion of rape. I want you to stand up and face the wall."

Unlike his coach the small amount of color drained from David Kennedy's face. He didn't or couldn't stand as Katherine directed. A commotion at the doorway distracted everyone in the room except Katherine. Her eyes remained fixed on the young giant. The athletic director had arrived from her office with her own entourage. The sergeant was not permitting her to go any farther, and her outrage rose for a moment before being quelled by the shiny badge of authority that the sergeant raised to her eyes.

"Stand up, David," Katherine repeated. She had her badge pinned to her shirt, and it was the first thing the football player saw as he turned back to the woman's voice that was telling him what to do. His coach and the director of all athletics at the far end of the room were silent.

The player stood and dwarfed Katherine, and Grace knew that this moment would determine if peace would reign or if all hell would break loose. They would be in trouble if it were hell.

"Turn around and face the wall," Katherine said.

Again the player hesitated. He tested a mocking smile, but it didn't last. Then he tried disbelief, but that didn't work either. He looked toward the entrance where the coach and athletic director stood. Finding no help there, he looked around the rest of the steamy room, desperate for help but not finding it anywhere. Finally he returned his gaze to the woman who was no bigger than the girl he had raped. The room where Alice had been was dark. This one was brightly lit, and he could clearly see Katherine's eyes, unlike the girl's eyes that he had not seen at all.

He turned around and faced the cage where all his armor was stored. Katherine unsnapped her handcuff case and removed the steel manacles. The noise startled the football player, and he looked back over his shoulder.

"Put your hands behind your back," Katherine said.

Kennedy's chin dropped to his chest as he offered his hands behind his back. Katherine closed the jaw of the first handcuff on one of the wrists, and Grace heard the ratchet click once and stop. She heard the same single click on the second wrist. Katherine grasped the left forearm of the handcuffed football player and turned back to the captain. She was done.

"Now it's your turn, Mr. Reed," Anne said. "You're under arrest for suspicion of rape. I want you to stand up and turn around just like your friend here."

Reed followed the example of his friend, skipping the mockery and disbelief, and hung his head as Anne fumbled with the cuffs. It didn't matter. She could take all the time she needed.

Katherine led Kennedy out first, through the clubless gauntlet of men and boys who did not speak or raise their hands, and Anne followed with Reed. Grace and the captain remained in the center of the room with one more arrest to make. She still had not seen Renzlau.

She could have asked where he was. She could have asked any one of the silent watchers, but she didn't want to ask. Instead she walked past the last caged locker and saw two boys in athletic shorts and bare feet standing in front of the open door of a side room. It had a large glass window in the wall that separated it from the locker room. She walked to the window and looked in.

Renzlau sat on top of a training table with his right knee encased in ice bags. There were other training tables in addition to the one he was on, but they were empty. Through the window she saw the recognition in his face. There was no surprise, no fear, no resignation even. She saw something beyond recognition. She saw what the captain who stood beside her was not likely to see. She saw contempt, and hate—subtle, strange, incomprehensible hate.

She walked to the door and with a silent command cleared the space so that she could enter. The captain entered behind her. Renzlau lifted his knee from the table and rearranged a piece of the elastic wrap that held the ice bags in place. He didn't look at her or acknowledge her presence. This was his room. She had no place in it.

"You're under arrest for suspicion of rape," she said. She didn't use his name.

"We've already been through this once," he said.

"No, we haven't."

Chapter 35

We thought she was a whore."

"Is that why she was crying?" Anne asked.

Reed was sweating. He wiped his forehead with his hand and transferred the moisture to his jeans. His hand was not an effective sponge, but he didn't have anything else. He was alone on one side of the table, and the two women sat on the other. He had trouble focusing on either of them. Anne asked the question, but he looked from her to Grace and back, hoping to find some sign of understanding. Grace understood him well enough.

"I didn't hear her crying. She wasn't making any noise that I heard."

"Is that why you hit her, so that she would make more noise?"

"I didn't do that. You can't put that on me. I'd never seen her before. I didn't know anything about her being a minister's daughter. If I had known who she was, I wouldn't have had anything to do with her. I thought she was a whore. Look, this wasn't the first time. He did things like that to show his appreciation. He'd take us out for a few beers or pizza, or he'd give each of us a CD. Stuff like that."

"And prostitutes. He bought you prostitutes, too," Anne said.

"I guess you could say that. A few times. I know it probably sounds bad to you, being a woman and all, but we were just trying to have a good time. That's why they get paid, isn't it?"

"I wouldn't know, Mr. Reed."

"Did he buy you prostitutes when you were out of town?" Grace asked. "Was he going to bring you a prostitute in Louisiana?"

"No, never on the road. We didn't know about that."

"About what?" Grace asked.

"About him leaving the hotel room before the game. It was just here in Seattle."

"Where did he bring the prostitutes? Where would you have these encounters?"

"Our place. Kennedy and I rent a house together where we live during the off-season. Twice he got a motel room. But it wasn't that often. You're trying to make it sound like we did this a lot."

Grace knew that what she sounded like had more to do with what Reed was hearing than what she was saying.

"Why did you think she was a prostitute?" Grace asked. "Did she dance like a prostitute? Is that how you knew? Do prostitutes dance certain ways?"

"I don't know the dance."

"Did you talk to her when you were dancing? Did she talk like a prostitute?"

"I don't remember talking to her."

"Did Renzlau bring other prostitutes to the fraternity house?"

"Not that I know about."

"Why this girl, then? Why did you think she was a prostitute? There must have been something. Did Renzlau come out of the room and say, 'Now it's your turn'?"

"No. He didn't say anything. He didn't have to say anything."

"So the girl came out and invited you in, you and Kennedy. She couldn't wait to get more. Right? That's why you went into the room together."

Reed looked away from Grace toward the interrogation room window. He was sweating as if he had struggled through a football game, but there were no crowds cheering his play.

"Were all the prostitutes black?" Grace asked.

Reed didn't immediately answer that question either. He looked at her, and she guessed he was seeing her the same way he was hearing what she said, with some distortion that she couldn't understand.

"You're trying to make some racial thing out of this—you and Flowers. You don't care when it's the other way around, do you? There's plenty of that, you know, but maybe you don't want to hear about that. Ask Flowers, why don't you? I'll bet he can tell you everything you want to know."

"What will he tell me?"

"Ask him."

"I'm asking you, Mr. Reed. What will he tell me?"

Reed was the last suspect still being questioned. They hadn't brought Renzlau into the holding rooms. On the drive into the station he wouldn't answer any of the questions from either Grace or the captain, who rode in the front seat of the car. Renzlau wouldn't answer even the simple questions about his age, date of birth, or where he lived. "You know all that," he said. "I want to talk to my lawyer."

When they arrived at the station, the captain told her to book him immediately. Renzlau expected them to wait for his father before doing anything—his father or the coach or somebody who would bring a check, legal stature, or political pull to circumvent the procedures they used for criminals. What about his phone call? What about his right to see a lawyer? They would be sorry if they didn't wait.

Grace wasn't sorry. As she led him through the tunnel that

ran under the street between the police station and the county building, she didn't talk to him. He wanted to talk then, but she was all through talking. The deeper they went into the tunnel the slower he walked, so that the officer accompanying her took hold of him from the other side in case Renzlau would try to stop completely or begin to resist. He didn't resist. He was only losing the will to move. She provided all the propulsion that he needed.

Kennedy talked enough to earn a temporary stay in a holding room. He gave them basic information. When Anne asked him what happened with Alice, he said that he had never raped anybody. He wouldn't answer any questions about what happened in the fraternity room or about Renzlau, and Katherine escorted him through the same tunnel where Grace had propelled Renzlau.

Reed was the only one left. It was the poetic captain who decided that only the women officers would ask him questions. When they went to court, the jury would be presented an interesting comparison—the women's questions, the football player's answers. In his worst dreams Reed had never imagined that he would have to sit before two women and explain his idea of a good time or that he would have to explain it to his mother, as Anne suggested he would soon have to do—as soon as he got out of jail, because that was where he was headed unless he gave them some reason not to put him there. She didn't want to do that, Anne said. She could just imagine how his mother would feel.

Reed wiped away tears with the same ineffectual hand that he had used to wipe away sweat, but the sweat and tears continued to flow as he explained once again that he thought the girl was a prostitute. He had stopped using the word whore. He began to cry noisily when Anne asked why it took two of them to hold that little girl down. Each of them was three times her size.

"I didn't know who she was. I didn't know."

They booked him, too—a two-hundred-eighty-pound crying boy who didn't know who Alice was. That was before the chief arrived but after the first television crew.

The chief nodded to Grace as he passed through the Sex Crimes office, where Grace was typing the report, and into the captain's office. Grace had known him since she was a little girl in Rigmor's store and he was Wes Micklelsen's partner on Ballard Avenue. He had left Ballard Avenue when he became a sergeant and went on to greater things, or quit being a cop, as Wes often said. But he still came back to Rigmor's apartment for the Saturday night poker game as did all the beat men who had worked Ballard Avenue. He wasn't the chief in Rigmor's apartment. He played poker with matchsticks like everybody else.

No one bothered Grace as she wrote the arrest report. And no one bothered her as she wrote her officer's statement. Katherine finished early, as she usually did. Katherine would finish early even when they had the same story to write. This time Grace had a lot more to write and wondered if she would ever finish.

The others may have wondered, too. Anne quietly removed each finished page from the desk where Grace placed it, copied the pages, and distributed the copies to the sergeant, lieutenant, and the captain's office where the chief remained behind the closed door talking continually on the telephone.

Outside, the rain had almost stopped, although the gale still blew strongly from the southwest as the final gasps funneled inland through the gap between the Olympic Mountains to the west and the Cascades to the east. She was sheltered from it like the coastal tribes in their sturdy lodges, built to withstand any gale. The permanence of the lodges may have been the reason she chose to study the coastal tribes rather than the nomadic people who lived farther inland. She imagined herself inside the sturdy lodges listening to the wind that could not reach her.

She finished the last paragraph of her statement, which had begun with Alice approaching Maria and her in the Student Union. She wrote about the fear that was evident in the girl's demeanor. She wrote the whole story that led to Louisiana and back to Seattle, and yet she told little. In her statement Maria was an acquaintance, not a policeman's daughter. She didn't write about the connection she made with Alice, the first eye contact of two people with a superficial commonality. And yet, would she have continued to think of the girl's fear without it? Would Alice have come to her without it, or would the football player have chosen Alice? It was still a mystery why Renzlau chose Alice. Reed gave a hint, but Reed was a liar.

She didn't write about her mother's cancer that had brought her sister, Evangeline, to Seattle, and who for all she knew was still in Louisiana talking to Miss Felicia about the slave girl, Rosalie. She didn't write about Rosalie either or the denominations of currency in Detective Beauregard's wallet. She didn't write any of that, but she wrote all that justice needed. She wrote all that could fit inside the courtroom where the elders were much less inventive than the elders who had long winters to think inside their warm secure lodges.

Her part was done, and she was ready to go home to Ballard where she had her own small lodge that would protect her from the wind. Anne and the other detectives would do the rest. There was already an evidence team in Renzlau's room in the fraternity house and another in his room at the crew house where he lived during the season. They were looking for any small piece of incriminating evidence. Maybe they would find a length of yellow rope or the belt that Alice described, the one with the large gold buckle that tore her skin. She wondered why Alice had not told her about the belt in the beginning.

It made no difference. Her part was done. Tomorrow she would be back on Ballard Avenue where the beer-flavored trouble in the fishermen's bars was nothing like the trouble the girl had. The fishermen on Ballard Avenue might fight one another with little provocation if they drank too much, but they would surely banish any Renzlau among them. If they didn't, Rigmor would sell them none of her pickled herring or her aged cheeses. She wouldn't even let them in the door.

Katherine had remained after finishing her statement. There was no need for her to stay, but Grace didn't try to persuade her partner to leave. There was no point. She knew Katherine well enough by now.

"Do you want to come over to my house and have a glass of wine?" Grace asked. "I think I need one. I have a few bottles stashed away in my cupboard."

"I thought you had a paper to write."

"I'm not writing another word tonight."

"Sounds good to me," Katherine said, "but I have to turn in the car at the precinct and change clothes."

"It's right on the way."

They walked out the door of Sex Crimes together. Bobby Flowers rose from the hallway bench when he saw her. Grace had forgotten about him. No, she hadn't forgotten.

"How long have you been here?" she asked.

He looked at his watch.

"I don't know," he said. "How long have you been here?"

She smiled at him, although she knew her smile wouldn't match the smile Anne had given him in the police car on the way to the stadium.

"Katherine is coming over to my house for a glass of wine. Do you want to join us?"

"I'll have that glass another day," Katherine said.

"No, you won't," Grace said. "Bobby is used to having other women around. He wouldn't know what to do with just me."

Then she smiled at him again. It was a smile that bore the memory of his ascent up the steps in the football stadium. It was a smile that remembered the beautiful song in Alice's church and his eyes as he stood behind Evangeline in the doorway in Louisiana. It was a smile that remembered her surprise when she saw his name, Harold Flowers, at the top of the newspaper story. It was also a smile that acknowledged all that she didn't know about him, that acknowledged the disappointment that might come, or the surprise that what she was looking for was not what she would find, and finally with the understanding that the surprise was not always bad. Not always. It was a smile that would surely make Anne Smith proud.

Chapter 36

Anne muttered to herself as she followed the western sweep of Denny Way as it turned north to Elliott Avenue. Who the hell was Elliott anyway? Probably some football player from the last century. It wasn't a woman, that's for sure. Not that it would make any difference.

A driver tried to sneak into her lane and interfere with her progress through the intersection. She responded with a loud resounding blast of the horn. When she looked up the light was red, and she cringed as she passed beneath it.

There must have been some yellow when she entered the intersection.

What the hell did an athletic director do anyway? It was bad enough that they paid a football coach twenty or thirty times as much as what she made, but did they have to pay an athletic director to direct him? If she was directing anything, she would have directed that pious hypocrite of a coach to defend the poor girl who was raped instead of running off at the mouth about letting the system work. Everyone was innocent until proven guilty, he said, which meant he wanted his football players back on the field.

The system was working, all right.

She placed her hand on the horn as the car in front of her turned on its blinker and slowed. "Use the turn lane," she said aloud, but she eased her hand away from the horn even though the driver didn't see the turn lane until he forced her and a whole line of cars that stretched back to Denny Way to slow nearly to a stop. By the time he finally moved over, the light at the next intersection had turned red. There was something about being the first car to get stopped at a red light that annoyed her.

She looked across at the driver who was responsible for delaying her. The driver was an elderly woman in a little pillbox hat, which had been in style twenty-five years earlier. She smiled at Anne, unaware that she had interrupted the flow of traffic.

My goodness, Anne thought as she smiled encouragingly to the other driver. She's just trying to get home. That's me in another twenty-five years.

It won't be me if there are many more days like this. Another one like this and I'll quit. I won't wait for the pension. I'll go into the chief's office and drop my badge on his desk and tell him I'm leaving this two-bit outfit. You don't expect much out of most of these guys, but it would be nice just once for the chief of all the police or the mayor or somebody to stand up and say that their cops did the right thing. If they couldn't see what was right, they all should be ashamed.

Nobody was ashamed, especially the athletic director who wasn't any different than the football coach, even if she was a woman. While she was telling the press that the University took the matter very seriously, she was pushing the prosecutor for all she was worth to drop the charges against her student athletes. Leave it to the phony liberals in Seattle to put a woman in charge of the athletic department so that she could talk about how seriously she took the whole matter while trying to stab the cops in the back, not to mention the poor girl who had been raped by these thugs.

When the light changed to green, Anne headed for the Ballard Bridge at a slower pace so that she wouldn't tailgate the next old lady in front of her, although there was no one ahead for at least a block. The cars raced by in the adjacent lane.

You would think a woman would understand. The coach was hopeless. The only violation that he was concerned about was the curfew violation, and Renzlau had already been sidelined half a game as punishment for that. Nothing mattered to him except winning the next game, but surely a woman could understand what the girl had been through. The director had read the report. How could she read that report and care where the suspects were arrested? The director knew about Louisiana, she knew about the girl who had fled from the rope, she knew all of it, and still she maintained that there was something improper about the arrests. Undignified, she said, when Anne called her on the telephone to talk to her, woman to woman. "How do you dignify rapists?" Anne had asked before the director hung up on her.

It didn't matter that she was a woman any more than it would have mattered if the street was called Mrs. Elliott Avenue. Maybe they would name the street after the rapist or the football coach when this was all done. They might even name it after the athletic director. She was doing such a fine job.

Cars began to brake ahead of her, and she said aloud, "Now what?"

It must be the bridge, she decided. Every time she tried to get to Ballard there was something in the way. She didn't want to wait for the drawbridge to raise and lower. One time, she remembered, she had sat in line for twenty minutes while a huge boat and a bunch of smaller ones passed in front of her. With her luck she would get stuck for an hour this time. She had told Katherine that she would be there in fifteen minutes.

Anne turned right on the first available street and started working her way up Queen Anne Hill. She couldn't find a

single street that went straight east up the hill. The hill was
steep, but it wasn't that steep. She turned south, then east,
south again, east, south, dead-end, back north, east, and finally reached the top. It was an equally uncertain route down
the hill where she found the ramp that led her onto Aurora.
The Ballard Bridge was probably long down by then.

The Aurora Bridge was high enough over the Ship Canal
that any ship could pass freely below it. It was at least a hundred feet down to the water. She didn't look toward the railing. She never did. There were four lanes, two in each
direction with a raised sidewalk on each side and no barriers
between any of them. The lanes were too narrow. She remained in the inside lane as far from the edge as she could
get. When she reached the end of the bridge, she took a deep
breath and looked back in her rearview mirror.

Sometimes now, weeks passed when she would cross the
bridge and not think about Jackie Mercado. Then other times
she would think of the young woman when she wasn't even
close to the bridge. She should have known before she ever
started up Queen Anne Hill that the memory would come
back today.

Anne still had the note in her desk drawer—Jackie Mercado's note that the patrol officers found tucked into one of
Jackie's shoes. The note was addressed to her. *Dear Detective Smith.* Anne always wondered if Jackie was addressing a
friend or if the greeting had been a simple formality. It was
the shoes that bothered her most.

I am sorry . . .

Anne remembered hearing the call come in over the F2
frequency speaker they had in the office—a jumper on the
bridge. Not common, but not unusual either. Then the patrol
officer at the scene asked for Detective Smith. She ran down
the stairs and commandeered another patrol car that was coming into the garage, and they were speeding out to the bridge
before Radio had determined which Detective Smith the pa-

trol officer was asking for. She was glad she wasn't driving. It gave her time to think about what she would say. She had known, without a second thought, who was on the bridge.

The trial had ended two weeks earlier, and the neighbor who had raped Jackie Mercado was a free man. He had cried on the witness stand—such a fine young man who had been lured into Jackie Mercado's apartment and enticed into sex when he knew it was wrong. His own will had been weak, but with God's help he had become strong again. His mother testified, his father, the minister at the church, his fiancée who had forgiven him his sin. If his fiancée could forgive, so could the jury. He carried a Bible with him every day to the trial.

Anne had testified for Jackie Mercado, and so did the physician who pointed to the faint bruises in the photograph of Jackie Mercado's chest where the fine young man had kicked her after raping her. No one testified about Jackie Mercado's character—not her father or her mother, not her brother or the boyfriend who would have nothing more to do with her.

Everybody knew it would be a difficult case, but they prosecuted anyway. They had to. Nobody could tell Jackie Mercado that they didn't believe her.

After the rape Jackie had locked herself into her apartment for five days. She could hear the neighbor in the next apartment, heard him knocking at her door, and finally she called for help. When the police arrived, Jackie still had in her possession the pink blouse with the two top buttons ripped away, and the investigating officers had taken the blouse as evidence. It was one of the few expensive items of clothing she owned, and one of the few pieces of evidence at the trial. The blouse was made of silk, and it was sheer. At the trial Jackie Mercado testified that the fine religious neighbor boy had ripped the buttons to get to her. The defense attorney picked up the blouse and held it up to the jury so that they could see his hand clearly revealed through the material. He showed the jury her black high-heeled shoes as well.

Jackie Mercado was preparing to leave her apartment for an evening of dancing when the neighbor knocked on her door.

At first the neighbor denied that there had been any sex, but after discussions with his attorney and before the trial began, he had a revelation. There had been sex. She had enticed him. He shouldn't have done it. He asked God to forgive him.

The day before the jumper call on the bridge, Jackie had come for the blouse and the shoes. It was a strange request, and it had worried Anne. Oh, child, why would you want these things?

Traffic had been stopped on both sides of the bridge. Idle drivers had gathered around the police barricade. The patrol car in which she rode drove in the empty oncoming lanes. They stopped beside the lone patrol car in the center of the bridge. It was strangely quiet when she got out of the car. So strangely quiet.

She saw Jackie Mercado outside the rail. Two patrol officers stood ten feet away from her. Jackie was wearing the sheer silk blouse. She had reattached the buttons.

Don't do this, Jackie. He wins if you do this.

No closer. No closer.

Jackie.

I'm sorry. It's my fault.

Jackie didn't jump as much as she simply let go. Anne could still feel the sensation in her stomach as if she were falling with Jackie Mercado. A patrol officer found the note in one of Jackie's black high-heeled shoes and gave it to her before she left the bridge.

> *Dear Detective Smith,*
> *I am sorry to bring you here, but you were the*
> *only one who believed me.*

For months Anne avoided the bridge. She drove through Fremont and crossed the Ship Canal over the low bridge. From there she could see the Aurora Bridge a short distance away. It was such a long way to fall.

Don't be sorry, Jackie. If I had to go through what you did, what all of you do, I might kill myself, too. But first I'd take my gun and blow that phony bastard to hell.

When Anne arrived at Ballard Avenue, most of the businesses had closed for the day—the furniture store, the secondhand store, the cabinet shop. It was after six, and the storefronts were as dark as the street would have been without the lights that shone from their old reflectors. Rigmor's store was brightly lit, and on the sidewalk outside were the two police officers she had arranged to meet. They were talking to a woman who had a shopping cart stuffed with garbage bags. Anne parked in an empty space across the street and got out of her car. There was no traffic to harass her, and she could walk across as slowly as she wished.

"Where are you staying tonight, Edith?" Anne heard Grace ask the woman with the shopping cart.

"I have a place," the woman said.

"It's getting cold," Grace said.

"Not as cold as where they take you. All they want is my secrets. They want to see my notebooks, but I won't show them. They can't find me."

Anne stood a half-dozen steps away from the police officers and the woman named Edith. Edith was not likely to feel the weather whatever it was. She wore two layers of sweatpants. The bottom layer, a bright blue, was stuffed into overshoes. On her right leg the red top layer had worked up so that the elastic cinched around her calf. It wasn't possible to tell how many coats or shirts she was wearing. A red stocking cap was pulled down over her ears.

"Do you have your medicine, Edith?" Grace asked. "Your daughter told me that you have medicine."

"It's poison. They're trying to poison me so that they can get my secrets."

"It's not poison, Edith. It makes you better. You don't hear the voices when you take the medicine."

"That's what they want. They don't want me to hear anything."

"Your daughter is worried about you. She can't come, but she still worries."

"I don't have a daughter."

"Yes, you do. I know you remember her. Do you have your medicine in one of these bags?"

"You're with them, aren't you?" Edith asked. "You want to get into my stuff so that you can see what I've written. I'm the only one who knows the truth. I'm the only one who knows."

"You told Rigmor."

"Did she tell you?"

Edith stared at Grace. Edith was a large woman, and Anne could sense danger in the piercing intimidation of the stare that she gave the young officer. Katherine moved a step closer to the two women. Grace didn't flinch, nor did she harden her face or return intimidation for intimidation.

"No, Edith," Grace said. "Rigmor didn't tell me."

Edith looked away from the young officer. She looked upward to the empty dark sky between the streetlights, and shook her head. "No," she said to something only she could see and shook her head again. "No," she repeated as she grasped the handle of her shopping cart and pushed it away. Edith turned at the first corner and disappeared from sight.

"She's getting worse," Grace said.

"The way she looked at you, I thought she was going to do something," Katherine said.

"I did, too," Anne said, closing the gap between her and the two officers. "What is this truth she knows that none of the rest of us knows?"

"The meaning of life. The voices have told her."

"No wonder she wants to keep hearing them," Anne said. "I would, too. Do you know what it is?"

"She won't tell me."

"But Rigmor knows?"

"Yes, according to Edith."

"What does Rigmor say?" Anne asked.

"She won't tell me."

Rigmor propped opened the front door and invited them in. The odor from Edith, one of the only two people in the world who knew the meaning of life, lingered in the store. Rigmor walked to the back where she had a large rectangular block of cheese on the counter.

"Take some of this to your father," Rigmor said to Grace. "Your mother called me today and said that Martin wouldn't bring home any *gammel ost* because he thinks the smell will make her sick. She doesn't start the treatment until next week, and she wants Martin to have his cheese before then. She sounded good. Strong. That's a good sign, *hvad*?"

"That's a good sign," Grace said.

"And maybe you would like to take a few slices home with you?" she said to Anne. "We call this *gammel ost*. It means old cheese. It's delicious."

"I think I'll pass," Anne said. She was no longer sure that the lingering odor was from Edith. Rigmor cut several thick slices of the discolored crumbling cheese and wrapped them in plastic wrap for Grace's father. "I heard Edith say that you and she are the only ones who know the meaning of life."

"Did she say that?"

"More or less."

"So then, I do. Now, dear," she said to Grace, "don't forget to take this to your father tonight."

Anne followed Grace into the back room. Anne heard Rigmor humming on the other side of the wall. Anne concluded that she would have to come more often if she were to have any hope of getting in on their secrets. She sat down in one of the three chairs in the tiny room, and the young officers sat in the other two. Three was an odd number to have. Weren't there supposed to be an even number of chairs in the kitchen? It was crowded, but surely there was room for one more chair.

"Something must have happened if you wanted to come all the way out here after work to see us," Katherine said.

No nonsense from this one, Anne thought.

"They released the football players this afternoon, just in time for practice."

"Did they post bail?" Grace asked.

"No bail," Anne said. "The prosecutor isn't going to charge them."

"What?" Katherine asked. Her voice was sharp with anger.

"He's not going to charge. He hasn't said so publicly, but that's what the deputy who's handling the case told me. Publicly, the prosecutor announced that he's deferring his decision until he has time to review all the facts, but he already has the facts. He'll wait until the football season is over, and then he'll announce that there isn't sufficient evidence to try the case.

"Our esteemed university's athletic department has been working overtime on the sidelines. I'm told that the alumni have been calling the prosecutor regularly, at least the rich ones with the special seats in the stadium. The whole team was planning to come to the arraignment to show their support—the whole team. Imagine what a circus that would have been—a hundred giant players in the courtroom against that one frightened girl. It's enough to make me sick."

"Jerome, too?" Katherine asked.

"I don't know. We could hope that a few would stay away, but there won't be an arraignment. Our sweet-as-pie athletic director and our pious coach have taken care of that. They're sticking up for the unfortunate young men who were trapped in a snare of questionable police tactics." Anne opened the newspaper she had brought with her and read the athletic director's words directly from the column, " 'The facts are being sorted out, but in the meantime, the reputations of three young men have been negligently tarnished.'

"It's all here," Anne said, unfolding the newspaper and spreading it out so that it covered the small wooden table. "It's enough to make you sick of this job."

Grace didn't look at the paper. Katherine picked it up and snapped it to attention.

A fourth chair, Anne decided, would have to be squeezed between the table and the wall. If the table were moved out to accommodate the chair, there wouldn't be room to pass between it and the shelves. The order of the room had been settled long before she arrived.

"What happens now?" Grace asked.

"It goes away. When the season is over, the prosecutor will announce his decision. He'll express concern for the girl and her family, of course, but he doesn't care about her. Why should he? He's not getting calls from the university president or the rich alumni telling him to stand up for the girl. No, none of them are calling with that message. He won't say that she made it all up, but that's what most people will believe. Or they'll think it was her fault, that she seduced him, I suppose. This is how every virgin wants her first time to be, isn't it? Isn't this the way you wanted it? She's on her own, God help her. And you guys will be singled out for special attention, too."

"What do you mean?" Grace asked.

"I've heard that your Captain Reimers isn't pleased with any of this. Lowery told me that Reimers has season tickets to the football games, and he's not looking forward to explaining to his buddies at the next game what happened. He wants a nice quiet precinct, and you made some noise. You didn't tell him that you were going to Louisiana on a police matter, and he thinks he's looking a little foolish right now. That's the way his mind works. He's a gutless old man who should have retired years ago. I'm sorry it turned out this way."

"Which way is that?" Grace asked.

"Captain Lowery told me that Reimers has decided the walking beat in Ballard is no longer necessary. You have too much free time on your hands if you can go all the way to Louisiana without telling him. You've forgotten what you're supposed to be doing."

"We're supposed to do police work," Katherine said. "Maybe he's forgotten what that's about."

"I'm sure he has," Anne said, "if he ever knew."

They became quiet around the table, and once again Anne heard Rigmor humming in the other room. It wasn't a melody that she recognized.

"Oh, well," Anne said, "at least we took a message out to all those guys in the locker room. They're not likely to forget that."

"There was a message, all right," Grace said.

Their call numbers came over the radio, sending out a message of a different sort. Their sergeant asked for a location to meet. Katherine pulled the portable radio out of its holder on her gun belt and set it on top of the table. She looked at Grace, and the two partners communicated silently.

"Make the meet somewhere else," Grace said. "I don't want to talk to him here."

Chapter 37

He bowed his head within the huddle and closed his eyes. It shouldn't be this hard. It shouldn't even be close. Behind by four. Stop thinking. Forget everything. Let it flow. Just let it flow.

Faintly, from the far end zone, he heard the band playing "Tequila" and hundreds, thousands maybe, clapping with the rhythm, their cheering sounding through the hostile shouts surrounding him on three sides. "Tequila!" came the cry. Louder this time. At home the whole stadium would be rocking. The chant would drown out the boos, the deep low idiot rumble of the enemy.

"Tequila!"

He ignored the antagonistic bugle calls and the incessant repetition of the one simplistic line, a call to arms from a dead civilization. It wasn't music, but it was all they played and it got on the nerves after a while.

That and the shouts he heard when he went to the sideline. He had stopped paying any attention to the shrill voices of the enemy—especially to the bitch who waited until there was a lull before she yelled. At first his teammates turned and looked for her. They laughed at her, then gestured with their arms and fingers until the coach told them to knock it off.

She didn't bother him. He ignored her when he went out

of the game. He stood on the sideline and the big guys surrounded him. After the first quarter the coach no longer took them to the bench to give instructions. He didn't need instructions. He knew what to do.

Beside him in the backfield Morrisey's helmet bobbed up and down with the rhythm of the far-off song. "Tequila!" came the shout from the end zone.

A long count to slow their rush. Let them come. Key off the backer. Wait, wait, wait. He took the ball and let the flow go around him. They blitzed inside. Wait, glide, open ground in the middle. He heard nothing, felt nothing except the rhythm in his legs, his feet on the soft grass. Strong, strong. Right. Find the sideline. Keep it in reach. Stretch it. Stretch it. Morrisey had the block on the safety. Fake outside, move in. The safety takes the fake, and Morrisey has him blocked outside. The corner has the angle. Get the last yard. The last yard. Sideline. Nobody touches me. Nobody gets a hand on me.

He dropped the ball at the feet of the opposing coach, who had moved back from the sideline to let him pass. How sweet it was. Routine. Thirty yards on a draw play. Routine. He heard the pleasure of his men. They were rolling now. They were in synch, and "Tequila" was closer and louder. They were all feeling the rhythm. Two minutes. All the time in the world.

He knew who she was—the black bitch in the stands, the same one who led the pathetic group outside the hotel with their signs. He knew who she was—the sister, the one in Louisiana. He laughed to himself as he ran back to the huddle. She could scream all she wanted and nobody would hear her now. Not with this noise. Not with the noise he had made. He knew who she was and where she was, and he wasn't going back there again. Not now. They were going to the end zone where the band played "Tequila" and the fans dressed in purple were standing and cheering. He was bringing it home. Bringing it home.

He could feel it now. He could feel the snap of the ball even if he couldn't hear the count. Jenkins dropped past him looking deep. Four rushing. Linebackers dropping into zones. He slid to the left, screened himself behind Anderson's block. Waited, waited. Jenkins looked left, deep left, then right and pumped his arm. The linebackers followed the pump, drifted right with the empty gesture of Jenkins's throwing arm. He moved out from the screen behind Anderson and stood in the clear as the ball dropped softly into his hands. Sidestep and the middle backer was gone. To the center. Plenty of time. Now the receivers were all blocking. So sweet when it worked. Glide with the wind, sail on home. This time, let him know you're there. Bury the bastard. Bury the son of a bitch.

He crushed his helmet into the chest of the safety who had worked free of Morrisey's block. He heard the gasp of the safety as he went down to the grass. Others grabbed at him, grabbed for the ball, but it didn't matter. He had buried the black bastard once and for all.

He placed the ball gently on the grass, pointed the tip toward the end zone, and got up on his own. Number 12 stayed on the ground gasping for air that wouldn't come. When it did he would feel the rest of the pain. Number 12 was done.

Three yards to go. The ball pointing the way home. The rest of the team running toward him, gathering around, knowing the touchdown was coming. They were in the groove, and the fans in purple knew it was coming, and the band playing "Tequila" knew it was coming. The other team knew it was coming, too, as they bent over to get the last bit of air into their lungs. Number 12 didn't care what was coming. He remained on the ground and didn't get up.

They had all the time in the world: time for three plays, maybe four, more time than they needed. Jenkins went to the sideline for the play. He knew what it was. They all knew. He had found his legs again. It had taken longer than he wanted, but he was in it now. This was what he wanted, what he lived for. This is what they wanted, the purple blur ahead of him. He would give it to them. They all knew what was coming. He was bringing it home.

Number 12 bowed his head as they dragged him toward the bench, a boy on each side. He wouldn't be back, and he would remember who hit him. He would remember.

He stopped watching number 12 and focused on the goal line. The ball was placed perfectly in the middle of the field. Nothing fancy now. No juke, no jive. Power. Straight-ahead power. They all knew, and it didn't matter. He had found the groove and there was no stopping. His team stood close, but nobody blocked his view. They knew what he was looking at. They all knew the line that he would cross, and nobody, nobody, would stop him.

In the bleachers directly behind the twin towers of the goalposts, a flicker of white caught his attention. He didn't intend to look, wasn't going to look beyond the end zone. He didn't raise his head, his helmet didn't move, but he saw the homemade banner with the purple letters being unfurled and hung across the wall at the bottom of the bleachers. He could have lowered his eyes before the meaning became clear. He had time. He had all the time in the world. It was there only a few moments before others tore it down—a blur of motion as the banner unfurled and was torn away. Nevertheless, he saw it. They all saw it. The painted purple letters were big enough that everyone in the stadium saw it.

RAPIST—GO HOME

The band played "Tequila," but the foot stomping wasn't as loud as before. Only those behind the banner who hadn't read the words kept at it, but the noise of their stomping gradually became fainter as the silence of those who stood motionless on either side stilled them, too.

He closed his eyes in the huddle and listened to the call. It was what he expected. It was what everyone expected, but it didn't matter. The bitch could paint all the signs she wanted, but it didn't matter. He was bringing it home.

He listened for the count from the quarterback, concentrated, waited for the snap. In perfect synchrony with the line before him, he sprang forward and felt the ball come into his grasp. All he had to do was hold on. Nothing else mattered. He followed the surge into the middle and held the ball as tightly as he could. Nothing else mattered.

He felt himself moving forward. One step, another. Shed the hands grabbing for the ball. It was his. It was always his. This is what he had lived for. He lunged the last yard and extended the ball out to the purple throng behind the goalposts.

The whistle sounded, and he saw the referee's arms go up to signal the touchdown. In the bleachers beyond the end zone he heard the noise coming back: drums beating, feet stomping, voices cheering the touchdown. His teammates lifted him off the ground, and he laughed as the big guys carried him off the field. He laughed as he looked back to the end zone and saw the last painted remnants of the torn banner still anchored to the bleacher rails. No one bothered to tear it away. No one had to. HOME was all that was left.

Chapter 38

Maria stared into the cold dark water, knowing what she had to do, knowing that she could, searching inside herself, inside her memories, inside the memory of her memories for the will to do it. Within the boat bearing her mother's name, she stared into the water and willed herself to plunge. She took a deep breath, a breath so deep that it would last until she surfaced again, leaned toward the water, leaned, tipped, and rolled.

It was colder than she had imagined, colder than anything she had ever felt as it surrounded her, pressed upon her and enveloped her. If she had not prepared herself, if she had not at least in some measure prepared herself, she would have given in to the cold, to the panic, and released the air too soon.

Remember the story about the sea otter.

With her eyes closed, she stretched her hands toward the surface of the water. Upside down, all sense of direction had left her. She would feel the air, he told her. Reach up until you feel the air. Her hands were freezing. How could she feel the air?

Do you remember when Otter could not swim?

She stretched her arms toward the surface. He told her to position the paddle parallel to the surface. She was upside down with her eyes closed, and she couldn't feel the surface any more than she could feel anything except the coldness of the water. She felt her heart. It was pumping harder and harder. Her body demanded air. She had to try now. She extended the paddle away from her and pulled it down with all the strength willed to her. The boat began to rise. She forced the air from her lungs as her face broke the surface of the water. She teetered on the brink a fraction of a second and gulped air before the boat rolled back under the surface of the water. Suddenly she felt herself rolling upward without any effort. She curled toward the bow and let the water drain away from her.

"That was good," her father said. "A lot better than the first time I tried it."

She opened her eyes and saw him standing in the water beside the kayak. He wore chest waders that he had borrowed for the day. She wore his dry suit, and her body must be dry, but she couldn't tell. She was too cold to know if she were dry or wet.

On the beach Katherine stood beside the fire. They had gathered enough wood to make a huge fire so that she could warm herself when they finished.

"Next time bring your left arm into your chest." He clenched his left hand into a fist and brought it to his chest.

She pulled the nose plugs off her nose and nodded her head. Next time she thought. She looked back over her shoulder at the fire. Katherine didn't or couldn't hide her worry. The fire looked warm and inviting, warm and sensible.

"You almost did it the very first time," her father said. "It must be in your blood. Next time I won't pull you up unless you tap on the boat. If you want me to pull you up, release the paddle and tap on the sides." He tapped the side of her boat with an open hand, and she nodded her head. He stood back and waited.

She fastened the nose plug back on her nose and stared

into the water. "Damn," she muttered as she rolled once more into the water.

Otter lived on shore with her cousins, Bear and Wolf. She loved to play games with them, but she could never run as fast as her cousin Wolf, and she was never as strong as her cousin Bear.

She expected the cold this time, the pressure. She waited until the kayak stabilized upside down and then reached up again with the paddle. This time her right hand felt the air. She curled her hands so that the paddle rose above the boat, parallel to it and the water, extended the paddle, and pulled once more. She forced her left hand to her chest and felt the boat rolling upright. She strained every muscle in her body to continue the roll, but she ran out of paddle before she was upright. The kayak rolled back under. She had enough air for one more try. Quickly she raised the paddle, pulled her left hand toward her, and her face rose from the water. Again, she strained with every muscle, every fiber, but she couldn't finish the roll. Again, she rolled back under the surface. She reached for the release strap of the waist skirt but remembered his instructions at the last second. She pushed the paddle away and tapped hard on both sides of the boat with her hands. A moment later, she rolled to the surface.

"You were so close," he said. "You leaned the wrong way, and you still almost made it."

Damn, she thought. So close, so far. It was all the same. She had watched him roll repeatedly, almost without effort. She had used every muscle in her body and couldn't make it.

"Don't forget your legs," he said and tapped the kayak where her right knee pressed against the shell. "The legs are the most important part. Hips and legs. Lean toward the paddle, not away from it. When you start coming up, snap the hips. Use your legs and hips." Standing in the water he wiggled his hips, which was meant to be some imitation of the snap she was to use with her head upside down or in some elevation on the way up.

Legs, hips, head, torso, shoulders, arms, paddle, hands. Too much to remember. Too much to work together. Some part was sure to work against the others and cause failure.

She took another breath and rolled slowly, reluctantly, unwillingly back into the water. She should have learned this during the summer. In the summer the air would be warm when she came up, if she came up.

Wolf played tricks on the otters. Do you remember what the tricks were?

He ate some of them.

Yes, but before that. What were the tricks before that?

It's cold down here, Mama. Is it always this cold?

She raised the paddle, willed herself not to panic, felt the air above the surface with both hands, shifted her head toward the side of the paddle, imagined herself snapping her hips. When she pulled the paddle toward her, she felt herself rising. All her instincts told her to pull with her head the other way, but she pushed against instinct, and when her head rose from the water she braced her knees tightly against the shell of the kayak and snapped her hips. The result was immediate and overwhelming. She rolled upright and kept rolling and plunged into the water on the opposite side. Her nose plug came free, and she could feel the water burning all the way up her sinuses. She pushed the paddle away from her and slapped the side of the kayak. Nothing happened except that more water ran up her nose. She slapped the kayak again.

She heard her father laughing as he rolled her up to the surface. Water poured out of her nose the same way it had poured in. It hurt in both directions.

"That was great," he said. "You're a natural at this. It's in your blood."

She wasn't sure if he were the Wolf or the Bear in her mother's story.

Wolf told Otter how dangerous the water was. He said there were killer whales waiting beneath the surface, ready to eat Otter if she ever jumped into the water. He told Otter that her webbed feet were made to slide on the ice, so that she could keep away from the killer whales. He told Otter that he would protect her if she stayed on the ice with him.

Her father retrieved the paddle that was floating a few feet away from the kayak and placed it into her hands.

"Next time," he said, "do everything the same but a little less of it all. Let it flow now. Don't think this time. Just let it flow." He tapped her shoulder and moved away.

The water was much closer than before. When she had rolled into it the first time, it had taken a long time to get there. It was much closer now. She reached down and brushed the surface with her hand. Then she clipped the nose plug back into place, took a deep breath, and rolled once more.

Bear was Otter's friend. He told Otter not to believe Wolf. He reminded Otter what had happened to her mother, what had happened to her brother. They went with Wolf onto the ice, Bear said, and nobody saw them again. Wolf said that the killer whales ate Otter's mother and brother because they jumped into the water, but why was Wolf so fat when he came back from the ice?

"Don't think," he said. "Let it flow." I'm upside down in the water, I can't see anything, it's freezing, and I'm to let it flow. What do you think, Bear? She reached to the surface with her paddle and let it flow. She thought that she wouldn't have the momentum to bring herself up. She thought she would sink back into the water, but she snapped her hips and rolled free of its grasp. This time she braced herself with the paddle on the opposite side. Her father held on to the nose of the kayak and whooped. Katherine yelled from shore, clapped, and jumped up and down beside the fire.

"Did you help me?" she asked her father.

"No. I was going to keep you from rolling all the way over, but I didn't need to. I think you got it. Another thousand rolls and you'll be an expert."

She looked at him with suspicion in her eyes.

"You have to learn to roll from the other side, too. But not today. Maybe you've had enough for one day."

He was beginning to look like a wolf in bear's clothing. She motioned for him to stand back. When he stood clear, she rolled into the water again.

Bear told Otter that she could swim like the fish. While she was slow and clumsy on the ice, she could dance in the water. The water was her friend.

She rolled in the water like Otter and came back to the surface. She filled her lungs with fresh air and plunged again.

Otter didn't listen to Bear. One day after the long winter, Wolf said he wanted to show Otter how the ice was disappearing into the water. Otter wanted Bear to see it, too, but Wolf said that Bear was still sleeping. Soon the ice would be gone. Now was the time to see it. Otter followed Wolf onto the ice. Just then the ice broke and began to float away. Otter ran from side to side but she was afraid to swim back to shore. "Wolf," she cried, "we're in trouble now." But Wolf only smiled and licked his lips. Otter knew then that Bear had told her the truth.

This time something was a little off, and she didn't make it upright: three-fourths of the turn and back into the water again. She held on to her paddle and made another attempt. She broke free of the water.

Wolf and Otter floated far off shore, and Otter ran from one side to the other of the ice that had broken away. The ice floe was her prison. Only the water could make her free. She looked into the water and decided that she would rather face the killer whales than be eaten by Wolf. She jumped, and it was like floating on air. She swam deep into the water and saw that there were no killer whales. When she came up to the surface, she called to Wolf. "Wolf," she said, "come with me. There are no killer whales here. Come with me. We'll swim back to shore."

Again and again she rolled into the water to imprint the motion into her body's memory the way her mother's stories stayed in her mind. Her father waded back to shore and watched her from the beach. Finally she was so tired that she didn't think she could roll again no matter how clearly the roll was imprinted. One more time, she decided.

Wolf tried to coax Otter back onto the ice. "It's warm here," he said. "I'll protect you. Come back, Otter. The killer whales will be coming." But Otter would not go back to the ice. "Come with me, Wolf," she said. "I'll show you the way back to shore."

She opened her eyes as the name *Gloria* rose out of the water. Her father had named the kayak after her mother when he learned that she had died, before he knew about their daughter. He offered to change the name when she came, but Maria didn't want him to change it. It was how she knew he still remembered.

She paddled Gloria toward the beach. She was glad that she wasn't far out on the ice. She would never have made it. Her arms were so tired they could barely lift the paddle. They were tired in a good way. Her father walked down to the shore and pulled in the bow. He was Bear after all.

"Enough?" he asked.

"Enough," she said.

"You can take her out now," he said. "Whenever you want."

Finally Wolf jumped into the water and swam toward Otter. "A little farther, Wolf," Otter said. "A little farther." Every time Wolf came close, Otter danced away in the water. "A little farther," Otter said. "A little farther." Finally there came a time when Otter looked back for Wolf and he was gone. "What happened to Wolf?" Otter asked her friend the sea. "Did he find the killer whales at last?"

Chapter 39

It was her job to keep the fire burning high, and it was burning high as the girl walked toward her, hair dripping with seawater and her face red from the cold—her hands, too, as she held them over the fire and rubbed them to get warm.

"You should wear gloves when you're out there," Katherine said.

"The bear said I couldn't," Maria said. "I have to feel the air when I raise the paddle out of the water."

"The bear?" Katherine asked.

"I was talking to my mother. She told me a story about the bear, the wolf, and the otter. My father is like the bear."

"Is it a good story?"

"It's from my mother. I heard her voice in the water."

Maria squatted beside the fire with her hands held out to the flame. She was a strong girl, and the muscles showed in her neck through the rubber suit cinched tightly around it. Katherine wondered if her mother had been strong, or if the strength, the muscles at least, had come from her father, who passed them on his way to the house with the kayak on his shoulder. He glanced at Maria, but she didn't see him. She was staring into the fire.

Katherine remained silent. She thought the thrill of seeing the girl come up from the water would last all afternoon, but it was already gone. She understood. The girl had heard her mother, and maybe Sam heard her, too, and she, who could hear no voice in the water, was on the other side of the fire as far from them as she could possibly be. The girl had asked her to come, to tend the fire, but why? She couldn't be more out of place—halfway between the years that separated father and daughter, halfway around the fire, halfway from everything.

She should leave. She had built the fire high enough that the flames rose above the girl's head as she squatted to warm her hands. From where Katherine stood, the fire was so hot that she had to back away from it. It was a beautiful fire, and she should leave so that the girl could look into it alone or with her father and talk about the woman whose voice she heard, or maybe they both heard. Her father had disappeared into the house. Before he returned, she should disappear, too.

"Thanks for coming," Maria said. "My father gets carried away sometimes. I thought you could balance him out if he started pushing too hard."

"It looked to me like you were the one who was pushing."

"I wasn't pushing," Maria said. "I was listening. I didn't want to stop."

Through the fire Katherine saw the tears gather in the strong girl's eyes and drop unhindered one by one down her cheeks. Where was Sam? she wondered.

Katherine circled the fire and knelt beside the girl so that the intensity of the flames rose above her. She took the girl's hands, which had begun blocking the tears, and looked into her eyes.

"I wouldn't want to stop either."

Like the little girl she had once been, Maria buried her face into Katherine's chest. Katherine put her arms around the girl and felt the cold slippery skin of the rubber suit. No longer did she feel awkwardly placed in time or space. The girl was almost as old as the mother she remembered, but not quite. This once, Katherine finally felt she was the right age.

She was the age of the mother Maria remembered, and Maria was the little girl who could cry in her mother's arms.

When Sam returned, she and Maria were sitting side by side in front of the fire that shot sparks high into the air before drifting away with the wind. Katherine held the girl's hand.

"I brought you some warm clothes," he said, holding out a bundle for Maria. "You'll feel better when you get out of that rubber suit."

Maria took the bundle of clothes from him. She laid the clothes on a rock. There were two sweatshirts, sweatpants, a pair of heavy socks, and a stocking cap. Maria removed a purple sweatshirt from the bundle and held it up in front of her. Then she dropped it onto the pebbled beach and looked at him.

"What?" he asked.

"It's the same color as the football uniforms."

"I know it is. Oh, I see," he said, but Katherine wondered if he did.

"You had only one sweatshirt left in your drawer, so I got one of mine. Look." He pointed to the sweatshirt on the ground. "It doesn't say anything about football. It could just as well be a sweatshirt for the rowing team."

"It's not from the rowing team," Maria said.

"No," he agreed. "I'm sorry. It will take us a while to get this figured out. Maybe you and Kat have already done that, but it will take me a while. Silve and I didn't listen to the game today, so that's a start. It's strange. You're loyal to a team for so long you don't even think why any more. I guess it's time we start thinking."

Katherine watched him pick up the sweatshirt with a huge dog on the front that looked like a wolf. Sam carefully draped the sweatshirt over the fire. Soon flames broke through the smoking purple material. Maria took a stick and pushed the burning remnants deep into the fire that consumed every bit of the fabric—every image, every word, every thread of loyalty.

Chapter 40

Grace looked up at the small white-frame house perched on the steep hillside. Heavy drapes were drawn across the front windows giving the impression of absence or mourning. On the hillside, a rock garden terraced the slope, and juniper bushes crept from one level to the next so that it was difficult to discern where the plants were rooted. Grace climbed the steep steps of the serpentine walk where short weeds grew in the cracks of the concrete.

When she pushed the doorbell button, she heard a three-note chime inside the house. The slow fade of the last note added to the emptiness. If she had not called, she would have thought no one was at home. She heard soft footsteps at the door and the deadbolt lock being retracted from the strike plate. The door slowly swung open, and Alice stood inside the entry.

They faced each other silently for a moment before Alice stepped back, motioning for Grace to enter. Grace stepped into the house and closed the door behind her.

"Are you alone?" Grace asked.

Yes, Alice indicated silently with a slow nod.

"I wanted to talk to you," Grace said. "I wanted to see how you were doing."

Alice led Grace from the small entryway into the adjacent

living room. Everything in the room was perfectly placed; there were no magazines or newspapers on the coffee table— not a pillow on the couch out of place, not a piece of furniture that appeared to have ever been moved. Alice gestured toward the couch, and Grace sat carefully so that she would not disturb the perfectly arranged pillows. Alice sat down in a straight chair facing Grace.

The drapes on the two side windows were open, and gray light from the overcast sky came through white lace curtains. On the wall opposite the windows were framed pictures of Martin Luther King and John and Bobby Kennedy. There was a painting of a mountain hung on another wall. It was too jagged, too pointed to be Mt. Rainier. Grace guessed it was Kilimanjaro.

"Your father told me that you stopped going to classes."

"Nobody believes me. They all believe him."

"There are a lot of people who believe you, Alice."

Grace's attempt to balance the scale of believers had no effect upon the girl. Alice's face remained as unchanged and closed-in as the room in which they sat. Grace wondered what Alice could do all day within such a room.

"I don't hear anything from them," Alice said.

Grace had heard little enough herself. The voices were louder from those who believed the football player—his lawyer and his coach and his athletic director and teammates and nearly everyone else quoted in the daily but declining pronouncements about innocence and justice. Perhaps a little of the luster had been removed from the university champion, but not much. Renzlau and the football players walked around the campus as if nothing had happened, while Alice stayed at home in the room where nothing was moved.

"My father tried to talk to the university president," Alice said, "but the president wouldn't talk to him. Somebody in his office told my father to talk to the university's lawyer downtown. The lawyer said that there was nothing the university could do because nobody has been charged with a crime. You saw what he did to that girl in Louisiana, and they still won't do anything."

"I know," Grace said. "I don't blame you for feeling angry."

"I don't feel angry," Alice said. "I don't feel anything."

"Have you talked to the counselors at the hospital?"

For a moment there was a ripple in the smooth surface of the girl's impenetrable expression.

"They offered me counseling—the university. They said I wouldn't have to pay for it. They said I wouldn't have to pay for anything at school. What's the matter with them? Do they think they can give me something and everything will be all right? Why would I need counseling if I'm lying about what happened? Why would I lie about such a thing? I'm not going back there."

"There are other schools," Grace said. "You don't have to go back to that one."

"My father just sits in his office all day," Alice said, as if she had not heard Grace. "He says that he's working on church business, but I know he isn't. He just sits there. Sometimes he's so angry at those men and at the university that I'm afraid he's going to do something that will get him into trouble. Sometimes he's angry at me. I disappointed him. He can hardly stand to look at me.

"My mother is afraid for all of us. She's afraid to leave the house. She calls from work and asks me to take meat out of the freezer for dinner or look in her room for her glasses. She's just calling to check on me. I wish she would stop. I wish I had never said anything to anybody. I just want everybody to leave me alone."

"I'm sorry," Grace said.

Was sorrow the reason she had come, or was it fear that she had made the girl's life worse? Grace wished she could reach over to the girl. The space between them was narrow, and yet Alice sat stiffly in the chair, untouched and untouchable. Grace couldn't leave the girl like this, not again. She remembered the first moment of eye contact with Alice on the patio of the Student Union on a day when she had wanted to enjoy the warmth of the sunshine, a gift from Indian summer. Grace had wanted to close her eyes and feel the warmth of a season that was certain to be short-lived and not think of anything else. She had imagined the contact with Alice to be like any other brief accidental connection of eyes, and she had dismissed it as she was used to doing. The girl had come forward, even after being dismissed, and had tried to warn Grace about danger. Alice didn't know what she was getting into. How could she know? No one ever knew.

"I told you at the police station that someday I wanted to tell you what else I found in Louisiana," Grace said. "May I tell you now?"

Alice's nod of acceptance was one of practiced politeness, the preacher's daughter responding to a member of her father's congregation. Grace had been in that congregation once, sitting stiffly in the pew behind Alice and watching the girl's reaction. Grace didn't want to be there again.

"My mother had breast cancer," Grace said before Alice had time to reconsider. "We found out almost exactly two months ago today. You think I went down to Louisiana to investigate Renzlau, but that was only half the story. Maybe not even half."

Grace watched puzzlement cross Alice's face. At least it was an expression, a relief from the unfeelingness the girl described.

"You think, 'What does your mother's cancer have to do with me?' I want to try to explain how you're linked to her and me and people you can't even imagine—at least how I think you are.

"My sister, Evangeline, flew up here from Los Angeles to be with my mother during the operation. She and I were never as close to each other as we could have been. Sometimes I thought she and I must have come from different planets, we were so far apart.

"After my mother's operation, my sister had one idea of what we should do and I had another. I thought Evangeline and I should clean our mother's house and make it as pleasant for her as possible when she came home. Evangeline helped a little, but she didn't think cleaning the house was important. She went up into the attic where my parents keep old papers and old clothes and everything else that they don't want to throw away. I think Evangeline wanted time to be alone, to think, to find pieces of the past that would bring back memories for her. At the time I thought she was just shirking her work.

"Evangeline found a land deed from Louisiana dated before the Civil War that she thought was some big discovery, but I was angry that she had spent her time in the attic instead of helping me. I accused her of not loving our mother as much as I did. We came really close to fighting and separating even more, but for some reason we didn't. There was a force that held us together. I thought it was my mother, but now I'm not so sure.

"That land deed had a name on it that we didn't know, but we were pretty sure that it belonged to one of our ancestors in Louisiana. We had always heard that our people were free even before the Civil War. Evangeline was sure that the land deed would prove it. She wanted me to go with her to find out.

"I wouldn't have gone to Louisiana with her if you hadn't come up to me to warn me about Renzlau, and I wouldn't have gone without the land deed Evangeline had found. I might not have gone if the girl I was with on the patio that day wasn't a policeman's daughter, if she wasn't my partner's friend. I might not have gone if Bobby Flowers had not helped me find you and a football player who told us some things about Renzlau. There were so many people and pieces of information that came together. If any one of them had been missing, I might not have gone.

"But I went. I went down there to follow Renzlau. And Evangeline went with me to look for the man on the land deed. My sister and I thought we knew who we were looking for from the document she found, but we found someone completely different.

"Our great-great-grandfather, Emile, the person on the land deed, was a Creole of color, as they called themselves back then. These people didn't think of themselves as black, and in fact, they were very light-skinned—most of them. We found out that he rented a slave girl to take care of his house. He didn't buy her; he just rented her. Something happened between them, between this free man of color and the black slave girl. They fell in love, or at least we think they did. He fell in love, anyway, and wanted to marry her. His family was violently against the idea. She was too dark, too African. This slave girl, our great-great-grandmother, was able to earn enough money to buy her own freedom. She must have worked herself nearly to death. From the few stories we heard about her and from the records we found, we think she was a strong woman, a very strong woman. Emile married her secretly against the wishes of his family, and they had a child. Then, one night, their house burned to the ground. Emile's family said our great-great-grandmother had caused the fire, but my sister and I think someone else did it, maybe someone from our own family. Emile and our great-great-grandmother left Louisiana and never went back.

"Miss Felicia, an old lady who was the great-niece of our great-great-grandfather, told us the story about Emile and the slave girl. She didn't know the girl's name. Nobody did. Evangeline and I went down there looking for this man, Emile, but we found the slave girl instead.

"Evangeline and I weren't the only people who went

down there to look for one thing but found something else. Bobby Flowers went to Baton Rouge to write a story about the football game and maybe about Renzlau. Instead he found the girl in the motel room, and maybe he found you when he wrote about what happened to her.

"What I'm trying to say, Alice, is that you don't know yet what you're going to find when you start looking for something or someone. You think you're going to find this one person, but you find someone else, and you're different yourself because of what you found. I just wanted you to hear this story. I don't think you know yet what you're going to find in yourself. Give it a little time"

Alice had remained perfectly still while Grace told the story that began with her mother, led to the slave girl, and ended with words about Alice. Grace couldn't tell if Alice understood why she was telling it. She wasn't sure she understood the reason herself.

"I'll leave now," Grace said, "but I want you to call me if you need to talk to somebody. I would like to talk with you again. Call me anytime, Alice—day or night."

Alice said nothing and made no motion to stop Grace from rising and taking a step toward the door, but then she reached out and held Grace's arm.

"Did you ever find out who she was?" Alice asked. "The slave girl? Did you find her name?"

Grace slowly placed her free hand on top of Alice's. She wanted this girl to hold on, however gently, however tentatively. Grace feared that any abrupt motion would be too fast for either of them. With her hand on top of Alice's hand, she edged back to the couch and sat down. From there she could look into the girl's eyes directly. From there she hoped the girl would see directly into her eyes as well.

"Yes," Grace said. Her voice was softer because of the touch from the girl's hand. "We did. Her name is Rosalie— Rosalie Stevens. She chose the last name herself."

Chapter 41

Sunlight shone through the tall stained glass windows—repeating a pattern that ran the length of the reading room. The last of the series began at Grace's table and extended high above the bookcases upon the east wall. The stained glass diffused the light, warped and subdued it. It had the same effect as the light that might have passed through the branches and fine needles of the Douglas fir trees that the Kwakiutl used to build their lodges or through the denser foliage of the thick and towering cedars from which they made their canoes and totem poles.

She had focused on the economy of the tribes, principally upon the bountiful runs of salmon. Her statistics and charts demonstrated that bounty. Her goal was to explore the consequence of excess.

For the Kwakiutl excess did not produce what she had expected—generosity, stability, or a sense of cultural ease. Instead excess produced rivalries that went on and on without end. Once begun, the thirst for rivalry could not be quenched, and the production of excess goods became the route to status and power, not to ease or to give peace or generosity. Goods could be given away or destroyed without threatening the livelihood of the tribe. Waste, according to Benedict, became a goal of the culture.

Grace closed her eyes and tried to analyze what it meant. How did her charts explain the rivalry among the chiefs? A scientist must suspend judgment and record the economic structure, puberty rites, marriages, births, and deaths as they are or as they were and not as she wished, for to wish was an act of judgment that interfered with the observation. A man can do what he wants, Schopenhauer said, but he cannot want what he wants.

Scientist or not, she longed for that one society, that one culture that offered a perfect balance of the Dionysian and Apollonian, freedom and responsibility, exuberance and restraint. No social order, Benedict wrote, can separate its virtues from its defects. Every culture carries within it the seeds of its destruction.

A shadow moved into the diffused light. She looked up from her charts that were not telling the whole story or even, as she was beginning to suspect, any meaningful part. The Adonis who had deceived her in the beginning and who continued to deceive so many cast the shadow. Her first impulse was to throw the books at him and follow with the charts and everything else at hand. Her second impulse was to reach down to the backpack on the floor beside her feet and place it on the chair next to her. She followed that impulse and rested her hand on the gun inside the bag.

He hadn't stumbled upon her. That much was clear. There was no surprise in his expression. He watched her pull her backpack close to her but didn't move. He must have known what was inside.

"What are you doing here?" she asked. Her question came through clenched teeth and was hissed more than whispered.

He crossed to the opposite side of her table and sat in the chair facing her. She looked around the room. No one was watching them. At an adjacent table a boy was asleep. He had spread his arms across the table and his face lay sideways in his open book. She recognized the faces of everyone around her. Most, like her, sat at the same table at the same time every day. Without knowing one another's names, without knowing anything about one another, the library users had established a pattern of familiarity. Renzlau was the only one who didn't fit into the pattern.

He hunched down in the chair so that he could see her beneath the shaded fixture that was mounted at the correct height to produce light without glare and shield from view the faces of all who sat opposite each other. No one had to sit opposite another. There were enough empty spaces for everyone.

"I wanted to talk to you," he whispered.

She gathered her charts and closed the two books she was using to provide information that she was now certain had nothing to do with truth. She didn't want him to see what she was reading. She didn't want him to see the useless information she had gathered. She didn't want him to see anything about her.

"I had nothing to do with those other guys," he said. "I didn't know they were still in my fraternity house. I thought they had left."

She would have to write a follow-up report. She would have to write what he said and what she said in return, and the thought of doing so revolted her. None of it would ever become part of a trial anyway. Her report would be as worthless as the charts of food production she hid from his view.

"Tell that to your lawyer or the prosecutor. Tell it to somebody who cares. I want you to leave, and I don't want you to come here again. I don't ever want to see your face again."

"I did tell him," Renzlau said. "Do you think I put them up to it? Do you think I would do that to her? I didn't mean for it to happen. It was all a mistake."

"You only meant to whip her and rape her yourself. Is that what you mean? Is that what you're going to tell us at the trial?"

Down went the mask that was earnest Paul Renzlau. Down went the mask permanently preserved and disseminated in the newspaper photograph of the football star and the boy with cancer. The face she saw now was different. It was the face Alice would have seen if the room had not been dark. It was the face the choking girl in Louisiana had seen, the girl from Jefferson Street, the face others had seen—no one knew how many others, except him.

"There won't be a trial," he said. "Don't you know that? Maybe they didn't bother to tell you. Nobody believes her. Nobody believes you—nobody who matters."

"Maria believes me," Grace said. "She sat in class with you for a whole week, and you didn't know that she couldn't stand to look at you. You didn't know that, did you? She couldn't stand the sight of you."

"I dropped the class," he said, the face changing even more. "I was just taking it for my enjoyment."

"There's something else you should know," Grace said, "a little piece of information that nobody may have bothered to tell you. If you ever try to hurt Maria, there won't be enough left of you for anybody to recognize. Famous Paul Renzlau, where has he gone? A little piece here, a little piece there. That's all there will be. We take care of our own. Maybe nobody bothered to tell you that."

It was a lie—mostly. She knew it was a lie, but maybe he didn't. The smile on his face, more sneer now than smile, faded a little. It faded as he pushed back his chair and stood so that the fluorescent light was below his face and did not illuminate it any longer.

"I just came to say hello," he said, "to let you know that I don't hold this against you. I won't have to do it again. You thought you had me, didn't you? You never did.

"We have two more games. After we win them, nobody will even remember what you did. We'll be perfect, and nobody will remember anything else. I knew that all along even if you didn't. Look," he said, showing her his wrists, "you didn't even leave a mark on me. You never will. I just wanted you to know that."

Grace stood so that she was looking him in the eyes, the man of many faces. The one he had now was triumphant. This was the face he showed when he scored the touchdowns and heard the crowd calling his name. Beneath the helmet and the protective mask, he could make any face he wanted and no one would see. She saw it.

Grace looked beyond him along the entire length of the hushed reading room. They had whispered to each other or had spoken in hushed voices in an absurd observance of the rules. No one had noticed them until now, until they stood face to face above the reading light. He couldn't see the others who were now looking at them. His back was to the others, but she could see them.

"This man is Paul Renzlau," she said in a voice just loud enough to break the rules, just loud enough for the girl two tables away to hear. "This man is Paul Renzlau," she said again, louder, loud enough so that the rules were shattered and even the readers at the far end of the enormous room would hear her. "Everybody listen to me."

Everybody did. Everybody looked up from their silent contemplation, from the books that gave them obscure pieces of information from which they were to create new ideas. All eyes in the room focused on her except for the two that belonged to the face that was now changing again and turning away from her.

"You have seen this man's face in the newspaper. Don't believe what you see. Don't believe what you read. He rapes young women. He beats them and then he rapes them. Women, stay away from him. He'll rape you, too. Men," she said, and by then he was moving away from her, walking down the long room through the center aisle of tables toward the door on the opposite end. It was a long walk from the table where she always sat. "Men," she said again as she followed him, "keep your sisters away from him. Warn them."

She began to single out upraised faces to warn them. "His name is Paul Renzlau. Remember that. He is a rapist. His name is Paul Renzlau. Remember that. He is a rapist."

By the time Renzlau reached the end of the room, he was not running. He was not running as he would run on the football field headed toward the goal line, but neither was he walking with the sure gait of the star on campus who confidently ignored the stares of others. She followed him out of the heavy bronze door into the foyer, which led to the winding marble stairway, warning everyone she passed with the same message. "His name is Paul Renzlau. He is a rapist. Remember that. He is a rapist."

He was running by the time he hit the bottom step. She stopped at the top of the wide marble staircase and watched him run past the information desk and out the doors into Red Square. She watched until the doors swung back and he was gone. Everyone else watched, too—everyone who was coming in or going out. All eyes remained focused on the door. She turned away and walked back toward the hushed somber reading room where she had left her books and useless charts, where she had left the startled eyes of the scholars, where she had left her gun and badge and the unposted rules of silence.

Chapter 42

Grace walked with Katherine through fog so dense that the streetlights overhead seemed to hover like flying saucers in an old science fiction movie. Strangely, the fog felt warm and cool at the same time as it touched her face with its light seductive fingers. She tasted the acidic fumes of combustion captured within it and smelled decaying seaweed from the saltwater side of the locks. Ballard Avenue was dark except for the hovering saucers and the occasional headlights from cars that moved cautiously and disconnectedly through the darkness. She sensed Katherine changing pace and stopping. Grace adjusted to the change and stopped beside her.

"Do you think they'll ever fix this window?" Katherine asked.

The gray duct tape on the ancient plate glass window of the hardware store had yellowed and melted into the crack that it covered. The window and the crack and the tape had been fused together as far back as Grace could remember.

"They have fixed it," she said.

Grace saw Katherine's and her own transparent reflections in the faint mirror of the cracked window. Their shift was almost over, their last shift working together on Ballard Avenue. As a result of Captain Reimers's notion of leadership, Katherine would be transferred back downtown where she had worked before, and Grace was going south, not as far as Louisiana but as far south as the city limits allowed.

Grace had been angry when she first learned of the captain's intentions, but a week had passed and so had her anger. Without realizing it and without intending to do so, Captain Reimers had done her a favor. It was time to move on. Eventually she might take the degree she was working toward and leave the department entirely. But that was for the future. In the meantime she would miss working with Katherine, but who was to say that they wouldn't get back together? Not the captain whose reach did not extend beyond the North Precinct, and not the partners who were already planning how and where. No, they would get back together. It was the street she was leaving—Ballard Avenue where she had grown up and never left: the hardware store, Arne's opera beneath the bell tower, Rigmor's laugh and the smell of her Manna brand cigars—cigars from heaven, Rigmor called them. She would miss all of them, but it was time to move on.

Grace looked beyond their reflections in the window to the small wooden counter at the back of the hardware store.

"I remember the first time I came here with my father," she said. "He needed a special galvanized fitting to replace a section of water pipe in our house. While we waited in line to get up to the counter, my father never looked around at all. I thought that was strange. There were so many interesting things to see in the store, but he stood in the line and looked straight ahead."

"Why did he do that?"

"I'm not sure. I do that myself sometimes. I think I know everything that I'll see, so I don't bother to look around. And maybe there's something else. I remember when I was a child I would close my eyes and pretend that nobody could see me. A child can do that. A child can close her eyes and believe that if she can see no one, no one can see her. Did you ever do that?"

"No," Katherine said, "but there weren't many people where I grew up. I could walk out into the pastures on my father's farm anytime I wanted, and nobody would see me. If anything, I imagined the opposite. I imagined that people would finally notice me."

"That would be strange," Grace said.

"Did they have the plumbing part your father needed?" Katherine asked.

"They have everything in there," Grace said.

Lit by a night-light on the wall behind the wooden counter was an outdated calendar from a tool company. It featured a young woman in a bikini holding an enormous crescent wrench. Her smile had yellowed with age, and the paper was curling off the wall as if it no longer wanted to be there. The photograph always bothered her. She wished somebody would take it down. The young woman in the bikini couldn't have known how long her photograph would remain on the wall.

As far as they knew, there was no photograph ever taken of their great-great-grandmother Rosalie Stevens. Evangeline had looked through all the photographs in Miss Felicia's possession and had sent word to Aunt Margaret to look for an unknown woman with dark skin. Aunt Margaret found a picture of Emile and his second wife, who was not a dark-skinned woman, but none of Rosalie.

The absence of a photograph left Grace free to imagine the slave girl's face. At first she couldn't help but remember the girl in her grade school class who had the same name—the girl she had knocked down on the playground—but over time, the image in her imagination changed. What she came to imagine was the pain she had seen so clearly in Alice's face—the recognition, as Miss Felicia said, that God was not a woman after all. The scars of the fire were there, too, but also the determination and strength of will that shone from her own mother's piercing blue eyes—a determination that could not be dimmed by cancer. Grace knew that she could never know exactly what her great-great-grandmother looked like, but the face she imagined and any that would follow in her imagination must have the determination of the freed slave girl who threw her baby out the window of a burning house and reached through fire for the piece of paper that had, a century and a quarter later, led them to her.

In the end, it was her own face she saw in the cracked reflecting glass—her face and Katherine who had waited beside her.

"Someday I'll have to tell you the whole story about Louisiana," Grace said.

"I'd like to hear it," Katherine said.

After they crossed the street into Rigmor's block, Grace looked down at the sidewalk and fit her steps within the rectangular blocks of concrete as she had done as a child. It was all in her mind—the game she had played alone, never with Evangeline. Evangeline would have marked the course or changed the rules of the hopscotch game. Grace changed the rules, too, but she was the only one who knew the endless variety of steps. The urge to skip through the course once more was almost more than she could resist.

Katherine looked at her with a quizzical smile as if there was something new about her partner that she didn't understand. Maybe there was. Maybe it was the memory of the hopscotch game and of the little girl who broke no rules, not even the rules she made for herself. Or maybe it was something else. Someday she would tell Katherine about the hopscotch game, too.

Edith's cart stood in a solitary heap within the translucent glow of Rigmor's store. Edith came through the door as Grace and Katherine stopped on the sidewalk, blocked from Rigmor's door by the cart. Edith ignored them as she made room among her belongings for two Styrofoam containers. One, Grace knew, held the last of the sailor's stew.

Edith rebalanced the load to accommodate the addition. Then she pushed the cart toward them as if she didn't see the police officers standing in her way. Katherine slipped in between Rigmor's tables, and Grace jumped off the familiar sidewalk onto the street. Edith stopped her cart at the second-hand store and picked up one of the miscellaneous pieces of wood that were left outside and priced "4 for $1." She shoved the stick into her cart and pushed the cart down the street.

Rigmor propped open the front door and watched Edith make off with her loot.

"Those sticks aren't worth a dollar anyway," she said.

Rigmor sat in one of the chairs on the sidewalk and removed a cigar from the pocket of her apron. Grace and Katherine sat in chairs on either side of her.

"Would you like one of these cigars, dear?" she asked Katherine.

"No thank you," Katherine said.

Rigmor laughed and lit one of her cigars from heaven.

"I don't like it that you girls won't be here tomorrow. But you can still come, you know," she said to Katherine. "Grace will come like she always has, but I want you to come and see me, too."

"I will," Katherine said.

"And now you are both invited to the poker game," Rigmor said. "Those are the rules. When you don't work here anymore, then you come to the poker game. You can teach those men how to play. We'll see how they like that, *hvad*?"

Far down the street Edith shouted something, but Grace couldn't understand what she said. For all she knew, Edith's words might have revealed the secret of life. If so, the words and the secret would remain with Edith and with Rigmor— the only other person Edith had entrusted with the knowledge. Grace looked at Rigmor, who blew out a stream of smoke that mingled with the warm and cool fog.

"Maybe we should close up, Rigmor," Grace said.

"No *ja*," Rigmor said, speaking the contradictory words that only she could say without contradiction. "We have to, I suppose, but let's just sit here together a little while longer."

Acknowledgments

I thank my talented advance readers who generously offered many different views and expertise but always the same encouragement: Sonya Senstra, Aage Clausen, Deborah Odell, Robert Vanderway, Captain Neil Low, Carol Brown, Marlene Blessing, Tammy Domike, David Ziskin, A'Jamal Byndon, Patricia Kunze, and Polly Partsch—especially Polly for her careful editing. Thank you to Guyneitha Clausen for her horticultural research and information about the struggle against breast cancer. Thanks to my Uncle Thorvald for the poker game research, although the game will wait for another day.

When I explained to my cousin, Amy Jorgensen, my vision of Grace, Amy told me that Grace wouldn't reveal everything about herself right away. It would take time to know Grace. She was right. The more I think about Grace, the more I write about her, the more I realize how much is still left to understand.

In the past there has always been another reader of my books whom I trusted implicitly. My sagacious aunt, Mary Youngdahl, died before she could finish reading this book. She was ninety-six. A retired English teacher with exacting standards, she never spared me from criticism because I was her nephew. When I began my second book with a tangential chapter, she told me to tighten it up. "The reader wants to know what the book is about in the first ten pages," she said. I tightened it up and remembered her advice.

I remember how nervous I was when I sent her a draft of my first book. I was more worried about what she would say than I would ever be for later editors. She sent me page after page of corrections. I knew she would. When I finally came to the end of her critique, she wrote a sentence that I'll never forget. The beginning of the book was good, she wrote, "but the last three chapters are the work of an artist."

I have never received greater encouragement or higher praise, and never will.

—*LC*

Lowen Clausen

FIRST AVENUE

Written with compelling authenticity by a former Seattle police
officer, this debut novel is the powerful story of a Seattle cop who
can't shake the image of the abandoned, dead baby he finds in a
seedy hotel—and who can't give up on finding the truth until
those responsible are brought to justice...

> "*First Avenue* is as moody as Seattle in the
> rain, and just as alluring. A skillful,
> memorable first novel."
>
> —Stephen White, *New York Times* bestselling author

> "I loved this book...[it] has an authenticity
> only a real cop could convey."
>
> —Ann Rule, *New York Times* bestselling author of *The
> Stranger Beside Me* and *And Never Let Her Go*, and a former
> Seattle cop herself

0-451-40948-5

Available wherever books are sold or at
www.penguin.com

SECOND WATCH
By Lowen Clausen

Katherine Murphy is new to Seattle's Second Watch and the Ballard Avenue beat. Her partner, Grace Stevens, grew up in the small Scandinavian neighborhood and introduces Katherine to its rhythms, its people, and its dangers.

When the body of a young boy is found in a trash compactor, Katherine and Grace are the first officers at the haunting crime scene. With only one clue to carry them, they take on a risky undercover assignment to search for the killer. But it may already be too late for them to save another child in desperate need of protection.

0-451-20819-6

Available wherever books are sold or at
www.penguin.com